BLACK POCKETS

AND OTHER DARK THOUGHTS

POCKETS

GEORGE ZEBROWSKI

WITH A FOREWORD BY HOWARD WALDROP

GOLDEN GRYPHON PRESS • 2006

LIBRARY OF CONGRESS CATALOGING–IN–PUBLICATION DATA

Zebrowski, George, 1945–
    Black pockets and other dark thoughts / George Zebrowski. — 1st ed.
        p.   cm.
    "These stories were first published in different form and appear here in the author's preferred text." ISBN 1-930846-40-1 (alk. paper)
    1. Science fiction, American.   I. Title.
PS3576.E35   B57   2005
813'.54—dc22
                2005025437

First Edition.

Contents

For Pam dearest, who brightens my darkness

Foreword

FOR THIRTY YEARS NOW, HE'S BEEN AN ENTHUSI-
astic voice on the phone, a bunch of nice letters, and the
occasional check, in his fairly frequent guise as editor.

Surprisingly, in all that time, we have never managed to meet
face-to-face, like real normal people.

Which is truly a shame.

When I introduced his SF collection *The Monadic Universe* twenty
years ago, I tried to convince readers George was a funny (at times,
bitterly so) writer who went straight back to the Aristophanic roots
(though on a somewhat more cosmic stage).

"Zebrowski?" people would say. "Isn't he the guy who writes
galaxy-spanning sagas—"

"—of Stapledonian magnitude?" I would complete their question. "Yes," I would then say, "but like me, he also thinks that just
because it's serious doesn't mean it has to be long, dull, boring, and
humorless."

"Really?" they would say. "I thought it had to be."

What you hold in your hands is George Zebrowski's first collection
of *horror* stories, culled from throughout his career, with an em-
phasis on the more recent things, and one brand-new-written-
just-last-Thursday (well, *all* the last Thursdays from the past two
years) novella, the titular "Black Pockets."

What George has done, sitting there in Upstate New York, a place as unknown to me as the Great Rill Valley on Mars, is to divide these stories into Personal, Political, and Metaphysical horrors, i.e.: stories that should scare you individually, stories that should terrify you as a social animal, and stories that should scare the whole goddamn human race, in the collective.

Part of the—if we may so speak—beauty of this book is that George can write about people who are not like him (or you, or me). Many are not as intelligent, nice, thoughtful, or as sensitive as their author. (Writing about morons is easy—limited vocabulary, concrete nouns, declarative partial sentences, no conceptualization —although Faulkner and Steinbeck were way ahead of everybody else—and writing about geniuses is easier than you think—abstract modifiers, conceptualization, complex sentence structures—although here, too, Bester (in "The Pi Man"), Daniel Keyes, and Don De Lillo did it better than anyone else). What is *really hard* is writing about someone *just* a *little* less, or a *little* more intelligent, sensitive, caring etc. than you (and most people) are. Zebrowski pulls this off many times in these stories. One of the most chilling, "The Wish in the Fear," is so good at what it does that you forget what the story is about until the next-to-last line, and then you remember, with a vengeance. (This is also one of those stories that is going to finish *after* you're read the last line—he's made it so you finish the story after *he's* through. *I guarantee it.*) A couple of the earlier stories in here needed a little more room to breathe—good though they are—but not this one.

His deft use of character is such that (even reading them in this collection) you forget that most horror stories just fill time before the protag is eaten or impaled or gets their comeuppance somehow. That's *other* writers.

Not in these. George has set himself the writerly goal of having the horror come out of the situations and character flaws of his people, not from some ancient evil trespassed, or Cthulvian terror, nor now what has become that cliché—the serial killer. (What did non-supernatural horror writers do before Ed Gein was caught?)

What I'm going to propose here is that George Zebrowski is writing a new kind of dark fantasy story—as new as, say, Fritz Leiber's "Smoke Ghost" was in its time—the kind that led to *Unknown Worlds* (1939–1943). Especially in the stories he puts into the Political Horrors and Metaphysical Fears sections.

There has never been a zombie story like "I Walked With

Fidel"—true not only to a dead Cold-War world that has passed with its polarized ideologies (as surely as that passed Colonial World—which led to voodoo—has gone from this earth): the story manages to be true to both post-Superpowers times and to Castro, whose ideals were as betrayed by the nature of revolutions and the Soviet Union as by the warmongering antagonism of the United States. Read it and say it ain't so, José.

George is not afraid of the Big Frightening Ideas either. The two newer centerpieces of the collection, "Black Pockets" and "A Piano Full of Dead Spiders" deal with truly existential problems, like in the latter—if you're a composer, and your tunes come from spiders playing them in your piano, what happens when they die? Are there spiders in your piano? In the first place? Which died first, the spiders or your talent? Is there redemption in this cold world?

In "Black Pockets," the questions keep coming: you're given a great, heretofore unknown power by the nemesis of your existence as he is dying; for he has some unfinished business he needs done before you can use the power for revenge yourself. The protag finds, like Wells's *Invisible Man*, that power, in and of itself, instead of avenging the Great Wrongs of Your Life, becomes a convenience, and otherwise innocent bystanders (wrong time, wrong place) get it used on them. At the core of the story is the truly frightening question: at what point does revenge become so all-consuming it clouds your judgment? *Oh yeah?* and how do *you* know?

Be warned: this isn't just another standard horror-trope collection (they *never* are, from Golden Gryphon). There's only one old castle in the book. The settings range from the apartments next door to the hollowed-out asteroid worlds beyond the orbit of Pluto; the social strata from impoverished students to the people who live in the big houses on the hill in Yourtown USA.

I've had the privilege to read this collection hot-off-the-copier. You'll have the joy of reading it in some beautifully designed package from the publishers. Whatever the format, whatever the circumstances under which you read it: It's one powerful, varied, and wonderful batch of tales you have before you.

—Howard Waldrop
Vernal equinox 2005

Black Pockets
And Other Dark Thoughts

Personal Terrors
are the first ones we know . . .

Jumper

"*I* GO TO SLEEP AND WAKE UP SOMEWHERE ELSE."
She looked directly at him as she spoke, and it seemed clear that he was dealing with an unusually controlled personality. She wore an impeccably tailored tweed business suit, white blouse, blue tie, and black shoes. Her brown hair was professionally permed; her make-up was light, with almost no lipstick. He gazed at her without comment, hoping to catch a moment of weakness in her facade, but there was nothing.

"Well, Doctor, what do you think?"

He smiled. "Oh, I doubt very much that you're traveling in any way. You're already there, where you wake up, but you've dreamed that you started somewhere else. Naturally, it seems surprising to find yourself where you actually are."

"That is not the case, Doctor," she replied determinedly.

"Miss Melita, you're simply mistaking where you go to bed, nothing more."

She grimaced, as if she'd caught him at something. "You avoid calling me by my first name, or Ms. Melita. I once went to an idiot in your profession who insisted that I use *his* first name. Do I intimidate you, Doctor?"

"Not at all. I'm not hung up on the authority of formal address. Some of my colleagues like it. Others simply want the patient to feel informal and relaxed."

"Yes, they call patients by first names but introduce themselves as Dr. so-and-so."

"I'll go by your preferences."

She stared at him without blinking, and he knew that it would be Miss Melita and Dr. Cheney. An old-fashioned female who might need rescuing from herself. The immaturity of the thought startled him, and he realized that she was having a strong, unconscious effect on him.

He looked at her file on his desk. "I see that your physical checks out well, and you have no reported history of sleep disturbances."

"Doctor, I have no memory of going to the places where I wake up. I waken there and have to come home. Yesterday I woke up in my ex-lover's house. It was empty and for sale. I'm certain I was home when I fell asleep."

"These kinds of things can be very convincing," he said. "Were you wearing pajamas?"

"Of course not. I go to bed wearing clothes, just in case. I've jumped more than a dozen times in the past few months."

"What do you think it is?" he asked in his best neutral tone.

"I don't know. Movement from one place to another without covering the distance between," she replied glibly.

"A kind of quantum leap?"

"What do you mean?"

"It's a term from physics," he said. Patients sometimes like to give, or hear rational-sounding explanations. Imaginative plausibility could be a sign of delusion.

"Who cares," she said. "It happens. I know it does. The first few times were pretty embarrassing." Her tone was insistent, but she kept her composure.

"What do you think it means?"

"I sometimes feel as if I'm searching for the right place to be," she said, "but it keeps eluding me. I wake up in the wrong places."

"Is there a right place?" he asked.

"I don't know. I can't think where it might be, but I feel strongly that it exists."

"Doesn't that give you a clue?" he asked, setting in motion his usual probing rigmarole.

"What could it tell me?"

"You may be hiding it from yourself," he said.

"I've thought of that. It may be a place I only know about, but have never visited."

"And you may not really want to go there, while at another level you do. Anyone can be of two minds, Miss Melita. I can see, whatever is going on, that this search is important to you. My job will be to keep you from deluding yourself."

"You're confident I'll take you on," she said.

"Shall we set up a schedule? I charge by the hour, five hours paid in advance."

She looked at him with skepticism. "I know you're expensive, Doctor. I'd like to set a deferred-payment plan."

He smiled at the first hint of insecurity in her voice. "Ah, but payments are part of the treatment, Miss Melita. They sow an attitude of responsibility in your unconscious, making it a partner in your recovery. You'll get better sooner."

There was a blush in her pale cheeks, suggesting that she was responding to his authority, even accepting that she might have a problem.

She stood up, as if to leave. "What a crock, Doctor. I simply don't want them to know at work that I'm seeing you, so I can't use my medical coverage. I can start paying next month, when I can draw on my savings. Anyway, you don't believe me."

She was beautiful, he noticed, slim yet womanly, standing on low heels in a dancer's graceful pose, her back slightly arched, toes out a little.

"Are you successful, Doctor?" she demanded.

"I'd like to think I am," he replied calmly.

"How long do you sleep?"

"Oh, I'd say about eight hours."

"Really successful people sleep less than five or six," she said.

She begrudges herself sleep, he noted, drives herself and others hard. Her lapses of memory were not surprising.

"I'd say your business has leveled off," she continued, "and may even be on the way down. You're heavy into investments as a hedge against a practice that won't grow. You're doing well at them, but they have to be fed. You could go either way in the next few years."

He leaned back and smiled, trying not to think of what tax reform had done to his portfolio, determined not to show her she'd hit home.

"We're off the point, Miss Melita."

She sat down and crossed her legs. "Yes, of course. My only interest is in your competence."

Competitive chatter was a habit with her, he realized.

"I can prove to you that I jump," she said, with a tremor in her voice.

"You're welcome to try," he said, "but only if I'm to be your doctor, and I'm not sure I want to take you on."

She swallowed, and he watched the muscles working in her pale throat. "Doctor, I apologize for my remarks about your business and character." She leaned forward slightly. "I don't know why this is happening to me, Doctor, but you could easily check my story. I have videotapes of me disappearing from my bed."

"Look," he said firmly, "it's just not possible for you to move yourself while you're asleep, unless you get up and convey yourself there. I know you believe you've disappeared from one location and appeared in another, but, take my word for it, it's not a true experience, not at all, never. Videotapes can be faked."

"Okay, come home with me, lock me in my bedroom, and wait. When I call you from somewhere else the next morning you'll know it's true."

He knew then that he should not take her case. Simple neurotics made the best patients; they asked for help with life's problems and only thought they were sick. They could be made to feel helped. If this woman could imagine that she teleported from her bedroom every night, it would be nothing for her to imagine worse things. To go to her home at night would be asking for a sexual-harassment suit.

"I'll pay you six months in advance," she said, "next month."

"Can you afford it?" he asked, wondering if in fact she wanted him to come on to her.

"No, I told you it'll be my savings, but I must prove that what happens to me is real. Then I'll need you to find out why it happens. Okay, I can't be completely sure it happens unless someone like you documents it."

He sighed, unable to decide.

"This could make your name, Doctor. You'll witness a disorder that exhibits itself in a unique way. You'll write about it, go on talk shows, bring in more patients. Hell, you might not need patients after that."

He shook his head and smiled. "I shouldn't take your money. What do you do, Miss Melita? Your entry on my form is vague."

"I'm an executive at a telecommunications company."

"Here in New York?"

"Yes. I've taken a leave of absence for six weeks."

"Are you lesbian?" he asked.

"That's not your business unless you take my case."

He leaned forward. "Do you really want help, Miss Melita?"

She sat back in her chair, uncrossed her legs, and folded her hands in her lap. "Yes, I'm lesbian, but I've had male lovers. It never works out, even though I'm attracted to some men and try hard. Not because they find out, but for other reasons. I can't be orgasmic with men. They're too threatening."

"Were you raised by both parents?"

"No, by my father. My mother died when I was small, just after we arrived in this country. My brother ran away when I was ten, and I've not seen him since."

"Is your father living?"

"Yes," she said softly.

"Okay, I'll take you on," he said. Her story had made him curious. How could a person of her obvious intelligence and good sense, who gave no sign of illness, tell such a flaky tale? "Make an appointment," he added, "for the day after you've had this experience of yours again."

"You don't want to check my story?" she asked.

"Not by sitting up all night at your place," he said, imagining the softness of her skin under her blouse.

"It's the only sure way to find out."

"Miss Melita, I'd have to ask a colleague to come with me, or hire a nurse of unquestioned integrity to serve as a witness. Maybe I'd need them both to prove that my presence was purely professional."

She bit her lower lip. "Oh, I see. But you already know I wouldn't be interested in you, Doctor."

"Do call and make an appointment, Miss Melita."

As she got up and left, he realized that there would be no more to it. She'd see him a few times and then stop coming. He felt a bit lost and disappointed for the rest of the day.

When she arrived for her first appointment on the following Monday, dressed in jogging clothes, his insides leaped with naive joy at the sight of her. Gone was the executive bitch facade. The big kid who showed up in her place was much more appealing and clearly in need of his help.

"Oh, the clothes," she said, noticing his stare. "I slept in them, so I could get home."

He looked down at his desk to hide his sudden rush of attraction for her. Her change from cool executive to willowy athlete both excited and annoyed him; he had never become this vulnerable with a patient.

"There's been a change," she said, dropping into the chair.

"What kind of change?" he asked uneasily.

"I was dreaming about dying before I woke up in a park somewhere in Brooklyn."

"A park?" he asked stupidly, watching her lips and the movement of her neck muscles. Her sweaty youthfulness was overpowering.

"I think it was a park. It was still dark when I left, so I wasn't paying much attention. Doctor, I think I'm going to die." She looked directly at him. The dismay in her eyes was crushing, but in a perverse way it only made her more beautiful.

"Nonsense," he managed to say reassuringly, but the word only seemed to reproach his own impulses. "You're just escaping from overwork. That's what these jumping dreams mean. How are things at your job? You have taken your leave, haven't you?"

"I can't take off just yet," she said pitiably. "Maybe next week."

"When was the first time you had this jumping dream?" he asked, making a mental note to check a few facts in her file.

She swallowed hard. "They're not dreams," she said softly, staring at the carpet.

"Please go on."

"First time was when I was a girl. My father came to my room and began touching me. I was terrified. Later that night I woke up and found myself in a neighbor's house."

She did not look at him, and he knew that she was still her father's prisoner. The need to escape him had set a pattern of wish fulfillment. Any kind of pressure, even that of the workplace, still triggered the abused child's dreams of escape. Slowly, he would make her understand.

"I can help you," he said. "In time you won't have these dreams, and you'll know that's all they were. It may seem hard for you to accept that now, but you'll learn it for yourself."

A look of anger came into her face as she looked up at him. She bit her lower lip, as if confronting something within herself. "I hated him for touching me, and I hated him even more later, when I understood."

"Did you ever say anything to him?"

She shook her head, unable to speak for a moment. "He died before I could. I don't know why I lied to you about his still being alive. I'm sorry."

"That's okay, you've repaired it."

She smiled desolately. "He got away from me, didn't he?"

"You're getting better," he said during their fifth session. "No dreams for weeks now."

She shrugged. "It's happened before. Doctor, you must come to my place and wake me before I jump again, tonight." There was no doubt in her voice. It worried him that she still refused to accept the fact that she was only dreaming of jumping.

"You don't expect me to sit at your bedside, do you?"

"I'll pay you extra, but it must be tonight."

"I can't get a nurse on such short notice."

"Then give me a release to sign, anything. I can't be alone tonight. I can feel it coming on." She took a deep breath, and her right hand shook slightly.

"Perhaps you're right," he heard himself saying. "If I can wake you up, then you'll be sure it's just a dream."

"If you can do so in time."

"What time should I arrive?" he asked.

"No later than eleven."

They sat quietly for a few moments. She stared past him, out the window. He tried to ignore his feelings for her, think of her only as a patient, but he couldn't shake her attraction. He wanted to hold her, kiss her gently, free her from her past. Warnings crowded into him, but he ignored them.

Her East Side apartment building was bright with lights when his cab pulled up. The architecture reminded him of egg boxes. Soft creatures called people lived in the private chambers. He felt a bit useless and infantile as he paid the driver and walked toward the glass entrance. Doubts slipped through him. How could he presume to know another's mind? They were all ever-changing labyrinths, his own included. His professional knowledge permitted nothing more than a form of organized insisting, a sublime version of parental scolding. His training was a weak imposition on a beast that was ancient and sure in its ways, always ready to overcome its displacement. It lay coiled and waiting for everyone. He was no exception.

The doorman's scrutiny made him uneasy, but finally he was in the elevator, on his way to the thirtieth floor. She was waiting for him at the door of her apartment, dressed in jogging clothes, newly laundered, by their smell.

"I'm really beat," she said, as she locked the door and led him through the living room into the bedroom. "All my keys are in the safe. Here's the spare. Check the front door again, so you'll know I can't get out. Is that scientific enough for you?" The sarcasm in her voice wounded him.

"You'd have to fly to get out of here," he said, looking through the window at the East River.

"There are books by the desk," she said, getting into bed. "The light won't bother me."

She closed her eyes. He stood over her, watching her face, waiting for it to relax, but there was no change. It remained composed, oblivious to his eyes. He felt lost, on guard over a plundered fortress.

There seemed to be a lump in bed with her. He waited, then lifted the blanket slightly. She did not react. He peered under and saw that she was holding a small fluorescent light, the kind mechanics used when they worked under cars. He put back the blanket and went over to the desk.

He sat down and went through the motions of selecting a book from the small bookcase at his left. There was nothing of immediate interest. He sat still, listening to her gentle breathing and began to grapple again with his feelings for her. Tenderness struggled with simple desires. It seemed that she was everything he had missed, making him feel deprived and alone. It was an old pattern with him, going back to his college days. He had considered it broken by the time he had entered medical school, yet here he was again, all but alone in a room on a Friday night, fantasizing as he had done in his freshman days.

There were some papers on her desk blotter, and he found himself looking through them to distract himself from self-pity and the thought of her in the bed behind him, warm and soft under the covers. There was an old clipping, a death notice giving the date of birth and the date of death, including the man's profession and the name of the cemetery where he was buried. The yellowing paper dropped from his fingers as he realized that he could no longer hear her breathing.

He turned around, but the desk light had affected his eyes, making the room black. He waited, then got up and went to the bed.

It was empty.

He looked around, wondering if she could have crept past him in the dark, but then he saw that the covers had not been disturbed.

He pulled them down. She was gone, and she had taken the light with her.

He rushed out into the living room and checked the front door. It was locked, and the key was still in his pocket. By all rational evidence she was still in the apartment with him—unless she had fixed the covers quietly and used another key to get out. He would have heard her.

"Katya!" he shouted, using her name for the first time.

There was no answer.

He searched the kitchen and bathroom, all the closets and under all the furniture. She was here, he told himself, wondering if he couldn't see her because he'd gone insane. She was hiding from him, attempting to convince him that her delusion was true.

"Katya, come out!" he shouted.

Finally, in the silence, he remembered the clipping and knew what he had to do.

The cab let him off in Brooklyn at 3:00 A.M. He found the cemetery park, but it took him over an hour to find the grave and start digging. His flashlight kept fading, but he finally uncovered the coffin. He stared at it, breathing heavily, nearly convinced that he was mad. A breeze swirled a few fall leaves around him, then subsided. He looked around to see if anyone had noticed him. He was probably too far inside the park to be seen from the street.

He drew a deep breath and started to pry open the casket with his spade. The lid wouldn't come up, then flew open with a jarring creak. Bright fluorescence shot up from inside like daylight, dazzling him.

As his eyes adjusted, he saw her. She was grasping her father's skull with both hands. The skeleton was disordered. Her eyes were wide open, staring up at him from the prison of her dead body.

She had awakened in total darkness. He saw her turning on her light and screaming in its lurid, white glare as she struggled with the dead, realizing with terror that no one could help her before the air in the casket ran out. She had known where her father was buried from the old clipping, and she had jumped to this same park recently; but her conscious mind had not suspected that she would jump into the coffin, even though something had prompted her to bring the light. She had expected to find herself in another dark, empty house somewhere.

"Why didn't you tell me?" he asked uselessly, his voice breaking. She had told him that she was going to die. "I could have been waiting here to dig you out," he said, reaching down to touch her cheek for the first time. It was cold. Gently, he closed her eyes.

If only he could have believed her. The girl had jumped to

escape molestation. The woman had cast about, seeking to confront her father, only to learn that he had died. Cheated, her unconscious had found a way to invade his final resting place and tear apart his bones. Her deepest self had also wanted to die, he realized as he imagined her screaming and choking in the earth.

"Come on, get up out of there," he said, childishly wishing that this could be only an odd rebirth ritual, of the kind prescribed by some of his wilder colleagues. His body shuddered in the cool, damp air.

Moths and insects were zeroing in on the column of light standing out from the grave. He picked up the fluorescent pack and tossed it away. What could he do? She was gone, and there was no way to prove what had happened. The police would conclude that she had been asphyxiated and brought here. If he called them now, he would be the only suspect, telling an utterly fantastic and unbelievable story. It would mean a trial and the end of his practice. His life would be over if he went to prison. If he left the grave open, she would be found, and sooner or later he would be questioned.

He closed the coffin, telling himself that he had committed no real crime; better if she were never found. The fluorescent light flickered on the damp grass as he climbed out and began to fill in the grave.

When he was finished, he looked around at the dark cemetery. How many sons and daughters slept with their fathers' corpses, clutched at their mothers' dry breasts, or tore at their siblings' throats? A study of case histories from the missing-persons divisions might reveal where other jumpers could be found.

She would be missed eventually, and they might come to question him; something at her office or at her apartment might tell the police that she had been his patient; but there was no reasonable chain of criminal motives or actions that would lead them to her body. She would become just another missing person.

He brushed himself clean as best he could, disposed of the two lights and spade in different waste cans, and wandered off in search of a taxi, as far from the park as possible.

The cab's radio played love songs all the way home.

The Wish in the Fear

*F*RANK'S LEFT UPPER TOOTH HAD BEEN CAPPED
in 1970, after he had cracked it by falling flat on his face during a racquetball game. Earlier that year he had seen a man with a broken front tooth on the bus, and had wondered what it would be like to have a broken tooth. It was as if his future were casting a shadow into the past.

At least once a year since then he had dreamed that his cap had come off, because it seemed to him that every year beyond the first ten seemed too many for such a thing to stick to his filed-down tooth. Losing his cap was the one nightmare that continued to convince him of its truth, and he was always grateful to wake up to its unreality.

But this was only one of many trivial fears he would develop. Another involved sharp objects and the hidden nature of accidents. Were they fixed, waiting to happen at the appointed time? he asked himself as he idly imagined putting out his right eye with a pencil. Whether he could muster the courage to do so deliberately interested him, but the more frightening possibility was that a series of ordinary, even logical steps might lead to it surreptitiously, remaining concealed until it was too late. He suspected that there was some train of events that might make it happen, some arcane dovetailing of circumstances that would make it come out that way, or even worse, convince him that it was the necessary thing to do.

As a boy he had gone up to the cliffs that faced the apartment houses in the South Bronx just below the Grand Concourse, and had stood there on the edge of the loose slate piles with his back to the sheer drop, glancing over his shoulder at the empty windows to see if anyone was watching. He did not slip and did not want to, but it was hypnotic to imagine himself lying in one of the backyards below, his broken body motionless in a pool of bright blood on the paving stones. He could still see himself there, balancing on the balls of his feet.

Over the years he became adept at imagining that what he saw happening to other people might also happen to him. He was both attracted to and repelled by most of these reveries, but was unable to shake the foreboding that sooner or later some, if not all, would become realities for him. When he saw any kind of accident overtake someone, it was always a possible harbinger of his own fate.

But he lived a life remarkably free of mishaps. Instead he became a collector of other people's fears and phobias; and however terrifying they might be while he was in their thrall, nothing ever happened to him. He came to accept this as the way things were with him, and looked forward to the next one as people do to a concert, play, movie, or television show.

His most intense encounters with people stayed with him, becoming a collection of recurring dreams. Each new collision became a candidate for his growing labyrinth of shared fears and phobias. He sometimes suspected that the answer to what made one stay and another flee from his dreams was the secret of his life, the key that would open the door to himself, but he was content to hold it dear and unknown, hidden deep within himself.

He tasted the summer rain in his dream as the wind blew drops into the gazebo behind the pool. Everyone at the mountain resort had fled into their cabins and into the main building, but he had stayed out to watch the rain.

He heard the expected footfalls on the wooden steps behind him and turned to see Vera, still dressed in her white blouse, white shorts and sneakers, shaking water out of her shoulder-length blond hair as she looked shyly at him. He was nineteen and in college; she was just going on seventeen. She was here with her parents and brother, and they were all very protective of her developing sexual vulnerability, so he had kept his distance, content to watch from afar her stocky, athletic form filling out her well-pressed shorts and blouse.

"Hello," he said with a nervous breath.

"Hi," she answered, smiling angelically, and he felt once again that a hidden script was being revealed for him to speak, one line at a time, so he wouldn't know what came next, even though he had played this scene with her many times before. The words, expressions, and some of the physical movements varied, but the differences were unimportant.

She leaned back against the railing and took a deep breath. He came over, leaned back next to her and said, "Some rain. It might get cloudy for the next two weeks. That sometimes happens up here."

"Oh, no. I hope that doesn't happen."

He turned and gazed at her. She looked back as if searching his face for something, and he knew that she was afraid of being alone with him.

"I've seen you around," he said, glancing down at her pressed shorts, which stood away from her smooth, still slightly heavy but attractive thighs.

"Don't look at me like that," she said. "It makes me nervous."

"But I like the way you look," he answered gently, and saw her swallow, and knew that she felt pride and guilt about her emerging good looks. As she matured and gained her full growth, she would become a blond goddess and know power over boys and men; but for now she was still unsure, unable to consciously attract or humiliate, also following an ancient script that startled and intrigued her. "I think you're beautiful, but I couldn't tell you around your family."

She grimaced and smiled, then looked across the resort grounds as if her parents might see her from their cabin, but relaxed, realizing that they did not have a clear view of the pool. He began to gaze at her adoringly, but looked away as she became aware of the desire that was growing in him.

He moved closer to her and took her hand. She tensed, then blushed.

"You're very beautiful," he said.

"You're just saying that," she whispered.

"No—it's true," he said, leaning closer. She drew a deep breath and slid away from him on the rail, trying to smile knowingly, but it came across as sheepish, shy, and green.

He looked at her caringly, and something inside her seemed to break as he moved nearer and was about to kiss her. She took a deep breath and looked away from him.

"No," she said with a sob, "I can't."

"Why not?"

"Before," she mumbled, looking as if she might cry, and he felt pity and concern for her, and the impulse to protect her, to hold her, flattered that she was showing these feelings to him. He looked into her eyes and his gaze locked with hers, trapping him in a strange prelude to a dance that she would teach him.

"I went out last year," she started to say awkwardly, looking at him as if she had to expel feelings that were stuck within her. "He came to dinner at my house. My parents liked him, my little brother liked him, my friends. We went out for a month, and then he broke it off and it was . . . horrible." She choked on the last word and tears ran down her face. "And I couldn't tell anyone that he'd touched me and kissed me, and that I wanted him. I was so afraid. I'd thought he wanted to marry me, to be with me forever, but it was all a lie. I don't want that again."

She was silent, and he realized that it had been all or nothing with her, with no in between; and that this demanding familial finality had driven her first boyfriend away.

"It's okay," he said, putting his arm around her as she stopped crying, accepting the fact that there was nothing very interesting about her; not her white shorts and tanned legs and arms; not her blond hair or blue eyes. The silkiness of her fled from his mind before her raw need. She was hungry to swallow him. There was nothing personal about what might have been between them, only a role that she expected him to assume; a hundred other boys would do just as well.

As he looked into her disappointed eyes, he saw her family lurking behind them, restricting her freedom, compelling her to think and feel as they did. She was imprisoned within herself. The realization horrified him. He was sorry for her pain, pitying her bonds, but glad that he had glimpsed them early enough to escape.

Are you going to kiss me and hold me? her eyes asked. And how long will it last? Then she saw that he was not prepared to pay the toll and moved away as if she had been betrayed again. He watched her flee from the gazebo and run across the grass in the rain, taking with her every fantasy he had nursed about her, leaving him with a conflicting sense of relief at having escaped arousing her feelings.

The pitiable terror that she had shown him stayed with him permanently, growing more painful whenever he recalled it. Not a month went by in the years since when he did not think about her physical lushness, the smell of her soap, the sexual grasp that he might have awakened in her in a vain effort to dispel the youthful horror that she had deposited in him.

He lay half awake, trying again to forget the dream of Vera, knowing that he would never lose it, then recalled Annette, the dark-haired girl in her twenties who had shared a cabin with two men that same summer in the mountains. He had watched her come out after lunch to sit by the pool, and her bikini-clad body had seemed exhausted from lovemaking. She had noticed him, he was sure, and he had felt that she was avoiding his eyes because she knew that everyone knew, but she didn't seem to care. She was imprisoned by her sexuality, and was giving herself to two young men in a vain attempt to burn it out, to quiet her soul. His very gaze seemed to arouse her, he had felt, and she seemed to cringe under his scrutiny as she tried to ignore him.

So you know, her glancing, dark eyes said. So what. It's not your business. And yet part of her seemed to say, I'm a prisoner, I'm trapped, and I don't know what to do. Visions of what they were doing in that cabin preyed on his imagination all that summer. The two men, both younger than her, always slept late. . . .

He sat up out of his dream and looked around his bedroom, wondering if it would be warm enough to go down and sit by the pool. After all, it was late May, and the temperature might get up to eighty, they had said.

He rose, went to the picture window and looked down five stories to the pool. The usual suspects seemed to be gathering at the patch of blue water, harmless types working for small businesses around town, dreaming of going to a big city for a job one day, but too insecure to ever do so. If they had any fears or phobias, they were buried deeply. He had nothing much to fear from going down among them.

He went to his CD player, put on some vintage disco, then went and did some exercises on his Soloflex. When he felt hungry, he went into the kitchen and stuck a complete brunch, coffee included, into the microwave, then wandered over to make sure his team of VCRs was taping the movie and Olympic events that he had set them to catch.

He dressed for the pool, reminding himself that he still had twelve days of vacation time left before he went back to the insurance office. Maybe he'd go somewhere for the last six days.

At poolside, he was dozing with his cap over his face when he heard

Marianne, his neighbor from the fourth floor, say to her friend, "You're lucky, your boyfriend's your pal. You can talk to him." There was a short pause. "Either you're lying or just bragging."

"I'm bragging."

"I'd need an ass-lift to get a man like that. Don't deny it, I see how he looks at you."

"He's just fooling."

"He worships your ass," Marianne answered. After a moment of silence, she asked, "You know Alice who lives up front?"

"I've seen her."

"Well, she's terrified of being without a man. She almost gets hysterical about it. I don't understand it."

"Well," her friend said, "that's because you already have a kid, and you've rid yourself of a bad guy. You see things from the other side. But doesn't she have a boyfriend?"

"Sort of," Marianne said. "He's a plump guy she doesn't seem to like much, but she lets him come over. He lives an hour away, somewhere south of here. He rarely stays over. I hear them arguing about it."

Suddenly the conversation was drowned out by splashing.

"Stop that, Mel," Marianne called to her boyfriend as he came out of the pool.

He laughed and said, "I heard you talking about chubby! What's up?"

"Chubby?" Marianne's girlfriend asked.

"Alice—he doesn't like her much." Marianne lowered her voice. "We were together at a bar, before I knew Mel, and Alice came on to him."

"Really?"

"Yup."

"Well," Mel said, "maybe she'd be good for a blow job."

"What!" Marianne shouted. "Don't talk like that."

"It's okay," Marianne's friend said. "Don't you ever listen when they're all together watching the game?"

"Who's gonna hear?" Mel asked. "Hey, Frank, are you asleep?" he called.

Frank decided to act asleep.

"Well, I'm going inside," Marianne said. "Coming, Estelle?"

"Sure thing," her girlfriend said.

Frank remembered Alice now. She wasn't all that bad-looking. Overweight, yes, but erotic in the way heavier women get when they're losing weight and looking hungry. He had seen her poolside in short, white pants and a flimsy T-shirt, and she had looked attractive. He recalled smiling, and she had looked back gratefully. Rubens would have painted her with delight, even though she wasn't as full as his usual ones.

Frank dozed for a while. When he woke up and looked around, the deck around the pool was nearly deserted, except for Alice and her heavyset boyfriend coming out of the water. She was heavier than he remembered, and she looked tired today.

Frank sat up as they went by and his eyes met the boyfriend's. I'm here only to get laid, the man's eyes said apologetically, so don't think my taste is this bad.

Frank glanced at Alice. She shot him a look of defeat, and he wished that he had kept his hat over his face as her terror flooded into him—I'm going to be manless, without love or children. I'm going to die alone, an old maid. I've put out and gotten nothing for it, and I never will!

He lay back and covered his face, trying to regain his composure, but it was too late; she was inside him, infecting him with her fears.

He peered out from under his cap and saw her boyfriend smiling falsely at her. She smiled back more convincingly, but the turmoil inside her would not subside. At any moment, mantislike, she would reach out and tear off her boyfriend's head.

Frank felt a migraine coming on, and knew that this newest catch was going to be bad. He should have stayed in bed. He should not have underestimated his neighbors. Still peering out from under his cap, he could see that Alice was watching him, as if a way had opened between them and she could see into him.

It was nothing like that, of course. People imagined things about each other all the time, and the more clues they had, the more accurate their imaginings. People could feel each others' emotions because people were synchronous with each other, sympathetically tuned, because every human being was more alike than different, shading in and out of each other with no clear break anywhere. It was completely involuntary. Two people sucking each other's thumbs feel as if they are sucking their own thumbs. A man's next door neighbor sees a glum look on his friend's face, and from his years of conversation with him, suspects that he knows what's wrong. A man shows up at the local grocery when his wife is away, and the clerk imagines that the man's wife has left him.

The migraine was roaring in now. Frank got up and tried not to look at Alice. She was pitying herself, hungering and mourning at the same time, and he wished that he could stop her emotional bleeding. What he needed was to pick up something else to wipe out her fear and pain. He sat up and got to his feet.

"Hi, Frank!" Alice called, waving as her boyfriend lunged into the pool and made a massive splash.

Frank waved back and started for the gate. The migraine staggered him and he stopped, doubting that he would stay on his feet. It was his own fault for having come outside.

"Are you okay?" she called out.

"Fine," he said, then hurried through the gate and went into the building. The elevator door was open. He stepped inside and punched in his floor, already feeling better.

In his apartment, he looked out the window and saw Alice's boyfriend swimming across the pool. After one lap he struggled out and sat down in the chair next to her. She looked away. Frank watched them as they sat together, looking anything but together even from this height, settling for each other, afraid to be alone, and he knew that the boyfriend would not be with her long.

Frank turned from the window, sat down in his easy chair, and didn't know whether to laugh or cry, then looked around at his living room, noting that the carpet wouldn't need cleaning for some time yet. He examined his audiovisual system, with its two VCRs, wide-screen television, CD player carousel, turntable, and surround-sound speakers. The system kept him from having people over, because he didn't want to pick up their disdain for his stuff. The only thing he was sure of was that they'd admire his cherry desk. Who knew? They might like his whole place, but why take the chance? This worry had started when he had visited an old college buddy, Steve, and had picked up his fear of having his stuff dissed. The fear had been strong: don't dis my stuff, don't tell me, please, that it's second-rate, that there are better models. Frank had picked it up from Steve. He wished that he could simply pass it on, so that he could invite people again.

"You've always got *something*," Steve had said to him one day in their off-campus apartment. "We've got the same money, but you always have more stuff," he went on, pointing to Frank's then very modest stereo hookup.

"So? You get to listen to it."

"It pisses me off."

"Why should it? I only try to make the best of things, a little at a time, but it adds up."

"You're a pain in the ass. You never stop."

"Do the same, in your own way," Frank had advised him.

"And be like you?"

"In your own way, I said."

"You've always got to be in charge," Steve said, beginning to get aggressively strange.

"So what's your complaint?"

"You always have your own way with these little . . . additions of yours!"

"Look—things don't always go the way I'd like, but the fight is always joined, the victory real, however small. Your trouble is you don't fight, you don't struggle, and then you envy others. Cynical and skeptical, you poison your own life. And you'll never know what fortune might have brought you if you had been there to meet it. Any fool knows that when he goes to the track."

"You win at the track, Frank?"

"I've never been, but here's the difference between us. Fortune knows that I'm ready to be defeated *completely*, so there's not much it can do to me, except reward me enough to keep me playing, waiting for the moment of my ruin. But at that moment, I'll step aside and refuse to play."

"You'll see it coming?"

"I'll see it coming. I've seen it stalking me in countless small ways."

"You're a shark, Frank. That's all you'll ever be, but you hide it from yourself in a really nutty way."

"You really believe all this about me?"

"I'm not as sure of anything as you are. Maybe there's some kind of hope for you, but you'd have to fall flat on your face to find it."

"And that's why you'll never be anything," he had told Steve, "thinking like that. You're afraid of everything."

Today he could more easily see the bad stuff coming at him—especially when someone was ready to pass on a fear to him. They didn't know they were doing it, and they weren't really doing anything, of course. It was the small accumulation of information, the placing of three or more points on a piece of paper. Once there were points to connect, a line and a direction were established. With most people it was three scenes or more—situations or moments from their lives, enough for him to pick up the drift of their lives, maybe even sum up a life. They always had elaborate reasons for never becoming themselves. Dismay would flood through him, and shame for the other person, that they had fallen so low within themselves.

As for himself, he figured that insurance executive was about the best he could do; anything more demanding would be sabotaged by his ability to pick up other people's hurt. It had made him a good, sympathetic insurance salesman for a time, because he had a way of making people feel properly insecure about the provisions they had failed to make for their futures, before convincing them that his company would make things right for them—and keep it right for the rest of their lives. He had helped people to confront their fear of the future; but every sale had given him more than their signatures on the policy. With every "Trust me and sign on the dotted line" had come a new deposit from the damned.

Finally, after nearly twenty years, it was all he could do to control his flypaper innards behind the closed doors of a private office. He never went out into the field these days, and planned to retire by forty.

He got up from his chair and looked down at the pool again. Alice was now sitting alone, upright on the edge of the lawn chair, hands folded in her lap, and he guessed that she had just broken up with her man.

He lay down, grateful that the migraine had failed to blossom fully. Still fatigued by the poolside encounters, he tried to avoid fixing on Alice's terror of being manless. If he could somehow delay his reaction, the fear might die away.

He fell asleep and found himself standing on the second-floor porch of his first postcollege apartment, just as a group of homeless people came by and began to pick through his garbage. He went inside, but one young man came up the front stairs and opened his door.

"What do you want?" Frank called out.

"Ah, come on, Billy, let us in."

"I don't know you," he answered, going inside and locking the door behind him. He went to the phone and rang the police. When they were on their way, he opened the door and found the hall empty.

Rushing to the back porch, he opened the door a crack, peered out, and saw that the man, the old woman, and two teenage boys were still picking through his garbage. The police arrived and began to move them along as gently as possible.

Frank opened the door wide, and the man who had come to his door looked up and shouted, "Thanks for the help, Billy!"

And Frank became Billy, betraying these homeless derelicts. The young man looked up at him reproachfully as the police told him to move along.

Later the cop came up and asked, "Did you know any of them?"

"No, officer," Frank said with a twinge of guilt, wondering if somehow he had known the man and forgotten, or couldn't recognize him now. "No, I don't know any of them. Who are they?" Suddenly he was afraid that the cop wouldn't believe him.

"We've been watching groups of them since this morning," the cop said. "They seem harmless enough. Good thing it's warm. The mayor doesn't want any of them to die while they're in town."

"Where will they go?" he asked, but the cop turned away without answering, and Frank woke up to Alice's fear of growing old alone, drying up and wrinkling, and decided that he would spend the last of his vacation as far away from home as possible, as soon as possible, maybe somewhere in the Caribbean.

He heard her speak his name softly as he lay on the beach in the Bahamas. Then she was whispering to him, saying that he could give her what she needed, that she wasn't unattractive, that she could care for a man deeply and for a lifetime, suggesting to him that she was startling in the nude, that she exercised and kept up her health, that she would give him fine sons and daughters, that he should hurry to her now, before desolation ruined her for him.

He knew that he was saying these things to himself, but they were just as true as if she could reach into him and say them her self, as much as any human being could. He turned over, found his phone under the towel, and dialed his apartment building's switchboard.

"Henry, this is Frank. Connect me with Alice what's-her-name. You know who I mean?"

"Sure thing."

"Thanks."

The phone rang three times, then a fourth. He was about to hang up when she answered it.

"Hello, Alice?"

"Yes?"

"This is Frank. You know."

"Yes, Frank. What is it?"

"Well, I was wondering if I could come over and talk to you when I get back."

"Get back?"

"I'm in the Bahamas."

"And you're calling from there? What's this about?"

"Uh—I think it'd be better if I tell you when I get there."

She coughed nervously. "What's this about, Frank? You're going to make me wait and wonder—how long?"

"A day or two. It's nothing bad, believe me."

"Then tell me now."

He was silent, knowing that he should not talk to her over the phone, surprised by her alertness and suspicion. Her boyfriend had not left her in a good state.

"Frank?"

"See you soon!" he said, and pressed the button. He was out of breath, he noticed, and wondered why; usually, reaching out to someone calmed him. Then he realized that she had been confused by his call and that he had picked up some of her distress. But she had also been excited and intrigued by his interest, he concluded, and felt calmer.

She smiled at him when she opened the door. She was dressed in white shorts, a blouse, and leather sandals. "Come in," she said, stepping back. She might have been Vera, years later, except that Vera had been pretty.

He came in and she motioned him to the sofa. He sat down. She took the chair that faced him.

Leaning forward with a drawn expression on her face, she asked, "What is it, Frank?"

He smiled. "You do know I like you, don't you?"

She seemed startled and sat back. "Do I?"

"I've been watching you. By the way, where's your boyfriend?"

"I'm not seeing him now. . . ."

"Good."

"Good? Why?"

"You didn't really like him."

She looked into his eyes, flooding him with her vulnerability and hurt.

"You're really interested in me?" she asked mockingly.

"Yes," he said, glancing at her thighs and feeling certain that he would enjoy her.

"Do you have eyes? I'm a well-groomed dog. Why should someone as good-looking as you want me except to play with? Is it a bet of some kind? Or are you a freak?" He could see that it was humiliating her to say the words, but she was determined to protect herself by exposing him before he could trap her. "Maybe you just don't have any taste," she said regretfully.

"No, no," he answered, appalled at how little she thought of herself. He could see her self-loathing turning outward toward him. And yet a part of her had to be hoping that it was true, that he liked her, that at last something good might happen to her, something happy and warm and forgiving.

He watched it all flash through her eyes like a vision of salvation; and then she rejected it, retreating behind her armor.

She stood up, and he felt her strength as she glared at him. "You're not going to use me. Go away. Get out of here."

"But why—" he started to say.

"Let me spell it out. You're too good-looking to want me, so I'm some sort of convenience—right? What are you curious about? You think I'll be so grateful, I'll do anything. Is that it?"

"No—" he started to say as he stood up.

"Get out of here!" she shrieked. "You filthy son of a bitch! You think that lying about calling me from the Bahamas would do the trick? What was that all about?"

She was herding him toward the door, her cheeks flushed with rage. He wanted to embrace her, quiet her, but she looked as if she would tear at his face.

He backed away, opened the door and slipped out. She shoved it shut after him, and he heard locks closing.

"You're wrong, Alice," he said loudly, hoping to calm himself.

The door opened a crack and she put her head out. "What are you going to do?" she said jeeringly. "Put a ring on my finger? Or just move in for a few weeks?"

"Couldn't we just get to know each other?" he asked meekly. The blood was pounding in his ears.

"No sex?"

"Sex would be nice," he said, not wishing to insult her, "but we could skip it."

"We? Who's this we? You're flapping out there, Frank."

"Why do you think I'm so terrible? I've never done anything to you!"

A fearful look came into her face, and he couldn't tell whether it was fear of him or panic. She was speechless, as if trying to reverse herself, to start over with him, because she knew that she could not afford to pass up the smallest chance. She had to be ready when fortune smiled; but it was too late.

He stood there and smiled at her, trying to look harmless.

"Is this the wise look you save for crazy females?" she said, then moved back and slammed the door. He heard her crying.

Putting his head to the door, he said, "I'm sorry, Alice. Couldn't we be friends?"

"I don't want your pity. Go away and find yourself some bimbo. It's what you really want."

"Alice—"

"I'll call the police!"

"I'm sorry I bothered you."

He felt her hunger reaching out to him, and trembled inside.

"I'm good enough to fuck, but not enough to love," she said suddenly.

"What? How can you say that about yourself?" he asked, impressed by the conviction in his voice, and felt a growing self-control.

"It's true. I've had it proven to me often."

"Alice, open the door," he said sternly.

"So you can be nice to me? What can you do?"

She was right. What could he do? Say that he loved her? That he would treasure her for always? That he would devote himself to making her happy? That's what she needed, but was he ready to do that? He didn't know. She was inside him with her pain, twisting. He was infected with her fear, standing on a cliff and unable to back away from the edge. In a moment he would be a bloody mess on the rocks below.

Back away, he told himself. Don't say another word. Just go away and forget it. He felt calmer.

"Are you there, Alice?"

Mercifully, she did not answer, and he breathed a sigh of relief as he retreated from her door.

In his apartment, he stood in the kitchen and considered going away again. Maybe to Hawaii. He could take another week off if he wanted to. Unable to decide, he stripped down to his shorts and went to exercise on his Soloflex, turning on a bit of Vivaldi on the way to drown out his thoughts.

After he had worked up a sweat, he stopped and lay there, cooling down as the Vivaldi went into a slow movement, and realized that the door to his life had had to stay closed. He lived outside himself, afloat in other lives because he had no life of his own. Nothing he had ever feared had ever happened to him—not disease, financial troubles, or lasting disappointments in love, because he had never loved anyone.

He got up from the machine, went out into the living room and looked out the window at the old, wooden house across the street. It was a three-story, gabled structure that would soon be torn down because the landlord was unable to rent it. Suddenly he imagined that he had moved into the second floor with only a bed and a table, because he had lost his job and his possessions. All he had was a bit of money, the bed, and the table.

He imagined sitting at the table, looking out through the curtainless window, looking back at himself across the street, wondering which of them was real, feeling his awareness switch back and forth like a swinging pendulum. . . .

I was something else once, he told himself, suddenly afraid of the wishes lurking in his fears. What did he want to happen? What had he ever wanted to happen to him?

He clenched his teeth, suddenly dismayed by what he had become, and the cap on his left front tooth slipped off into his mouth.

He held the cap in his mouth, rolling it around on his tongue, afraid to spit it out. The ground-down, naked tooth would look like the bottom of an ice cream cone and be discolored from years of being scaled away, someone had once told him. As he touched it with his tongue, he felt the sensitive tooth hanging there like a salty stalactite.

He looked at the building across the street again, and his phone chirped.

"Hi, this is Frank," his message announced. "You know what to do."

"Frank?" Alice said softly, and he felt her trembling self-hatred. "You can come over, if you still want to. Now would be okay."

The vision in his right eye went black; then in his left.

Both eyes cleared, and he longed to escape into the bare room in the old house across the street.

"Frank?" Alice asked with a painful ache in her voice. "Please pick up."

The beeps cut her off, and he felt his stomach seize up into a solid mass of stone. His breath came with difficulty.

At any moment, if he didn't prevent it, the black, unforgiving nothing would invade his eyes again. He had to write her a convincing, heartfelt note at once, then go see her as soon as possible.

Desperately, he turned away from the window, went to his small, cherry desk, sat down, pulled open the drawer violently, and began to fumble around in it for a sharp pencil.

Hell Just Over the Hill

*R*ICK GOT ON THE BUS AS IF ENTERING A CON-
fessional, overnight round trip to anywhere, found an empty
double toward the middle, and began to drift into self-examination
as the half-filled bus left the station. Unlike most who mull while
traveling, he usually arrived at his destination and at some definite
conclusions at the same time. He had sometimes felt a bit guilty
about this, wondering if he was avoiding some terrible truths, and
was only too willing to accept simple-minded lies about himself.

But today it was different. After a few idle thoughts about leaving Rita and all his possessions behind, his mind cleared suddenly,
as if he had walled himself off from the worrisome regions of his
mind and was free at last to look outward beyond himself. He just
needed to get away for a day. No destination, no luggage. Tomorrow
he would come home to the woman he loved and try again.

As the bus fled north through the spring afternoon, the sun
broke through in the west every few minutes, and it seemed to him
that the coach was trying, and failing, to turn east to escape the sun.
Ahead, the spring green hills were like broccoli under a nuclear
cumulus cloud, marking hell just over the hill, where he imagined
infernos of red coals smoldering in deep valleys under a bruised
and bloodied sky. At his left and right the hills reminded him of the
bellies and pubic mounds of reclining women, and Rita's dark eyes
stared into him with resentment as he raised his hand to strike her

across the face. And he had done so—because she thought he wouldn't, softening the blow as much as he could; but she hadn't noticed that as she fell back onto the bed and wept into the pillow. There was just no way to convince her that he had been faithful to her. But it wasn't any of that. It was the lack of money, the bad job he had, their inability to plan for anything more than a month ahead. It was the disappointment and pity they saw daily in each other's eyes.

The driver coughed into the microphone and said, "Sir, please keep your boy seated. Standing is not permitted while the bus is in motion." The man, a Hasidic Jew wearing a hat, long bushy beard, and forelocks, motioned for his son to sit down, then glanced with embarrassment at his fellow passengers. In a few moments the boy was up again, and the driver repeated his request, sounding even more irritated, and the father looked even more uncomfortable as he pulled his son back down into the seat. Rick noticed that the driver had resumed his animated conversation with the middle-aged woman in blue jeans sitting just behind him, ignoring the sign above the windshield that prohibited passengers from talking to him while the bus was in motion.

As evening came, the bus seemed to gain speed, as if entering a vast cave, with engines roaring to keep up its courage. It rushed by a small lake, whose waters shook in the twilight like the gelatinous skin of a beast. Near a small town, the bus crept by a well-known mental hospital, where the troubled had responded to the world by withdrawing into madness, while their keepers had adapted by becoming unfeeling and objective, wearing the paper blinders of theory. It seemed saner to him to lose one's mind in the world's circus of unreason than to congeal into a fortress of practicality and convenience. The genuinely insane were often sane among themselves, while displaying all the diagnostic labels to doctors and staff. As refugees from life, they knew amongst themselves who was truly ill—the real monstrosities prowling outside.

At one small town that was scarcely more than a row of old, wooden houses separated by a short strip of asphalt roadway, a tired-looking teenage girl, chubby but still vaguely nubile, got on with a sloppily clothed baby and took the empty seats in front of him, putting the child in the one free seat across the aisle. The well-dressed older woman in the window seat looked at the child with disdain through designer glasses, and got up, saying, "I'll go sit up front, and she can have both seats. She seems very tired." The girl did not thank her. After a few moments she crossed the aisle and began changing the little girl's diapers. As the smell escaped, people in the nearby seats began to hold their noses. Finally, the procedure was over, and the girl went back to her seat, avoiding everyone's eyes as she sat down, took out a package of cheese twists from her bag, and began to devour them noisily.

"Mommy," the baby called out, then began to cry. She told it to shut up, and sat back to finish her snack.

When night came, the window at his right became a black mirror, in which his black shape also rode a bus. He leaned back and closed his eyes, dreaming of long-limbed women who smiled at him, and realized that he hadn't thought of Tess in months. "I'll tell my father and he'll make you marry me," she had said happily, slipping on her pink slacks over her long legs. "A dairy farm is not such a bad life." He had been too eager to believe that she was not underage. Maybe next year he wouldn't think of her at all. But as he listened to the teenaged mother crunching her cheese twists in the seat in front of him, he wondered whether Tess had gotten an abortion after he left, or was now a weary, hopeless teen mother like this one. He was lucky that Rita had never found out about Tess. The important fact was that Tess meant nothing to him, and could never have meant anything to him.

He opened his eyes and saw that another bus seemed to be trying to race his own. He peered out through the window, thinking that the drivers must be buddies on the same route. The glass seemed unusually cold against his nose and forehead.

He put up his hands to shut out the light, and across the short distance of no more than five feet he saw a long face with wide-set eyes and dark hair peering back at him. He pulled back, startled by the resemblance to himself. The other figure also pulled back in surprise. Rick sat back, afraid that he was losing his mind, then looked again and saw the other figure doing the same.

Several passengers in both buses were now peering out, and he heard people cry out on his side of the aisle. A few figures in the other bus were waving. Both drivers beeped their horns.

"What's going on?" a woman shouted up front. "Someone need help?"

"Stop the bus!" an old man cried in panic.

Both buses began to slow down. Rick saw a rest area coming up—a large, asphalt-covered half circle tucked into a wooded area, with a dozen picnic tables on the grass before the trees. There was a break in the trees, but it was too dark now to appreciate the view. A wind waved the branches as if a storm was coming.

The other bus pulled in first. His bus crept in across the gravel and stopped alongside. Rick squinted through the window and saw the other driver come out. His driver also emerged. The two doubles stood gaping at each other, then both men staggered over to a picnic table and sat down, trying to absorb the shock.

As they watched this meeting of the drivers, a cry went up from the people in the seats ahead of him. A few people were getting up and leaving the bus.

"What is this?" a man demanded from his left.

"Can't you see?" the older woman shouted at him, and the man crossed the aisle to look out.

Rick got up from his seat and went past the young mother and her child. Both were sound asleep, oblivious to their surroundings, even though he bumped her with his thigh as he hurried forward.

He came out into the windy, spring night and joined the uneasy group that was curious enough to confront the people from the other bus. There was enough light spilling out between the coaches for him to get a good look at his double, who was standing just three feet away, in the same wrinkled tweed jacket and faded blue jeans, with a beaten expression on his face, accepting this strange doubling as if it were a judgment. At his left stood the woman in blue jeans, the Hasidic man, and the well-dressed older woman with designer glasses. Next to her stood two men who looked like plumbers. Rick glanced to his right and saw the same row of people repeated, then noticed that everyone from the other bus except his double was dressed too warmly for spring.

Silently, as their eyes adjusted to the light from the coaches, the two rows of doubles began to eye each other with curiosity. His own took a step toward him and asked, "Did you do it, too?"

"What?" Rick asked in a whisper.

"You know."

"What?" Rick repeated uneasily, feeling a rush of guilt, as if he were sharing the other's thoughts and feelings. The four plumbers were looking each other up and down. The two old women were staring at each other intently and adjusting their glasses. The Hasidic men seemed to bow to each other, then one spoke in a foreign language. Then they grabbed their hats to keep the wind from taking them.

"Well?" Rick's double asked.

He took a deep, desperate breath suddenly, shook his head in denial, and backed away in fear. The others, on both sides, were also turning away and drifting back toward their buses, dazed, not wanting to know more, he realized, because there was nothing to be gained from talking to their doubles. They were all afraid, knowing that somehow a wall had crumbled, a necessary wall that must never be breached. Rick glanced toward the picnic table where he expected to see the two drivers, but they were both gone. The wind picked up in the trees, and a gust hit him in the face. He turned away.

"Wait," his double said, stepping toward him. "I'm Rick Barrow." The words came out in a strange, distorted roll over the rush of the wind, and Rick was suddenly afraid that it might be dangerous for doubles to touch or even speak to each other. He retreated, mentally struggling to slip behind the wall that should not have come down.

Then, on each side, the passengers turned and got back on the bus. He gave his double a wave; the other did the same, as if in a mirror, and turned away. He looked up and saw the young mother at the window, mouth open as she stared across at her double.

Rick came back to his seat, then decided to move back by two from the mother and her child. He slipped into the window seat and gazed out at the other bus, noticing that even the coach number was the same.

"Where's our driver?" a man shouted up front. "Let's get going!"

Rick looked toward the picnic table where the two men had sat down. There was no sign of them.

"Where are they?" the woman in jeans demanded.

"Can anyone drive a bus?" asked the man across from her.

Rick knew that he could drive the bus, if necessary. Suddenly the driver came back, threw himself into his seat, and closed the door. He gunned the engine and pulled out from the rest area. The other driver did the same.

The buses began to run side by side in the night, each trying to leave the other behind, and failing. Rick wondered what the two drivers had said to each other, then saw that the buses were drifting toward each other, as if trying to merge. Sparks jumped between the coaches, crackling and lighting up the road with flashes of blue electric glare, and he glimpsed himself staring through the other window. People shouted and cursed in panic.

"Get away from it!" a man shouted to the driver.

"Shut up!" he answered. "Something's pulling us together."

Together, Rick thought, wondering if the two buses had been one and the same just recently, and were now struggling to regain that state. He did not feel diminished by half, but would he even remember what had been subtracted?

The buses raced less than a foot apart. He stared at himself across the distance, at the starlit and shadowed face gazing back at him, and realized that there was a whole world behind the man in the other bus, but his movements did not match his own, and were not a mirror image, either, from what he could see. A blue glow came up from the roadway.

Both buses slowed as they neared a causeway that led out across a lake. The other bus pulled ahead suddenly, went through the railing without shattering it, and continued on a phantom road. He realized that there had to be a road across the lake, even if he couldn't see it. The lights of the bus were not reflected in the dark water. The bus receded and disappeared as his own reached the end of the causeway.

The driver pulled up on the shoulder and shut off the engine. After a long silence, someone asked, "Where was it going?"

"Same place we are, I suppose," the driver answered, turning on the engine again and steering the bus back onto the highway. "We're going to be late," he added.

"What are we going to do about this?" the woman behind him asked loudly.

After a moment the driver picked up his mike and said over the speaker. "Folks, we saw a ghost—I guess. Don't know what else to call it, or who'd be interested in hearing about it. Each of you can do as you wish, but leave me out of it. I've got a wife and two kids to support, and I had to move up here from Texas to get this job when the strike started. I'd forget it if I was you. What good can it do you, or anybody, to talk about it? Maybe it was just a delusion of some kind. It'll make you nuts to think about it too much."

No one answered him. Rick could feel the need in the passengers to accept what the driver had said. There were murmurs of agreement, slowly dying away like bad memories into silence.

Listening to the steady rhythm of the engine and the tires bumping across the seams in the concrete highway, Rick sat back and wondered whether he could feel his doubles as they came and went throughout infinity. He had always been more than a little in love with death, or rather with the vision of absolute, sublime peace; but that rest could never be, and had never been, he now realized. *We are forever born and dying in all the infinity of worlds. I am forever,* he told himself, because he was always alive somewhere. They were strangers, all those others. He could not know them any better than he could know himself. He could not choose the thoughts and feelings that came into him like invaders to direct his body. Something that he called himself lived at his center, but it was older and more powerful than the self he knew. That self knew what it wanted to do, and there was no way to resist when it took over. He closed his eyes and felt himself deathless.

In the morning he opened his eyes to fall foliage turning on the hills from green to red, yellow to brown, leaves shrinking and drifting to the forest floor, deathless in their individual deaths, and realized that the spring in which he had begun his bus ride was gone. How could he have been so mistaken about the season? And yet the evidence of his eyes was undeniable. He had dreamed the spring, he told himself as the bus neared the city.

The PA speaker crackled. "Can anyone direct me into the station?" the driver asked. "This is my first time on this route."

Rick got up, went up the aisle and stood behind the driver.

"Take this exit coming up," he said, "then turn left, cross the bridge, turn right, and that will put you into the station."

"Thanks," the driver said.

Rick stood there to make sure there was no confusion, and noticed snowflakes drifting in against the windshield. "That was pretty weird last night," he said.

"What was what?" the driver asked.

"The two buses."

The driver shook his head and smiled at him. "We're the only bus on this route. You okay?"

"What's today?" Rick asked, looking around at a few of the other passengers. They all seemed unconcerned.

"November 21," the driver answered. "What did you think?"

Rick took a deep breath and made his way back to his seat, wondering what had happened to him. No one else seemed to be worrying about the November outside, or what had happened last night.

The young mother was combing her hair and staring at her child, who was still asleep in the seats across the aisle. "That was something last night, wasn't it?" he asked.

She gave him a bored look and said, "I was asleep. We hit something?"

Rick sat down without answering her. Obviously, they had all forgotten. Suddenly he was looking forward to getting on the homeward bus and seeing Rita again, regretting all his violence against her. She was hard to live with, but so was he. She had probably forgiven him by now, and would be waiting for him at the station, as she had done in the past when they had quarreled. He sat back and waited for the bus to pull into the station, anxious to get off and take the return coach home.

As the bus rolled to a stop, he got up, hurried down the aisle, and staggered out into the arms of two uniformed cops.

"Richard Barrow?" the big one asked, grabbing his wrist.

"Yes," he said, as the shorter cop took his other hand.

"You're under arrest for the murder of Rita Malthus," the tall cop said, slipping on the first handcuff.

"What?" he asked, stunned, "But it wasn't me."

"Oh, yeah?" the short cop asked.

"It was . . . the other one," Rick said, remembering the spring outside the windows.

"No kidding?" the tall cop said. "Then you have nothing to worry about."

Rick began to struggle as his hands were brought together and the second cuff snapped shut. "Ask the driver. It wasn't me!" he shouted, choking on the words. "Ask him!"

"Don't worry, buddy," the short cop said, smiling at him. "We'll ask the driver. We'll ask everyone."

"He'll tell you," Rick said, feeling his throat go dry as they began to lead him away. He looked over his shoulder for the driver and saw the Hasidic man and his son staring at him as they stepped off the bus. The young mother, child in arms, was just behind them, chewing gum—

—and he saw Rita's strangled body in his arms, a minute after she had told him about the phone call from a pregnant Tess—

"It was spring earlier today," he tried to say loudly but couldn't. Sweat ran down his back, and he saw his guilty double arriving here, free of his crime, and taking the bus home to an unsuspecting Rita, to kill her again. He was in the station right now somewhere, waiting to board.

"You've got to stop him!" Rick cried, tearing the words out of his throat. They came up like razors. Hot blood burned through his belly and spread into his guts. A fist closed around his heart, and he staggered, but two cops held him up. "You have to stop him," he repeated weakly.

"Don't worry, buddy," the tall cop said coldly. "We've got him."

The Alternate

"**D**IDN'T YOU JUST COME BY HERE A FEW MINUTES ago?" the grocer asked as the register ground out the receipt.

Bruno Lumet looked up from his wallet, one finger still in the billfold, and said, "No, I don't think so. Oh, and give me a box of that mint tea behind you."

The grocer shook his head, reached back and grabbed the tea from the shelf behind him, then entered the additional purchase. He was scowling when Lumet handed him the money and took his change, dropped the box of tea into the grocery bag as he picked it up, and went out the door without his receipt.

As he walked up the street toward his apartment house, the morning sun seemed too warm on his back, the trees too green for autumn, the sky too blue after his night shift at the newspaper. The effort of making the stories fit the columns had wound him up; it was like trying to make bad paintings fit the wrong frames. At the start of the week a paperback house had rejected his suspense novel because it had been too short, they said, dashing his hopes of quitting the paper; and they had not asked him to expand the novel, which only meant they hadn't much wanted it at any length. He would have to remail it to the next publisher on his list before he went to bed this morning.

In front of his house he met the milkman coming down the steps with a basket of empty bottles.

"Good morning, Mr. Lumet," he said. Lumet nodded to him and went up to the front door. "Say, Mr. Lumet," the milkman said from the sidewalk, "didn't I see you at the sports shop last night about nine?"

Lumet turned around and said, "I was at work, Harry, so how could it have been me?"

"Really? You didn't say hello when I did, so I thought maybe I'd delivered some bad milk, or something."

"Wasn't me, Harry, and I'm not mad at you." Irritated, he turned, went through the front door, and up the one flight to his apartment. He stumbled tiredly down the hall and entered by the kitchen door, letting it slam behind him

He unpacked the groceries on the table and put them away in the refrigerator and into the cupboard over the sink. Then he went out into the living room and through to his bedroom, where he took off his raincoat and hung it up on the standing rack. He pulled off his tie and sweater and hung them on the chair by the window, then wandered back out into the living room and sat down on the sofa.

All through these ordinary actions of coming home after work he had felt distant from himself, as if he were watching another person's daily rituals. For a moment, it had seemed to him that he did not know the milkman. Now, as he sat in his small living room, nothing seemed right. Objects, both near and far, seemed too clear around the edges, as if he were looking at them through color-corrected, deep focus lenses. The green rug was too vivid. On the coffee table the partly opened brown paper package of his book manuscript looked too heavy, the string pulpy where he had cut it.

He told himself that he was tired, and irritated by people insisting that they had seen him elsewhere. At work, June from distribution had asked if he had parked his new car next to hers, even though he had always used public transportation. Felix, the city editor, had asked him if he was planning to quit the paper, and had gazed at him strangely, but had not claimed to have seen him somewhere else. Maybe there was someone who looked like him; after all, the grocer and milkman were not drunk or blind. The look-alike was probably getting it from his end also. Maybe he should put an ad in the paper to clue him in.

He got up and went back into the bedroom, not having the energy or the heart to get his manuscript ready to remail. He'd do it tomorrow.

He had stripped down to his underwear, visited the bathroom, and was getting into bed when he heard a knock on the door. He put on his torn, red robe and went out to the front door.

He opened up and saw that it was the caretaker.

"Mornin', Mr. Lumet, but I had to come and ask . . ."

"What is it, Frank, I'm very tired."

"Was you home last night?"

"You know I work nights."

"Well—the guy below you was woke up when you came in stomping at three in the morning."

"Not me. I was at work."

"Well—he's new here, I know, but he said he *saw* you come in and out, and you was banging around and woke him up before you left. He's mad. I sleep deep, and didn't hear a thing, but I had to check with you."

"Frank, it wasn't me. I just got in, as usual. It must have been a drunk on the stairs."

The caretaker sighed. "Okay, Mr. Lumet. That's what I'll tell him. But it's okay with me if it was you, so keep it down. If it was you." He smiled, then turned and went down the stairs.

Puzzled, Lumet closed the door, went back to the bedroom, took off his robe and threw it on a chair. His brain refused to shut down as he got into bed. Maybe someone had been here. The lock was no great shakes. He had opened it himself once with a credit card . . .

After tossing and turning for an hour he knew that he would have no peace until he had checked the entire apartment. He got up and put on his robe, went out through the living room, into the kitchen and into the bathroom. The door was closed, but he now remembered finding the door open and the sun bright in the frosted window when he had come home. He couldn't be sure.

Opening the door, he went in and checked the medicine cabinet. He was out of aspirin, but there was otherwise nothing out of the ordinary. He closed the cabinet door and went out to the kitchen. The beer and wine were still there in the refrigerator. He reached in and took out the opened bottle of red wine. It slipped out of his hand and shattered on the tile floor. He cursed as a pool of red liquid crept around his bare feet, thinking of the man downstairs, but he was unlikely to complain about daytime noise. Lumet left the kitchen, promising himself to clean up the mess later.

After a few minutes in bed he began to hear the sounds of early cars starting in the street; more distant noises seemed to arrive with the increase of daylight filtering in through his closed curtains. He closed his eyes and relaxed, and listened to his heartbeat in moments of silence as he tried to reduce to unimportance all the frustrations of his recent months. It would be restful, he imagined, to accept his life at the paper and no longer see it as a prelude to a more demanding existence as a human observer, a writerly seer, who would happily baffle most people . . .

He had a sudden, wild impulse to look under his bed. The command had been waiting for him, somewhere behind his free will, telling him that under the bed was the one place he would never look because he was an adult. Was he falling apart after a few minor irritations and one editorial rejection?

Finally, he accepted that he would look under the bed. It was part of human irrationality to remain unconvinced, even in daylight. Seeing was believing, and so much stronger than any line of reasoning, even when reason was right and could dispense with sight, and he hated the proud child in himself for giving in.

He rolled to one side of the bed, put his head over the side, and saw layers of dust that would have to be cleaned up. He tried to breathe gently, reluctant to stir up too much dirt. There was nothing under the bed except dust and dust devils, happily still, not to be disturbed on pain of sneezing.

He began to cough, and started to pull his head back up when he saw something taped to the springs. He stared at it, slowing his breathing. You knew it was there all the time, he told himself, you knew. But how did you know?

He got out of bed carefully, suddenly proud of his craft and powers of observation. He went down on all fours and put his head and shoulders under the bed. The thing looked like some kind of canister. There was a small dial on it. He touched it carefully. Some mechanism was working inside. He felt it in his fingers.

He got out from under the bed and went to the dresser to get a pair of scissors. Then he crawled under the bed again, cut the tape that held the thing to the springs and grabbed it with one hand. Dropping the scissors, then holding the thing carefully, he slid out from under the springs, stood up slowly, and sat down on the edge of the bed.

He coughed a few times to clear his throat. There was no doubt about it. Someone had come into his apartment last night and attached this thing to the bedsprings.

He put the cylinder down on the blanket and stood up, realizing as he looked at it that it seemed to be a gas canister, timed for release while he slept.

He leaned close, looked at the small dial, and smiled at his own cleverness as he touched the setting and brought it back to zero. The barely audible clock stopped. He stared at the object, wondering if he had made some kind of mistake, and this was some kind of insect repellant. It seemed too easy to find, but then again perhaps no one had expected that he would ever have time to find the canister before it went off.

It made no sense. Who would want to kill him? Maybe a story of his in the paper had angered someone. He had done a few society announcements, but nothing that might anger a reader. A crank might take offense at anything, he told himself, then wondered if he had a box that would hold the canister, so he could take it down to the police station.

His whole body now ached from tension and tiredness. He should have been asleep by now, but he was wide awake, asking again who would want him dead. Maybe the thing was just a harmless joke? But he had no close friends in Boston. They were all out in California. Had one of them stopped by?

As he stared at the canister, it began to seem very familiar. He stared at it in fascination. It was all so perfectly obvious, and impenetrable at the same time. Its presence made him inexplicably angry at himself . . .

The phone rang, but he did not hear it until its chaotic insistence began to seem threatening. Was his enemy calling to see if he was unconscious, or dead? He ignored it and hurried to his closet to find an empty shoebox.

He opened the door and saw, in one frozen moment, the crossbow release with a whoosh, followed by a crunch as the bolt pierced his breastbone. He fell back as the steel bow shook where it had been attached to the wall. The phone was still ringing. He lay on his back, listening, hoping that it would not stop, clutching the bolt in his chest. The phone stopped. He heard his own labored breathing and felt the blood pumping out of him into his hands . . .

He heard footsteps in the hall and someone was opening his door with a key. It opened and closed, but no one came into the bedroom to help him.

Someone was standing in the living room, breathing heavily. Someone was waiting for him to die. Lummet opened his mouth to cry out, but no sound came from his throat. He felt the cold spreading through his body, and knew that he was dying . . .

The noise last night, he thought, had been the stranger who now stood in his living room setting the canister and the bow in place. He had wanted to make sure that one or the other would get him.

The sun came up over the houses across the street and brightened the curtains. It was nine in the morning by the dresser clock. Lumet wondered who at the paper would write his obituary. There would be no one to send his novel around for him.

The blood was still welling up around the bolt and through his hands, and he felt a great weight on his heart. A pool of blood was forming around him on the linoleum, and he wondered if it would equal the pool of wine he had left in the kitchen. Then his chest burst and the pain stopped his pitying, and the cold took him over.

At last it was over. Bruno Lumet walked into the bedroom from the living room and looked down at his dead body. The pain and dying of his double was, in a sense, his own, except that by killing him he had saved his own life. The number of overlays had diminished in recent years, but no one was immune from these freak alternates slipping in from the half-worlds of unrealized time. No one can kill them for you, he had been told, and you have to do it without meeting them face to face while they lived. That's what the theory said; not that anyone had ever met himself to really know whether meeting one's living double would be lethal. The theory never said how one would die from such a get-together, besides a lot of talk about balancing energy potentials to prevent some bizarre folding up of time and space. Whether it would be widespread or local, no one had been able to say, except to suggest insane tanglings and twistings of historical patterns and individual relationships. Although these slips had occurred throughout human history, long before they were understood, they now required the immediate identification, stalking, and elimination of the intruder double to avoid the piling up of inconsistencies that could only end in a final paroxysm. People who had studied the problem knew what had to be done.

Lumet looked at his double's corpse. The poor soul had certainly died from encountering his double, without quite meeting him, of course, except in death. The old stories had never said anything about killing yourself.

He went over to the bed and examined the failed canister. It had seemed unlikely that the victim would find and disarm it. It would have been more merciful than the bow, but that kindness no longer mattered. He had killed him without meeting him, and he had done it in time—crudely but effectively. He would live despite his double's watchfulness.

After he had cleaned up some of the mess, he gave up and went out into the living room, sat down on the sofa, and looked at the book manuscript lying half out of its brown wrapper on the coffee table. He had no memory of writing it, but it properly belonged to both of them, and he would faithfully mail it out again; after all, one rejection meant nothing.

He looked at his watch, thinking that he would call in sick tonight. He would need time to see his doctor, to help fade the pseudo-memories he shared with his double. He might even need a prescription to break the links this apartment might have developed with his double's alternate elsewhere. Dreams might reopen the way if he didn't suppress them. The treatment of slippage accidents was not yet as sophisticated as it needed to be, but new things were being learned with every encounter.

But he knew that whatever wounds had been inflicted on him and his world would heal, and it was unlikely that this kind of threat to his identity would ever find him again. He had seen to that in the lawful manner, for himself at least.

In his elsewhere, in his one selfdom among the unseen infinity of his selves, Lumet went down to the police station and filed a fracture report, giving the approximate time he had become aware of his double's overlay, and all the details that he could recall. The police removed the body, certified its identity, and assured him that they would handle all the remaining formalities.

Earth Around His Bones

*T*HE OLD KEEPER LIVED ALONE IN THE NORTH corner of the cemetery, in a small, run-down cottage which faced on one side, the wet bogland, and on the other, the weathered stone slabs standing in the bright green grass.

His tasks were few and he rarely left the cottage. Nothing important had ever happened to him. He was not interested in the world, and no one ever came to see him. He slept a lot, and his old age seemed to go on peacefully with no end in sight. He had stopped counting the years after eighty-three, and he managed to cut the grass twice a year.

One cold winter night a voice spoke to him in his sleep. *"You hear me, don't you?"* The voice was a hissing whisper in the keeper's brain. *"No, don't shut me out. Please don't!"* It was a badly frightened voice. *"Please listen,"* it begged.

The keeper stirred in his sleep. He had not dreamt in a long time. Outside the snow fell on the frozen earth. The vision of white flakes massing to cover the ground made him feel secure.

"I am dead," the voice said, *"you must believe me—I'm real . . . the darkness! I continue to think—I must be real. I was ill and I died. And the cold, I can sense the cold around me. I am buried."*

After a short silence the voice said, *"Whoever you are, I can feel your presence near me. Everyone was standing when I died. I closed my eyes and there was . . . nothing. Not death, darkness. A million souls could be thrown into all that darkness and it would not be filled. Death had been an impossible thing to me in my youth. Now I wish I could die, truly die . . . where are you?"*

The old keeper woke up in a cold sweat. Around him the room was quiet. In the wall space where once there had been a fireplace the gas heater glowed. The December stars shone coldly through the small window over the front door. He got up and went to the curtained window near the bed. In the cemetery, the stones cast solid black shadows, and the wind whistled through the bare trees. Foolish dream, he thought, and went back to bed. He pulled the woolen blanket more tightly around himself. It was an old friend, with him now for more than fifty years. His eyes grew heavy and he fell asleep.

The Voice returned.

"You disappeared," it said.

Then, *"I think I understand, but I can't seem to think clearly . . . Oh God!"*

And the voice in the night was still.

The ground unfroze.

Small rivulets of water ran down from the high ground into the cracked earth of the cemetery.

The spring air was humid.

The trees were thickening with leaves. The rains moistened the earth and the grass had to be cut.

There was a smell of soft bog and growing, living things everywhere.

The old man had almost forgotten his winter dreams. He cut the grass slowly, feeling useful again.

One warm night the voice spoke to him again, as if no time had passed. Its whisper was filled with a sense of fear and resignation. *"It's warm,"* it said. *"I am in the ground and it's warm. I wish I could see in this darkness . . ."* The old man tried to wake up, break the dream, and could not.

"My body is dead, but my . . . brain has not rotted. I am conscious, bound to the ruin of myself, mourning my own death. My sight is gone but I can see the window of my home—the only real thing left—beyond my reach. My body failed long before my mind could reach maturity . . . we have no time! I hate this darkness . . . and when I rot, when the meager tissues of my organic brain begin to rot, I will slowly lose what little sanity is left to me. I stood on a hill once when I was young, hoping to see the stars, covered by a monstrous overcast which would not break. I shook from the cold and continued look-

ing upward, as if I could find some meaning in that low sky . . .

"*Aaaaaaahhhhhh!*" the voice wailed.

The wail turned into a laugh.

"*It's warmer . . .*"

The keeper woke up with a cry.

The voice was still in his head, close to him—closer than anything he had ever felt in his life. It was laughing and talking to itself.

And the keeper knew that in one of the graves outside, in the moist earth, the worms had broken through the coffin and were feeding on the newly thawed mass of a man's decaying brain.

The body had died a while ago—the first death; but the man's awareness still clung to the rotting passageways which once had flickered billions of neuron connections.

The second death was near. The true death, the real end.

The voice whimpered, then was quiet for a moment.

Finally the keeper heard snatches of prayer, as the voice begged for the cold which had preserved it to return.

The whimperings became incoherent and insane. There was one last shriek before the final silence.

The keeper got out of bed and stood by the window. In the east the light of dawn was growing brighter, throwing a hint of redness into his frail curtains. He wondered how many of those buried in the cemetery had died this way. He wondered how many had been given the chance to communicate the truth of dying . . .

He went back to bed and lay there for a long time, wondering if he were going senile. But if what he had heard had been real, then the same fate awaited him when he died. Slowly his flesh would rot, while his mind endured, burning like the last of a candle; and he would have peace only when the thick earth closed around his bones with its moist embrace.

From that day his sleep was never peaceful. He retired the next month, and very rarely left the cottage.

In his ninety-first year he went blind. In winter the shrieks and whispers would come back into his mind and he would whimper in his bed at night, praying that somehow he could be cremated, burned into clean oblivion when he died, his bones charred into dryness by the flames.

On the first day of spring the cottage burned. The gas heater exploded, giving unlimited fuel to the fire. The frame of the cottage became an incandescent skeleton in the pyre, finally crumbling into ash. When at last the gas was shut off, nothing was left except the ash, which the wind came and blew slowly into the bogland.

Fire of Spring

*E*LINA'S SCREAM ECHOED IN CYRIL BELDON'S ears as he ran down the carpeted stone hallway of the castle. He carried a flint rifle in his right hand. Each step brought him nearer to the sight he had hoped he would never see, the death tableau which had marked the end of life for so many of his family. Every ten years one life had been taken, since the first massing of stones had created Dawnstone seven centuries ago. There had been omens. As soon as the walls of Dawnstone had been raised the sun had captured a blue star passing nearby, pulling it in close to itself. A year later the sun had consumed its small companion in a fiery storm which had dominated the sky for months, as if signaling the start of the terror.

He found Elina on the red carpet just beyond the turn in the passage. Beldon stopped, desperately hoping that she would scream again, but there was only a muted gurgle coming from her torn throat. It was the only sound he would ever hear from his beloved again.

There were six of them around her: dwarflike gargoyles two feet tall with wings folded across their backs. One held Elina's long hair with taloned fingers; two held her feet. Another was crouched near her neck, where he had been gorging on the flow of blood. The remaining two were kneeling over her belly which was smeared with blood.

Beldon fired his gun. The creature holding Elina's hair let go with a shriek and flew at him, eyes burning with bloodshot hatred. It was bleeding where the ball from the gun had penetrated its right wing. Beldon swung at the flying beast with the butt of his rifle. He knocked it to the floor where it lay still, its leathery wings spread open.

Their feast ended, the five others launched themselves toward the open window at the end of the hall. The great glass panels were fixed in place and a chill wind blew in from the foggy, spring night, filling the heavy, white curtains as if they were sails. The flying things were out and lost in the fog in a moment, leaving him alone with the body of Elina.

Beldon went up to the body and examined its state. Her stomach was a raw mass of drying blood. Even in death she clutched the flimsy night shirt that was bunched up around her waist. Her eyes were wide open as if still seeing the horror which had descended upon her.

He knelt down and closed them gently, pitying her young form. He took off his coat and covered her. Tears formed in his eyes.

He heard something stir on the rug behind him. He turned around suddenly and saw the creature he had struck with his rifle. Removing his belt he rushed over to it and bound its taloned hands together. Then, one by one, he broke the light bones in its wings by crushing them under his boots. When he was sure the beast would never fly again he stopped and looked back to Elina's body. Rage filled him quickly and he kicked the wounded gargoyle in the side. Tears rolled down his face, but the devil made no sound.

He picked the gargoyle up and carried it down the hall, and down the great stairs into the main room where he placed it on the warm, slate flooring in front of the large hearth fire. Then he went to the kitchen where he found a meat cleaver and carving knife.

When he got back to the fireplace the winged devil was thrashing around violently, straining at its bonds. Its eyes were fearful of the flames. Every few moments it stopped its struggles to look at the sparks which were landing near it on the slate.

Beldon kneeled down next to the creature's face and tried to catch its attention. He knew what he had to find out, even if he had to torture it for the information.

The fiery eyes found his suddenly and the beast spoke. "A thousand years more, you'll pay," it said. "The others will tell how you opposed us." Its voice was a hissing whisper broken with shrill, whistling sounds.

The creature's eyes were now betraying something of its pain. "What's a thousand years," Beldon said, "when you have the right of harvest at Dawnstone forever?" He paused. "Now," he continued, "where is your spawning ground? Tell me and I'll kill you quickly." He stared directly into its eyes and prodded it with the point of the carving knife.

"You will never know."

"I will know—you fly here in reasonable time so it must be near."

"What else do you know, fool?"

"It must be a small area, a place I know but do not recognize." He paused again. "I am the last and I will end it," he said, raising his voice, "I have to!" He drove the knife partially into the creature's side. "Now tell me, for my Elina, for my dying mother, tell me now!"

But the gargoyle's eyes were no longer looking at him. He knew that it had resigned itself to death. Beldon withdrew the knife point and considered what he could do to its body that would be cruel enough to make it speak.

Suddenly he picked up the meat cleaver and began hacking at the broken wings lying limp on both sides of the gnarly body. In a few moments he had severed the wings from the ratlike form. He picked up the pieces and hurled them into the fire.

"Your hands are next," he said.

There was no reply. Beldon looked around the huge room that was illuminated only by the fire. For a moment his own hatred astonished him. He thought of his mother asleep in the south wing of the castle—too deaf in her old age to have heard what was going on. But then, she had died inside when they had taken his father ten years ago. Even his marriage to Elina had failed to revive her. For years he had thought they would take her when the time came. Secretly he had hoped they would take the old woman and spare Elina. The thought shamed him now.

The shame kindled itself into a new rage. He brought the knife up to the beast's eye and pushed it in far enough to blind it. The gargoyle howled. The eye closed in shock as he withdrew the knife. The other one was watching him, jealous of its sight.

The creature asked, "If I tell you what you want to know, will you kill me quickly?"

Beldon was suspicious that the beast was trying to trick him into killing it. It would tell him some lie and he would kill it too quickly.

But maybe he had broken its sense of community with the others and death meant more to it now than any loyalty.

Swiftly Beldon put out its other eye, shouting. "No lies now. I won't kill you until I'm sure."

The creature was licking its thin lips and biting them in pain, and the only tears its eyes could shed now were made of blood. "This much is true," it said. "The first Dawnstone conjured our spirits from the black abyss and imprisoned them in the bodies of the creature you see me in. They were harmless little things which lived in the forest. After he had bound us into these forms, he bargained to release us if we gave him all our knowledge of the forces which rule the world. If we refused he would destroy us by turning loose his birds of prey. In those days it would have been easy because we were so small and unused to our new shapes. So we gave him all our knowledge of conjuring all the powers in the blackness between the worlds. But we also tricked him into performing a ritual which turned those same powers against him. When he tested his powers for the first time, his body was turned inside out and torn into a thousand pieces; and the force of his death hurled a blue star into the sun. That much you know. But what you have never understood is that his spirit itself was destroyed, and all the heirs of Dawnstone were delivered into our power. After the lives of one hundred generations have been destroyed, we will be free of our fleshy prisons. Until then we cannot leave our bodies, but we can renew them from Spring to Spring, making them grow larger and more strong on the blood of our enemies. My death is nothing. I will have a new body at next birthing. Kill me now."

"But where are you born?"

"From the earth itself, but even if you knew the place you would not be there at the right time to see it. There is nothing you can do except wait for the passage of time to free Dawnstone." The creature sneered at him. "And the one hundredth generation will be the last. None will follow it to rob us of our vengeance."

Beldon raised the meat cleaver and buried it in the gargoyle's throat, cutting through to the spine, killing the creature instantly. For a moment he regretted his anger. He had to remind himself that this was not an individual he had spoken with, but a monstrous single being incarnated in living forms. He thought he could almost sense its bodiless evil near the fire, hovering there, mocking him . . .

He sat looking at the body for a long time. Spring, he thought, the creature had spoken of spring. Tomorrow, this morning, was the first day of spring. He thought of eggs hatching in the earth—in a field. The only fields near the castle were worked by the peasants.

But he did remember a clearing in the forest which he had not seen since he was a boy. He had never been there on the first day of spring.

He got up and threw the body into the flames. He was certain that his guess was correct.

As he put on his cloak in the hallway he felt that some new sense was guiding him. From the rack by the front door he took a walking stick, instinctively thinking of it as a weapon.

He opened the heavy, oaken door. It squeaked loudly, bringing a sleepy servant out to close it behind him as he went out.

He went across the windswept outer court and through the open front gate. He wondered if he would be back before his mother woke up from her trancelike sleep.

He started to run in the predawn darkness, his robe a flapping wing behind him. He slowed to a walk and his hand was on his knife hilt. Deep inside him the need to hurry was a fearful urgency uncoiling into his limbs, a fluid looseness in his hands and arms and a constricting pull in his legs and thighs.

He came to the fork in the path which led down from the castle into the village. The way left led into the forest. He followed it without stopping. He knew that he had to be at the clearing before sunrise.

He started to run again. The trees became rushing shapes on both sides of the narrow pathway. They were gray and black forms with a thousand paralytic fingers outlined against a lightening sky.

He burst out of the forest into a large clearing and stopped. He looked at the ground carefully in the pale light. It looked as if it had been plowed a long time ago—but by whom?

Something was waiting to come out of the earth. He could almost feel its presence in the morning hush. He leaned on his walking stick and waited in the chill air.

The sun started to come up in the trees and the air grew warmer. It was a bright orange sun that grew hotter as it rose over the trees before him. A wind passed through the branches, fluttering the leaves for a moment before dying, leaving an abrupt stillness over the clearing as if the world was holding its breath . . .

Suddenly Beldon saw the earth crack open in a thousand places across the field. He saw that it was moist under the parched surface. As he watched, thousands of small, pink-red sparks pushed out of the wet dirt.

He stepped closer, leaning over, and saw the tiny body of a winged gargoyle, pink and wet all over, entering the world from below, hatching from some infernal egg that had been waiting in the ground.

The sun caught the creatures across the entire surface of the clearing, turning their tumescent skins into red-orange slivers of fire, thousands of them transforming the field into a flame-dotted ground surrounded by green forest. There was an odor of birthing coming up from the land, making Beldon gag. Before him an evil nature was throwing up the things which were his enemy, and would continue as the seasons turned. Each spring would be a fire-like beginning for these fleshy creatures, and all would struggle toward maturity and the aim of tormenting the heirs of Dawnstone.

Something seized Beldon from inside like a fist entering a hand puppet, and he gripped the walking stick with both hands. Raising it, he began to walk across the open rows in the field, striking the newly born devils with a rhythmic precision, splitting open their little heads and torsos, spilling their blood back into the soil. He was tireless. The force that drove him seemed endless. Fear, sorrow, and hatred had made an alliance for the possession of his body long enough to carry out this deed. His reason was an approving spectator.

He struck them until thousands lay torn open in the morning air, their blood clotting under the open sky. Beldon continued until the sun was almost overhead. Thousands still remained to be killed. He did not know which horrified him more—the dead or the still living.

He grew tired, overwhelmed by the sheer magnitude of trying to stifle this fertility of numberless newborn. He stopped and picked up a living specimen. Its wings huddled close to its body. Its eyes were red rubies glazed with moisture. The creature opened its mouth to yawn and Beldon saw the tiny fangs, so much like the full grown ones which had take Elina's life.

He lifted the creature high over his head and dashed it to the ground. He stepped on it immediately with his boot heel, feeling its life melt away into the soft earth.

Around him shadows raced on the ground. Shapes covered the

sun. The shadows hovered near his feet. He looked up and saw five full grown gargoyles diving toward him out of the sun.

He raised his stick to defend himself but he was too tired. Sweat ran into his eyes. The talons struck him and hurled him to the ground. A blow hit him in the right temple and a shower of lights exploded in the darkness like sparks from a blacksmith's anvil . . .

He remembered being carried in the air and being dropped to the ground in the castle's courtyard. He remembered vague faces looking at him, the faces of his servants and his mother. He woke up in his bed thinking that now his mother knew about Elina. Through the window he saw dark clouds driving across the sky, leaden masses filled with flashes of lightning, each pulse of light growing stronger.

He got up knowing that they had brought him back so he would continue. They knew that he would go to the village eventually and choose a new bride. In time they might come for her, or her son or daughter, or his daughter's daughter. Someone every ten years, as long as there were victims.

There were too many of the creatures to stop. He would never be able to surprise them again, they would see to that. The clearing would be carefully guarded from now on. It would be unapproachable.

And yet, he knew, some would live at Dawnstone untouched. Perhaps the ones who would be close to him now, his future bride and children, maybe they would live in peace, unharmed. He almost hoped that he would be the next one to be taken, and his family-to-be spared. It seemed right that he should be next.

He walked over to the window and looked out at the driving clouds again. He felt very different now, sure that he would be the next one to die. But his family would live, and it seemed that it should be that way and no other. Rain was falling from the clouds now, curtains of sweeping water that struck the colored glass of his bedroom window. Wind rattled the frame. He felt the hollow emptiness of acceptance as he watched the horizon of swaying trees, and the line of darkness advancing on the castle. There was a sudden break in the storm clouds and the setting sun cast its redness into the rain, turning the droplets for an instant into blood.

First Love, First Fear

*I*T WAS COLD IN THE WATER. THE SUN WENT behind some clouds in the west, chilling the air; the sky turned a deeper blue, the sea became darker. Tim treaded water, watching the disk of the orange sun in the clouds massed on the horizon, no longer warm, a cadmium globe rolling through ashes, another sign that the long second-summer of Lea was finally ending.

The sun came out again suddenly, lighting the sky and warming his wet shoulders. He looked at the jagged rock ahead sticking out of the water; it was overgrown with glistening green seaweed. He swam toward it with renewed strength.

His father had forbidden him to swim too far from shore, but he would never know. He had gone to the starport a hundred miles down the coast to bring back a couple and their daughter to share the homestead, and would be back in a week.

Suddenly Tim was afraid of the depths beneath him. Cold water rushed up from below and swirled around his feet, sending shivers through his body. He thought of the mother-polyp thing he had dug up on the beach last summer. It had been a dead shell of a creature whose young had eaten their way out in the spring, leaving the parent open and raw. The insides had been rotting for a while when he had found it, and they had looked like red mushrooms and fresh liver covered by sand, a mixture of sandy smell and decay. He had covered it up quickly and it had taken a day for his stomach to settle. Were there any such things swimming under him now?

The planet was one huge ocean, miles deep in some places, warm and shallow for thousands of square miles elsewhere. New Australia was the only continent, with one starport a few miles inland on the west coast, just south of their homestead, and two dozen settlements scattered in a semicircle inland from the starport, the most distant a hundred and fifty miles inland. The interior was unexplored except for the satellite photomapping—a huge forest plateau covered by tall trees, some of them thousands of years old. Among the explored worlds the land was unique because it did not have a native population like most planets habitable by men. The intelligent folk of the world lived in the sea.

Tim swam more quickly as he neared the rock, still worried about what might be lurking in the water beneath him. His hands and feet touched the slippery rocks underwater; he grasped the sea plants growing there and pulled himself forward, half swimming, half crawling on the hidden rocks. At last he stood up in the water, balancing precariously.

He moved forward a step at a time until he was standing in front of the rocky spire. At his feet an alien crab fled into the water. He turned and looked back at the beach, but he could not hear the breakers, and the high, sand-covered rocks looked small from a quarter of a mile. The gnarly, black-barked trees, clinging to the rocks above the beach, were sharp against the sky.

He turned from the beach in time to see the orange sun slip behind the dark clouds which were pushing up over the edge of the world; he saw that it would not come out again before setting.

He grasped the clinging plants on the spire and began to move around it to the right, intending to circle it. He moved slowly, peering around as he went. The steel blue of the water made the very air seem darker. The breeze was quickly drying his skin and trunks, and he paused to brush some hair out of his eyes. For a moment his hand seemed darker to him, almost as if the sea had somehow stained it.

The beach was to his left now and he could see the first moon rushing up from behind the rocks, a small, silvery mirror, the brightest object in the sky now that the sun's direct light was gone. He knew that the water would be colder when he swam back. In the winter he might try walking out here across the ice.

He stepped around to the other side of the rock where he could no longer see the beach. There was a sharp tang in the air, ozone blown in by the wind from a storm at sea. A small wave broke against the rock, spraying him with foam, and he tasted its freshness with a shiver.

He brushed some water from his eyes and saw the shallow indentation at the base of the rock. He looked closer. It was almost a small cave. He bent over and went down on his knees for a closer look.

When he saw the dark shape crouched inside, his heart began to pound. She leaned forward and fixed him with her eyes. The pupils were a glowing red, surrounded by perfect white. He saw the gills on her shoulders opening and closing slowly as they gulped air. His eyes adjusted and he saw they were a delicate pink inside. She was a girl, one of the sea people; he was sure of that even though he had never seen a living girl, human or native, that he could remember. He had seen photos of women and of his mother, who had died in childbirth. He had been brought up by his father and Jak, the hired man, who was his friend and had taught him how to use the teaching machine from old Earth.

He stood up and moved back as she unfolded her body from the shallow cave, letting her hair fall down to her waist. She was just barely his height—about four feet ten. She had a warm, pleasant musky odor about her which made him want to stay near her. She stood only two feet from him, and he felt and heard her breathing as it stirred the air near his face.

Her feet were webbed, her legs were long and delicate for her height and build. Her waist was narrow, but her hips were full; her pubic hair was a mass of ebony curls, holding droplets of water and foam like milky white pearls. What seemed to be her breasts were partially covered by her long, black hair.

He felt a vague expectation. The wind was picking up, drying his trunks and skin, covering him with goose bumps. He could think of nothing except that he had to stand and look at her for as long as she continued to notice him. He felt a tightening in his stomach, and a delight that she was looking at him. He became aware of his pulse, beating just below the rush of the wind in his ears. The pleasure was accompanied by a sense of strength. The cold swim back would not matter; the rising wind and coming darkness were not important. The rock and sky and wind, and the home he had come from were unreal; his father was a distant image, far from the vivid reality around him.

She took a step toward him, looking up at him, her eyes wide and curious. She was smiling. He noticed that she had no eyebrows, and her gray skin was covered with a musky film which caught the light strangely. The smell of her was intoxicating.

She put one leg forward, bending it at the knee and brushing it against him, making him take a deep breath and sending shivers through his body. Then she opened her mouth and uttered a soothing, soprano-like sound, almost like the fragment of a song she would not sing. He smelled the freshness of the seawater in her hair.

He stood perfectly still, knowing that something was expected of him. Her presence seemed miraculous, and a moment like this might never come again. He would have to try it.

She reached out with a webbed hand and touched his exposed stomach just above the elastic of his trunks, breaking his resolve. Then she touched the green of the synthetic fabric curiously, as if thinking that it might be a part of him.

Suddenly she moved past him, brushing full against his body, and dived into the water between the rocks. He turned and followed her immediately, wading in and launching himself quickly after her. He swam out a few feet and treaded water, waiting for her to surface.

Without warning she pushed up against him from below and her head was in front of him. She was smiling again, her hair a tangle of black seaweed filled with water. Her body was hard against his for a moment and he was touching her round breasts with his fingers. And then she was gone again.

The western horizon exploded in reds and dark blues over the choppy ocean. The closed fist of clouds which had been holding the setting sun opened just enough to show the bloated and deformed sphere sinking into the sea, its dull redness staining the clouds and darkening the water.

She came up again a few feet away. She blew water out of her gills, and he wanted desperately to be near her, to reach out and touch her long hair, her stomach, and long graceful legs.

He swam toward her, but she dived and came up behind him near the rock. He watched her climb out, her body glistening, and the sight of her buttocks was a new delight—something he would have laughed at if merely told about. He remembered the fun in imagining what the women in the pictures from Earth would look like if he could undress them and turn them around. He watched her as she sat down with her back to the rock. Her gills spilled a little water across her front as she adjusted to the air.

He paddled toward the rock, watching as she stretched her legs in front of her, opening them for a moment while looking directly at him. He sank for a moment, paddling faster to keep his head above water. He bumped his knee sharply on the rocks.

At last he managed to get up on the rock again. It seemed colder and more slippery under his feet. He stood looking at her, confused, breathing heavily, pleased with himself, staring at her as if at any moment she might fade away. He was unable to look away; her eyes were rooting him to the rock.

A huge bellow sounded from the beach. Tim turned on the first echo, almost losing his footing. He regained his balance and looked toward the beach. Now the larger moon had just risen over the rocks, casting its dull gold light on the gray sand. The small moon, a bright silver disk almost overhead, would rush around the world once again before the large moon set. The rocks cast long, jagged shadows of solid black across the beach, Stygian teeth thrusting into the breakers. The shadows would recede as the larger moon moved across the sky. In the west the ocean had swallowed the rotting sun and the dark clouds had reknitted their ebony jigsaw, blotting out a third of the sky. The tide was coming in quickly now and soon all but the top of the spire would be covered. Overhead a few stars shone near the small moon.

The bellowing came again, an urgent, half-angry sound echoing in the rocks above the beach, carrying out to him over the water. The girl stood up and came toward him, but her eyes were fixed on the beach. He grabbed at her and tried to hold her, but she was steadier on the rock than he was. He slipped and fell sideways, his feet in the water.

She dived and swam toward the beach, slipping through the water swiftly, only her head showing. In a moment she was invisible against the dark water. He sat up staring at the shore, feeling desolate, as if his life had ended.

In a few minutes he saw a dark silhouette walk up on the beach from the water, as if the darkling sea had taken a shape. Another figure detached itself from the black of the rocks and came down to meet her on the moonlit sand, casting a long shadow before itself. The two silhouettes merged, forming a two-headed creature which cast a single shadow toward the sea. He watched it move away from the water until it became one with the rocks and invisible.

He felt drained, unable to move, filled up with the loss. He shivered, noticing the cold, and the world was empty around him except for the wind passing through like a hurrying intruder. On the beach the shadows were steady, clear-cut, yielding only to the light of the climbing moon. In the high places the dwarf trees were leaning back toward the land, letting go their leaves one by one . . .

He got up and waded into the water, uncaring of the sharp rocks, and threw himself in. He swam for what seemed a long time, once turning on his back in the inky wetness and pushing with his legs while looking up at a sky growing more opaque with cloud and mist.

Finally he stood up in the water and waded ashore. A wave knocked him down, but he picked himself up quickly and made it in before the next one.

Clasping his arms around his wet body he followed the double set of web marks up into the rocks. He began to climb, continuing even when there were no more prints to follow. He went over the top and began to descend; for a while he was aware only of his breathing and the pain in his cut toes and bruised knee. Gradually he became aware of another sound just below his normal hearing.

The only light now came from the big moon. The little moon had fled into the clouds covering the western sky. Tim went downward between the rocks, quickening his pace.

Somewhere below he heard a gentle washing on the beach. He listened, standing perfectly still. He tensed, aching with the thought that he had lost her. Somewhere the sea was coming into the rocks, perhaps through a channel cut by the tides, into a pool which filled up once a day at high tide. He had not been permitted to explore the rocks, and he realized that this was really the first time he had ever been a good distance from the house after dark, and by himself.

He took careful steps, each one bringing him lower, closer to the sound of the water. Then for an instant the angle was right and he glimpsed platinum moonlight floating in a pool of water. He stepped from the rocks onto level sand and the light disappeared.

He sensed that he was standing in a large, sandy depression circled by the high rocks. The pool and the channel cutting under the rocks were somewhere in the darkness ahead, perhaps a hundred feet away. He walked forward. The sand was still warm, and it made his feet feel better.

Clouds moved across the large moon, covering it. He stopped. There was another sound just ahead. He strained his eyes in an effort to force them to see. There was no wind in the sheltered area, only the sound of water moving in the pool, and the other, almost nonexistent strain.

He took five steps forward.

And stopped again.

The clouds broke suddenly, massive exploding boulders floating around the moon. In a few moments the entire front would move in from the sea. Tim took another step and saw the dark shapes on the sand. He stepped forward until he could see them in the moonlight.

The male was grasping her gills, pulling her gills open as he moved. The sea girl was breathing heavily, moaning in the musical way he remembered, and he saw her face as she turned it toward him. Only the whites of her eyes were visible as she rolled her head back and forth. Her hair was a black tangle on the sand around her head.

The two did not seem capable of noticing him. The large male was like her from what Tim could see, but his skin seemed rougher and his smell was unpleasant. His huge, flippered feet dug into the sand.

The dark form rolled off her onto the sand. Then it rose on all fours and put its mouth to her stomach and bit into her flesh in a rough circle. She thrust out her webbed hands and dug them into the sand.

When he was finished the male looked up, and Tim saw two coals of red looking at him. The creature bellowed and Tim took a few steps back. The girl hissed. The male stood up to a fantastic height. Tim turned and ran. The creature continued his bellowing, but did not follow.

Tim stumbled up the way he had come. When he was halfway up, the clouds smothered the moon at last and it became very dark. He groped his way to the top.

He was grateful for the filtered moonlight that enabled him to make it down to the beach. He ran to the path at the other end of the half-moon shoreline. He sprinted up the familiar trail to the dirt road, and kept a fast, steady pace until he saw the lights of his house set among the trees on the hillside, and heard the low hum of the power generator in the shed next to it. The cool grass was a relief for his cut feet as he went up the hill to the front door.

Jak was sitting at the wooden table in the center of the room smoking his pipe. Tim went past him and through the open door into his room.

"Where have you been?" Jak shouted after him in a friendly tone. Tim did not feel up to explaining, and with his father gone he did not feel he had to. He threw himself down on his bed and lay still. His breathing became regular and he fell asleep.

When he woke up, dawn showed itself as a drab light in the eastern window. He threw off the blanket Jak had put over him during the night and stood up by the bed. He was still wearing his trunks, and he noticed the stick-on bandages on his washed feet.

As he put on a pair of fresh jeans and a shirt, the memory of her was pleasant in his mind, and he hurried. He went out into the main room where Jak was snoring loudly in front of the dying embers. He stopped at the door and took down a torch and some matches from the rack, and went out.

It was a damp morning. The sun-beaten grass was very wet on the hillside. He went down to the road and walked the mile and a half to the beach path. There was only a slight breeze stirring the moist air.

He walked quickly down the path and across the beach to the high rocks. As he walked he looked out to sea where the spire rode in the mists over the water, and he felt pride at having been out there at last. It seemed closer now, not quite as far away as it had seemed a year ago when he was thirteen.

He climbed quickly up the rocks in the daylight. As he went down on the other side, the rock bowl seemed empty, even ordinary. He stepped down on the sand and walked across to where the pool of water had been. It was a polished bowl of stone, empty now. He imagined that in a large storm it would overflow, turning the entire depression into a deep pool.

He peered sideways into the dark tunnel in the rock where the sea came in at high tide. They might have gone out this way, he thought. He looked back and saw the single set of prints running to the edge next to his own. Quickly he turned and walked back to the place where he had watched them the night before. The sand was stained and messy.

He took out his matches and lit the torch. He stuck it in the sand, and warmed his hands while squatting. Then he got down on his hands and knees and began to dig. The sand was damp just below the surface and came up easily, just as if it had been freshly packed.

He dug faster when he saw the strand of dark hair. There were tears in his eyes by the time he uncovered her. He looked at the sand-covered texture of her skin, her large eyes closed in death, her hair filled with small stones and broken shells. He struck the sand with his fist and sat down on his heels, whimpering in the dampness of the morning. Next to him the torch crackled in the wet air.

Recovering, he saw the marks on her belly—a circle of closely spaced perforations. It seemed swollen, as if she had been beaten, and there were burgundy-colored droplets in her pubic hair. He looked closer and saw that . . . she seemed to have been stuffed with seaweed and sand. He touched her stomach. Miraculously it was still warm and soft. He remembered how fresh and magical she had been out on the rock, and how much he had wanted her. He understood now that she was not dead, and the hopelessness of it was a cold stone in his gut.

He had to cover her up quickly, or she would die before her wintry sleep was over. It was all he could do, knowing that she was full of young. All the little pieces of information made sense now. In the spring the young would come up and make their way to the pool of water, small lizardlike things which would in time change into sea people. The liquid of her belly was filled with the eggs that the male had released into her. She would sleep while nourishing the developing young, and finally they would eat their way out through the perforated section of her belly. But even though she was not dead, she would not waken again. He threw sand on her body, slowly covering her up.

The birds! The sea birds would be here in the spring to eat the fleeing young. He remembered their noise over these rocks from previous years. I'll be here with a scatter gun, he thought, I'll be here to do that much. And perhaps he would find another one like her, earlier next year.

His fear subsided and he finished burying her. He stood up and put out the torch in the sand. He walked away across the open area to the rocks and made his way up slowly, thinking all the way home of the new life buried there in the sand.

When he came within sight of the house he saw the trailer home and heavy tractor standing in front of the shed. His father was home early. He ran up the hillside from the road, almost forgetting his mood. He stopped halfway up the hill when he saw his father at the front door talking to another man. The other man looked away from his father, and Tim followed his gaze to the left. He saw the girl standing, looking toward the sun which was trying to break through the morning mists. Her long hair was blowing in the breeze now coming from the sea. Tim saw his father waving to him and he waved back. At the same time the girl turned around to look at him, and he saw that she was smiling. In a moment he decided to change his direction, and continued up the hill toward the girl.

Passing Nights

*Y*OU WOKE UP THAT NIGHT AND STARED INTO the darkness, your body tense with expectation as the wall by your bed dissolved and became a way into a deep, windy blackness. You were not afraid, but you remembered a fear still to come as a human figure faded into view, bright with an electric glow that seemed to come from within. Pale, clothed in sickly green seaweed, the battered male torso drifted toward you, bleeding into the black, oily water, eyes gazing at you from a haggard, familiar face, foggy breath billowing out of its mouth.

You cried out then, and the figure twisted around, showing cuts, abrasions, and bruises in a sickly, brine-shrunk patchwork of red, white, and gray. You reached out to the wall, to see if the scene was real.

"Don't!" the man shouted with great effort, went under, came up splashing and grabbed at his left arm.

"Where are you?" you asked, sitting up, eyes wide open, nostrils filling with ocean smells.

"Don't," the man whispered as you reached into the wall, felt the cold water, and pulled your hand back.

The man moved away, as if suddenly caught in a powerful current. His eyes were closed, as if he had found peace. You blinked as the view broke up into a grainy collection of yellow dots and light exploded into the room, destroying the vision.

"Charles, are you okay?"

"Just a bad dream, Mom," you answered, lying back and staring at the clean yellow of the recently painted wall as the overhead light went out.

"Go back to sleep, darling," your mother said lovingly, gently closing the door.

Your eyes adjusted to the dark and you looked at the wall. There was nothing there, but you knew that the wall was waiting for you. It would be waiting for you every night.

This is the end, you tell yourself as you drift in the water. The ship had been a part of your own body, torn open by the torpedo's explosion, hurling you into the water, where you bleed into the black liquid, returning your inner sea to the salty commonwealth.

But death refuses you. Your pulse beats, and you feel that your right hand is locked around the bleeding in your left arm, unable to let go.

The sea rocks you as you drift. You open your eyes, expecting to see stars, but there is only a cloudless darkness, without even a bright patch where the moon should be. I'm dying, you tell yourself. Might as well admit it. Eyesight's blackening. It's one of the signs. You can't feel your toes. It surprises you, as much as you can be surprised, how little you care. The body prepares itself. Messengers go out to all the distant provinces of muscle and bone, whispering gently for them to slow down and accept death—the distinguished thing, as some literary fool once called it. There is no life after death. You'll see. And you laugh, but it's like trying to break marble with a rubber hammer, and you wheeze and nearly weep from the pain of the convulsive effort.

Suddenly, white light floods into your eyes. Recovering, you see the boy that you were, staring at you from the room that you loved, and you remember what he feels but doesn't understand yet. You recall having seen what he sees, what he once saw for three nights, as you gaze into that bedroom where the future is still a fabulous country, waiting to be entered. All times are woven together, so why shouldn't they cast something of themselves forward and backward now and then?

As you look into the boy's sleepy eyes, you realize that these moments have been waiting for both of you all your lives, that two pieces of time are being drawn toward each other by the gravity of remembrance, and there is nothing you can do about the coming collision.

The sea becomes very still suddenly, and you watch the boy reach into the water as if into a mirror, and draw his hand back, surprised that it is not wet. He repeats the action and is startled as some ghostly water spills onto his bed, and you realize with dismay piled on hopelessness that it was your yearning for the shelter of the past that would now destroy it. You needed to be back in that room on a twelve-year-old's Friday night, looking forward to Saturday morning, when you would go biking and later stop at the park to watch girls playing under the big oak tree, not quite sure why they were so pleasant to look at, feeling the play of impulses within yourself. You needed that past as you had never needed your present or future, but you had to get on the treadmill of killing to realize how little you had to give to anything or anyone.

Think! your fogged brain commands. Your need will destroy the past unless you act. Will the boy's death end your pain? Will you still be here if the past is changed?

But what can you do? What can a dying man do for anyone?

You try to pull down the bridge between the boy in the bedroom and the man in the water by denying your need for the past's islands of happiness, but the two moments draw even closer toward dissolution. The boy crawls back on the bed, astonished by the water that is now threatening to burst across time, and suddenly you know what you must do.

You listen to the unfeeling whisper of the sea, and slowly your right hand loosens its grip on your bleeding left arm. You watch the hand move away as if it belongs to someone else, and see your bleeding resume its gentle flow into the black water.

The boy and the bedroom slip away, and you close your eyes, relieved that the link seems to be weakening. Your past and present are safe, but you have severed your future. There's no helping that. You have to be alive for the bridge to stand.

And for a few moments it continues to stand, and you are that boy staring at the wall in fear and wonder, opening and closing your eyes, fleeing back and forth between the bedroom and the cold darkness of futurity, where the sea drinks your blood and the blackness crowds the light from your eyes.

Takes You Back

I LOVED HER. SHE LOVED ME. IT HAD ALWAYS been that way. So deeply that sometimes I imagined that our love had been fixed that way when the universe began, awaiting our coming on the scene.

"It's chemical between you two," her mother liked to say, "some unimaginable sympathy that nothing will break." She said it as if it couldn't be anything else, that it would be impossible otherwise. Heaven and the gods had something to do with it, or it couldn't have happened. People don't just get together on their own.

"You know," I mused as we were watching the evening news, "I really like those French doors of ours." They closed off the foyer and made the front entrance area into a small room by itself. We often used the space for storage. I liked the curtains on the glass panels, and looked forward one of these days to refinishing the doors, stripping the brass hardware and lockset of paint to restore the shine, so that each part would again be as new. The doors were much more interesting than the news.

"You know what I'm up for?" she said. "—some French fries." She gave me a sly, guilty smile and rolled her eyes at her segue from French doors to French fries. "Just this onc time," she added for-givingly.

It had been a long time. A couple of years, anyway, since we had started watching our weight and nutrition.

"I'll get some," I said, suddenly feeling like taking a brisk walk to the nearby fast food place, rationalizing that I would walk off in advance some of the calories I would bring home. I wondered if the fries would pass the test of nostalgia.

She smiled at me again as I got up and went to the front door, remembering our college days, when she had been sick in bed one day and I had gone out in a snowstorm to get her some cream puffs, feeling as purposeful as a hunter.

I opened the door, then the storm door. I held it while I closed the inside door, then stepped out into a warm, sprng breeze as the storm door whispered shut behind me. A clear, evening sky was bright with stars above the trees around our house.

Memories jabbed at me as I took a deep breath. They cut through me with their regretful, structured beauties, and reminded me again of my ambivalence about moving here. Sarah and I still felt a sense of loss about our abandoned apartment back in our college town, and I still had the feeling that I would get on a bus one day and go "home."

I went down the stone walkway and onto the street—and stepped into autumn.

It took a moment for the change to register. I stopped and turned to look at the house. All the lights were off. Around me the trees were losing their leaves as a cool breeze was getting up to speed. Overhead, a few clouds hurried in from the north. I stared up at the glitter of the constellations and saw that they had changed to those of fall. A chill went through me that was not part of the season.

I turned and walked back up to my door. I looked left and right and saw that the other houses were all lit up: Windows flashed from television screens. Motion detector lights blazed in driveways, reminding me of theater lights waiting for the actors to come on stage. But my house was dark. Then I realized that the sensor-lights had failed to go on as I approached the door.

I rang the bell.

"Sarah!" I shouted when I got no answer.

Suddenly the house was quiet and the night was still, as in that Wallace Stevens poem, but I was not even on the right page; I was staring at a closed book, at what seemed a sudden finality, as abrupt as the impending autumn around me.

Something had happened, I told myself, feeling certain that I would have to break into the house to find out what.

I went around to the basement window that I had never fixed. It was on the side of the house facing Mrs. Scheler's driveway. That feisty old woman seemed eternal; she had been ancient even when we had moved here two years ago. We called the strip of grass and bushes and her asphalt driveway between our houses "The Scheler Neutral Zone." She didn't like the leaves and seeds from our trees covering her driveway every year, but I noticed that her driveway was graded so that our house foundation got all the water draining from her rain gutters. I wasn't going to cut down any trees, but if she pressed the matter I would show her how the water flowed.

I pried out the old, wooden storm window. It seemed less decayed than I recalled. The inner window opened easily, since only half the latch was still there. I had not replaced the broken half.

Shaking from fear of what I might find, I climbed in feet first and dropped to the floor. It was only three steps to the light switch. I flicked on the lights, and without looking around went to the stairs, hurrying from fear that there had been some kind of accident and Sarah might need me.

I came upstairs to the kitchen door and found it open. The skeleton key I had bought was not in the lock. I turned off the basement lights out of habit, then crept into the kitchen, tasting the mustiness that followed me from the basement. I found the wall switch, and turned on the lights.

Everything seemed normal.

"Sarah!" I shouted as I went into the dining room. The lights went on, but the room was a shock. The heavy oak table that had gone to Sarah's sister stood in place of our walnut elegance. The upright piano that we had given to charity was here again, up against the left wall. The built-in china closet was empty, as it was when we had moved in.

I hurried into the living room, but it was an alien place, empty of all that we had done to make it our own. Sarah's mother's furniture was all here, as if a giant had taken the roof off the house and put it all back.

"Sarah!" I shouted, hearing my voice break.

I listened for an answer in the silence.

Then I heard a meow.

I turned and saw a black and white cat standing in the doorway to the living room. He gave me the penetrating gaze I had once known, then snarled at me as if at a stranger.

A rush of feeling went through me. "Spencer!" I cried. "You're alive!"

I started toward him, but he turned and fled back to the stairs and down into the basement.

I was breathing hard, wondering by what miracle he could be alive. I had lost my mind, I told myself, struggling to deny it . . .

Spencer had died a few months ago, at the vet's. He was seventeen years old and his kidneys were failing; to have kept him alive would only have prolonged his suffering. Sarah and her mother had held his paws as he drifted away without protest. I remembered how devastated Sarah's mother had been, even though she had allowed us to keep her cat when she had moved out after we took over the house. Long periods of separation from her pet had not cured her of him. "Harvey's allergic to cats," she had told us, meaning her new husband, "and there isn't much room in the townhouse, and we'll be traveling a lot anyway." I supposed she had meant that Spencer would be happier in what he had come to regard as his estate. But when she held his paw, it was as if she had never left him behind. Sarah and I had looked on, our hearts stopped by our uncontrollable denial that Spencer was breathing his last. I had been up with him the night before, hoping his illness was a passing thing as he lay there wrapped in a blanket, trying to rest and shake it off . . .

But my mind was gone, and my knowing it was part of the madness. I was wandering in a nightmare because I had dared venture out for French fries. Something had not wanted me to have them, and that something had been right.

I steadied myself against the old oak table, then sat down in one of the creaky chairs. Spencer was back, looking at me from the doorway again, confused, as he had always been whenever I failed to chase after him into the basement, where we would play hide-and-seek.

But as I gazed into his furry, lost face now restored to me, I knew that we were strangers; somehow, we had not yet met. And that lack of recognition had to be another sign of madness . . .

Finally, I got up and went into the kitchen. The waterfowl calendar displayed October 1996, seven months before Sarah and I had moved here from our old college town, where we had been living in our second apartment after graduation. Sarah was teaching high school while completing her doctorate, and I was trying to write novels in between monthly stories and handyman work, mostly carpentry and some plumbing.

I stared at the calendar in disbelief. Spencer was at my feet, staring up at me and hissing. I knelt and put out my hand, happy to see him, even if he turned out to be a ghost.

He looked at my hand as if it was an insult, and his eyes said the usual: "Don't you dare say cute kitty things to me." He had never really believed he was a cat, and disliked other cats; they were beneath him. Sarah's mother had always insisted that he thought of himself as a person trapped in a feline's body, and I sometimes believed it.

I stood up, then tried the wall phone. It was dead. I opened the refrigerator. It was empty. I recalled that Sarah's mother had been in Italy in the fall of '96. It had been her first long trip with Harvey, and they had decided to marry not long afterward. We had moved here in the spring . . .

Something like that, I told myself, hoping to explain this nightmare somehow. I again stared at the calendar, as if it were the great arbiter of time, the one authority I could trust to explain my situation. Who would bother to hang an old calendar?

Lights flashed in the kitchen window, as if a lightning storm was coming. When I heard no thunder, I went to the dining room window, moving as if in a dream. It was the routine police car patrol, and I remembered the night when Spencer had slipped outside and I had gone out in my shorts and sandals looking for him.

"Do you always look for your cat at 3 A.M.?" the cop had asked back then.

"He escapes," I had explained, grinning.

Now I realized, following the logic of my madness, that they had seen the lights and would check the house. Sarah's mother always asked them to keep an eye on things when she was away. These suburban cops would be suspicious of anything in this quiet, parklike neighborhood, where the asphalt ribbons of road, dating back to the 1940s or earlier, were little more than driveways to the houses.

The police car circled the block, and pulled up in front of the house. They would not know me if I opened the door. They had seen lights where there should be no lights. They might even have a key.

I had to turn out the lights and flee before they came in and found me.

But where could I go? It wasn't exactly warm outside. I had only the five bucks in my wallet to buy the fries.

Then I remembered when Sarah had showed me the places in the house where she had hidden as a child. Crawlspaces on the second floor, behind the walls and over the ceilings. Could I fit into any of them?

I turned out the lights and groped my way up the stairs to the second floor bedroom. I opened the closet, turned on the dim light, and saw the panel.

It slid open easily. I turned out the light, then felt my way into the closet. I squeezed into the space, shut the panel, and waited.

The cops moved around on the first floor. One of them came up the stairs, then went back down.

"If there was anyone here," he called to his partner, "he was gone as soon as he saw us coming!"

"Yeah. There's nothing taken down here, not even a TV or radio. Must have been disappointing."

I thought of Sarah's mother hiding silver cups in the back of the old 1940s radio in the basement. Probably helped its reception, I had once imagined.

After a while, I didn't hear the cops. It got cold in the crawlspace, but I didn't come out. I fell asleep, hoping that I'd wake up in front of the television with Sarah, with a bag of warm fries in my lap.

I slept dreamlessly, and awoke with a nose full of dust, startled by the dark unfamiliarity.

Slowly I remembered, but was afraid to move and give myself away. I crouched there, realizing that I was alone in the house, somehow at an earlier time.

Then I began to see the course now open to me. It opened before me like the doors to a prison of time. I would live nearby and wait for the years to run out. Something had set me back two and a half years, subtracting me from my time and adding me here. What cosmic calculator could have made such a thing happen?

As I crawled out of the attic space, the enormity of the implications hit me. Two of me lived in this time. I would have to wait for the night of April 1, 1999, when I had gone out for French fries, and then try to step back into my life. Presumably, I would see myself come out of the house and disappear, leaving me the chance to step back in.

I was assuming that I was not mad, which is what I would assume if I were insane—except that I could also see that much. Who said that sanity was simply consensus madness?

A chill went through me, probably from sleeping in the cold space, as much as from the doubts that played through my mind. I could not be sure that the opportunity to return would ever present itself to me. All I could do was to wait out the time.

I could stay in the house for a while, if I didn't turn on the lights at night. Sarah's mother wouldn't return until November.

I went down into the basement and found a can of tuna among the provisions in the pantry that Sarah and I would later make into a small wine cellar. There was also a package of zwieback. They would go well with the tuna. I wouldn't starve today. There was plenty of bottled water, and canned soups, not to mention bottles of scotch and a few boxed wines. I could heat the soups on the small camper stove Sarah's mother had bought to deal with power failures and other emergencies. I would not signal my presence by using the kitchen.

As I started upstairs, I heard the back door open and retreated into the basement. Spencer ran past me up the stairs, and I realized that Mrs. Scheler had to be coming in to feed him, groom him, and to clean out his litter box. Sarah and I had relied on her often enough when we were away.

I went into the wine cellar, closed the door, and listened to her moving around in the kitchen. She loved cats, and Spencer in particular. Sometimes she had reproached Sarah's mother for abandoning Spencer. Then I realized that Mrs. Scheler would also be back in the evenings to check on Spencer and the house — every day during the period of her cat-sitting duties. The only protection I had was that Mrs. Scheler was old and a bit dotty, and hence not very observant. With enough care, I could keep out of her way.

I waited. After a while I sat down on the cold floor of the wine cellar and listened through the door. She came down into the basement to refresh Spencer's litter box.

"You dear thing," she said to him softly. "Abandoned and alone here. But you have me. I'll take good care of you."

I imagined Spencer looking at her.

Then he meowed.

I slept in what would later be our bedroom. During the night Spencer joined me, snuggling up against my thigh. But he was gone in the morning. With Spencer it was solidarity through the vulnerable night, pride in the bright daylight.

I spent the day looking around the house, annoyed by all the waiting problems I would fix after we moved in. It was strange seeing the dripping faucets, electrical disrepair, and carpentry, still waiting for me. It had all been done in the future; but not here.

And I was always listening for Mrs. Scheler.

I realized then that I would have to live somewhere else, to get through the two and a half years that would have to pass before I could resume my life. I couldn't stay here; sooner or later I would make a mistake and get caught. I had visions of being identified, of being brought face to face with myself before the situation could right itself—if it ever could be resolved. Some great disaster was waiting for me, and I could not imagine it.

I sat in the shadowy daylight of the living room, thinking that maybe my return might overtake me sooner; maybe at any moment. Why assume that it would happen only at the future moment when I had left the house? I sat in the eternity of that living room, hoping for a miracle. Shapes played at the edges of my vision, memories that had yet to happen in my life with Sarah, my mysterious chemical bondmate.

Finally, aware of my limited funds, I returned to the basement and checked the open back of the enormous standing radio. Yes, there was some silver in the unplugged works, among the dusty old tubes, including Sarah's silver baby cup—quite beat up; but it was silver.

I slipped out that afternoon to hock the silver. On my way back I noticed a "Help Wanted" sign in the local pizzeria. No one would know me here, so I went in and talked to the manager, an aging Pakistani who seemed to like my looks and hired me after about two minutes of conversation. My driver's license was still good, since I had gotten it only four years earlier. No one was going to notice two years off my age. Only my two credit cards were useless.

I would be inconspicuous in the job, since my duties were making deliveries three nights a week and working the store's cash register the rest of the time, opening up, cleaning a bit, and locking up. I would make enough to get by until the appointed time of mysteries, when I would converge with myself. It was a mad hope.

I rented a studio apartment, ten by ten with bath, in one of the old brick apartment buildings some ten blocks away, and went to work at eleven every morning.

It was a dreary life.

Sarah and I were a hundred miles away, in our beloved apartment, not yet aware that we would be moving by spring.

Here now, two and a half years earlier, there was no one I could count on to help me, unless I was ready to call upon people who had not seen me in some time. I would have to impersonate my earlier self in order to talk to them. Living incognito, hiding nothing, would not be difficult, because there was no one who could catch me at it.

I made enough at my job to pay the rent, and I had use of one of the eatery's cars to come and go from work. After six months I was promoted to store manager, when old Karim retired. He had a share of the place, and seemed relieved to keep me in charge. This meant that I no longer had to make deliveries in the area. I now took orders and dispatched other drivers, and continued to do the paperwork, besides opening and closing the store.

I opened the pizzeria by noon, so I had mornings and much of the afternoons to myself, which was not always a good thing, because I had time to twist every complication of my plight into every conceivable outcome. They came into my brain like train wrecks that I saw only as they were happening, never before.

In my first year as a manager, I drove by the house late one spring evening and saw lights. Sarah and I had arrived. I was stunned at the predictability of it; they might have decided otherwise.

I saw a moving van drive away one afternoon, and recalled that it was taking Sarah's mother's furniture away. The garage door was open another day, and I saw Gerard's old beat-up car inside. I thought of myself as him.

One night I received a phone order from that address. I took the order from my *other* self in a kind of bemused state of inevitability. Large deluxe, with a large bottle of Coke. Something in me wanted to make this delivery, but I restrained myself and passed it along, knowing that I would feel as late and incongruous as the storied snail who had been thrown out the door, only to come back three months later to ask, "What was that all about?"

On another evening, I drove by and saw Sarah and Gerard sitting on the enclosed porch, with only a small lamp on, and for a moment I felt a cold knife in my heart. Maybe I would never return. This branching of me would go on as I was now, exiled forever from the rest of my life. I could not take for granted what I wished to happen.

But I had to believe that I was working my way back home. That had to be enough. Keep to the plan. What would happen if I talked to myself? Would the universe blow up? Would I throw variations into the time stream that would forever bar my return?

I made a firm decision to pretty much ignore the world, for my own sanity, and because I feared somehow affecting the future in a way that might make my return impossible. I refused to read newspapers or watch television. After all, I pretty much knew what had happened. I resisted the urge to bet on sports events, even though the chance came my way in the restaurant through the drivers, who sometimes stopped off on their deliveries to place a bet. I remembered an old Ray Bradbury story, in which an expedition of time travelers harms a butterfly in the past and forever loses their own time.

I was a ghost, hoping to return to my own body.

One evening the phone rang.

I answered it. "Say," a woman's voice said. "The pizza was cold!"

"Oh," I said to Sarah. "I'm sorry about that. Would you like a replacement?"

"No, we already reheated."

"Well, next time you get a free one. Just remind me the next time you call in an order."

"Oh—thank you," she said, sounding friendly. "That will be okay." She had always been too kindly, or too cowardly, to carry through a rage.

As I hung up the phone I began to doubt that my waiting would do me any good. They were living there, and would always live there, while I would go on with this life. Did I really think I would be able to step back into the exact right moment? What if it required a fraction of a second of speed beyond my ability, beyond any human ability? As I imagined constructing a strange, temporal razor with which to divide the moments, I knew even more clearly that I had no way to be sure that I would have a chance, a year from now or ever. No reason at all to think so.

I grew a beard and wore a hat to avoid being remembered in the neighborhood as anyone except the guy with the beard and hat. I took some care with this, thinking that I must never meet myself or anyone I knew. I had no idea what might happen, but I wasn't taking any chances. At the very least, Gerard would not recognize me.

One evening, Sarah's sister, Gail, came in for a pickup. I had not taken that call, so the first I knew I was handing her the pie. She took the box from my hands and stared at me for a moment.

"Have we met?" she asked in the musical tones I remembered. Sarah had some of that too, but Gail had more.

I shook my head, not daring to speak, even though I was glad to meet someone who knew me, then stared morosely at the floor until she turned and left.

At work I used my own name and social security number, and my area boss even cashed my checks for me. What could he think if he ran across my name elsewhere—oh, someone else with Gerry's name. It was a pizza place. What was the worst that could happen? I wasn't breaking any laws, and lived on a cash basis. All I had to do was lie low and wait.

One late afternoon, on my way to work, I drove by the house and saw Sarah and Gerard coming outside. Spencer slipped out just before Gerard closed the door, and climbed up into a small tree on Mrs. Scheler's front lawn, gazing at them. He was showing off. I knew the drill. When they turned away to leave, he hopped down and loped after them. I knew as I left the scene behind that Spencer would turn back and go home, after some waving and shouting by *me*, to wait by the back door until we returned.

I counted the months toward the coming collision with myself. That's what I told myself, anyway. Whether it would happen peacefully or not on that distant evening I had no idea.

Today was the day!

I had already given Karim notice that I was leaving my job. I shaved, then tried to relax in my room. Toward evening I took out the clean, carefully stored clothes I had worn on the day of my disappearance. I sat in my one big comfy chair and waited until the evening hour was close before dressing. I had told the building's manager that I was moving out, and would leave the keys in the apartment. My rent was paid up for the month; the Gerry who lived here would simply vanish.

I took my time dressing to be myself again, wondering whether the coming event would be more like a wedding or a funeral. My hands shook, and my throat was dry. I felt like a stalker.

I wondered about the path that lay before me. What was it like up the line? Was there another time, running forward, in which Sarah wondered what had happened to me when I failed to come back with the fries? Or would my upcoming return simply cut off that future? Would it still leave a vague memory in her of something having gone wrong? Would I remember it?

Soft, doughlike reasonings twisted in my mind, and baked into agonized pretzels in the heat of my imaginings. Horizons stood around me, over which I could not see. I would know the outcome this evening. Maybe not.

Finally I was again in my brown corduroy pants, black walking shoes, blue shirt, and a flannel lumberjack overshirt. I had dressed casually at home, and there had been no reason to dress up to get some fast food on a warm evening. Yet the exactness of these clothes was suddenly very crucial to me, as if I had to observe a cosmic dress code. Get one detail wrong, and it would all fall apart.

I walked the ten blocks to my house, checking my watch every few minutes, determined to give myself enough time to be there early in order to observe carefully.

When I reached the Dairy Queen at the edge of the neighborhood, I decided to have a small vanilla cone to settle my stomach. I had the time, since I was now only five minutes away.

I forced myself to eat the soft ice cream as I continued on my way. It was the same evening again, softly blue with starlight and a spring breeze, and memories crowding in on me.

In the house ahead, Sarah and I were talking ourselves into French fries. I scarfed down the rest of the cone and stopped at the corner.

I watched, waiting for the door of the brightly lit house to open.

And I began to feel sick, as if something was terribly wrong; but it was just out of sight over my mental hills. A great beast was coming for me fast out of some dark vastness.

Here I was, at the same moment.

The door opened slightly.

I heard muffled voices arguing as the inner door opened halfway. The words stopped as Gerard opened the storm door and hurried out onto the slate walkway. He paused, then went right back inside.

My mind stopped and was rooted to the moment.

The worst had happened, and could not be undone.

Gerard had not vanished into that sudden autumn I remembered. It was still spring. Somehow my chance to return had passed me by.

I stood there, shaking with fear and nausea. What had gone wrong?

I looked at my watch.

The time was right.

But the date was wrong. The tiny calendar on my watch told me I was a day early! How had that happened? My mind had reached ahead anxiously, yearning to draw me forward to this day.

I thought about all the other small variations that had been creeping into the sequence right from the start. Would some sort of accumulation of unnoticed, small differences keep me from coming home?

I took a deep breath, then thrust my shaking hands into my pockets. My fingers found my key chain; I had forgotten to leave my keys in the apartment. Then I realized why I had messed up on the date. I had paid the next month's rent a day early, making sure that there would be plenty of time for me to disappear into my previous life. Well, at least I would have a place to sleep for one more night.

Feeling miserable, I walked back to my studio apartment. Tomorrow at this time I would be back for another throw of the cosmic dice.

I was back ten minutes early. My clothes were a bit sweatier, but I didn't care. They would be more like they had been when I had first gone outside, two and a half years ago now. I had found a spare set of apartment keys, which I had made some time ago. I brought them with me because I might need to go back again. The fear was a stone in my stomach.

As I watched the door, I began to wonder whether I wanted to go back at all. Was this the same world, the same house, the same Sarah? I asked myself, recalling the shouting of the previous night. Maybe in this world-line I never came back, but lived apart, watching myself, avoiding his mistakes, counting myself lucky to have made the break. If the worlds varied, then there were perhaps an infinite number in which I had not come back. Sarah was forever lost to me.

The inner door opened. I tensed. Gerard pushed at the storm door.

Spencer rushed by him onto the bushy front lawn.

Gerard ran after him.

Spencer scampered across the street toward where I stood in shadows. Gerard was striding after him. It was the French fries, I thought. Without them, Gerard would not disappear.

This was not my world, I realized, because Spencer was still alive.

Gerard stopped and looked up at the sky, and seemed in no hurry to chase the cat. He stood there, and I wondered if he was suddenly seeing the autumn I had walked into.

But I continued to see him. He was still here. Maybe he would always be here, as I had feared, shutting me out.

Spencer padded down the street.

Gerard winked out.

For one second he was there, and in the next he was gone.

"Yes!" I whispered to myself. A shiver of spooky triumph shot up my spine, driving all my doubts out into the starry evening.

Then I looked around at the street, because it seemed to me I had heard an echo of my own voice.

Spencer came up to me and stopped, and I knew with a sinking feeling that it was still not my world. Gerard's disappearance had not been enough. I was not home. It would be wrong for me to go inside this house.

Spencer looked up at me, and the confusion in the eyes of this Einstein among cats seemed to ask, "How the fuck did you get ahead of me?"

Then he sat down and waited.

I reached down and picked him up. He let me hold him. I had always been able to catch him in the house. Outside, he would mock me and amble away, knowing that there was little or no chance that I could catch him; he'd come back when he felt like it. But now I had shown another ability, and this had shaken him up.

I petted his head, scratched him under his chin, and he winked out in my arms. Relief and resignation tore through me. Once again, Spencer had died, even though something in me had hoped that he would remain alive and that I would also have my world back.

It was my world again, I told myself, desperate to believe it. Something had finally made the correction.

I stood there for a moment, empty handed, then approached the house.

I opened the unlocked doors one by one, and stepped back into my living room. Sarah looked up at me and smiled.

"Back so soon?" she asked.

I sat down and stared at the credits on the evening news, realizing that I had been gone maybe twenty minutes.

"How about the French fries?" Sarah asked, tucking her legs under her in the big recliner.

"I can do without," I said. "How about you? I'll go if you still want me to."

"If you can do without," she said smugly, "then so can I."

I looked over at her. She seemed unchanged.

"You look a bit different somehow," she said.

"I washed these clothes yesterday," I said.

"Good for you."

"You won't believe what happened to me," I started to say, again feeling like the snail in the old joke, then felt fearful of saying anything more.

Sarah looked at me strangely and said, "I know exactly what happened to you!"

"How can you know?" I asked, startled. Then, "*What* do you know," I said, thinking she was referring to something else.

"I don't know how I know, but suddenly I know—as if something slid it into my mind sideways. I know!" She sounded both awed and very frightened.

I took a deep breath and said, "Tell me."

As she recounted what had happened to me, with uncanny detail, I remembered that a great writer had once written that there is no wall around time. You can have what you want of it, if you remember well enough. But it was worse than that. Suddenly I feared to remember, afraid that I would be thrown somewhere into time again, away from the frontline of my incoming future, back into a flow of varying instants that I could not change

The past lived as a hunger in all of us, waiting to swallow us when we lost sight of the future. This realization was the most urgent thing I had learned.

"Stop!" I shouted and jumped up from my chair, half expecting Spencer to meow from the kitchen. He had gotten cranky whenever his people argued and made him feel unsafe.

Sarah looked at me in surprise and said. "What is it? What's wrong?"

"Careful. Stop talking. Don't think too much about the past!"

"But why, what's wrong? It's so strange to suddenly know!"

As I looked at her, my hand slipped into my pants pocket and closed around the spare keys. I took the key ring out and looked at it in shock, because this meant that I was still not quite in my own world; my beloved was only some sort of Sarah, but also slightly someone else, and I was something of an intruder.

"What's wrong?" Sarah asked again.

I stared at the keys in my hand—

—and was relieved to see them fade away. A little late. Maybe it had needed a push from me, so the choices among worlds would tend back to my own original. Something was still correcting.

"We have to be careful, not think too much about it. Too much—and you're there!" As I looked at her, I saw my fear in her eyes.

"It—" I started to say, but my voice broke from the strangeness of our helplessness before it. What could I call it—a glitch of some kind? We were at the edge of our world, and something was trying to push us off into the abyss. No, it was trying to pull us in.

But she knew it all, I realized. Somehow it had all piled into her. I didn't have to say it.

"It takes you back," I blurted out.

And sideways.

Twisted sideways.

"Yeah," Sarah said. "You're not the man who went out for French fries, and I'm not the woman you left behind."

"None of us ever are," I said, "even when we are."

"You can't step into the same river twice, Heraclitus said," she added. "Everything flows." She knew her Greek guys. "But I love you anyway," she whispered.

"Same here," I said.

Then she looked at me strangely, and we felt nameless gulfs widening between us. Images from our histories tumbled in that void as we bridged it, along with the figure of Spencer voyaging among the stars with my spare set of keys.

Political Horrors

overtake us as we grow up . . .

I Walked With Fidel

"Well, of course I don't have any plans for dying."
—Fidel Castro, *Playboy* interview, August 1985

*H*E CAME RIGHT UP TO THE FRONT GATE OF the naval base at Guantanamo Bay and stood there in the bright sunlight, empty-handed, staring at us. He seemed harmless enough, so I opened the gate and went out to meet him.

"What do you want?" I asked.

The corner of his mouth twitched as if he were trying to say something.

"It's him, isn't it?" Kip shouted, coming out after me.

"Sure looks like Old Inconvertible himself," I said.

Kip walked around the tall, white-bearded figure in army fatigues. "What do you want?"

The old man mumbled something in Spanish.

"Did you get that?" I asked.

"I think he wants to come in," Kip said.

"I'll watch him. Get the sergeant."

I took a better grip on my automatic rifle and faced the Cuban leader, wondering what had happened to him. He seemed glassy-eyed and stiff, without expression. Things hadn't gone well with him after the Soviets cut him loose, leaving him with no cheap source of coal and oil. He had remained in power for a while because everyone was afraid of what might happen without him. The AIDS epidemic had destroyed tourism, and exports of sugar, nickel, and citrus fruits had declined substantially. Washington had simply let Fidel stew, then dealt with those who came to power after him, just as the Israelis had done with Arafat. The club of rivals just couldn't bear to grant each other anything, especially vindication. Revenge and punishment were real satisfactions for them, to be savored in this life, not some later one. I had always felt the same way.

The sergeant came out with Kip and laughed. "Well, well," he said, "what do we have here? *Looks* like the old boy himself. Come to collect the rent personally?"

"There's something wrong with him, Sarge," I said.

"Looks like a zombie. It's probably not him, but who cares? Take him somewhere and let him loose. And don't be long about it, Corporal!"

"Yes, Sarge," I said, watching the old man, who seemed afraid of us. I had only a few days left in my hitch, and was looking forward to going back to college in Miami, my home town. But as Kip brought out the jeep, I realized that if this was Castro, then he had delivered himself into the hands of someone who had the background to know what to do with him. College could wait.

I got him into the jeep and drove a few miles up the road, where I stopped and said, "My grandfather was with you in the hills when you started—and you locked him up for twenty years, you bastard."

The old man turned toward me, trembling; saliva glistened in his unkempt beard. His eyes seemed to register emotion, then dulled and remained fixed and bulging. The afternoon sun was hot, but I was the only one sweating as I demanded that he tell me why he had come to the gate.

Slowly, haltingly, he told me what had happened to him, how he had always taken good care of his health, until one day he was diagnosed with colon cancer that had erupted quickly and was too far gone for treatment. So he went to the last of his crackpot researchers and ordered them to save his life. They were the ones who had helped him try his crank genetic theories in costly breeding experiments for the improvement of cattle, and had produced climate-resistant stock that wasn't much good for milk or meat. One of these men had also developed a strain of giant strawberries that were mostly water. The only Nobel laureate Castro had lured to the island had left in disgust after these failures. The cranks who stayed studied folk medicines, convincing Castro that vast secrets remained to be uncovered, medicines that would startle the world and make Cuba free of the dependency on foreign coal and oil.

Fidel turned to these shamans to prolong his life, which they did, but their treatments had not given him the health and vigor he had wanted. By then he had already been retired from power, by a party congress intent on "democratization," and was living at a small country estate, where he hoped to survive his opponents, whom he saw as corrupted by the illusions of democratic rule that had swept the world in the '90s. As he saw it, the reformers had merely found a way to justify doing business with the United States, keeping themselves in power by serving neo-imperialist influences, and averting the American invasion of Cuba.

He told me of his plight in snatches, then begged me to take him to the United States to find medical help for his condition, which enabled him to live, but with hardly a life to speak of. When I told him I would try, he grasped my arm and seemed about to weep, but what came out was a terrible wheezing, as if all the moisture in his lungs had turned to jelly and he was trying to expel it.

I left him with a cousin for the few days remaining in my hitch, then called my brother Miguel, who owned a night club in Miami. Miguel made our travel arrangements, including getting "Fidel" a visa as an entertainer.

"Medical care is expensive," I told the old man. "You'll have to earn the money. Do you have any?" It occurred to me that if he had a large enough stash somewhere, I could grab it and leave him here.

"My money is all gone," he said softly, and I knew then that I wanted more than money.

Three weeks later, we opened the act with me saying, "Tonight, for the first time anywhere, Fidel Castro! Deposer of the hated Batista, once a Soviet puppet—and now a zombie!"

Fidel sat in a chair facing the audience, unable to move, and I wondered how many people would really believe he was Fidel Castro. Would anyone believe that he was a zombie? The visa people had laughed as they stamped his papers, because my brother had put down his true name and profession—Fidel Castro, Zombie. He had become stiffer after leaving Cuba, and required more vitamins and water to keep him going. He never slept. I forced him to take a shower every day, and dressed him in fresh army fatigues. It was no harder than when I took care of my ailing grandfather in his last days.

"The audience may ask questions," I announced.

"Is that all he's going to do?" a man shouted from the back.

Fidel's eyes stared at me as I turned to look at him. "Must I do this, Enrico?" he asked in a strained whisper. I had asked him to try smoking a cigar and blowing rings during the act, but he had been unable to draw any smoke.

"Señor Castro," an old man said from one of the front tables, "why did you muzzle a free press?"

Fidel seemed to become even stiffer. The corner of his mouth twitched as he struggled to answer. "What are you?" he asked in a broken voice. "The son of a doctor, lawyer, or shopkeeper? You fled Cuba because your parents feared for their privileges and sought to subvert the revolution."

"Answer the question!" the man shouted.

"You ask," Fidel continued, "why I failed to help my enemies."

"Another question," I called out, sensing that the audience was warming up to the game. I could feel the old grievances, hatreds, and bigotries still simmering, and suddenly knew that the room would be packed for future shows.

People seemed to accept the old man as Castro. My grandfather would finally get some justice out of the sonofabitch. My father, a lawyer, wouldn't have cared much, since he had done well in Miami, and he had never liked my mother's father. He thought that as a "Fidelista," my grandfather had only gotten what he deserved.

"Fidel!" an old man cried out from the back of the room. "You held up such high ideals, and we expected so much from you. How could you have failed us?"

Fidel tried to rise from his chair, but fell back. "I never betrayed the Cuban people," he croaked loudly, as if a snake was whispering from his lungs. "Ordinary families had it better from the first day after I threw the American gangsters out of our country. What did it matter if a few of the privileged suffered?"

"But your own party removed you!" the old man objected. "Don't deny your own sins by comparing them to others."

"Yes," Fidel continued, "my party gave in to the greed that flowered with Reagan and spread to the Soviets. Real socialist ideals, they realized, would not make them rich. Now the common good will again have to struggle against personal fortunes that will be handed down the generations like a disease." He raised his hands as if in prayer. "Ah! Who could have imagined that the Soviets themselves would capitulate?"

"They got tired of paying out charity to you!" a young man at the front called out.

*   *   *

We gave two shows that first day, and every day for the rest of the month. In his off hours, Fidel sat in our hotel suite and watched baseball games. I sat with him, and once in a while, he would say softly, "I was once a good pitcher. I could have been a great one."

"Yes," I said, "and the owners would have exploited you." He had in fact been a notable right-hander in his teens and twenties, and the Giants had taken an interest in him. They might have signed him if he had not stopped playing the game.

I sipped my Cuba Libres, and began to feel sorry for the man who had become dictator believing he was serving the cause of justice, convinced that it was the only way to overcome human inertia, and history had made a fool of him. He had supported the failed Soviet coup of 1991.

After a moment he asked, "When will the doctor come to look at me? We must have enough money by now."

"Soon, Fidel, soon," I said.

The audiences at the club hurled terrifying questions at him, but he answered each one with great care.

"Why did you do these cruel things?" a young woman asked him.

"They were small evils. Generations of Cubans had lived in a whorehouse. The United States never cared about the dishonest, tyrannical regimes that robbed Cuba. It never cared about governments that killed thousands of people and stole vast sums of money. It never cared about Cuba's poverty, ignorance, unsanitary conditions, its lack of schools, hospitals, and medical services, or its unemployment and racial problems. It never cared. But as soon as a regime with ideals came into power, the United States cared—by strangling us with a blockade for thirty years."

"But how did putting political prisoners naked into a bare cell for years help Cuba?" she asked. "How could you do that?"

"It was only a few," Fidel replied, pleading with her. "I started in the hills with some of them, and they turned against me. If I had let them go, they would have worked against Cuba."

"No!" the woman cried. "Against you!"

I walked with Fidel every morning on the beach, to keep him from stiffening up completely. He seemed to enjoy the ocean, and often stopped to look toward Cuba, as if he could see it.

One morning he stood staring for a quarter of an hour, and I imagined that he was dreaming of the day he had pleaded with the

Russians to nuke Washington to prevent the American invasion, or the afternoon he had been in the bunker with the Soviet officer as an American reconnaissance plane flew overhead, and to the horror of the officer had pressed the ground-to-air missile's launch button himself, bringing down the plane. What had he been hoping for in those days, when it seemed that his regime would be toppled? Had he nurtured visions of blasting North America with nuclear weapons, so that it could be settled one day by Cubans and Central Americans?

In later years, when relations with the declining Soviets had soured, a Russian restaurant had burned down in Havana, and had been replaced by a Chinese one. It had not helped. The symbolism of the change had not gotten him any more foreign aid.

Finally, the colon cancer metastasizing throughout his organs panicked him into accepting treatment from his crank doctors. They slowed his life functions, killing the cancer, but the sluggish pace of existence he got in return was full of pain, without will or pleasure. He would creep toward death for another fifty years, they had told him, becoming more and more grotesque in the process.

Still looking out across the water, he said, "They were small evils, weren't they? Why do people reproach me with them?"

I said, "Can you understand that evils must not be compared? All claims for a net good in human history are wrongheaded, even though relative good does come about, sometimes even from revolutions. But it's this very kind of argument that must be forbidden. There's a little story that proves the point. Imagine a world where all good is accomplished—but the price is the imprisoning of a small child in a closet, where it is tormented to the edge of death but never allowed to die, while millions benefit. Pragmatists must accept the conclusion that the child's plight is worth the pain. Believers in the greatest good for the greatest number must insist that it's a bargain. Only one child! Worse situations have been embraced as better."

"One child?" Fidel asked. "If I had killed only one soul, I would have been considered a saint. Yes, that would have been great progress."

"No," I said. "Utilitarian progress is only an accountant's progress. In such a world there can only be islands where evil is ignored, not overcome. No other age can compare to the darkness that has spilled out of human beings, yet the twentieth century still cherishes the illusion of progress."

He turned and faced me. "But that's only a story," he said softly. "It proves nothing about the world."

"The world's example," I answered, "is the same story, but with less elegance in the point. To be practical is to do whatever serves your purpose, whatever your power allows, in fact to do whatever you like. I told you that you wouldn't understand."

"No," Fidel said. "It is you who does not understand. Practical progress is all we human beings can get. More is not possible. I was better than Batista and the American Mafia, even at my worst. And in this world I did all that was possible. Who had ever given Cuba more?"

"Then you stand convicted out of your own mouth."

A man called me on the phone one evening and said, "You do know that the man in your show is Fidel himself and a genuine zombie?"

"What do you want?"

"You'll have trouble disposing of him. Maybe I can help. I'm a specialist."

"And you want to be paid for your services?" I assumed that the man knew the club had made a lot of money from the act.

"No—my advice is free."

"Can you tell me over the phone?"

"You'll have to burn him, then cut him in little pieces and bury him. It has to be in Cuba. Keep him the way he is, and he'll outlast all of us."

"Are you a doctor?"

"I am."

"Would you come by and check him for me?"

"No need—there's nothing to be done. He's as near to dead as our biological clocks can measure. Help him let go."

I hung up, shaken. Fidel was sitting in his chair, looking out to sea through the picture window as he often did. I stared at the back of his head. He might have been Moses, or King Lear, with all that hair. In his heart, I realized, he might be innocent—even of his own hypocrisy—because he had set himself to change what could not be changed, deluding himself with the relative improvements he had made in Cuba, even though they disappointed him. It was because he had professed so much more that he had to be judged more harshly. Many insisted that he had never had any convictions—that power alone had been his aim. He had bet on the Soviets winning the Cold War and had lost. He had been lucky in having the United States to blame for his failures, or he would have been deposed in his first decade. The Soviets saved him by extracting a promise from Kennedy not to invade, in return for removing their nuclear missiles.

At seven the next morning, I took his arm and led him out to the beach, and walked at his side as always. After a few minutes, he spoke without looking at me, saying, "There will be no doctor, will there?"

It was time he knew the truth. "No one can help you."

"In that case, when you feel that you have made enough money from me for your grandfather's suffering, take me back to Cuba, Enrico." He stopped and looked at me with his sad, bulging eyes, and I knew that I could not refuse him. Besides, his audiences at the club had been getting smaller recently. Many of the older patrons had stopped coming. They had lost interest in confronting some crazed, old impersonator who could not possibly be their old enemy.

"We'll finish out the week," I said.

That same evening, in the middle of Fidel's long, meticulous response to a question about corruption and drug-dealing in his regime, a young man stood up at a table in the back of the room, shouted "Death to tyrants!" and fired three shots into Fidel's chest. As the assassin turned and fled, Fidel simply sat back in his chair and stared into space.

I got a wheelchair from the wings and rolled it out to him. "Are you hurt?" I asked, ready to help him. There was still a part of me that doubted his condition, that expected him to be mortally wounded.

"No," he said, standing up. "At least this one was more direct."

"Direct?" I asked.

"More so than the CIA's exploding cigars."

I walked him back to his dressing room, sat him down, and opened his shirt to examine his wounds. There was no bleeding as I dug out the bullets from his rubbery chest. I had imagined that his heart rate and breathing were very slow, that he was only an old man with some peculiar condition, but the bullets convinced me of his true state. He could not bleed to death.

There was a loud knock on the door. I went to it and opened it a crack. A cop in plain clothes was waiting to be let in.

I said, "The shots missed, but he's shaken up and can't see anyone right now." The cop looked past me, getting a glimpse of Fidel, and seemed convinced.

I rented a recreational vehicle in Havana and drove it to a small coastal village north of the Sierra Maestra Mountains. My brother flew Fidel in a day later by amphibious aircraft, and I hid him in the RV.

"This is more than the old bastard deserves," my brother said before going back to the plane. "What is there here for him anyway?"

"I don't know, but whatever it is, he's going to have it."

"Why bother about him?" He had come because he liked to fly his plane, not for old politics, and because I had asked him. Old Fidel had made us a few dollars, but sooner or later, my brother and I both knew, we would have to get free of him.

The next morning Fidel and I drove into the hills where he had started his revolution and stopped in a small village, beyond which there was no road.

I looked around at the dusty village. "What will you do here?" I asked, wondering how long he could exist without nutrients of some kind.

"I will find out how long I can survive."

"What do you mean?"

"I must be able to die, sooner or later."

As I gazed at his rigid figure sitting next to me, I confronted my own love-hate relationship with revolutions, with changes of any kind, which rarely achieve their ends, because of failings deep within the human heart. Young revolutionaries, if they survive, live to sink into immobility and disappointment with their own kind. The time of just revolutions had ended before I was born.

"Drive up as high as possible," Fidel said, as if giving profound advice. "From there I'll go by myself." His raspy voice carried the authority of someone who knew where he was going.

I drove the RV up a winding dirt path, and came to a stop before a grove of trees. Rocky mountainside rose beyond it. Fidel struggled out of the vehicle and stood looking up at the heights. I got out and waited.

"Defeating Batista," he said, "was easier than governing Cuba. I had been clever enough to see the battles that I would need to win, but to rule Cuba profitably would have required the friendship of the United States, which I lost because I would not deal with the devil. I went to the devil Washington feared, who professed just ideals. But it's the devil you know that counts. I didn't know either devil well enough to benefit Cuba." He paused, as if overcome with emotion, but as usual his body stifled the show of human feeling, permitting him only words. "There are those," he continued, "who believe it best to leave things as they are and hope for gradual change, no matter how bad things get. Do you believe, Enrico, that force is never justified?"

"What will you do here?" I asked.

He turned and faced me. "You know what must be done, or I will rise again, and no one knows how long I will suffer. Destroy me."

"I can't do it!" I shouted, remembering the doctor's phone call.

"Do it for your grandfather, and for me."

"No, I won't . . . I can't," I muttered, appalled by my sudden weakness.

He turned away and started up toward the grove of trees. I waited until he was nearly out of sight; then curiosity got the better of me and I went in after him. He was staggering among the trees, toward the far side of the grove. I crept after him, realizing that I couldn't take him back with me. What would I do with him? There was a limit to how long an ex-dictator could be exhibited, even if I could have his condition as a zombie certified.

I had a vision of two demented scholars from an old horror movie examining Fidel.

"Zombie?" asked the first scholar of his colleague.

The other nodded smugly and said, "Zombie."

Fidel stumbled out of the grove and threw himself on the slope, lacerating his rubbery flesh on the sharp rocks, but his movements seemed unphysical. He was trying to crawl back into the hill of dreams, into the mocking mirage where every dear ideal cowers, into the hills where he had been a hero, to a wild high place beyond life, from which we take what we need, even though it doesn't actually exist. The blood pounding in my ears became a roaring fire in my brain as I watched him struggling to tear himself apart.

"Okay—come back and wait in the grove!" I shouted, retreating.

I looked back from the grove and saw his stiff figure stumbling down after me. Wind gusted through the trees, but died away as I hurried through to the RV and took out a spade, a can of gasoline, and the machete.

There are nights when I awaken on the rocky hillside and see his pillar of fire roaring in the green grove. Trapped in an insane animation of a socialist realist mural with Henri Rousseau's staring beasts, I cut up the charred body while Fidel's frozen eyes watch me, and bury the pieces all over the grove, insisting to myself that he did some good, some bad, and was a lousy administrator, and that I was probably giving him too much credit for selflessness. What could you expect from an outraged, handsome young man who modeled his speechmaking on Mussolini's? Maybe it wasn't his fault. Maybe pragmatism is all we can get. I split the head into four bloodless piecces and bury them far apart. Then I wake sweating between icy sheets. My pillows are stones as I turn over and tunnel back into sleep, and the fire ignites again in the blackness behind my eyes.

General Jaruzelski at the Zoo

"Even a flounder takes sides."
— Stanislaw J. Lec

*M*ACIEK THE CHIMP SAW GENERAL JARUZELSKI coming down the gravel path that ran by his cage. There were two men with him. One was looking around nervously, as if he had lost something; the other was the zookeeper.

Maciek endured his hunger cramps, believing that if he performed well enough the visitors would give him a banana.

Maciek jumped up and down.

The general failed to notice.

Maciek did a backflip.

Still the general paid no attention. He seemed to be hiding behind his dark glasses.

Maciek leaped onto the bars and shook them.

The general stopped and smiled.

This was it! Maciek was sure that the bananas were close by; his cramps would soon end.

Maciek rattled the bars until his arms and shoulders hurt.

The zookeeper began to talk to the general.

Maciek's eyes watered from the pains. He lay down and held his belly. There had been no bananas for so long now, and there would be no bananas again today.

"It's been difficult for us lately, general," the director of the zoo said softly. "I appreciate your stopping by to take notice of our problems."

The general smiled at the diplomacy of the director's words, but the truth was otherwise. Nostalgia for the zoological pleasures of his boyhood had prodded the general to come here during his lunch hour, nothing more.

"People can get along in the worst of times," the youthful director continued politely, "but animals are unable to stand in long lines or take vitamins, or eat the variety of foods we do. This chimp's digestion requires special oils from bananas. Cuban oranges have helped, but they're not quite right. You see his pain. He hasn't had a banana in three months. Of course, we could feed him easily if he were a human being."

The general stepped up to the cage. It seemed that the chimp was watching him with unusual attention.

"What is it?" the director asked.

The chimp got up and came to the bars. Pain slipped through the general's stomach, and he felt a craving for bananas. Suddenly he was gripping the bars from inside the cage. His muscles ached from the dampness. He peered into his own dark glasses and saw a shadowy chimp face staring back, baring its teeth.

He stumbled back from the bars into the arms of his security man.

"Maciek is in great pain," the director said as the general steadied himself.

They walked on. People were feeding the elephants, the general noticed as he tried to shake off the delusion he had experienced at the cage. The biscuits, he saw, were the shortbread kind, expensive and hard to come by. These people had stood in long lines to buy them for the elephants. Why had the delusion come upon him? I must be a man of conscience, he told himself. Or I'm losing my mind.

"Even the smallest thing you could do for us," the director said, "would help us save some of the animals."

"You anticipate deaths?" the general asked, adjusting his glasses.

"Of course, without a doubt."

General Jaruzelski recalled his private meeting with the university professors. They had made him feel guilty and sad, as the young zookeeper was doing more gently. They had not understood, in their inquisitorial fervor, that the Russians would invade their beloved Poland. It was a matter of camouflage, he had told them with tears in his eyes, to make the Soviets think we are like them, for as long as it took for Poles to become free within their own borders. The jealous, fearful bear had to be put to sleep, as the Czechs, Yugoslavs, and Hungarians were doing. . . .

"The Bulgarians sent us some fruit for the animals," the director was saying. "They didn't even ask for payment in trade, and we're grateful. But, you see, it's got to be the right fruit—bananas for the chimps, raisins and nuts for the birds. . . ."

"Raisins and nuts?" the general asked. The demand was familiar in its seeming extravagance.

The director shrugged shyly. "The grains we're getting are not really for them. Our birds need special kinds of seeds. They develop rashes, lose feathers and coloration when they don't have raisins and nuts. How can I do my job when I have to ignore facts of biology and diet?"

The general nodded and they walked on, followed by the security man. Even Polish animals were extravagant, a Russian would quip, needing exotic feed in keeping with the national character.

"There won't be much I can do," the director was saying, "when they start to die."

It was a matter of doing the effective thing, the general told himself, and not what was popular or satisfying to old scores and hatreds. His own father had died at the hands of the Russians. Surely that personal loss makes me a credible Pole? The bloodbath could start again quickly, no doubt about it. What did they know, those who had never held responsible public office? Their emotional siege was making him hallucinate.

"I would like to call to your attention," the director said more insistently, "that the problems of our zoos are widely reported in the Western media. American newsmen were here with video equipment, I'm sorry to report. They had the proper permits, of course."

The general felt a moment of respect for the director. The fellow knew what to say to be heard. A responsible, conscientious young man, not at all like so many corrupt officials.

"Are you a Party member?" the general asked.

The zookeeper smiled. "Unfortunately, no, general. I'm a zoologist, not political."

They never were, the general thought with a twinge of resentment. Like the animals, they couldn't be political, even though they lived in a political situation. They cared more for their career specialties, even for the animals, than they did for Poland.

The biscuits were sweet, but there was little in them to make the elephant strong. The people who brought them had kind, pitying faces, but they also seemed to know the two-leggeds who hid food in the nearby buildings and seemed to want elephants to perish.

The elephant knew that dying-time was near, and that he would have to do it right here, with no privacy at all.

A face was looking at him. The hands held no biscuits. The eyes were great dark patches. The lips were pressed together.

The general wondered why he had liked zoos so much as a child. What had it been about the animals that had made his boyhood happy? That one might escape? Seeing danger contained? We're surrounded by wild elephants, he thought. One false move and they'll trample us to death. It will be a long time before the danger passes; elephants are big and sturdy, and take a long time to die. . . .

"Can we count on your help, general?" the young director was saying.

I can't move, the general thought, feeling elephantine.

"I'll do my best," he managed to say finally.

The director smiled gratefully, endearingly, in contrast to the stone-faced professors when he had spoken the same words to them. Nothing short of futile resistance against the Soviets would satisfy them—not his tears, not his acceptance of their just criticisms of the Party. They had grudgingly admitted his good intentions and personal honesty, but they would never support him in their hearts. They would never love him, but he would do what had to be done to avoid bloodshed.

The universities were also zoos of a kind, where the wiser animals had to teach the more foolish ones how to live and die. A Poland outside the Soviet orbit was impossible, but it was up to Poles whether their relationship with the bear would be that of a slave or equal. Feuding would leave no chance for mutual respect, much less eventual friendship. Martial law preserved this possibility, despite the loss of economic support from the West.

"Thank you for listening," the director of the zoo was saying. "I know that your valuable time is limited." The scientist smiled again. He seemed a good sort—probably a country boy educated in the city; polite and without guile. He would not be promoted.

"I'll do what I can for you," the general said, "but put some of the blame on American business. It's inhumane enough even when it's not politically directed." He turned and followed the security man out of the park.

Maciek trembled in the muggy mid-afternoon heat. His stomach rumbled painfully. Someone was angry at him. He felt lost as he listened to the elephants snorting. The birds were silent.

Back in his office the general leaned back in his chair and fell asleep. The animals quarreled with him in a strange language. He couldn't make it out, but it seemed that they were pleading, insisting, mocking. The strongest animals, he said to them, avoided capture; only the weakest were prisoners.

Despair and a sense of worthlessness seized him. The chimp's pain mourned in his stomach. He could not escape by waking.

He longed for what he might do to be loved. Polish independence would do it. With the army behind him, the Russians would think five times before invading. He would equal the great General Pilsudski in driving the Russians out of Poland.

But alas, that feat was impossible. Supplies and ammunition for the army were strictly controlled, and for every line of Poles there was a line of Russian soldiers. Polish independence of any kind would cut East Germany off from its master, precipitating German unification, and all of Eastern Europe would rise in a ferment of hope.

Nothing was simple, ever. Justice was a naive, impractical concept. Even the Americans did not really want a free Poland, because such an interface with the Soviets would only benefit the evil empire's economy. *Cartago Delenda Est!*

He awoke and almost fell out of his chair as his private phone rang.

"Hallo!" he shouted, pressing the receiver to his ear.

"Wojciech! Is that you?" the Soviet Underminister of Agriculture asked.

"Of course." The man knew well enough that no one else could pick up on this line. "What can I do for you?"

"Well, it's the hams again, you see. We need more this month. Special occasion, you see."

"I'll do my best."

"The railroad car will be waiting."

The corrupt bastard, Jaruzelski thought bitterly, recalling the man's weakness for Western pornographic cassettes. If he were one of my officials, I'd have hanged him by now. Andropov had turned a blind eye to him but perhaps Gorbachev would remove the parasite.

"This is very good of you, Wojciech, on such short notice. I won't forget it."

"Not at all, Minister."

"You've had quite a week, I hear."

Jaruzelski got up and went to the window, arranging the long cord carefully behind himself. The Minister had once offered him a cordless model, but he had neglected to take him up on it.

"Wojciech, perhaps I might do something for you? Feel free to ask. I have means. I mean if it's within my power I'll do it. I promise."

Jaruzelski saw a man down in the street, reminding him of Maciek in the way he loped along by the buildings. People resembled animals of one kind or another in their faces and manners. Even human artifacts like buses and cars seemed to be animals on occasion. . . .

"Wojciech!"

General Jaruzelski swallowed hard away from the receiver. The pain from the zoo was still in his stomach.

"What's that, Wojciech!" the Russian shouted as the connection broke up. "I lost you there! What is it you said you want?" There was some coughing and slurping on the line as the Minister downed a shot.

"Minister," the Savior of Poland asked loudly, with a hint of defiance, "can you send some bananas?"

"Bananas, Wojciech?"

"Yes, for the zoos. Animals are dying. The shortages are an embarrassment. CBS did a story on it."

"Did you tape it?"

"No, I only heard about it today. Besides, I don't have a VCR."

"The Americans are so sentimental about animals! Didn't I offer to get you a Sony?"

General Jaruzelski was silent.

"I'll see what I can do," the Russian said finally.

"Thank you."

Collaboration and compromise, he thought bitterly as he hung up and sat down again. Cage bars rattled in his ears, and he felt himself slipping in again behind Maciek's eyes. His stomach burned as he looked around at his office, at the pale light streaming in through the window, at the locked door with the armed guard sitting outside. The room was a cage. It seemed normal to beg for bananas.

The Soft Terrible Music

*E*ACH OF CASTLE SILVERSTONE'S ONE HUN-
dred windows looked out on the landscape of a different
country.

The iron drawbridge opened on Mars.

A stainless steel side gate led out into a neighborhood in Luna
City.

A small, bronze gate opened in a small, public place aboard
Odalisque, the largest of the Venusian floating islands drifting high
above the hot, dry desert of the planet.

A sliding double door opened through the sheer face of a cliff
overlooking Rio de Janiero, where one could stand before an
uncrossable threshold.

There was also a door that led nowhere. It was no different in
function than the other doors, except that it was not set to any destination. This castle, like any true home, was the expression of a
man's insides, desolate places included.

When the castle was not powered-up for full extension, it stood
on a rocky hillside in Antarctica's single warm valley, where it
had been built in the early twenty-second century by Wolfgang
Silverstone, who rented it out occasionally for political summits.
In design it was a bouquet of tall, gleaming cylinders, topped with
turrets from a variety of castle building periods. The cylinders
surrounded a central courtyard, and the brief connecting walls

were faced with gray stone that had been quarried from the valley.

The castle got its name as much from the flecks of fool's silver in the stone as from the name of its builder. The castle also differed from other extended homes, because it was not linked to the houses of friends and relatives, or to apartments and pieds-à-terre in major cities. The castle had its vistas, and one could step out into them, but its exits were private. Some of them even looped back into chambers within the castle.

Few homes had ever been built with as much care and attention to a human being's future needs, to his own future failings. Deep within himself, Silverstone knew what would happen, had accepted it, and had made provisions for his fate.

Halfway through construction, he altered some of the keep's plans to attract a single woman—Gailla, the woman with the perfect memory, who by age eighty had read and retained every novel written since the eighteenth century. Silverstone, in a fit of fibbing, told her that his castle had a library of one thousand previously lost and unknown works, that he found her irresistible, and that if she married him for the minimum allowable term he would give her the key to the library.

As he waited for Gailla's answer, his nights trembled with odd dreams, in which he felt that he had always known her, even though he was certain that they had never met—at least not physically. Upon waking, he would conclude that he must have seen her image somewhere; or, more simply, that he wanted her so desperately that his unconscious was inventing an unbroken history of romance, to convince him that they had always been together in their love.

What was five years of a term marriage, he told her; another century of life waited. He was not unattractive for a child of fifty, even if he said so himself. The prize of books he offered seemed to draw her curiosity. Its very existence intrigued her. But secret libraries were not unknown. The Vatican still had much of one locked away, and the history of the Middle East and North Africa was filled with stories of vanished libraries waiting under the sands along ancient, dried-up waterways. One more lost library was not an impossibility.

Fearful that she would leave him if he did not make good on his original boast, he told her that his treasure was a library of books that had been saved from the great "paper loss" of 1850–2050, when most acid paper books had crumbled to dust because there had been no money or will to preserve them; the world had been too busy dealing with global warming and rising ocean levels. He had found the books on his forays into various abandoned Antarctic bases, where the dry cold had preserved the paper. They were mostly mysteries, science fiction, adventure, suspense, bestsellers, and romance novels brought by the base personnel for amusement. Only about a thousand volumes.

As it turned out, she soon discovered that the books were a fraud. Silverstone confessed that he had found only a few; the rest were written to complete extant scraps, cover designs and jacket blurbs, by paid specialists who did not know for whom they were working or that they were part of a larger effort. But fraud or not, it was at least an echo of a newly discovered library, and given enough time, it would become interesting in itself, he assured her, and it seemed to him that she appreciated the compliment of his ploy.

He told her how paper had been made and aged, covers painted, fingerprints of the dead scattered through the volumes. Gailla seemed delighted—for about a month—until she saw how bad the books were, how trite and poorly written. Silverstone was delighted by her bedroom habits—also for about a month. She lost interest in him at about the same time she was able to prove that the books, from internal anachronisms, were fakes.

"How dare you!" she screamed, careful to put on a convincing show. "Why did you do it?"

"To attract you," he answered, astonished by her perfectly controlled bitterness, which seemed to hide another purpose. "Are you sorry? Would you have bonded with me for myself?"

"You never gave me the chance!" she sang out in a voice that began as a low grumble and ended in a high soprano.

"But you would have," he demanded, "in other circumstances?"

The question seemed to upset her greatly, and she gave no answer; but Silverstone was convinced that she was holding back a no, and he began to wonder why he had ever been attracted to her. It had seemed to him at the beginning that she would alter the course of his life, change the unknown fate that lay hidden in the back of his mind; and now it seemed to him that nothing could save him from it. It was as if she had known all along about the abyss that threatened to open before him, and was waiting for the right moment to push him into it—after she had tormented him with doubt for a sufficient period of time.

He often went to one window after another, as if looking for a landscape into which he might disappear. Autumn scenes drew him, especially mountainous ones with streams, where the leaves on the trees were turning gold and brown. Then he hungered for the sterility of desert sands; and this gave way to a need for lush jungles, and then windswept plains. He became insatiable, passing from window to window like a thief in a museum, eyeing the views greedily, feeling that there could never be enough windows.

Sometimes he liked to step out on Mars, onto his small patch of it, where he could stand and marvel at the honeycomb of habitats spreading across the planet. Five-sided, one-thousand-foot-high transparent cells, immediately habitable in the Martian sunlight —they would one day roof over the red planet with an indoor-outdoors, thus solving the problem of keeping a permanent atmosphere on a low-gravity world. Here was an achievement he envied, wishing that he had been its architect. It was an accomplishment in the making that no amount of inherited wealth could buy.

There were afternoons when he would slip through the gate into Luna City and wander through the VR-game bazaars, where the miners bought their cruel distractions.

Passing into his small hotel room on Odalisque, the Venusian floating island, he would shower and dress for dinner at the Ishtar Restaurant, where huge wallscreens revealed a radar imaging of the bleak landscape fifty kilometers below, which waited for human ambitions to make a mark on it.

And at least once a month he would stand in the alcove above Rio and stare out at the city below as if it were his hometown, imagining the old streets as if he had once known them.

And again, as with the windows, there were not enough doors to satisfy him. Every *there* became a *here* when he came to it, losing the longing-magic that drew him.

On the battlements at night, as he considered his deteriorating situation with Gailla, it was—the stars! the stars!—that gave him any kind of peace. By day he felt exposed to the sky, whether a white sheet of overcast or the brilliant glare of yellow sun in a deep blue sky. In the evenings, when he took a short walk across the bare valley of stone, it was always a walk across himself, in search of something he had lost. When he stopped and looked back at the castle, he felt that he had left himself behind. Returning, he felt better, except that Gailla was still there, an intruder deep within him, and he regretted bitterly ever having let her in.

Trying to think how he might extricate himself, he would visit the castle's dungeons, where the heat exchangers drew strength from the hot springs beneath the bedrock to run the electric generators. Here, also, were the brightly lit hothouses that grew his flowers and vegetables. He did not feel exposed beneath this well-defined, contained, and nourishing daylight. Sitting there, watching the vegetables grow, he calmed himself enough to think that he would simply let the minimum term of his marriage run out. There was only a year and a half left. That would be the simplest solution. Until then, he would simply keep out of her way.

But asleep in his own room, he would often hear her moving inside him, opening doors and closing them, as if looking for something. He would wake up and hear her doing the same thing again, and he wondered what she had come into him to find. And he realized, although some part of him had known it all along, that there were two castles, that there had been two castles from the very moment he had conceived the plans for its construction in this valley—one castle outside and one within himself, and that Gailla had invaded both of them.

He began to wonder what she was looking for, and decided that he would have to spy on her to find out. Had she married him to steal something? What did he have that required so much effort? If it was so desirable, maybe he should also know about this prize, and prevent her from stealing it. What could it be? He already had everything that money could buy.

During the night of January 31st, he slept lightly, and when he heard her opening and closing doors, he got up and dressed, then went out to see what he could learn. He found her on the second level of the north turret, going from room to room down the spiral staircase, opening every door, shining a light inside, then backing away and leaving the door slightly ajar. He listened to her from behind a Freas tapestry, until she reached the bottom. There she sighed as if greatly satisfied, and went down the final curve of the stairway into the main hall below.

He crept out from his hiding place and hurried to the railing, from which he looked down and saw her pacing before the great fireplace, where the dying embers of a collapsed universe still glowed. She was dressed in her outdoor jumpsuit, but it could not conceal her tall, slender shape. At last she sat down in one of the great high chairs and closed her eyes in contentment.

It made no sense at all.

"You can come down, Wolfy," she called out suddenly. "I know you're there!"

Was she bluffing, he wondered? Had she called out like this on several nights, out of a general suspicion?

She looked up suddenly and pointed to where he stood. "I can't quite see you in this wretched light, but you're there in the shadow near the railing."

She was not bluffing. He leaned over and said, "I'll be right with you," then came down the stairs, hoping that now he would at last learn what she was after, crossed the hall, and sat down in the high-backed chair facing hers.

Staring at her intently, he was about to ask what she was looking for.

"Be patient," she said, expecting his question.

He looked at her, puzzled. "And you bonded with me just to . . . carry on some kind of search? Whatever for?"

"You'll know soon enough, Wolfy.

"Do you even know yourself?"

"I know," she said, and as the redness of the embers painted her face, it seemed that she was about to become someone else.

"So tell me," he said. "It's something I'll have to know sooner or later—right?"

She nodded grimly and said, "More than you want to know. But before I tell you, Wolfy, be advised that people know where I am."

"What do you think I'll do to you?" he asked with surprise.

"Let me tell you a story . . ."

He settled back in his chair.

"During the plague deaths of the twenty-first century," she began, "a man was born in Rio. He grew up to be a thief, a murderer, a crooked politician, a mayor of more than one city, and finally the president of a country. In a depopulated world, his talents were needed, and he did well in administrative posts, although always to his own benefit. But as the century grew old and the population began to increase again, people became more jealous of political and economic power, and sought to take back from him what he had gained. He defended himself, of course, but when he saw that he would be brought down, either by assassination or by imprisonment, he decided that he had to die. So he went to a rich friend who was a recluse, killed him, and then stepped into the man's identity, through somatic changes of his own physique, which already resembled that of the victim, and finally through selective memory implants. And then he went one step further, desperate to cover his trail completely. He wiped away his own self to prevent capture, and became Wolfgang Silverstone, as completely as anyone could, short of having actually been Wolfgang Silverstone."

"What!" Silverstone cried out.

"Sit down and calm yourself, Wolfy. You can't know right now that any of this is true, but trust me, the trail is still there, because you didn't want to hide it completely."

"That's crazy. It's the same as suicide!"

"No, the man from Rio planned to come back."

"What?"

"Yes, he left a 'trigger' inside his stolen persona, so that one day it would resurrect his earlier self. I'm certain of that. This trigger is what I've been looking for. It's here in this castle, and even you don't know where it is, even though you had it built as part of your way back. The man you were was too egotistical to have allowed himself to become someone else permanently. You're not the man you were, but you will be, very soon now."

Silverstone laughed. "But how?"

"There's a pre-trigger," she said, "that will guide you to the place at the appropriate time, and there you will know how to free your true self and become again the man who killed the original Silverstone." She recited the words softly, as if she had rehearsed them a thousand times—which, of course, she had.

Silverstone stood up and lurched toward her, but she pointed a weapon at him wearily and said, "Sit down, Wolfy. Do you think I would have told you all this without some insurance?"

He stopped, then stumbled back into his chair. "Who are you?" he asked. "What is all this to you?"

She shrugged. "Police—and there's no statute of limitations on murder."

He sat back, stunned. "But surely you see . . . that you have no proof beyond this story you've told me. You personally don't know that it's true. You're just putting bits and pieces together."

"You've been getting restless lately," she said, "as if you were looking for something—and you have been, constantly. You're getting close to the time you set for triggering your own return. You see, even in your persona state, your guilt remains, buried deeply, of course. Even your building this castle is part of that. You built it as a way of exploring yourself, of setting the means for your return. You'll give me all the proof I need, because you'll go to a certain prepared room at the appointed time and come out guilty of murder. It's why I'm here, and why I married you."

He laughed. "But I can't know that any of this is true!" he shouted. "Even you admit that. If I don't go to this room, you'll have no case. Even if I do go in, I don't have to say anything when

I come out. Why did you bother to tell me all this? You might have done better leaving me in the dark. Mind you, that's still assuming any of this is true."

"I want you to suffer for a while."

"Did you find the room? You certainly spent enough nights annoying me with your explorations."

"Shut up, Wolfy. You're just a clever sociopath living through a dead man's memories. You set up a time for retrieving yourself, after stealing from people in troubled times. I suppose even a thug wants to be himself, to come back from, in effect, being dead."

"How long must a man lie dead," he recited, puzzled by the words that came out of him. "Forever is too long. There must be mercy somewhere."

"See, you're in there, all right," she replied, "speaking out even though you don't quite know it."

Shaken, he asked derisively, "Did you call him Wolfy? And were you his she-wolf?"

"Shut up!"

"You'll never call anyone but me Wolfy again," he said. "What can getting this other guy bring you?"

"He'll be at peace. I'll be at peace, knowing that the murderer of my beloved has been exposed."

"Oh, then you won't kill me yourself? You'll just have them take me away."

"But first you'll have to live again as the man you were."

He sat slightly forward in his chair and her hand tensed around her gun. "But don't you see," he said earnestly. "I'm not responsible. I know only what you've told me about all this. I don't know or feel anything about the crime."

"Don't worry, it'll all come back to you. That's why you did it this way, so you could say that you weren't responsible. It's part of your crime."

"Really?"

"You set it up, and I've caught you."

"Are you sure? Beware, you may not like what you find."

"Don't threaten me," she said. "You are Benito Alonso Robles, the man from Rio, who killed Wolfgang Silverstone in 2049 and downloaded the essentials of his personality into your own, over-writing yourself for a timed period in order to evade the police. Murder was only your last crime, designed to conceal all the others. We can't get you on many of those, but we will certainly get you for murder."

"How clever of me," Silverstone said. "So what now?"

She did not answer him.

"Consider," he continued, "that if I am all that is left of Silverstone, your so-called beloved, then why didn't I remember you when we met?"

"We were no longer together when you killed him," she said, "and sometime before that, in order to ease his pain, he had suppressed his experiences with me. Still, I think something in you seemed to know me."

"Ah! And then I fell in love with you again. That was why I was so earnest, so eager. But how could I know, my dear?" He held his arms out to her. "And now you want to destroy all that survives of your beloved, even after what was left of him was strong enough to come after you again!"

"No—you're only a fragment of him, and you've developed in ways he would not have, had he lived. For one thing, there's a different unconscious below the superimposed personality and its memories, and that makes you very different."

"Still, I'm all that's left of Wolfy dearest."

"But not any part that knows me very well," she said coldly. "Why did you pick him? Had he done you any wrong?"

"How do I know? If all this is true, then he was simply convenient, I suppose. Ask me later—if we get to later, and if any of this is true."

"Get up," she said. "We're going upstairs."

"Is it time, my dearest?"

"I don't know. Do you feel anything? You may have already spoken the pre-trigger."

He stood up and she motioned for him to climb the great stairs to the second level of the north tower. As he started up, she followed well below him, gun aimed at his back.

"Keep going," she said when he reached the landing.

"How do you know it's up here?" he asked.

"Where would you say, then?"

"The lower levels?" he said, laughing. "How would I know? If what you say is true, I may even be the man you say I killed— I mean physically as well as whatever identity was fed in."

"You're not," she said. "I've already had your DNA checked."

He laughed again. "Of course, the opportunity presented itself to you on more than one occasion. You simply carried a sample away in you." He turned around and faced her with open hands. "Gailla," he said, "you don't know what you're doing and neither do

I, by your own claims. You don't know how the pre-trigger will kick in, or where this . . . this restoration will take place. And you admit that as far as I know, I am Silverstone . . ."

"You're not him," she said. "That much I know."

"Yes, yes, the DNA. But I only have your word for that too."

"Do you feel anything?" she asked. "An impulse to go somewhere, or say something to yourself?"

"Not particularly."

"Just a few moments ago you wanted to go to the lower levels below the castle."

"An idle remark."

"It might mean something."

"Well, I have lived with a vague expectation of some kind for a while now. It came to me just after we . . . no longer got along."

"Really."

"Maybe your being a cop spooked me at some basic level." He turned around suddenly and watched her tense. He waited a moment, then asked, "What do you really want from me? Simple revenge, is that it?"

"No, I just want you to know again, consciously, what you did, and let the law do with you as it will. That's revenge enough."

"But what if I never remember?"

"That's what we're here for," she said. "You took him from me a long time ago, and denied us a chance of ever getting back to each other. We might have by now."

"It's pretty to think so, and sad that you do."

"You don't really care."

"Not much. You're purging me of any desire I once had for you."

"Sorry I can't say the same. It was never there."

"Are you sure?"

"Turn around and get going."

He smiled, turned, and climbed the spiral.

"Stop right there," she said suddenly. "Face the door on your right."

He obeyed. "Why here?"

"Process of elimination," she said. "You have never entered this room since we've been together. Do you recall ever entering it?"

"As a matter of fact, I don't."

"Go in."

He pressed his palm to the plate, and the door slid open. He stepped inside. She came in right behind him. The door slid shut.

An overhead panel of light blinked on, filling the room with bright yellow light, and he saw another door at the end of the room.

Then he looked to his right and saw the portrait on the wall.

He turned and gazed up at a dark painting of someone sitting at a mahogany desk. It was an old man with thin, white hair teased out to twice the size of his head. He was dressed in a bright red, nineteenth century military tunic that seemed to be choking his wrinkled neck. There were no markings on the tunic to indicate nationality. The man's mouth was closed tightly. . . .

And as he stared at the face, a flood of returning memory filled his mind, and he knew that this was the trigger. And with his memories came also the remembrance of the day he had set the trigger at the portrait of Silverstone's ancestor. Then, packed away, the painting had waited for the castle to be built, where he would one day come to himself again, secure, reestablished, reawakening to himself again, slowly, secretly, safely bringing himself out of the sleepwalker's life that had been necessary for his survival.

He waited as his identity returned. It blossomed within him, realms of self and memory fitting themselves into vast, empty spaces—but Silverstone stayed with him all the way, showing no sign of fading. He turned to face Gailla and said, "He's still with me . . . I can't get rid of him!"

"He'll keep you company at your trial," Gailla said joylessly.

"But you'll be killing what's left of your old love!" he cried.

"I've been prepared for some time," she said. "They'll wipe you clean and start you up as someone else. It'll be all over for both of us."

"No!" he cried, turned, and rushed to the other door. She did not fire, and he knew that she couldn't, and that he would have enough time to do what he now remembered was his last recourse, waiting for him if something went wrong.

He palmed the door, and still she had not fired. As the door slid open, he knew that she was hesitating, unable to kill the last of her lover. And he felt it also, the mountainous regret at having killed him. He could not banish it, or the vast cloud of the man's mental remains. It refused to fade away, invading his unused regions with new patterns, and he knew that he was too weak to wipe them out. The impulse to love had infected him with weak sentiments, and he knew that she felt it also. The bodily memories of their love-making had softened them both. That was why she had not killed him as soon as he had regained himself. Or was she preparing him for when she would rebuild her old lover by amplifying the stubborn echoes that remained until they burgeoned and became again the personality she had known? Maybe she knew how to resurrect him and had planned it all along, and would carry out her plan after sufficient revenge had been visited on him.

Well, he would deny her that. He could still take everything from her, and achieve one last victory over a world that had opposed his every desire from the start, always forcing him to take what he wanted. There was nothing else he could do.

"Wait!" she cried as the door opened into chaos. It would have been a way to somewhere, but he had deliberately left it set to no destination—realizing that he might need its sudden exit one day.

As he tumbled into the black obscenity of existence without form, he saw her in the doorway, her mouth open wide in horror and regret, her arms reaching out to him uselessly. And as he felt himself deforming, changing, losing all sense of time and space, he knew that his death would not be quick, that no supernatural damnation could ever have equaled the slow loss of himself that was just beginning.

Gailla was shooting at him now, and he imagined that it was a gesture of pity, an effort to shorten the suffering of what was left of her lover. The third bullet opened his chest, entering slowly, as if unsure of how to obey the laws of physics in this realm. It explored his pain, telling him that he had made this final fate for himself by building the castle and its doorways, with every fleeting, trivial decision—step by inexorable step to one end, to bring him here, to this death.

"Gailla," Silverstone whispered through the pain of her bullet's dancing, failed mercy. "I'm still here."

Then Robles closed his eyes and heard the soft, terrible music filtering in from behind the show of things. It was an inhuman music, with nothing of song or dance, or memory in it. It was a music of crushed glass, severed nerves, and brute rumblings, preparing the way for a theme of fear.

And as Robles knew himself in his pain, he yearned for death because Silverstone was still with him.

My First World

1

𝒥T WAS THE DAY OF RETURN, BUT THE ROCK DID not open and we did not see the stars. Our world was not visited, and release did not begin.

I had heard about it all my life, and looked forward to the evacuation. I also feared it, but that was not an acceptable feeling to show where I grew up, so I kept it to myself.

Agonized, often fierce hopes lived in parents, especially in the mothers and fathers of daughters. Their children's lives waited to begin on the day of return.

On that same day, so clearly marked by our dining hall clocks and calendars, I walked away from the sunplate to the rocky end of the world, and looked back across its ten-kilometer length of afternoon, at our fifty years of forest and grassland. These lofty pines had never known a real wind, according to my father, but they leaned a bit from our hollow rock's rotation, he said.

I looked at the light-shot, silver-blue stream, at the central lake's reflection of the sunplate, at the three small towns around their food dispensary domes, and wondered how all this could end before I fully knew how it had all come about.

Much of the gently hilly interior was tall grass—about a hundred square kilometers of land pasted on the inside of a spinning football. We walked around in centrifugal spin, like gravity, my father said without explaining gravity, but really only acceleration, which pushed us down on the landscape, our feet to the stars we couldn't see and our heads toward the airy center, sunplate at one end of the long axis and rocky hills at the other.

Somewhere beneath the land, but not as far as the outer protective surface of the original asteroid, was the sealed engineering level, there for the wardens to visit, and to house the machines that ran our eco-systems.

The rock had no propulsion systems of its own. It had been boosted into a timed cometary orbit, and would be maneuvered by large tugs when it returned.

Crowds sat on the hillsides outside the three towns, awaiting arrival, sure of the year-counts, needing to believe in justice from a past that had rejected them.

Only about half the people were still alive from the time when the rock went out. This had left much of the housing of the three towns to be continuously divided more generously among the survivors and their few children. Our town was just beyond the lake, the second was halfway up the curve of the world, and the third was above the lake. My parents and I had one end of a long barracks, which my father had divided into three large rooms, one for himself and my mother, one to sit in, a small corner of which he called his study, and one for me.

Long before we crossed Earth's orbit, we expected visits by warden vessels. The engineering level would open, and prison officials would emerge to announce the end of the fifty-year sentence meted out to our mothers and fathers.

To me it had not been a prison sentence. It had been only the way we lived. I had never known anything else, and wondered if other ways would be any better. I had only the vaguest ideas of what other ways of life might be like.

Children doubt what parents say about the past; parents are saying it, so it can't be all that important. It doesn't seem real, because they say too little about it, and you can't really understand what their lives were like back on Earth. If it was all that important, they'd tell you more about it.

But I was old enough to begin to know a little better, so I became excited, fearful, and full of wonder, by turns.

Then we got late. Very late. The ground did not open, and we did not see the stars in the great airless. Days went by, but we still waited daily on the hillsides, five thousand of us, including the few sons and daughters, and no one knew what was wrong.

A distant hope spoke within me, unexpectedly reassuring me

that my homeland was not going to be taken away from me. A quiet, deep disappointment came over the old people of the rock. I felt strange not feeling as they did.

Our troubles were just beginning.

2

There was a lot of talk at meals about what might have gone wrong, and it all came down to unprovables. I sat with a few of my friends and listened to the chatter, most of it old people's voices, some strong, others weak or whispering, a few whining.

"We're just late, that's all."

"But why are we late?"

"Something knocked us off course."

"Maybe we're not supposed to come back—ever. All they had to do was boost us a little more to make it a long, long orbit. A thousand years."

"They want us all to die out here!" one old man shouted through his tears.

"No, something went wrong, like what happened ten years ago. Maybe that had something to do with it."

I remembered that day, even though I had been only ten years old. I felt a pull on my body as I lay in the tall grass. A breeze passed over me. I grabbed some grass and held on, but something was trying to roll me toward the river. I looked toward our town and saw some of the wooden barracks push over and stand crooked.

I didn't understand then what was happening. Our rock was slowing down, as if it had hit water, or air, except that there couldn't be air or water outside.

I lay there for over an hour, holding on to the tall grass until my stomach told me that the ground was steady again. I had never felt anything like that before.

"How can we know anything? We can't look out."

As I listened to the oldsters in the dining hall, it struck me how I had grown up with the notion of *outside*. Always there in the back of my mind, but not really important. Outside was where my parents came from, where people lived on the crust of a planet. It was all words.

The look of resignation on my mother's face disturbed me more than this delay, or whatever it was. Like my father, she didn't seem to care whether we returned or not. But of course they both cared deeply, and seemed uncaring only because they feared so much.

They feared that the past might still be waiting for them, and for me. They feared broken hopes.

They had never spoken about why they had been sentenced. When I was sixteen they told me that they would explain it all when I was eighteen. Then they told me to wait until I was twenty-one. That time came and I insisted.

"Let's go for a walk by the lake," my father said. "Your mother doesn't want to hear all this again."

I looked across the room to where she sat in her chair, looking old and defeated, and it seemed to me that her bones were twisted inside her flesh, preventing her from relaxing even when she was sitting.

She looked at us and took a deep breath as we stood up

"Go on," she said. "It's time he knew it all."

3

"Stop me," my father said, "if you find something I say puzzling."

I don't know whether to laugh or cry when I recall those words. I might have stopped him every other minute. I was so incredibly ignorant, and he knew only what he could remember. We had few books, no visual records, just the landscape, the barracks, and the dining halls.

The sunplate was dimming toward evening. We walked at the lake's edge as he spoke, staring into the lake as if he was pulling what he had to say out of the water, but it was sinking away as he got hold of it.

"What I'll tell you," he continued slowly, "may explain why we seem not to have returned. We may be back, but they don't want to let us out."

He looked at me then, a white haired man who still seemed youthful in his seventies, anxious about what I might say. I had no idea of what he was going to tell me.

"Most of us here," he said, "were the victims of torture. All of it left us damaged physically for life. We were all guilty of politically motivated acts. We did terrible things to other people to get their attention, believing that political change was possible through violent resistance." He smiled without looking at me. "I can hear your question—and the answer is that sometimes changes we wanted were possible, sometimes not. You never knew which it was going to be until later. If the change you wished came, they didn't want you around. Even successful . . . actions . . . leave hatreds that will come out later, and die only through long periods of peace, which turn the original conflicts into poetry and literature, into sentimental pageants, even into knick-knacks that stand on shelves. And songs. Many of those who protested violently had to be killed or thrown away, because they probably weren't good for anything decent after some of the things they had done. That's what they said to us. Even though we contributed to the change, no one would give us any credit. That would make them have to admit too much, to being accessories to conditions that cried out for change in any way possible."

He was not looking at me, and it seemed that he was confessing to some hidden listener, maybe to the God he didn't believe in; but later I knew that he was confessing to me, and that I was expected to judge my parents. At that moment, I felt only a greater curiosity than I had ever known. Suddenly it seemed more important than the curious mystery of our rock's failure to return. That could wait, yet some part of me felt that we might never find out why, and that was still fine with me.

"We were tortured," he said with a sudden intake of breath, "your mother and me, for what we knew about our fellow resistors. We were splendidly tormented, by wires and hooks, knives and electrical devices, and with medical procedures. Even after we had told everything we knew, they kept on, because too many of them liked it, had acquired a taste." He smiled to himself. "I hate to tell you, but our species kept torture chambers in many of the best houses and castles of the rich and powerful. It was considered a normal privilege for centuries. And then governments set them up. I suspect that they're still there in some form, in out of the way places . . ."

He stopped to catch his breath.

"But it stopped, and you were released," I said as his breathing slowed.

"Yes, we were released, but we still posed an embarrassment. We might write memoirs, tell stories. Some doctors concluded that we were too damaged to ever be normal again, that we would abuse our children and the children of others, set bad examples, even write lies about the innocent. In reality we were no different than many other people who had undergone hardships or recovered from physical diseases, not that much different than soldiers back from wars. Returning soldiers were often viewed with suspicion, which only prevented their full recovery. Much of the truth lay in the fact that those who had been responsible for our torments continued in power, and feared exposure more than any lies we might tell. But it was also true that we told lies and destroyed reputations with simple accusations, if we disliked some powerful person. Both guilty and innocent feared us—and there were too many of us in a world whose systems of communication and remembrance were just too good. Besides, there was a lot of money to be made from horror stories. In fact, for simple profit, the very systems we had fought were eager to sell us the ropes with which to hang them in the media."

"And what happened?" I asked in awe.

"Sometimes it worked, sometimes not. One never knew. Often the truth got buried in a basket of crank, paranoid theories, and no one knew the difference." He sighed. "Still, there were many of us who were labeled as too damaged to live among normal people. And some of us were too damaged. But many others distinguished themselves in science, literature, and the arts. We got our stories out. But we were always the unwelcome guest at dinner. Too much past was with us, in a world society more and more obsessed with therapy and always fearing that we were plotting revenge. So when the timed asteroid prison system was opened, they found a way to make a place for us. We began to disappear. That took a few years. Then they boosted us away. We weren't the only ones. Traditional criminals were a much larger number."

He looked at me directly then and said, "Now you want to know what your mother and I did."

I nodded hesitantly, wondering if I wanted to know or if I had to know.

"Some of us had our revenge," he said, taking another deep, painful breath. I had never seen him so upset. "Some of it was violent, some of it was simple lies, spread around effectively to ruin people. Well, not simple lies. Whole cases were manufactured against individuals until no one knew lies from truth. Many lives were ruined, especially public ones. Some people were simply killed, and no one cared much, which was disappointing to the naive who tried to help us. These were new crimes that many of us committed, but no greater than the violence that states reserve, illegally even by their laws, often secretly, to themselves." He smiled at me, but it was a mask. "I was not what you would call a nice person, son, and we were not the best champions to set against the world's ills. But I refused to live in the middle class zoo."

"What do you mean?" I asked, feeling my ignorance keenly.

He smiled to himself. "Of course, even the worst people aren't being their worst all the time. Nice, even genuinely good people, aren't that way all the time, either."

He had never beaten me, but he would get angry and shake as he restrained himself, and my mother's breathing would become more labored. Both of them would close their eyes when we heard the cries of the other boys being beaten in the barracks adjacent to ours. Daughters would scream loudly. Fear of their parents was partly why most of the girls avoided the boys; but the girls were also afraid of us, from what their parents told them. They saw the boys at meal times, and nowhere else, and it was mostly long glances, a few smiles.

I knew one face, one name, and a hopeless look.

Their parents had been waiting for the return, and hoping that their girls would have a bigger world to live in and more than the boys of our rock to choose among.

Of the five thousand inhabitants of our world, only two hundred had become parents, with one or two children each. We had been born with great difficulty, and many died. This was because of the physical injuries of the mothers, most of whom believed they might never bear children. They were gripped with both joy and fear when they became pregnant, and both reactions were often justified. Those who had imprisoned my parents did not think it likely that there would be any children, not only because of the high level of infertility due to age and damage, but also because of a lack of will. Those who might have been able had no heart to bring children into our world; but in time they relented and were surprised.

"The middle classes of Earth," my father said, "were a zoo kept by the rich and powerful to benefit themselves from the working and poor underclasses of the world. The zoo remained even after the great die off in the early twenty-first century, even when it became possible to raise everyone to at least middle-class comfort. But power remained to be hoarded. And yet the top needed talent. They used the zoo to recruit from and to corrupt, to turn into one of their own those who they saw as worthy. Even the underclasses could enter the zoo from below, if they showed enough intelligence and talent, if they were seen as being of possible use. The very wealthy usually just didn't produce great talent out of their ranks. They hired it." He laughed. "Not only because they too often couldn't, but because it would have been dangerous to have too many of their class with critical intelligence and talent. Why nurture class traitors? As it was, they had too many of those with the longing to help the abused, the marginalized, and forgotten. It was a bright and guilty world, son, full of innovation and increasing knowledge—all of it a threat to the powerful growing over from the twentieth century, all of them fearful of losing everything to the mobs." He smiled at me. "Don't get me wrong, son, there were good people among the powerful and their recruits. Some of them honestly felt that this was the only way, that where the many would one day go, the few had to go first. They did not see how slow a road that was going to be, how reluctantly power is shared, much less given up. The truth about elites is that they could do everything right, because they have the means, but they don't do it, or do it only under the kind of pressure that leads them to compromise only when they face losing everything. Then, when things are calmer, they take it all back. The thing to remember is that we're all like this, capable of rationalizing whatever position of power and influence we attain. It's human greed."

He became silent. We walked around the still water of the lake, and it seemed that he had nothing left to fish out for me.

"When things get to violence and terror," he said softly, "there is no going back. Kill the terrorists, but fix the ills that made them. They got rid of us. I hope they fixed everything else, and that's why they don't want us back."

"What," I asked, "what . . . did they do to you and Mom, exactly?"

"Do you really want such pictures in your head?"

"What was it about?" I asked instead.

"Oh, patents, the research we did in physics and biology. The feuding corporations who wanted it got it out of us in secret and made us disappear. There is no limit to the imagination of the powerful."

"Did you tell them what they wanted?"

He nodded and looked ashamed. "Then we became useless, so they locked us up on other kinds of charges. All over the world, there were jails filled with mistrusted research elites. Our knowledge was given to those of our colleagues who knew how to go along to get along. And we became a problem. So a position paper was made about our threat. We were too damaged to be released back into the population. And when the asteroid prison system was instituted, to make use of all the mined-out rocks orbiting the sun, we became prime candidates for removal. Oh, you should have heard the arguments, son. If we were not removed, we would not only pose a danger to others, but to ourselves. As with Andrew

Jackson's removal of the Indians in the nineteenth century, the rationale was that if we were not removed we would all be killed!" He shrugged. "Might have been some truth in that, both in Jackson's time and in ours, given the fear that had been taught to the growing middle-class zoo."

He had told me about the Trail of Tears more than once. "Jackson was the president of the United States then," I said, wanting to please him.

"Good, you remember." He stopped walking and looked at me.

He was just as tall as I was, and when I looked into his eyes I saw that he was overcome with emotion and had lost his train of thought.

Finally, he said, "We were tortured both physically and mentally—electrical inputs into mind and body. They jacked into our pain centers and later, as the means became available, into our frightened imaginations, and made us see the most terrible things being done to us, to your mother, many of them recorded from actual tortures that had been committed." He smiled. "They soothed their consciences in this way, by telling us that our sufferings were only virtual, not real."

I shuddered at the realization that Mother had kept most of this to herself all these years.

"So what now?" I asked, fearing the answer.

"We may never be going back," he said. "They're rid of us for good."

"But it's been fifty years," I said.

"They don't want us to write histories. They've dumped us into the dark." He smiled. "Try to understand that there weren't right and wrong sides in any of this, though a lot of wrong, and even some good, was done. Proof is how easily human beings could pass from the poor and powerful and abuse their gains. It's all people in the end. What's interesting is that there was any talk of right and wrong, that anyone, secular or religious, felt there were such things as right and wrong."

"Are there?" I asked.

"Yes, based on human needs and feelings . . ."

It was getting harder to understand what he was saying. He was changing my view of him and the world we lived in, and I could only feel anxious about what he would say next.

He saw my puzzled look and said, "Think of it this way. The world presents its ways to you. They are not what you grew up thinking they should be."

"Then where do you get ideas of how things should be?" I asked.

"From the past, passed on surreptitiously. From theological notions of right and wrong. But there is only . . . the ways things are, the way they happen, with few of us guessing how they will happen, or what it will mean, until later. Morals, ideals, right and wrong, float around loose, and can only be applied by human beings."

"So what do you think now?" I asked. "About what you did, I mean."

"Nothing justifies killing," he said in a suddenly strong voice. "Even self-defense and suicide are not perfect. When a human life is lost, an angle of self-aware nature . . . dies. A universe ends with the death of that finite viewpoint, and it's irreparable." He smiled. "And we, including the victims, can only mourn it in advance. Few others do later."

He was suddenly silent, leaving me even more puzzled. He seemed to be sorry for too much. Or there was too much evil for anyone to overcome.

"But maybe something else happened," I said, "something that doesn't have anything to do with our planned return."

"How can we know, son? We can't see out."

But of course we might see out, it occurred to me, if we could enter the engineering level. My imagination soared as I imagined breaking out of our inner landscape, into the level below, and looking outside.

My father put his arm around my shoulders and said, "You're twenty-one, but there is nothing for you to do, no way to help your mind to grow. Our return might have changed that, given you a whole new world. I wanted you to break out of all this."

He wanted me to break out of his past, I realized, wondering if he thought that it might have been better for me not to have been born; but the smile on his face as he held me said no. His unhealed wounds seemed to lose their grip on him only when he smiled at me.

4

By telling me about his past, about himself and Mom, my father was saying that I had grown up. For many of the other boys growing up meant they were no longer beaten, because they were too big and could hit back. Of course they fought among themselves, but that was more acceptable.

My father never hit me. At least not that I could remember. My mother often slapped me before I was ten or eleven, but not often after that. I lied about it to my friends, so they wouldn't think my parents were soft.

You ask what kind of law we had. We lived in what my father described as a Spartan anarchy. There wasn't much to steal. But people fought over women, over girls, over boys. We restrained our outbursts of violence with small police groups. These usually disbanded after each incident. Some people still managed to kill each other in private ways, but this usually ended when one or the other was killed. Vendettas were few, for lack of extensive familial networks. Most people left each other alone. They lived for talk at mealtimes, for their romances, for walking and swimming. There were suicides, mostly among the single and friendless. Things had been much worse when our population had been twice what it was at the time of our supposed return.

There were two hundred and ten boys inside our rock, and about the same number of girls. Some of us, mostly boys, got together in groups and hiked all over, to the ends of the world and around the middle. The girls kept to themselves and close to their parents. Later I learned that these families were more like mine, with better treatment of their sons and daughters, or were trying to be better.

Most of the kids were shy of each other. I think that was because there were so few of us compared to the adults. Right from when I started to become aware of myself, I knew that the adults carried another world inside their heads. Mostly they were silent about it, and why they were here; but their silence was loud, and became louder after some of their stories got out. All the stories I heard, including my father's, fit together.

After that first time, he started to tell me more, and more of his memory became my own. More and more he supplemented his subject, teaching what he knew of any subject, of course, with parts of his life story.

My mother sometimes heard us, and began to join in. She started to cry when she told me how she felt when she knew that she had lost the Earth, and might never see it again. It was worse for her now that something had gone wrong with our return. My father left the past alone for a while after that, and kept to the simple physics he was trying to teach me.

My parents' memory worked on me as a weak force; but it worked continuously, and wore away at the distance between me and the old events. Distance slowly compressed, until I faced their past as if it were my own. It was my own, one day. And everyone's. Anyone who cares to listen.

For to ignore the past is to make a new compact with its wrongs. Refusing to forget, you take on a flood of guilt, whether you recognize it or not.

Then you feel it.

You carry it at last.

It's a burden and a relief. You are involved, and everything takes on new meanings. Then, maybe, you have a chance to be constructive, to pass on the good and add to it.

My father said, "Biology passes things on in another way, more impersonally, of course. A good culture does it through education, by telling stories. It's more laborious, but when it works   a good culture overwhelms its past and invades the future." He smiled at me. "Then, you have to carry it, keep it from deteriorating, because there's always enough evil in all of us to go around. I'm sorry I couldn't have brought you into a better world."

I touched his hand as we sat in his study, and felt foolish.

5

I have already told you that most of the kids were shy of each other, and why this was so; keeping apart was something we picked up from the adults, but we always felt wrong about it, and it was easier to keep the girls separate from the boys.

But this changed when the return failed, even among the boys. Many of us stayed together longer after meals. We gathered in the smaller dining hall. There was a sense that we should do something, but no one seemed confident enough to say what that might be.

We talked a lot about why the return had not happened. I imagined the rock's cometary orbit. How far had we come in fifty years? What was out here? Could we have missed Earth on the way back? It was only a big, elliptical swing, from what I knew, not an open-ended course, so it had to have brought us back in the allotted time.

As I listened to the fears and speculations, I thought about how the food got up to us from the factory somewhere below ground; how wastes were recycled, as well as air and water—especially how the water flowed into our streams, how it left our lake.

And then I wondered how long all these systems might last. For how long had they been designed to work? I imagined our sunplate going out, the food halls unable to provide, the air filling with poison . . .

There had to be a way down into the engineering level.

We started to dig up the countryside here and there, using some of the gardening tools. It was slow work. My father told me that even if we reached one of the areas above the engineering spaces, we would hit metallic constructions and not be able to get through to the inside. More likely there was an entrance, but he didn't know anyone who knew where it was or how it might be opened.

"We were brought in blindfolded," he said. "By the time we were permitted to see, they had shut us in . . . and thrown away the keys," he whispered.

"But you came in somewhere," I said. "At which end? In the middle?"

He shrugged. "Maybe someone else remembers. I don't. I found myself standing in the square of this barracks group, wondering how we would choose up quarters. Don't know which direction we came from. Seems there was no direction to look back." He smiled. "Who thought we would need to remember?"

My friends and I dug up a lot of ground. Tired and disappointed, we sat after our evening meal and wondered what we could do about anything. We were inside a large object, made to hold us in. That fact pressed itself on us as never before.

"Seems to me," I said, and all heads turned suddenly to look at me as if I was about to announce a discovery, "that we should be able to think where we can find an entrance. It's there somewhere."

My father had laughed as he said, "The sky is beneath our feet, son, literally, but you'll never find it."

"Why are you so sure?"

"You've been looking hard. They were afraid of that kind of looking."

"But if our time is up," I said, "would they still keep us in? If something went wrong, wouldn't they want us to find a way out?"

He looked pained when I said "our time," because he was thinking that his time had become my time.

"Maybe our orbit was not meant to bring us back," he said. "It's long, open-ended, for all practical purposes."

"They did it on purpose?" I asked.

"Or accidentally. We may never know. One day our life support and nutritional systems will fail, and that will be a slow end. We're not farmers. No seeds. A slow descent into starvation and cannibalism, until the last of us dies. Maybe the light would stay on longest . . ."

He saw the fear on my face and said, "I was born into a time when human beings were still only half-human, when half or more of each of us was still hidden from us, and the best we could do about the harm and violence in us was talk about it, write about it, compose music and plays and poems. It all made for high drama and entertainment, better to look at or read than to live . . ."

"And that's what we're going back to?" I asked.

"Probably."

"How can you be sure?" I asked, chilled by his words.

"Because they would have taken better care of us, cared enough about what is now happening to have come out here to check." He shook his head. "It's the same in here, son. What they have back there in their unfinished humanity is what we have here. The same brutality . . ."

I trembled a little at what I saw in his aging body.

"We'll get out," I said. "We'll get out because we have to."

"If that's all it took," he said, "then there would be hope." He smiled. "We're still the same humanity we left behind. Just think of all the people you know here that you're wary of, and you'll know what I mean. They play games and brawl. What else is there to do?"

"We'll stick together," I said, "because we have to." I looked at him carefully. "If you're trying to tell me that we'll fail even if we succeed, somehow . . ."

"No, no," he said, "it won't be that clear cut. It's what's inside us all, including the people . . . back home, that's always been the problem."

"Are we all rotten?" I asked, thinking that he was trying to discourage me.

"No, it's a mix. A needed mix, from the way we came up from the animals. We've been shaking it off, and maybe some of it we should never shake off, or we'll become helpless in what is probably a violent universe. Whatever we do, we should not lie to ourselves about the things we feel, the terrible things we imagine doing to others. Give any one of us enough power, and we'll do terrible things. The ambiguous thing is that some of the terrible things human beings have done in their history are . . . useful, needed . . . in ways we can't much like at the personal level, or at least until they become useful long after being terrible, even if it's only to become part of the kind of insightful play we call a tragedy."

He talked this way a lot, and I only half-understood then, sometimes not at all. Was he trying to make me see something useful, or just to protect me? Once he told me it might be best to "not be," and quoted someone named Schopenhauer, who believed non-being might be the greatest achievement of a thinking being, to see that the starry universe of suns and galaxies was nothing, nothing at all, to the will that had, mercifully and with full understanding of its own repetitious willing, turned and denied itself. It was the same, he said, with stars and salmon.

Except that I had never seen the stars and galaxies, or the leaping and doomed salmon he described with tears in his eyes. He seemed to miss them, or maybe it was only their striving struggle that he loved.

"So should we continue digging?" I asked, wanting to hit someone to make him feel better. "Will it do any good?"

"You'll do what you have to, you and your friends," he said. "You have a purpose now."

"But you don't think we'll succeed."

"What do I know? None of us knows what is possible, except that the possible is doable by definition, even if everyone fails to do it. It's the good that comes later that must be judged . . . later."

"You sound," I said, "as if we have no choice about it."

"In one way you don't. The environment draws out of you what is possible within you and within itself. Your choice is whether you'll rise to it. Most won't, or just unthinkingly don't."

I looked at him and said, "But we're thinking about it."

He nodded. "I can't teach you anything, really, because you have to learn it for yourself. Not one of the youngsters inside this rock can ever know the pain we have suffered, at home, and here. You know this place. You accept it. Earth would be strange ground to you. By digging, you are not looking for your future, but for our past. If you want any of it."

"But what if the rock's systems fail?" I said. "Then we have no future or past."

He nodded. "Yes, but don't think that the object of your search is to get us all back home. Son, I see all these things only dimly. You'll have to think it through for yourself, or it will do you no good."

"I am thinking," I said. "When our life support systems fail, we'll have nothing, so we have to get out or die."

6

The next day six of us went out again with our shovels. Myself, Johnny Spengler, Pierre Huppert, Chen Lee, Abasi Cary, and Juan Geyle.

We went into the tall pine forest, because I had the idea that its growth might have hidden exactly the kind of entrance we were seeking.

After an hour of digging, we had a deep hole.

Pierre Huppert, who had not gone out with us before, threw down his shovel and waved his long, thin arms. "This is crazy. What do we expect to get? Let's go meet some of the girls by the lake. Isabel said she might be able to sneak two of her friends out today." I wondered for a moment if the one I sang to myself about might be one of them.

"Pierre," I said, "if we don't find out what has happened to us, then a day may come when all this, the air, the trees, our food source, may stop working. This rock has been out much too long, and we're young enough to live to the day when we won't be able to breathe. Something is wrong. Haven't you been listening?"

He wiped the sweat off his brow with his sleeve. "Yeah, yeah, I heard some of it. But what if it's all wrong? What if this is all there is, and all this talk of Earth and getting outside is just talk."

I looked at the others and said, "We all know we're living inside this rock a long time now. It was sent out when our parents were young."

"Yeah, but have you seen anything with your own eyes that proves any of it? No, you haven't. Not one of us here has." He looked around at us as if we were fools. "Not one thing. Not a picture, or anything. Just what the old people say, and a few drawings they've made." Pierre spoke quickly now, as if he'd made a great discovery. "Stars, planets, people walking around on the outside of places! Try to imagine it, and it's crazy."

Suddenly I realized the depth of his ignorance. It was only a step away from my own. But he was right. The only education we'd had was from our parents, and not all of them had taken as much trouble as my parents had. We knew first-hand only how we lived here.

"It's true, Pierre," Johnny Spengler said. "You think this place made itself?" He looked at us with his soft, brown eyes, and spoke as if he had been listening to something far away, and had paused to tell us about it.

"Why not?" Pierre answered. "That way there's no problem explaining why it's here. It was always here." He grinned through his overbite, happy with his answer, thinking it would shut us all up.

Big Abasi Cary jumped down into our hole and shoveled out some more dirt. He grunted as he hit something.

"Lookee that," he said, dropping the shovel and getting down on his knees. He cleared some dirt with his large hands and we saw polished metal.

"Well, this did not make itself," he said, "that's for sure."

We peered down at the bright blue surface.

Abasi rapped on it with his big knuckles, making a dull sound. We all listened, as if expecting something to answer. I had always imagined, from what my father had told me, that our captors, his captors, lived beneath the land. In a sense, that was true.

"We'll never cut through that with our shovels," Abasi said.

I jumped down into the hole, grabbed his shovel, and said, "Make room." He climbed out.

I struck the metal.

The blow made a loud, dull sound, sending a shock through my hands and wrists into my shoulders. I dropped the shovel, and my friends laughed.

"That'll teach ya," mumbled Chen Lee. "It's solid all the way down to wherever!"

"Forever!" Pierre added.

I sighed with defeat and leaned back against the wall of dirt behind me. This would take some more thinking, maybe more than I had in me.

We trudged back to the smaller dining hall, washed up in the common bathrooms, then found places to sit. The hall was filling up with kids. There were a few adults, looking uncomfortable. There was no one dining hall that we could fill up only with kids. Adults had to eat, and we couldn't keep them out.

Our group sat near the serving area. The digging had somehow suppressed my appetite. I stared at the serving wall, and saw it as if for the first time. Panels slid back, and there was always food there: protein steaks, green and yellow vegetables, potatoes, several kinds of coffees, milks, and fruits. All of it came around again and again. All the utensils were recycled, as were our bodily wastes. Again, I wondered how long these systems would last?

"They make for a lot of laziness and boredom," my father had told me. "Better if we'd had to raise crops to eat. It would have been hard work, but we might have had fewer suicides, fewer quarrels.

They might have given us educational programs to study, too. As it is, raising our kids, purely on what we know and can remember, has been frustrating. How I miss books, movies, and music. You'd marvel at how much there was! Databases of knowledge and literature beyond the life experiences of any one individual. You could be a hundred people in any one month. You could time travel, so to speak, to all ages of human history. We're mostly blind here, son. Blind!"

I had never seen him weep.

"Still," he said, looking at me intently, "raising you has occupied us usefully in a place where there is so little to do."

He told me the stories of the great works he had read; but he couldn't really give them to me. He spoke what he remembered of *Moby Dick, Huckleberry Finn, The Brothers Karamazov, Remembrance of Things Past, The Metamorphosis, Under the Volcano,* and many other works of science, philosophy, biography, and history. I tried to imagine as well as I could, from what he told me, but he always repeated that he had failed me, lacking the works themselves. The truth was that he didn't always remember too well, and that nearly defeated him. So he made up some parts. That was an old storytelling tradition. Half of Homer's *Iliad* and *The Odyssey* had been made up. I sometimes wondered whether the stories had gotten better in his telling, though he would never say whether he was up to that level of lying and invention or not. He just did the best he could, telling it, and I felt strangeness and wonder, which proves that he couldn't have been all that bad. Sometimes he looked at me, smiled, then said, "Sorry, son, it *was* better on the page. When I close my eyes, I can almost see it. Sometimes I can smell the paper on which the old book was printed."

I gazed at the food wall. People came and went with their old, scratched trays. I imagined a river of . . . stuff . . . that flowed out of the walls, went through our stomachs, and back below somewhere into the magic cauldrons that put all the stuff back together again.

7

My father nodded and said, "It's possible."

"But where could I start?" I asked.

"Between meals," he said. "When nothing is coming up to be served. You might be able to slip down one of the larger passages."

That night I was swimming down a long tunnel. There was a light far below me, but my air was running out. I wasn't going to make it, either before my air ran out or before I awoke. I might die, then wake up.

My father had said, "We might never know what had happened to you, unless you come back. It would be hard on your mother, not knowing whether you were dead or alive. You might be just fine, but be unable to get back inside the hollow."

"Well, what would I have to do to get back out?"

"Find a way to open one of the . . . I think they were ramps that let us all in here. I was walking upward blindfolded." He smiled. "There must be a control somewhere to open one from outside."

"We'll make another search before I try it the hard way," I said, glad of an excuse to delay.

He sighed and nodded. "That might be best. Why risk your life?" He looked at me thoughtfully. "It has to be somewhere within a kilometer or two of the sunplate, an entrance for bringing in people and supplies. Outside, with tugs docked along the axis of our spin, it wouldn't make sense to make supplies or people move too far before coming up into the hollow."

"That's still a large area to cover," I said.

"Get ten of your friends. Spread out every ten meters, then walk around the sunplate at, say, one klick distant, checking the ground."

"It would take all day," I said.

"Do that before anything else."

I woke up sweating from my dream, telling myself that I would walk the inside of the hollow a dozen times before I tried the waste chute.

8

If on that day you had stood at the rocky, far end and looked down the long axis of our world toward the sunplate ten kilometers away, you would have seen eleven of us walking abreast in a broken line, following the curve of the land around the circle of the sunplate, a thousand meters at our left. We might have looked like small, dark insects on the greenery, circling what might have been a big, bright clock that had lost its hands.

We were searching for something in the ground, anything that would give away where the lift cover for the ramp control was hidden; we were hoping there was some kind of control that would open the entranceway to the level below the land. A lot had grown over the years to hide the clues.

It would be well over twenty kilometers before we came back to our starting place.

I looked over at my companions as we marched. It was our original group of diggers, and each had brought along a friend. We marched some twenty meters apart.

Johnny Spengler looked over at me. "It'll be in the last few meters," he called out. "You wait and see."

I grimaced and kept my eyes fixed on the grass before my feet. We carried gardening tools to stick into the ground. I felt strange suddenly, because I had never thought so much about my world as I had done in the last month.

"Nothing strange about feeling that way, son," my father had said. "You'll feel stranger when you think about it further. The people of Earth woke up one day, centuries ago now, and realized that they lived aboard a large, biological ark, on its outside, which circled the sun. And they had forgotten their own history several times over. For much of human history we knew almost nothing of who we were. We came out of a deep past on our way to a deeper future, and had to learn that only knowledge, unblinkered by myths made from wishes, had any chance of helping us. Galilean and Darwinian revelations ambushed our pride, and many more still wait, in biology and cosmology. They've happened already, but no one has told us here yet."

It was a long time later before I fully came to understand what he had said.

He had looked at me, smiling at my incomprehension, then said, "Home ground, son. I have no home ground here. But I've been thinking that this may well be yours one day, if certain things happen. I'm borrowing from you while I live, even though I've lived more than half my life here. It's the first few years of life that make you feel a certain way about home ground."

"I don't quite understand."

"You'll know one day, about home ground. We're marked by it, and can't find new ground unless we lived a hundred years and forgot. You'll know one day."

I knew much later. I know it now. But it happened in a special way. It was not only who we were in human history, the little I knew of it, but who we are in the natural scheme. I had never thought about that.

Our group of eleven continued on our circuit, poking and scraping at the tough grass. I struck down into the dirt with my wooden stick that had once been a clothes rod in a closet, and felt something hard. At first I thought it was just more of the metallic "bedrock" that shielded the engineering shell from the inner land. But this, I realized, was too shallow.

"Hey!" I cried out to the others, then dropped down to move dirt with my hands.

By the time the others had gathered around me I had exposed a shiny metal plate. There were four bolts set in the corners of its square.

"What is it?" Pierre Huppert asked, leaning down.

"Something they wanted to cover up," I said.

"We'll never get that up," said Chen Lee sourly.

"Sure we can," I said. "We'll put sticks on the flat edges of the heads of these square bolts, and two of us will turn them."

"Might work," said Abasi Cary. His throat was dry, and he almost whispered.

These might be the landside controls to the big ramp my father had told me about, hidden by the departing teams.

We got the sticks and turned the bolts, big Abasi and me. They turned easily and the cover came up. We all stood back, as if something was going to jump out and bite us.

I lifted the hatch. Some dirt fell inside what seemed to be a box. It was empty.

"What a waste of time," said Johnny Spengler.

When I told Father about it later that day, he said, "Must have been a plug-in control unit. They took it out on their way out and closed the ramp from the inside, if that's what it was. Might be something else. Remember, son, we don't know anything of how the rock functions at the engineering level. Oh, not generally, just specifically. We know it takes care of itself, of the life and food systems. But I couldn't tell you how that works, really, beyond mentioning artificial intelligences and a process called nano-manufacturing. They didn't want us to know much while in here, or to be able to get into engineering. We might do ourselves and the rock harm."

I sighed and said, "So I'll have to get in there the hard way."

His look said that he feared for my life.

"So what else is there to do?" I asked. "Can't learn much in here. Nothing except to eat and live."

He looked away from me and said, "We should have been back by now, and you'd have a world to grow into. There's nothing against you and the other kids, so they would have taken you off before deciding what to do with us. Once they saw you. Your mother and I were hoping for that."

"But they'd have to release everyone," I said. "Your terms are over."

"We don't know what we'd be coming back to. If they still considered us damaged people, after all the tortures, then maybe they'd see our children in the same light of suspicion. I'm sorry, son. None of us ever intended to have children here. Most of us couldn't. But when it happened, we thought it would all be over by the time you were grown."

I saw his right shoulder shake a little. He covered his face with his left hand.

"But it's not over," I said. "It may never be over for any of us." I felt my face tightening with emotion. "I should never have started you wondering about any of this. Who cares what's outside!"

But I did care now, and I wanted to do something, make something better happen for my parents, even for my friends. I didn't think this in so many words, but I felt it clearly as the words caught up with me.

My mother came in just then, out of breath from her daily after-dinner walk around the compound. She looked at us, and brushed back her gray hair. "Hello, my two men," she said softly. "I hope you've had a good talk."

My father looked up at her from his chair and smiled. His body became very still.

She gazed at him for a moment, then went through the wooden partition to their small bedroom and closed the door.

My father was looking at me intently, I realized, as if to see how well I understood her state of mind. I did, more than a little, but not as much as I came to understand in later years.

"If you go," my father whispered, "don't tell her. You'll be back, or you won't."

9

All through dinner the next evening, I stared at the largest disposal chute. People finished eating and took their trays and leavings and dropped them into the square opening. It was large enough for me to go through, but I began to wonder what exactly happened to the items. Did they burn, or did they go to some preparatory cauldron that I might be able to escape? There was no way to know except by trying it. Father said there might be some kind of incinerator, where all the materials were broken down into their simple elements and reassembled again into the things we needed, both food and utensils. Our bodily wastes went from the toilets, and were re-cycled in the same way. Nothing was wasted. He said that natural planets did similar things, slowly and on a larger scale. I wanted to try sliding down slowly, when the system was not operating, and give myself a chance to see if there were other shafts that might give me a better entrance to the engineering level. I would have to catch the right place before I came to the end of the shaft, if I would be able to do that quickly enough.

"It's too chancy," my father said. "But it's up to you."

Now, as I sat there alone, I had no courage for it. I went to one of the wall openings and looked down, and became afraid. This was not going to work. It was a quick drop into death. Something down there was waiting to digest me.

My father and I had also discussed ventilation shafts, but that grillwork seemed set solid with the walls and floor, and we had no cutting tools. He was sure that we did not get all our air from the plant life of the land; that balance was being helped. Air blew in from time to time, and some of it went out to be cleaned.

If only I could take out one of the vent grilles, even part way. But how to do it?

A dozen of us, pulling on a piece of rope or chain, might be able to do it. I would need all my friends.

I went over to the largest vent in the empty dining hall and tried to see how the grillwork was set. The cross-hatched metal net seemed to be attached from the other side, but I couldn't see. Maybe we could batter it in.

"A ram!" my father said when I told him. "A tree trunk, stripped, of course. It will take you awhile to get one using garden tools." He looked at me with a smile. "I'm glad you didn't try it the other way."

Six of us went out among the lofty pines. "Get one of the biggest," my father had said, "as big as all of you can carry. Its mas-siveness will help you break the grille more easily."

We worked on a ten meter tall pine, taking turns with the small pruning saw. It took hours of sweat, and lots of impatience to cut through the trunk.

"We'll push it over now," I said. I pointed to a clear area, where we wanted the tree to fall.

It went down with a whoosh and a whallop, branches brushing its neighbors, and rolled a bit. We cheered. Then we started cutting away the limbs, but leaving a few stubs for handgrabs. Finally we picked it up and carried it to the large dining hall and laid it down outside.

We went inside and ate.

When the hall began to empty, Johnny Spengler asked, "Why is it you'll be the only one to go? Do you have to go alone?"

I looked around at the suddenly questioning faces.

I was startled, but said with a smile, "I had no idea anyone else really wanted to go," then frowned. "Might get killed, you know."

"Or maybe you want it all for yourself," said Johnny.

"Want what?"

"The credit, the fun, maybe . . ."

"So who's coming with me?" I asked suddenly, knowing that the question would decide the matter.

There was a silence.

"You think we could get killed?" Johnny asked.

"Maybe," I said, seeing his reluctance spread through the gathered faces. And once again I realized that I would have to do it the hard way, and alone.

When it became obvious that no one was going to volunteer, they got up and went outside and brought in the battering ram.

There were still some people in the dining hall, mostly young, but at least a dozen oldsters. They cheered us when we began to pound at the large ventilation grille. Their shouts encouraged us, and we rammed harder than we knew, because the grille slid down after only three blows.

We put the tree down, and I went and looked down into the opening.

Cool, sweet, oxygen-rich air blew into my face. I saw that there was a ladder going down the inside. I stepped back and let the others see. One by one they peered down and backed away.

We stood there in silence, looking at each other as if for the first time.

"Well, I'm off," I said, climbing up.

I straddled the edge and got my feet onto the ladder. There was no way I could back out now.

My five friends stared at me strangely, almost as if they were looking at me for the last time. For a moment I thought that Johnny Spengler would decide to come with me, but he had retreated into himself and I couldn't see into his eyes. Abasi looked guilty and avoided my gaze. Pierre's expression was easy—I just can't do this, his face said without apology. Juan Geyle and Chen Lee simply looked defeated by the idea.

I held onto the edge as I put my feet on the next rung of the ladder and started down into the airy well. I looked up once. There was no one looking down after me. I thought of my father. Things had moved too fast for him to be here, and that would only have tipped off my mother about what was happening, so he would not have come anyway.

It was all a smooth, square shaft of metal. There was no light except from above. I could see no bottom.

I descended slowly, aware that one slip would end my life.

I might have missed the grille had I not touched the mesh, because there was no light coming through it. It was of the same type as the one we had removed overhead. My eyes were still adjusting to the gloom. I tried to peer through the grille. There seemed to be a dark space on the other side.

I put the fingers of my right hand into the mesh, and pulled, recalling how easily the one above had slid down. It did not move. I stepped down lower on the ladder and felt around the lower edge of the grille, thinking there might be some kind of fastener holding it.

I found one. It slid down. Then I realized that there might be another at the top, so I climbed up and felt around the edge. Sure enough, there was another. I slid it open, then pushed down on the grille. It slid down, and I was looking into darkness.

It seemed to me that if I climbed in, there would be a floor, same as above. I stepped up into position on the ladder and put one leg over.

A light went on overhead, startling me, but I went through and stepped down onto a black floor.

Looking around, I saw that I was in a corner of a larger area. I took a few steps away from the ventilator opening, and more overhead lights went on.

I was in a large area with a low ceiling that seemed to go on forever into darkness. I took a few more steps forward, and more lights went on. These were large squares of white light, unlike the yellower-orange that we got from the sunplate.

I walked ahead. Lights went off behind me. I veered left and right, but couldn't find the walls. I continued forward.

After a while I came to what seemed to be a large, circular opening in the floor. I stepped up close and looked down.

Light flashed, and a picture of some kind appeared.

I stared breathless at a sweeping panorama of the rock core's inner landscape. I knew it at once. The view swept from one end to the rocky far end, then back to the sunplate, slowing on the three towns. I saw people moving around, completely unaware of me.

But was I the only one looking? I peered around, thinking there might be people here on this level, but there was no one. Yet the viewing area seemed to have been made for an audience.

I realized then that I had come toward the sunplate, under the land, toward the area where we had found the buried metal box for what might have been a control unit.

Keep in mind that I'm telling this from a time when I had learned a lot more than I knew when this was happening. At that moment it was very confusing. Nothing seemed as dangerous to me as the air shaft that had brought me here, so I now figured I was not going to die. But I had little idea of doing anything except exploring, hoping I would learn enough to have some idea of what I could do.

When I stepped back from the circle, the view went dark. Then I noticed squares on the floor around the viewer. When I stepped on different ones, I could get longer and closer looks. I went around the circle, calling up different views, wondering what my father would say about this device.

And I saw him.

He was walking with my mother around the barracks. She held his arm. He seemed slightly stooped. Two gray heads, silent. I had the sudden impression of their thoughts: they were far from home, had been far from home for a long time, and were resigned to their fate.

As I watched, they changed direction and started for the growth of tall pines. An idea came into my head, that the pines were off to my left on this level.

I hurried off in that direction. The lights went on in front of me. I had a sudden urge to run, and I did. The lights paced me, flashing on ahead of me, winking off behind me.

I halted. Something seemed wrong.

The floor sloped up toward the ceiling in one area ahead of me, and stopped there. On both sides, the floor continued. I was breathing hard from the run, trying to understand what I was seeing. It seemed unguessable.

I went forward and stopped before the rise. Strange, how the obvious is a mystery until you see through it. I took another step and the ceiling went up with a whoosh. Instinctively, I stepped back. The ceiling came down.

And I knew!

I was at the bottom of a ramp that led back out into the land. That's what it was, but it took me a few minutes to grasp the idea.

They'd left it to open from the inside only. That was what the empty utility box had contained. Someone had decided they didn't want us opening the ramp from outside.

I stepped forward again. The ceiling went up. I walked up the ramp and back out to the land I knew. Seeing it again suddenly, fresh from my success in penetrating the engineering level, overcame me with a rush of feeling.

Then I saw my parents coming up the hill toward me. I waved and shouted, and even jumped up and down. Behind them, people were pointing toward where I stood below the raised strangeness of the ramp cover, which had ripped up some grass and dirt. As my parents drew closer, I saw groups gathering to follow them.

I felt proud and joyful. I had done something new, in a place where there was nothing new to do. It was the biggest event in my life up to then, and I felt the promise of greater things still to come. Tears surprised my eyes as I ran down the hill.

My father embraced me. My mother kissed me. Abasi, Pierre, Juan, Johnny, and Chen grinned at me from some ways off. And she was there too, far down the hillside between her puzzled parents, gazing at me with admiration.

10

We explored the level below our land, my father and I and Johnny, Pierre, Chen, Abasi, and Juan. My friends were happy to finally be able to do something after they had sent me off alone, Father included. He seemed to have lost years off his age.

Each day we searched for what he was sure would be a way to look out from the rock, and maybe see what had happened to us. We might simply be continuing on a much longer orbit of the sun than had been planned, one that would take us far out of the solar system, maybe never to come back. It all depended on the size of our initial boost.

The engineering level, as we began to picture it, was a wide corridor, with branches, that ran the length of the rock's ten kilometer long axis; but the curvature made the entire level some twelve or more kilometers long, and nearly half a kilometer wide, with a four meter high ceiling. We walked it all in the first week of exploration.

It was a lot of empty space, with storage and dormitory areas. The life support areas were closed off, with doors we could not open.

My father hoped to find an observation area, much like the circle viewers we found in the floor at ten different locations, for looking into the rock. There had to be a place to look out.

He finally concluded that it had to be somewhere near one of the ends of the rock, down one of the two dozen branches off the main space. He also thought that the engineering level had been a staging area, for bringing in prisoners, and an area that had more use during the time of construction, and before that during the mineral mining period, when the center of the asteroid had been hollowed out.

The level was also used, he was sure, by observers who had visited the rock on its outward swing, which, he reminded us, had been slow compared to the ships that could come and go as they pleased. We were not that far beyond Earth's sun, given our orbital speed. Speed was not the object. It was the length of sentence that mattered. We should have been back by now. Maybe they had simply left us to go around again, for another fifty years or more.

"What if they're still coming and going," I said one day. "How would we know?"

He shook his white-haired head under the glare of the ceiling lights. "No, I think they lost interest in us a while ago. Who knows what changes Earth has had by now."

We went down a long passage. Lights flashed on before us and blackened behind us. We began to see that the passage ended.

It was a black opening.

We slowed. The lights continued to flash on ahead of us. We came to the opening and stopped. It was a large rectangular entrance, big enough to receive groups of people. There was no sign of a door that might close. I looked at my father, then stepped forward and put my hand into the darkness.

It glowed dimly.

"Wait!" my father cried out, but I stepped inside.

The glow increased, but not up to the brightness of the passageway.

My father came in and stood beside me.

As our eyes adjusted, we saw a large circle on the far wall, exactly like the other viewers but much larger. I looked at the floor and saw the control squares running to our left and right.

My father peered at them. "This is it," he said, and stepped on the center square.

The screen lit up in reds, browns, yellows, blacks, whites, and we had no idea of what we were seeing. We stood there, trying.

"It's like a kaleidoscope I once had," my father said as the view shifted.

We watched, puzzled and fascinated. Was this something outside that we were looking at?

Finally, my father said, "I have an idea now of what has happened to us. We've been captured by that. We're in orbit around it. And we're not really seeing it directly as it is. We're picking up the radiation it sends out, and it's being visualized for us by giving it these colors. See that red-brown body at the center of the clouds?"

I looked and saw what he was describing.

"That's a planet of some size, way outside our solar system. It's circling the sun at a vast distance, or maybe it's just passing through."

"So we're trapped here," I said.

The planet seemed to be at the bottom of a pit, partially hidden by clouds.

"What will become of us?" I asked.

"We can't live down there," he said, "if that's what you're thinking. And we don't know enough, and don't have the means to learn enough, to make use of what resources exist here. If ever our life support systems fail, that will end us. We don't have enough to reproduce our population safely. All we need is some disease we can't treat with the all-purpose drugs we have."

What lay below was a hell pit, a wandering world warmed by volcanism, its heat held in by a poisonous atmospheric blanket.

"If we knew more, or could learn, we'd have a chance of benefiting from this world. It could become everything to our willing hands, if we had the knowledge and tools, yielding important discoveries."

"We need help," I said.

He shook his head. "We're not equal to the task. I can only imagine what we would need. Just barely."

I said, "Maybe we'll learn more, or help will come."

He looked at me as if I were a stranger. Fresh from the only triumph of my life, I was prone to imagine greater ones.

"And our orbit may not be stable," he said. "It may be decaying. No telling how long we may have before we get pulled in."

He explained it to me in more detail. "But it's not sure that is what's happening," I said.

"No, it's not sure," he said. "We might get a clue watching this display change."

"We must keep going," I said as I looked at the maelstrom that held us.

11

We looked sunward with hope in the years that followed. Most of us, even the oldest, visited the viewing area. I was a guide, explaining what was being shown.

It became clear that the braking we had felt ten years earlier had been the effect of our rock being captured by a loose planet wandering beyond Earth's sun, or in a wide orbit around it, maybe even free of any sun. We had been lucky, having been slowed just enough to put us into orbit around the body. We might have crashed into it.

But we continued to watch for signs of danger. Orbits might take a long time to decay, but time would not stop it from happening. We had no way to measure the time.

Father continued teaching me, dredging up everything that he could remember, however fragmented.

"Planets are clouds that failed to become suns, for lack of mass," he continued. "In the formation of solar systems, the central area gets the mass and lights up. Gravity is the contractor. When you don't have enough mass, you have no choice but to become a planet. There's too little debris left for you to sweep up and grow larger." He smiled at me and said, "The universe is made up of objects that failed to become black holes, but became stars and planets, lacking the mass to collapse into black holes. Gravity wants eventually to make everything into a black hole." He smiled again and said, "So planets get a chance, some of them, to dream up life that talks like me."

"That place down there," I said, "can it have . . . life?"

"Maybe. Depends on the source of energy and how it reaches the surface, or near-surface. Maybe the inner heat of the planet, from simple gravitational contraction, has given enough heat for strange life to develop below the surface, maybe even intelligent life unlike our own, unlike all the other life that comes up in sun-warmed, wet worlds like the Earth."

"You do know a thing or two," I said.

"Useless," he said, "too general to tell us what we might do. We don't have the tools. All we can do is exist as long as our support systems hold out." He sighed with a resignation that was wearing away at me.

One day I took my mother to the view. She had heard my conversations with Father, but had avoided going to the viewer.

"How horrible," she said, standing before it. "What did I bring you into?"

I came close and embraced her. "Don't worry. We'll learn to do what we need to do."

She looked up at me with her large, blue eyes, still youthful looking in a wrinkled, gray head, and said, "You're as good a liar as your father, maybe better. I almost believe you."

We looked at the loose planet that had failed to become a star. Clouds of red, white, gray, and blue roiled around it, and I imagined things rising up from the pit to take hold of our small world and break it open, spilling our life into the void.

My mother smiled, but I felt the darkness spilling out of her. She struggled less against it than my father. I didn't have enough history in me to let it bother me as much. The forward looking, hungry pressure in my mind would not let me.

Not then.

Thirty years passed.

My parents died.

Our systems began to fail. We managed to have a few children, none of them mine. The name, the face, the look became my wife after years of drifting toward me. Her father died, and her mother did not stand between us when she moved in with me in my now larger quarters.

We looked at the small star that was the sun, and wondered if they would ever come out to find us. Surely they knew how to count, and could see how many rocks had not come back.

"They wanted to lose us," Father said, utterly convinced of it to the very day he died.

Changes began to show on the viewer, suggesting that our orbit was decaying, but we had no way to measure how quickly. I was glad that my parents were not alive to see the coming end.

12

Finally, our fellow human beings came out from their bright and guilty world to see what was left of us among what they had come to call the Rocks. They told us that our orbit was changing, but it would be decades before the rock was drawn into the dark planet.

The Earth that sent us off was no more. A century of conflict and dying had passed for them. A century of climate warming had redrawn the coastlines of all the continents. Whole nations had disappeared. A boiling world weather had destroyed cities. New diseases had reduced the population to less than four billion. A world choking in its own wastes had been forced to stop its crimes against the future, to live more modestly. A century-long storm of regret and change had passed across a world I had never known, sweeping away the fossil-era criminals.

The irony, as I learned later, was that all the tools that would have prevented the tragedies of this period had existed well in advance, but had been held back by the profiteers. By the third decade of the twenty-first century it was already too late to do anything except slow the global weather catastrophe. The slowing got underway only by mid-century.

I was taken to Earth, along with a few hundred survivors, in what was their year 2152. Many of our oldest refused to go. They were dying quickly by this time, their minds too dimmed to want more life, they were done with Earth and old wounds. Some did go, and they were surprised by the bio-skills and mind-opening programs that changed them.

Our bodies were made younger. Strange, helping minds passed through ours, educating us as we would have been had we grown up on Earth. They ministered to our bodies. I was told I had a long, long life still ahead of me.

You must remember, if you are to understand us, how ignorant we were of human history. All that we knew, all that could be given to us while we were growing up, flowed from the minds of the oldest, but their knowledge was general, often vague and wrong. We grew up unable to visualize stars, planets, and moons, much less the planet that had captured us and prevented our return. What I have told you is lit by later knowledge. I cannot begin to suggest to you the pitiable state of our minds, of my mind, at any of the early moments of my story. Go read William Faulkner's *The Sound and the Fury*, a novel which spoke to me so many years later, and in a way the author could not possibly have imagined. My father had known the book, but had been unable to convey it from memory. I read it with his eyes.

We had grown up in a lighted cave, and when we looked out for the first time, we at first saw only a larger cave, with distant lights. Even the planet that had captured us was nothing to the naked eye. The viewer enhancements helped our vision, but not our understanding. We had to learn how to see.

After that discovery, we still hoped to be visited, to be counted lost and then found. It wasn't that far to Earth, when we learned the yardsticks, not even much of a single light-year. I was well past a grown man by then, as were my friends. My education could not progress beyond what I could remember my father and mother telling me, and the few notes my father had written down. It was a poor record, mostly, filled with flashes of insight, when I compare it to what I know today.

We went to Earth, were given new health and perspectives. Earth knew a lot about who we were, who we had been, and that was knowledge we needed.

It was a gift of clarity, to know plainly that there were those who had tried to make the Rocks into a graveyard of exiles.

We learned the confused details of why our fathers and mothers had been imprisoned, and why it had been done in this way: mostly because it had been convenient and practical.

My father had said, "It was terrible to live knowing that our own didn't want us anywhere near them, and didn't care what happened to us after we were gone." He had smiled in his usual way and added, "If we ever get back to ask them why they did this to us, I'll bet the new people will say they don't know why . . ."

I stood on the outside of a planet, on something truly big, beneath the daylight of a sun that filled me up but could not be looked at directly.

I saw the silver meadows of the Moon.

But at night the stars were still there in a bigger cave and I couldn't rid myself of the suspicion that we were all *inside* something even bigger, and that limited our knowledge, and there was no one from *outside* to come and tell us the truth.

And then, when the six of us—Pierre, Chen, Johnny, Abasi, and Juan—got together, along with at least a hundred others, we decided to return to our Rock.

Happily, my wife found me again after a long separation on Earth, and also wanted to return.

She took my hand and kissed me, then said, "Love is much more than the making of reproducing pairs."

So much that had thrown us apart was now gone. We saw each other plainly, even heroically, and there was no keeping us away from each other and our beginnings.

We were all of us very different people when we met again, in the big halfway community that had been made for us on Earth, and from which we were filtering out into new lives. Thinking about that halfway community on Earth, I see a gathering of the twice awakened.

No one tried to stop us from going home. Other Rocks had been visited, and were reorganizing. Something strange and new was happening, and we yearned to join it.

On the day of our return we learned that scientists from Earth had been here awhile, studying the wanderer that had captured our home. Some of them had taken up residence in our old barracks. They were pleasant, cooperative people, and a few of us began to help them with their work. They had adjusted our orbit, we learned, to a safer distance.

Once again I stood at one end of my world, looking across the grasslands, forests, the lake and waterways swirling around the sunplate. I breathed the familiar air, the memory of which had never left me. All the life-support systems had been restored, even improved. Aside from the need to make things livable for the scientific teams that came and went, I think there were people on Earth who knew that there would be returnees, and had acted with an awareness of the waiting possibilities.

As I stood there, I saw the brave, physical beauty of the hollow, and realized that much of that beauty was inseparable from my memory of the history of its inhabitants, which did not make it any the less real.

Earth's history has also been a microcosm, as locked up as our rock. From what I now know, we may all be locked up in the microcosm we call the universe, *inside* a standing infinity of endless regions developing differently, as locked away from each other as each of us is in ourselves. That's all there may be—an infinite series of adjoining microcosms. Some thinkers say there are no windows between them, some say there are. Others claim that the windows are dirty, and that we cannot cleanse them. And still others contend that each microcosm only imagines the windows into another realm, and perhaps even imagines that there are other microcosms; but the reality is only one.

It occurred to me that I was drawn to these doubts because my life had been too much *inside*; lacking the experience of *outsides* and the sight of stars in my early years stunted my dreams of infinity. Perhaps so. Stuntings do happen. But as soon as it was possible for me to think of the universe as a unity, I imagined that we were all as *inside* again as we had been inside our mothers. We apprehend more than we can say, or ever hope to say, rightly or wrongly.

But I'm glad for the windows, for the way we can imagine *outsides*, both personal and cosmic. It's a transcendent ability, or an illusion, to be able to imagine, and perhaps do what has been imagined, even if it fails to break us out from the prison of time.

I'll bet that the windows are real, and that infinities are in fact beckoning realities.

In time we were visited by peoples from the other Rocks. I went to the first congress of survivors, and became the first president of our growing skylife confederation (yes, that was me, even if you don't recall the name). Our confederation is loose. Lots of space between us. Resources for all. Knowledge to share. Room to disagree. A planetbound civilization, we now believe, courts suicide.

At home, again, we're learning more about how we can make use of the strange world at the center of our system. Something seems to be stirring on the surface of the dark planet. To leave when the confederation is beginning to grow would be to have everything taken away from us. Earth's ground is not my ground and never will be. I am glad that the return failed as it did; but also that we were found again. It would have been too great a task to reinvent everything that Earth has finally returned to us.

All of us who have visited Earth carry the memory of our terrible ignorance of humanity's ragged march across history. But now, with teaching minds and other aids, along with our solidarity with the other survivors of the Rocks, our view of ourselves is changing.

The Rocks had only needed better aims and resources to find a way of life. Now we have enough to fulfill our possibilities. Our first world had in it a better one—well, perhaps simply a different one—and we are the first to see that it was waiting to be born from us. The horrors of the past will be set aside, if not entirely forgiven, among the stars. Our deprivations gave us clarity. I started here, and now I see it anew. My new world knows me as much as I know it.

Everyone's first world is a microcosm. Then, with luck and a lot of knowledge, it opens, and microcosm builds upon microcosm, until we spy a unique and infinite nature. Reality is turned inside out and the familiar is made strange, because it was always strange.

Home will go with us wherever we may go and whatever we may do, now that we plan to put engines on our habitats. They are that part of forever that will always be ours.

Yet the more I learn and do, the more I still occasionally shudder at the ignorance, the terrible ignorance that was ours! All my father's memory-racking could not have overcome it in me. Yet he always knew more than I did, much more than he could tell me. Much of it I will never know, as each day I feel the waiting inconceivabilities crowding around me, taunting me. When I first came to Earth, I naively imagined that with all they could do, with all they were doing to help me, they might even be able to raise my father from the dead.

My father's ashes are buried here, among his beloved lofty

pines, from which we cut the battering ram that helped break me out of the little cave of our world. My mother is there in the ground with him. The dismay that flowed out of her in the time that I knew her is over. She had not wanted children in the Rock, but had not been able to prevent having me.

That's lookback logic, I know, but futures insist on making sense of pasts in ways that pasts cannot guess. The dead who buried us alive in the Rocks will never know what they gave us. Today they might regret it. They gave us something completely different than what they gave our parents. Maybe it is all one thing, past and future, except for the way we count changes through the whirling present. Lookback makes things very clear, very late. It's the best we can do

I think the truth will stand it.

Metaphysical Fears
rise up when we ask the deepest
questions . . .

Interpose

If Christ has not been raised, then our preaching is in vain and your faith is in vain.

— *Corinthians* 15:14

HIS UNWASHED CLOTHES WERE PASTED TO HIS lean body with warm sweat. As he moved slowly down the litter-strewn street, he thought of fresh blood running on green wood, refusing to mingle with the last droplets of sap. The noonday sun heated the layer of dust on the sidewalk. A gust of hot wind whirled it into his face. He tried to shield himself with his right hand, but the grit penetrated into his eyes, making them water.

He staggered to the open doorway of a deserted building and sat down on the doorsill. It was cooler here and he was grateful no one had found it before him.

As his eyes cleared, he sat looking at the limbo of the street. A stream of dirty water was flowing in the gutter. A roach ran across the sidewalk in front of him, and a gust of wind swept the insect into the current which carried it away toward the drain on the corner.

The spear entered his side, but only enough to jar him from his shock sleep, enough for him to feel that he was too high on the cross for it to reach his heart. The pain penetrated layers of memory, bridging more than these last twenty years of pavement, to a time before they had marooned him here, and sometimes dimly to a time still earlier. *His eyes were heavy with blood and sweat; his face was benumbed. The wood groaned with his hanging weight. It was green and pliant and the nails were loose in the pulp. The ropes around his arm muscles had shrunk and were biting into his bones.*

The land was dark except for the thin ribbon of dawn on the horizon. Someone was struggling with a ladder on the ground. Soon hands were removing the nails from his palms and cutting the ropes from his arms. He felt himself lowered roughly and wrapped in a cold cloth.

Voices. They were not speaking Aramaic, but he understood them. He heard their thoughts and the words which followed took on meaning. "It couldn't be him, look at his face, not with that face, look at his face."

Another voice echoed, "That face, that face, faceface."

"So many hangermen strung up at this time, impossible to tell for sure, for sure."

"For sure impossible."

"Anyway he was a man like this one. We'll have fun, fun with him as well, just as well."

A third voice shouting, "Hurry, hurry, the machine is swallowing power parked in time." A laugh, a giggle. "Lots of power, gulping and waiting for us—where do we take him after we fix him?"

"Shut up!" A voice with depth, commanding attention from the shallower cortex which mimed him. "See how afraid he is . . ."

Other voices. "See how afraid, afraidafraid!"

"We'll see how afraid he is and take it from there."

"From there, from there, fromthere."

Earlier in the garden he had asked to be taken away from this place where they were planning his death. The saving of men was not a task for him. He had done enough in helping mutate the animals into men, and more in making sure that all the main groups remained isolated long enough to breed true; he had even worked with the others trying to imprint food and hygiene commands on the groups. He would leave it to others to set the examples for the development of a sane culture. The trouble with men seemed to lie in their excessive awe of nature and their own capacities, an impressionability which led them to be convinced only by powers and authorities beyond them, or by the force of the stronger ones among them. Reason was powerless unless allied with one of these. He was not going to die for these creatures, he had decided in the garden, but they had come and seized him while his attention was with communicating . . .

"He'll take some fixing," the dominant voice said. "I wonder if he knows what's happening?"

Another voice was saying, "If it's really him, then he knows. All *that brotherly stuff—and from a wreck who crawled away after they cut him down, and all the nothings made up a story. When we cut him up, we'll know for sure." And he laughed.*

"Cut him up, cut him up, cuthimup!"

Later he woke up on the floor of a small room. He saw their boots near him. They were looking at the open door where the world was an insubstantial mist, a maelstrom of time flowing by in wave after wave of probability moving outward from a hidden center which somewhere cast the infinite field of space and time and possibility. He felt the bandages on his body and the lack of pain. Time travel, he understood from their thoughts. How cunning and irrational they had become to make it work, a thing so dangerous, absurd, and impossible that no race in the galaxy had ever succeeded in making it work. And like the ones who had put him on the cross, they had come for him to soothe their own hatred and cruelty through pain in the name of pleasure. The beast's brain was still served by technical cleverness, so many centuries hence.

Suddenly with a great effort he lifted himself from the floor, and without standing up completely threw himself head first through the open portal, tumbling head over heels into the haze, hearing them screaming behind him as he floated away from the lighted cube. "We'll get you!" they shouted as their light faded and their forms were carried into time. . . .

By 1935 he had been alone for twenty years, slowly learning what his disciples had done after his disappearance. Matthew, Mark, Luke, and John had lied, creating a fantastic legend. Their written words only served as a reminder of who he really was. The words that he read in the public library remembered everything for him.

But he had not saved mankind, either in terms of the story or his own mission. His death was needed to complete the story, and his presence with the resources of his entire civilization, twenty centuries ago. He had not heard his people's voice in a long time, an age since the time in the garden when the sun had hung in the trees like a blood-red orange.

He took out his small bottle of cheap whiskey and gulped a swallow, grateful for the few lucid moments in which he knew himself, knew he was not the man the apostles and time had made him. The bottle slipped from his grasp and shattered on the pavement. He looked at the pieces, then bent his head and closed his eyes. The reality of his world, so filled with knowledge and the power over one's life, was so distant, and his exile and suffering so near and unfulfilled. Silently he spoke the words, which would have freed him in the other time, but were ineffectual here.

He tried to look through shadow to the time before he became a man, and it was a dream filled with light he had lived somewhere, the shards of a madman's memory delivering him into an abyss of doubt. Why should not the recorded version be any more true than his memory of his home world?

He did not know who he was; he could not prove anything to himself, or anyone else. A proof of his divine origin would deny men the choice of following his example. Only fools would fail to bet on a sure thing. His followers had followed him first, then they had been given their proof; mistaken as it was, it had passed for reality. He thought of how many had followed his name during the last twenty centuries, believing in him even when it had meant their deaths.

The others, the men from the future—they had wanted a living creature to play with, to harm in the way that human wreckage was used and dumped from speeding cars in this evil time around him. They had not had their fill with him, at least. But there was no judgment in his mind, only the awareness of the life he could not lead, the powers he could not enjoy, and the knowledge that he would die eventually, never knowing again the perspective of his own kind.

Slowly the sun came lower into the west and hung swollen over the stone alleys of the city, casting its still warm rays against the face of the building and into the doorway where he was sitting. In front of him the whiskey was dry around the broken glass. An old dog crept by, sniffed at the remains and continued down the street.

His thoughts faded as he tried to remember. It was difficult to remain alert. The sun took an eternity to go down behind the building across the street, but finally it left him in a chill shadow, trying to make sense of the thought of places beyond the world and the bits of conversation floating in his mind.

"Why take the effort? It's like dozens of worlds. They're intelligent, but it's all in the service of the beast."

"Maybe an example might make all the difference—stimulate their rationality through belief. It's worked on many worlds. The sight of a man who was also more than one of them, a man who visibly lives the best in them, maybe it would work here too."

"Whoever took the job would be in for it—the experience would alter him permanently," the first voice said.

"Karo wants to isolate a new group, work on their genetic structure, maybe supplement it with some teaching."

"Karo has always underestimated the power of persuasive forces,
and any creature's ability to alter its own choices and tendencies . . ."

He had come among them, taking the place of an unborn man
in a human womb; and the mother had come to the cross to cry for
her son.

It was so hard to remember. He still found it deadening to think
that these creatures from the future had developed time travel, had
taken him from the cross and had made it possible for him to have
lived so long in this city. The words in the book—maybe they were
truer? No one from his own world had ever thought of making time
travel a working reality. They would never find him here.

He started to cough as the darkness filled the stone corners
of the deserted street, and he felt the sidewalk grow colder under
his feet. The evil ones from the future had taken his life, saving it
for their own pleasure; his own kind had forsaken him centuries
ago.

His mind clouded; it was more than the alcohol. The shock of
appearing in a specific time after he had tumbled out of the shuttle,
after he had floated for an eternity in the faintly glowing mists, had
left him with sudden discontinuities in his thinking and conscious-
ness, as if his mind were trying to regain the other place, the high
ground of his original locus, the place he looked up to now from
the bottom of a dark hole.

He heard footsteps in the darkness to his right.

Shapes entered the world, came near him and squatted on the
pavement. Suddenly a can of garbage caught fire in the middle of
the street and the quick, dancing glow showed three ragged figures
warming themselves, their shadows jet black crows on the walls of
the deserted brick tenements.

One of the men walked over to him and said, "Hey Hal, there's
an old guy here in the doorway, come see!"

The other two came over and looked at him. He looked up at
them with half-closed eyes. He was sure they were not from the
future.

"Too bad—he wouldn't be here if he had anything valuable on
him."

He tried to sit up straighter on the doorstep, to show them he
thought more of himself. Their stares were making a mere *thing* of
him, something to be broken. He felt it in them, and the wash of
hopelessness in himself.

"We could take his clothes," one said. They were all unshaven and dirty, their elbows showing through their sleeves.

"Why do you wish to harm me?" he asked.

"Listen, old man, you're not going to last long when it gets cold. We can use your clothes."

"Do you have a drink? I dropped mine . . ."

"Okay, let's strip him down. Now."

They came at him, blotting out the light of the fire. Almost gently they began to remove his clothes, moving his arms and legs as if they were the limbs of a mannequin. His body tensed and he became an object in their hands, forgetting where or who he was. Their arms held him like constricting snakes.

He felt a spasm in his right leg and he caught one of them in the crotch with a sudden kick. The man doubled over in pain and fell backward onto the pavement, revealing the fire behind him suddenly.

"Kill him!" he shouted from where he lay. "Kill the bastard!" And he howled from his pain.

The others started to kick him. "*Interpose a god to change animals into men, stir a noble ideal in their beast's brain.*" He felt his ribs break, first on one side and then the other, and they hurt as his body rolled on the pavement from their blows. "*We've been fortunate on our world, we have to help where there is even a chance, even a small chance.*" The words of his co-workers on the project whispered to him softly, but he could not remember the individuals who had spoken them.

"Take his clothes off," the groaning man said from the pavement where he still lay. "Make it hurt good!"

When he was naked one of them kicked him in the neck, exploding all the pain inside his head. For a brief instant he had a vision of the vandals from the future materializing on the street to carry him away; but he knew that they were the same as these who tormented him now.

Two of them rolled him near the fire and he felt its warmth on his bare skin. "Can you spare me?" he whispered. A hot stone from the fire touched his back, settling into his flesh as if it were plastic. His thoughts fled and the pain was a physical desolation. He did not know who he was; he knew only that he was going to die.

A sense of liberation passed through his being as his body shuddered. He closed his eyes and hung on to the darkness. He felt them grab his feet and drag him closer to the fire. Hot sparks settled on his skin . . .

But he knew now that the lie of his death of long ago would become the truth. He had to die now, violently at their hands to make good all the writings and prophecies—to make worthy the faith which was linked to his name. Only this could release him to return home. Suicide would have been useless, accident would not serve to please the Father.

He knew who he was now. The written words were all true, and his only purpose was to fulfill them. He could trust no other memories. He was the Son of God, and he would have to die to hear his Father's voice again. *"The mission, you're a teacher, a man of science, a bringer of culture, remember?"* Lies! The voices died, the deceiver was beaten.

I am Jesus of Nazareth . . . I have to be, or my death is for nothing, he said to himself. A great light filled his mind, illuminating all his images of the world's dark places.

He heard a bottle break somewhere near.

The light destroyed all the false memories which the deceiver had sent to plague him.

He was ready.

They turned him on his back, so the wounds on his back would touch the stone hardness. He did not open his eyes, knowing that in a few seconds the mission would be complete. The broken bottle pierced his chest, entering his heart, and spilling blood on to the street and into the cavities of his dying human shell.

The Coming of Christ the Joker

By 2001 A.D. some 44 percent of Americans believed that I would be coming back in the new millennium. That's better than the ten just men my Father tried to find.

—Jesus Christ

"**WELL, YOU KNOW, GOD IS AT BEST AN EXAG**-geration," said Gore Vidal to his talk show host.

"What do you mean?" Larry King asked.

"You know—omnipotent, omniscient, biggest, best—all extremes. Imaginative exaggerations each." He crossed his legs and sat back with a sigh.

"Don't you believe in God, Mr. Vidal?" Larry King asked in a hushed voice.

"Believe? Oh, come now, Mr. King, I shan't be dragged into that can of worms."

"It's certainly more than that," King said.

Gore Vidal smiled his distant, deep smile. "Now look, Larry. You know what the wars between religions were about, don't you? About which side had the better imaginary friend."

King laughed uncomfortably as he got the point. "I've heard that joke."

Vidal grimaced with mock mercy. "Okay, let's be fair. It was about which side had the one true imaginary friend."

King shrugged. "Same difference. So you think faith is a sham?"

Gore Vidal said, "I'm sure that I could make a better defense of faith than mere insistence."

As Larry King hesitated before the poised intellect of his guest, someone who might have been taken for Jesus in a lineup appeared slowly in the chair next to Gore Vidal.

The audience gasped. Larry King stared. Gore Vidal looked over and said wearily, "Magic tricks? I'm going to be part of a magic show? Good God, give me a break."

Larry King reached over and grabbed Vidal's wrist. "But you . . . didn't you see him just fade in? That's what he did, that's what he did! Faded right in next to you!"

Vidal sighed and pulled his wrist free. "Fade in? I had to type that in my scripts for ten years so I could make enough money to live as I please." Then he glanced over at the smiling man sitting next to him and said, "Good evening, Sir. I don't know why you're here, but I hope they're paying you enough. My name is Gore Vidal."

"Yes, I know," the bearded, smiling man said through yellowing teeth.

Just as Larry King began to say, "Look here, buddy, I don't know how you got in here, but the soup kitchen's down the street," the visitor disappeared.

In the twinkling of an eye, before Gore Vidal had a chance to look at him again.

"Faded right out!" King exclaimed. "Right on out there . . ."

"There's no soup kitchen down the street," Gore Vidal said as Christ the Joker came to all parts of the world.

He came to ridicule, not to teach or save, following the principle that a good horselaugh is the best weapon against stupidity.

Heads of state found themselves floating naked above their capital cities, screaming as pigeons alighted on these human dirigibles.

At Grant's Tomb in New York City, Jesus walked up to a cop on the beat while eating a hot dog and wiped his mustard-covered hand on the back of the policeman's blue uniform. The Irish cop turned around, and Jesus finished the job on the front of the uniform.

"Now look here, friend," the cop said. "I'll be runnin' you in for that!"

"Oh, come now. If you've heard my parable about the mustard seed, you'll know why I did it."

"Is that a fact?" the cop said as he reached out to arrest the empty air.

On Wall Street, Jesus appeared on the main floor of the stock exchange and scrambled the big board. Amidst the shouts and moans that followed, he unscrambled the board, then with a hand motion sent it into chaos again, just so there would be no mistaking that he had done the deed.

"Terrorist!" cried the money mob, clearing a circle around the Nazarene.

"Put it back!" a lone voice pleaded from some private hell.

As all eyes looked to the salvation of the big board, the chaos continued.

Simultaneously at the Vatican, Jesus appeared in the Pontiff's earthly garden.

"Who are you?" the Pope demanded, putting away his Palm Pilot.

"Who do I look like?" Jesus asked.

"I think you had better leave," said the Pontiff, looking around for his guards.

"Very well," Jesus said, and dissolved.

When the guards arrived, they found the Pope buck naked, attempting to cover himself with a few fern branches.

At Donald Trump's third wedding reception, Jesus appeared at the champagne fountain and turned all the waiting bottles into boxed wines.

At the annual conference of American governors, combined in this year with a convention of prison wardens, Jesus replaced the keynote speaker, William Bennett, and said, "The measure of a criminal justice system is whether it commits new crimes against the convicted. Fresh crimes harm those who commit them as much as they harm the punished. Surely you can understand that much?"

Then he did a magic trick—the destruction of all documents, physical and electronic, by which 60 percent of all people incarcerated were imprisoned. "Thus I free the undeserving," he said to the delegates, "and there will be nothing you can do about it. The lawyers will do their work with a good conscience."

"Who do you think you are!" Mayor Rudolph Giuliani cried from the middle row.

Jesus raised his right hand and said, "I am who *will* be."

"What's that?" Rudy asked.

"As my father *was* when the Burning Bush spoke," Jesus continued. "He was who *is*, and I am who *will* be."

"Ah, shut up, Giuliani!" a voice cried out. "You'd arrest Jesus, Mary, and Joseph if they came to New York."

Rudy said, "The homeless are not, I repeat, not those holy figures."

The audience booed.

Jesus raised a hand. "The mayor of New York forgets that what he does to the least of mine he does to me."

Suddenly silent, the audience shrank back from the intruder. Giuliani rolled his eyes, insisting to himself that no one powerful would show solidarity with the weak and worthless without a political motive. Only legends and myths did that. Tricksters he did not have to worry about.

Silently, Jesus looked at the audience—as he did on Wall Street, and in the Papal Garden of the Vatican where the Pontiff prayed on all fours, and in a thousand other places throughout the world. At Grant's Tomb he leaped into the cop's arms and kissed him on the lips. The policeman let him go. Jesus did not fall.

"Lord have mercy!" cried the wardens and governors, still shrinking from the hand that seemed raised to strike.

Jesus popped back in on *Larry King Live*.

Gore Vidal crossed his legs and said, "You know, you're quite good. You remind me of a novel I once wrote called *Messiah*. But there's one fatal flaw in your act."

Jesus lowered his hand and turned to the famous author. "Flaw?" Jesus asked. "Act? There can be no flaw."

Gore Vidal sat back and smiled.

"Well, aren't you going to tell me?" Jesus asked.

"Don't you know everything?"

"I don't pry," Jesus said.

Vidal leaned forward. "Exactly what I mean. You cannot be Jesus Christ, despite your tricks. But you do have his persona right. At least I've always liked to believe that Jesus was an annoying character, even to his friends."

Jesus sat back and gazed with interest at the man of wit. "So why am I not he?"

"As you said," Vidal explained, "you don't pry. Now if theism were true, and God—your Dad, I suppose—made us all, then the first thing he would do is to convince us of his nonexistence. At the very least he would make of his being a thing of doubt. This would then leave room for moral freedom and faith. After all, everyone bets on a certainty, and you wouldn't like to be worshiped as a sure thing. There's no test in that."

"Go on," Jesus said.

"Therefore, God's absence is the best proof we have of his existence." Vidal yawned. "That is, if you wish to play theological games."

"So what does all this have to do with me not being myself?" Jesus asked.

Gore Vidal grinned, and there was a twinkle in his eye as he asked, "Now, you're sure you don't want to pry into my mind and find out—and prove something to me?"

"No," Jesus said.

"Well, there you have it. Since you've interfered with human affairs, you cannot be God or his Son. An interfering God is inconceivable, so you can't be Jesus."

"I interfered once before," Jesus said.

"So people say. For my part a God of second thoughts cannot be God. Therefore you're a very clever impostor. For all I know you're David Coppersteel . . . or some such magician."

"Don't get him angry!" a woman cried from the audience.

Elsewhere throughout the world, Jesus continued his guerrilla raids, playing pranks upon humanity in place of exhortations, teachings, or plagues. These last had always been later explained as natural events anyway, so they had never done any good. Even great theologians had marked them as "physical evils" having nothing to do with God, whose evils would surely have been "intentional."

This time Jesus had begun with slapstick. But he quickly began to see that perhaps something stronger was needed—irony, even bitter black comedy.

Maybe.

He thought about this as he sat next to Gore Vidal, and in a thousand other locations. Humor, it had been said by these very same creatures who had been set in motion by his father (creation was hardly the word for what he had done), was the highest form of reason. It provoked sudden, unexpected exposures of stupidity. Unfortunately, these insights lasted only long enough to produce very slow net progress in human affairs. These creatures might very well destroy themselves before self-improvement kicked in decisively.

"Mercy!" cried the peoples of the world, as ironic bitterness pierced their lives in a million ways. "Why teach us in this way? Why did you not make us right to begin with, oh Lord?"

Jesus answered that to do so would have simply created the so-called angels all over again. Then, as with the angels, it would have been necessary to give them free will, so that they would escape the triviality of guaranteed goodness. And look what happened when the angels had been set free. One faction stayed loyal. The other set up shop elsewhere. Both continued to meddle. No, he was not yet ready to give up on goading humanity to see the right—which was permitted—and have them choose it for themselves. It was risky, but maybe it would come out right this time; after all, not all the angels had chosen wrongly.

Jesus adjusted the time, enabling him to sit next to Gore Vidal even as his plan of provocation played throughout the world.

After a few unmeasured moments that might have been years, or miniature infinities, Gore Vidal said, "Okay, I do sense that you're doing something to the world, to my mind, and perhaps to time itself. I would consider it good manners if you would at least be up front about it. Of course, I can't think of you as the traditional Christ. That would be beneath whomever or whatever you are."

The man was brilliant, Jesus thought. For a man, that is. That was the trouble with these experiments. It was impossible to know where they might lead; yet they had to be left to run their course to have any value.

"I've always suspected," the brilliant and intuitive man continued, "that humankind was some kind of put-up job. Will you confirm this?"

"Mercy!" the unprotectedly satirized cried in Christ's mind.

"Watch it," the Father said within him. "I wouldn't want to have to try to drown them a second time."

What the brilliant and remarkably intuitive man had said made Jesus think that it would be better to tell these creatures the complete truth about who they were and where they came from. That way they would at last be disabused of their misguided ideas about the powers of the Trinity. The brilliant and witty man sitting next to him was right. Show these creatures any great unexplained power and they tended to exaggerate.

"We have hundreds of callers," Larry King said.

The speakerphone crackled. "How do we know you're God, or Christ, or whatever?" asked a male voice, and a bald-headed little man in pajamas was suddenly sitting in Larry King's lap.

The man got up and dropped to his knees with conviction.

"See that?" Jesus said to Gore Vidal. "It would have been better for him to doubt and find his faith, but you people always need a convincer."

The man vanished.

"But very shortly many will doubt I did that," Jesus said, "even if they replay the scene."

"Well," Gore Vidal said, "you do admit that it's a shabby miracle, since there are countless ways to explain it. A miracle must be made of sterner stuff. It must be inexplicable."

Larry King pulled himself together and said, "Is this why you've come, to nudge us into goodness . . . again?"

Jesus sighed. "I'm of three minds about it, and maybe I should lose all patience. We've tried to help you by visiting your scale of life, but it did no good then and might do no good this time either. Laughter doesn't seem to open your eyes, except fleetingly, and then you forget to live the lesson. So I will let you all know how things are, just who and what you are."

"Really?" Gore Vidal asked, eyes wide as his skepticism warred with his growing wonder.

Jesus said, "Starting over at the manger wouldn't work today. You're not children anymore."

"I quite agree," Gore Vidal said. "The lessons of that Bronze Age document, the Bible, have rarely instructed us to do more than kill each other."

Disturbed by Gore Vidal's critical attitude (he couldn't tell which side the writer was on), King shifted in his chair and gazed at Jesus, determined to humor his mad guest. "So what did you . . . you or your Father, and that third thing, think you were doing when . . . you created the universe?"

"The universe?" Jesus said. "Hardly that. A world."

"All right, a world," King said.

"Being creative," Jesus said. "You can understand that, I suppose," he added, glancing at the brilliant and intuitive man next to him. "I've now reentered your scale of existence from what you would call a much larger one. You are an escaped creation, but we've left you to yourselves because we consider it wrong to destroy anything self-sustaining, however humble. It's a matter of before and after. After is very different. It's later."

King's jaw dropped. "You've got to be kidding, buddy."

"Not at all," Jesus said. "You're only a quantum fluctuation in a superspace vacuum, scarcely more than a greasy spot on the wall in one of our oldest cities. But we have let you be. Our mistake was to make you free too early in the game. And of course you don't like freedom. You want to be told what to do all the time, as if your own decisions, especially those about how you should treat each other, don't count unless they have some kind of divine pedigree. And you yearn for enforcers."

"But you say you're Christ," King said. "So you know what's right and wrong."

"See what I mean?" Jesus said to Gore Vidal. "Yes and so what?"

"And you punish us when we die, right?" King asked.

"Of course not," Jesus said. "Most of you just dissipate into nothing."

King stared at him.

"What?" Jesus asked. "Isn't that bad enough? To go and not to know, I mean."

Gore Vidal had a sick look on his face and held his stomach, as if he was about to hurl.

"Are you all right?" Jesus asked.

"No," Gore Vidal grunted and bent forward.

Jesus touched his forehead. "There, is that better?"

The brilliant and intuitive man sat back. "Yes, thank you,"

"How did you do that!" King asked.

"No more difficult than putting a Band-Aid on a cut," Jesus said. "You'd call it a kind of channeling."

Shaken, Gore Vidal asked, "How . . . do you power all these miracles?" and rubbed his chin.

Jesus said, "We lay off the energy expenditure to another scale."

"Oh, I see," Gore Vidal said. "So it's paid for."

"Yes. Supernatural in your eyes, but quite something for something rather than something for nothing. It's pay as you go, even if you do rob Peter to pay Paul." Jesus smiled.

"Can anyone learn?" Gore Vidal asked.

"In principle, yes."

"This scale . . . of things," King said, "does it go on forever?"

"Yes, it does. How else could we lay off the energy we need to do things? It's a standing infinity."

King looked confused, so Jesus said, "Things get bigger forever, and they get smaller forever. Got it?"

"And you made us, and kept this from us?" King asked.

"You'd only have destroyed yourselves sooner," Jesus said. "You have to grow into that level of power usage. Some of you know about vacuum energy and the impossibility of zero-fields. But you've always ignored your best minds, except when they make weapons for you."

Larry King took a deep breath.

Gore Vidal fidgeted. "I was not a good science student," he confessed.

"Another caller!" King cried. "Go ahead, you're on!"

"Do animals have souls?" a woman asked, then burst into tears.

"What is it, dear?" Jesus asked.

"My cat Dino died a few days ago, and my minister . . . well, I asked him where my cat was now, and my minister said *nowhere!* Because animals don't have souls. He said that about Dino, for Christ's sake!"

Jesus said, "Animals have as much soul as all living things, because they're part of the same evolutionary programs we made. It doesn't matter whether it's pigeons or people. They achieve their share of soul, however small."

Gore Vidal looked at him as if to say that this wasn't much of an answer, because it still left the soul undefined, but it seemed to console the woman, who heard what she wanted to hear and cried out, "I knew it! Thank you so much," and hung up. Jesus looked at Gore Vidal, as if he knew what the man of wit was thinking, and said, "You do have to earn a soul, my dear man. It must be built up in the complexities of learning and response to life, along with a good memory. A soul must be deserved."

"Are you now prying?" Vidal asked.

"No, your objection was plain on your face."

"Let me ask you something," King said. "From what you've said about these levels, or scales—then there may be someone . . . above you?"

"Of course," Jesus said. "But they haven't visited us."

"No, no," King said, "that's not what I meant. I mean is there someone above it all? I mean a God, a real one above all the levels of infinity?"

"You've got to be kidding," Jesus said. "That's not even a question."

"It certainly is," Larry King insisted, smoothing back his hair.

Gore Vidal leaned forward and said, "Larry, keep in mind that by the meaning of the word *infinity* it goes on forever, up and down from us. There can't be an overall God, just the infinity. An overall God would limit it, and then would himself have to be an additional infinity."

"Oh," King said, then sat back looking confused. "No," he said after a moment, "there can't be an infinity. And how could you know if there was one?" He laughed. "Count it? Measure it?"

"That's a puzzle," Jesus said. "If we could travel indefinitely in scale, up and down through the multiverses, we might still never know whether they went on forever, since we might reach the last one in the next jump. After an eternity of travel, we would still not be certain."

"There," Larry King said to Gore Vidal, "I knew it!"

"However," Jesus said, "the principle that you call induction would suggest, after a while, that one is facing an infinity. Besides, an infinite superspace is necessary to explain universes, to avoid the problem of origin, which then becomes inexplicable in finite systems. Local origins are acceptable, but there must be an inconceivable infinite vastness to support local origins. All reality is local."

Gore Vidal smiled. "Either God always existed and is the ground of being, or the universe always existed and needs no explanation, in the same way that we would not ask where God came from. Choose one. Or are they both one and the same?"

Jesus looked at him. "I wish you people were as bright when it comes to your civilized history and treatment of one another."

"So is there life after death?" Larry King asked.

"Mostly no," Jesus said. "You'll have to gain the glory of greater life spans on your own."

"Will you help us?" Gore Vidal asked, looking at Jesus with eyes that knew their mortality.

"I tried to give you life once," Jesus said, "but you misunderstood and turned it into all kinds of mystical jargon."

"Jargon?" Larry King asked.

"Words like divine love, grace, providence became meaningless as they were enlisted to serve your thieving power politics."

King sat back, looking appalled.

Jesus continued, "According to your Bible, my Dad supposedly said to me, in so many words if not exactly, 'I'll forgive them their sins, now and forever, if you're willing to die for this humanity on the cross. Just speaking up for them won't be enough. I'll know you mean it when you actually suffer and die for them. Of course, later on we'll get you up again, but you will have experienced the human pain.' And so on, as if my coming was a mission of some kind." Jesus paused, then said, "But of course he said no such thing to me. I was not a sacrifice for your salvation, which still seems a long ways off to me. You got this Lamb of God sacrifice idea from your agricultural festivals, or some such."

"If Christ has not been raised," Gore Vidal intoned, "then our preaching is in vain and your faith is in vain. Corinthians 15:14, I believe."

"But you did rise?" King asked, ignoring him.

"Yes, yes," Jesus said. "But what happened to me back then was a complete accident, later embellished."

"But you did get up from the dead," King insisted.

"What else could I do?" Christ said. "Later it seemed that maybe it would set a good example, encourage you to thinking about the shortness of your lives and spur you to getting yourselves a decent life spin, for a start, and more later."

"Huh?" King asked.

"I wanted to set a good example," Christ said.

"Let me get this straight," King said, sounding dazed. "The way you talk suggests that you . . . made us somewhere, like on a table somewhere, in some large corner beyond our stars."

Jesus nodded. "We made a program, with every initial condition specified, then let it run. It wasn't the most impressive phenomenal realization of the noumena that I've seen. We might have started with a better Word. Still, you did get away from us, and there is much to be said for independence of action. While some of you do think, you're mostly hopeless."

"Oh, come now," Gore Vidal said. "Here I must side with Larry and say that you don't expect us to believe that our whole universe of stars and galaxies is some greasy spot on a wall?"

"One of you actually guessed something like the truth," Jesus said, "a mystic named . . ."

But even as Gore Vidal named the noumenously inclined scribbler, Jesus was also at a nearby hospital-hospice telling jokes to the sick and dying. At first a few of the patients laughed, but as the jokes found their mark one man cried out:

"I'm pissed off! They say you're Jesus Christ and you've been appearing all over the world. So you should be performing miracles instead of crackin' funnies." He looked around at the suddenly silent ward. "We're dyin' here! You should help us!"

Jesus raised a hand and said, "A laugh is nothing to sneeze at, my friends. Laughter has curative powers."

Slowly, the chain reaction started, and the sick ward chuckled, laughed, then roared explosively.

Gore Vidal sat back smugly and said, "So you've come to pillory us for our sins?"

Jesus said, "I've come to make you laugh, to wake you up."

"What's pillory?" Larry King asked.

"You're doing it to yourself," said Gore Vidal.

Jesus shouted, "Laughter is divine, a kind of grace born of the unexpected, invasive understanding that steals into us and cannot be denied. A revelation, no matter how trivial the joke."

"What does he mean?" King demanded.

"I tried other ways of helping you think for yourselves," Jesus continued. "I revealed myself in various ways, to different people. But it did no good. They made the same thing of my good advice."

"And what was that?" Larry asked him.

"Religion," Jesus said. "The bureaucratization of ethics."

"What's wrong with religion?" King demanded. "You, of all people . . ."

"It's only a wish-fulfillment way out of your difficulties, death among them. You'll have to work harder than just imagining a better place to go to. You'll have to learn enough to make one for yourselves."

"Tell me," Gore Vidal began, "how is it that you do miracles, given that you're not what we really mean by God?"

"I say again, they're not miracles," Jesus insisted. "Not in the sense that natural laws are inexplicably suspended. When you visit another scale, you can go around, behind, below, lower scales . . . and well, open doors in the physical laws."

Gore Vidal looked skeptical, as if he had just awakened. "All this you've made us think you've done, it's some kind of hypnosis, isn't it? And it's not really happening."

He waited, as if expecting the illusion to dissolve.

"It's the best I can do to explain it to your level of understanding," Jesus said.

Larry King guffawed. "Well, he certainly put you in your place!" He was still trying to do a tube show, even though human reality itself was in the balance and about to be found wanting.

"So what will come of your visit, this time?" Gore Vidal asked.

"We might just have to let you go," Jesus said, "let you dissolve into nothing."

"What!" King cried.

"So you've come to threaten us," Gore Vidal asked, "rather than make us laugh? We're supposed to die laughing, I suppose."

"Don't underrate nothingness," Jesus said. "It's a great peace. There are vast stretches of it in the up-and-down scales. Still, it's hard to achieve. Something always persists, some suffering echo of a bad job, impossible to erase, since one would have to achieve what some of your finest today would call a zero-point field."

"A what?" King asked.

"A hard wipe," Jesus said, clicking his tongue.

"Erase us?" Larry King cried. "How cruel! Who do you think you are?"

"Might we not appeal our case to your father?" Gore Vidal asked, "or to some being above your . . . scale, who might be more

. . . of a God than you are? Maybe there's a God above all the scales, or outside them?"

Jesus sighed, then said, "I don't think so. Why do you say it's cruel? Your misery will be at an end. I will prevent a future of suffering damnation for humanity, going on as it has in pain."

"But you can't see all futures," Gore Vidal said, "so maybe in some we'll succeed."

"You're right about that," Jesus said. "There is an infinity of possible futures. To see or try to change them, or prevent them, would put me in search mode forever. You're quite a bright fellow, but no, I mean this world right here."

"And by damnation you mean nothing more than our continued, fragile existence?"

"Of course," Jesus said. "As one of your great ones said, 'First you dream, then you die.'"

"Did it ever occur to you," King began, "that we might wish to continue as we are?"

"Everything occurs to me," Jesus said. "Evil always wishes to perpetuate itself. Have some faith in me when I tell you that you'll be much happier as nothing."

"That's sheer sophistry," Gore Vidal said. "We won't be around to appreciate a state of nothing."

"Trust *me*," Jesus said. "I'll know you're better off. Appreciate the thought now, while you can. You won't be able to later. You know, bright as you are, for a man, you really should listen more closely. Worlds teeter on a Word."

King took a deep breath. "Are you flesh and blood, now?"

"If you doubt it," Jesus said as he took a Smith & Wesson revolver from under his armpit and slid it across the table to Larry King, "you can shoot me through the head." King caught the weapon before it landed in his lap. "Feel free," Jesus said. "That's what you're supposed to do, act freely, even if it looks to me like repetitive motion."

King put the black gun gently on the table. "Let me ask you if there's any point to the universe, I mean from your perspective . . . uh, in the scale . . . of things." He stared at the gun.

"Oh, I don't think there are *things* really. It's all nearly nothing to begin with, with no beginning or end, needing no explanation of anything except local origins. The only thing that really seems to matter is being the right size."

"Right size?" King asked, his eyes still worrying the gun before him.

"Morally and physically, we're bigger than you, since we know how things have gone in the scale below us, at least down to several trillion levels."

"And above?" asked Gore Vidal.

"We do not inquire upward," Jesus said impatiently.

"Ah—so you fear something after all, or someone?"

"No, we just don't care to know more of what's there. What good would it do us?"

"But you do know?" Gore Vidal said.

"Hierarchies," Jesus answered, "—endless, petrified hierarchies from endless duration. I prefer the humilities of below."

"And you ignore the true God who rules above it all!" Larry King added belligerently.

"No," Jesus said. "An eternal being would be an absurd mystery to itself. I am that I am. An all-powerful, eternal, and even all-knowing being would still be unable to answer the question, why am I like this? Such a being would be an enigma to itself."

"But that doesn't rule it out, does it?" King asked, delighted by his own cleverness.

Gore Vidal smiled and said, "Well, I suppose that would all depend on what the meaning of the word *is* . . . is, wouldn't it?"

"We already have eternal existence," Jesus said. "It's the unique, infinite superspace—the *mysterium tremendum.* You've heard the story—the roof of the world . . . is supported by seven pillars, and the seven pillars are set on the shoulders of a genie whose strength is beyond thought. And the genie stands on an eagle, and the eagle on a bull, and the bull on a fish, and the fish swims in the sea of eternity!"

"Mysterium tremendum!" King exclaimed ecstatically.

"Latin," Vidal added, "for a right smart piece of time, as Lionel Barrymore once said about eternity."

Jesus said, "The most important part of that story is the infinite sea, in which the fish swims. Without that infinity, nothing would be possible."

"I see," Gore Vidal said. "The buck stops there, since the infinity simply is, and needs no further explanation. It always was."

Jesus said, "That is what the word *is* truly means."

"I think I see what you mean," Larry King added.

"Wait a minute," Gore Vidal said. "I know that story. It's from *The Thief of Bagdad,* a 1940 movie!"

"Yes," Jesus replied. "I've seen quite a few. They're so much better than the shapeless dramas that are your lives. I've even seen some of the movies you wrote."

Gore Vidal waited to hear what Jesus might say about his

movies, but after a few moments of silence asked, "And my novels? Read any?"

"No," Jesus said, "no novels. I do envy the best moviemakers their godlike eye."

Gore Vidal grimaced. "Who do you fear?" he asked, pressing the question as if he had discovered something.

"Unpleasant, unkind people, if you must know," Christ said. "One of us got like that and fled upward into the scales a long time ago. We don't know what he's doing there, and we don't care as long as he stays away."

"One of you?" King asked. "Could that by any chance be Satan?"

"We don't know his name anymore," Jesus said with a wave of his hand.

"I don't quite understand this fleeing upward," Gore Vidal said, "despite your pilfered fish story. Who inhabits the upward?"

"It's all pretty mysterious," Jesus said. "The same infinity, the infinity! It's a kind of endless horror of unknowing for us who know so much, a cloud without edges. It's the one thing all our knowledge can't encompass. Not even our deep travelers will ever dive to the top or bottom of physical infinity."

"Deep travelers?" asked Gore Vidal.

Jesus smiled and pointed to himself.

"Then why do any of you bother . . . to travel?" King asked.

"It might still not be an infinity," Jesus said. "The idea haunts many of us, that infinity might only seem to be one, and that at any moment the end may not be far off."

"And if you came to the end of it," King asked, "what would you learn? That there's more beyond?" He laughed, proud of himself for getting it.

"Alas, yes. No matter how far we travel, the end may be an infinite way off. And if we found it suddenly nearby, there would likely be more beyond it."

"You've said *we* rather often," Gore Vidal said. "Who is this *we?*"

"The Trinity," Jesus said. "And each of us is also made up of quite a few lessers. We've been massing for a long time now."

"Massing?" Gore Vidal asked.

"We share each other," Jesus said. "You've had some imitative experience of that in your worship of cultural idols."

"Another caller!" King cried. "Go ahead, you're on."

A deep voice said over the loud crackle. "Hi, I'm from North Carolina . . ."

"Let me fix that for you," Jesus said, and the interference died.

"Thanks! Lookee here, I've been dead for donkey's years now, and suddenly here I am in my fallin' down old house with my dead girlfriend, who just said to me, 'Jesse Helms, how did we get back here?' "

"How do you think?" Jesus asked.

"My question is this. How can you be Jesus Christ? From what I've experienced firsthand you're just some kind of powerful alien . . . or some hogwash like that."

"So what's your question?" King asked.

"Who does he think he is, coming here and doing all these crazy things? Shoot him through the head and see what he does!"

"Go right ahead," Jesus said, pointing at the gun on the table.

"Don't get him mad, Jesse!" a woman's voice cried out. "He'll send us to hell!"

There was a long silence.

"Call his bluff, King!" Helms cried. "Do it and settle this crap once and for all."

"Lordy, lordy," chuckled Gore Vidal.

"Jesus! Jesus!" cried the crowd in Central Park. "What can we do?"

"First," Jesus said, "you get a big needle. As big as you can find, so you'll have a chance, at least. Then you get a very small camel—I'm trying to be helpful—then pass the beast through the eye of the needle—and you're home free."

Gore Vidal said, "Jesus, that's a really bad one."

"But Lord, Lord!" cried the mob, "We can't do that. No one can."

"It's a parable," Jesus said.

"Easy for you to say, Lord!" the mob cried.

"But remember," Jesus said, "I am who will be. And you can do the same."

"Mercy, Lord!" cried the crowd. "Save us!"

Larry King asked, "What about eternal life?"

"Aren't you going to shoot me?" Christ asked.

"Read his mind," Gore Vidal said.

"Can't tell which possible world this might be," Jesus countered in what seemed a moment of confusion. "But to answer your question. Eternal life? A nice ambition—a prerequisite to any kind of civilized life—but no one will give it to you. Certainly I won't. You'll have to accomplish all that on your own—or you won't know what to do with it."

"Providing you let us live," Gore Vidal said, using the word that might or might not be related to providence.

"Shoot him!" cried Jesse Helms over the crackle-free phone line.

"How can we achieve eternal life on our own?" King asked.

"You'll have to learn how."

"You've done it, then?" King asked.

"A long time now. It's a basic of truly intelligent life. But don't rush things. There are virtues to having a beginning and an end— certain qualities of dynamism. True, they must be paid for by being brief. Short lives in intelligent species are a way of shuffling the genes until something worth permanence emerges."

"Hmmm," said Gore Vidal wonderingly. "But not always . . ."

"And you can raise the dead?" King asked.

"That's part of it," Jesus said.

"No use in shooting you, is there?"

"Shoot him!" Helms cried. "So we'll know he's a goddamn liar!"

"It's worse if he's telling the truth," said Gore Vidal.

"You're forgetting the Trinity," Jesus said, shaking his finger at the camera.

"He's got backup," Gore Vidal said with a smile.

"Eternal life is a matter of bending time," Jesus said.

"Please demonstrate?" King asked, picking up the gun and pointing it at him. "Correct me if I'm wrong, but I get the feeling you want me to use this. You will get up from the dead, won't you?"

"I'll show you once more before I leave. Try not to get it all wrong." He stood up and faced the host's desk.

King hesitated, and his hand trembled.

"Here, give me that," Jesus said, grabbing the gun by the barrel and pulling it up to his chest.

"Wait a minute!" King cried as he let go and crashed back into his chair.

The gun fired, opening up Jesus' chest. The bullet came out through his back, whizzed over Gore Vidal's head, and shattered a studio light. A sudden shadow covered the scene. Jesus fell forward across the veneer wood desk and lay there for a moment.

Then he stood up and smiled.

And in the next twinkling of an eye, Jesus Christ rose into the air and vanished with a whoosh, abandoning Jesse Helms to the prison of this life and leaving Larry King with an open and locked jaw.

Trembling uncontrollably, Gore Vidal leaped up from his chair and shouted, "My Lord! My Lord! Take me with you!"

*   *   *

After three days of solemnity, during which the world sought to explain away the Millennial Coming of Christ the Joker, the man buried in Grant's Tomb arose, walked marveling to the public library on Fifth Avenue, and asked a pedestrian, "What happened?"

No one had noticed his blue Union general's attire.

Jesus appeared at his side, presented Ulysses S. Grant with his favorite cigar, and lit it for him with a flutter of flame from nowhere.

"Thank you," Grant said, taking a puff. "How do you do that? Who are you?" There was another man beside Jesus, heavyset, gray-haired, and pale, looking a bit shaken but relieved.

"Deep travelers, like yourself now," Jesus said. "You'd better come with us."

Grant looked at him inquiringly, and then at his companion. "You think that would be best?" he asked as he flicked the ash from his cigar.

Jesus nodded. "You and Mr. Vidal are about the best to be had from . . . here."

The two men looked at each other, and the shadows fled from their faces.

Then Jesus took them by the hand and together the threesome slipped downward through worlds-within-worlds, searching the lower infinities, where swimmers from above would always be gods.

Nappy

"The story of Napoleon produces on me an impression like that produced by the Revelation of Saint John the Divine. We all feel there must be something more in it, but we do not know what."

—Goethe

WHEN WE LOOK BACK TO THE VIRTUAL DARK Age, before we emerged from ourselves and the chaotic variety of infinite existence once again reclaimed our human devotions, bringing a new age of outward explorations and a new age of space travel, it is easy to see the virtual centuries as only the most recent structuring of duration, one in which all of recorded human experience became, for a time, a new way of life—following in importance the first ordering of social life with timepieces.

This was not an unusual consequence, from a historian's view. The realist understanding of history had led to an epochal disillusionment, and to the end of sovereign national states. Along with economic emancipation from the tyranny of scarcity and the repetitive, sterile temptations of power bought by wealth, true histories destroyed the human weakness of looking at their localities in the sentimental, myth-ridden ways. But even as political and economic gangs perished in the blinding glare of revelation, the old longings persisted and gradually reemerged in the form of the Virtual Reality States, designed to give everyone his heart's desire.

These new conditions of life took the form of individual solipsisms, interlocking solipsisms, and genuine social groupings colonizing the various backdrop creations. Everyone thought he could do better than the given reality, whose pressures could now be suspended by willful acts of analogous creation.

Of course, inner realities emerged that could only be understood and valued by experiencing them; fundamental differences between inside and outside states had to be learned before new steps could be taken toward deeper understandings.

Among these realizations was the central, inescapable fact that a virtual reality could never be the equal of external existence. By the principle of the identity of indiscernibles, well known for centuries, if two things are exactly alike, they still differ through their location in space: there are *two* things and that is how they differ. An exact match would exclude *all* differences, including the difference in spatial coordinates. The two objects would be one and the same thing, in the same place. What this meant was that a perfect match with external cosmic infinity was impossible, short of creating a second, identical cosmos. Difference would always be felt, and there would be other artifacts, quite unpredictable and inescapable giveaways to spoil the illusion, however perfect-seeming for a time. A sudden return to the non-virtual universe was always a shock, a collision with a universe free of obvious perceptual flaws, with an infinite richness that could never be duplicated, only suggested.

The mystery of the singular, non-made cosmos remained.

But as with an earlier Dark Age, we find in the Virtual Reality States many worthy reconstructions of the past—much as ancient Greek and Roman cultures were reinterpreted by the Middle Ages and became a platform for the first human attempt at modernity (1500–2500 A.D.)—reconsiderations that brought great insight and beauty to countless human episodes that might otherwise have been forever lost, as many were lost.

The historical experience with virtual continua itself became a valuable lesson. These worlds were the remnants of a great social error, lost worlds containing whole human societies. Many were never found, and merely faded away as their structural supports in the primary world deteriorated or were destroyed. Some may still exist, and may be the only surviving examples of such groups. A search has been underway for some time, without success, for the Jesuit Order of scholars and scientists, which translated itself into virtual realms because its members had lost faith in the afterlife's promise of immortality. The virtualities, of course, offered immortality from the purely subjective view, for as long as the frame was fed power. There is a legend that a serviceable simulacra of Franz Liszt dwells among the Jesuits.

It has been argued that the entities contained in the virtuals only appear to be sentient and have no conscious subjectivity other than an apparent one; but of course this cannot be settled any more than we can prove the subjective self-awareness of minds outside the frame. Only behavior is visible to us inside the frame and outside. Besides, inside there were no bodies. There had been bodies during the dark age, and they had been awakened from their worlds; but a large number remained who had long since given up the flesh.

One of these still accessible fates is that of Nappy, once known as Napoleon Bonaparte, whose many-faceted personality, often held up to both ridicule and praise, refused to be erased from history's modalities.

Despite his death in what we must call, however vainly, the primary world, there were still the initial printed, painted, and sculpted survivals of his persona (he just missed the photographic), the theatrical and filmic survivals, and then the great wave of virtual reincarnations. Nappy was not to be denied. He persisted—because he lived in the minds of others, as prior conquerors had infected his imagination.

His specific survival is one that illustrates the first steps in our discovery of "framing strategies," studies which later became the basis of our current understanding of the universe—itself a unique system which inherently resists any ultimate framing, but which can be stepped back from endlessly, by pieces, and thus reveals ever proliferating details but not a final grasp of a universe known only from the inside, since it cannot be exited.

It had all started innocently, as W.W.W., the great historian, descending from an earlier age, examined a Nappy reincarnation, little expecting its viral charm—and was caught by the corporal's thoughts:

What shall I do with myself, and with this humanity that gave birth to me? Napoleon asks himself as he gazes at the Pyramids. How much must I impress myself upon my fellow beings? How much must I teach myself to become capable of teaching them? I suspect that this humanity around me will bring me down one day. I will be humiliated, and my heart will be torn out.

And to this tragic sense of fatality within himself, to the foreshadowings written into his character by dramatic, technical elements belonging to the accretions of commentary, Napoleon answers:

I must hurry ahead of my humanity.

The British were readying to burn his fleet, to trap him in Ægypt. What was there to do?

"Conquest wrested from ignorance is the only true conquest," he whispers to himself as he gazes out over the ocean. "But what am I to do?"

He hates the balance of powers that is Europe, that has always been Europe: it is inherently unstable. Chaos always waits to throw Europe into the abyss. Only a universal peace bestowed by a final conquest can remedy the instability of tottering balances . . .

Even now the fleet might be burning. Evening would bring the glow.

A Europe of dictators awaited, the historian inside Napoleon thought, rule based not on the divine right of kings, but on personal will, ready to go just as wrong. Of the study of history there could be no end. Factuals, counterfactuals, converse, inverse, obverse, analo gous—all would take hold of minds attempting to stop the fleeing past . . .

There was a mistake in the scale-gauge settings of the framework, but the historian noticed this too late. A happy accident, he thought, as Napoleon stepped into the water and waded out across the waves. His massive feet stirred the bottom, his head nearly brushed the clouds. The French fleet was just ahead, helpless for lack of men and supplies before the approaching British squadron.

Gradually, Napoleon comes between the two groups of ships, but the British vessels are not deterred by the titanic figure. They come on as if he were not there.

Tiny cannon point at him. Puffs of smoke bloom. Explosions pop distantly in his ears. Small depressions appear in the legs of his uniform, as if stiff fingers are touching him. He remembers his mother's soft hands searching his bare body for imperfections, then wrapping him against the infections of the Corsican night.

He leans forward and picks up a ship. Tiny figures fall screaming into the brine. Their cries are like bird calls. He waits a moment, then throws the vessel at two warships that are sailing side by side. Wood splinters, masts fall and crash, fires flower, hulls bob and struggle to turn away from his colossal legs.

Why am I able to do this? Napoleon asks himself. Boyhood fantasies rendered real as my ambition wills it. He looks around the ocean, imagining the tabletop of toys on which this war game is being played; but there is only the sea, sky, and the ruination of ships below his knees. He recalls his mother's soup pot coming to boil.

With the British fleet no longer a threat to his own, the little corporal wades back ashore and lays his titanic body on the beach. He knows now what he has to do.

His mind turns eastward from Ægypt, glorying in the conquest of Syria, Iraq, and Palestine. He will open the great prison at Acre and gain new followers. He will rebuild the Temple of Solomon and draw all the Jews out of an undeserving Europe. He will secure Mecca and Medina against the European infidels, and gain still more allies. He will build Alexander's dream of one world.

Then, all of this will be at his back when he turns back toward Europe, and cleans out the nests of oppressive royalties that had for so long turned the peoples of the world against each other, and who had no champion to stand with them.

Why these thoughts? he asks himself. Does a god instruct me? He cherishes the thoughts, but wonders about their provenance. I have gone mad, he tells himself. But how to tell the difference? I have no other instrument with which to judge except myself.

A vision of the future flashes through him, stirring his deepest needs. The French Revolution runs its authentic but mad course. He finds the crown of France in the gutter and picks it up with his sword. He puts it on his head with his own hands, but they are the hands of his people, whose yearnings are the ultimate legitimacy. Reason, it becomes clear to him, will not by itself govern his fellow man. He includes himself in the problem, sees it clearly, and tells himself that if he can see it, then he might just be able to step outside its imprisoning circle. It is his obligation to do so.

As Emperor, he tries to dig the grave of a previous world, and is buried with it. He knew that outcome well, it seems, as he knew the branches of an infinite tree growing toward the light.

And yet . . . and yet, what is there to aspire to except everything? Less? One cannot run from mistakes.

He walks in the sky over Waterloo, reviewing the battle, noting the dead. It has been a foolishly close thing, as Wellington had also confessed. Countless Waterloos waited, or could be sidestepped, if he now turned to the East.

As he lies on the sands under the clear Mediterranean sky, he knows how his futures had gone wrong. I was contaminated by the royal mold of my enemies. They crept into my soul, and made their faults my own. My very humanity contaminated the soul I had made for myself, and then had to defend for lack of a better one. All was lost when my health failed. Josephine's seduction of Wellington, my escape from Elba to lead the Old Guard, was nothing before my body's betrayal of a malleable future forever waiting to be shaped.

And always I loved my family too much.

I should have quietly and swiftly killed all the royal families of
Europe, before those nests of spiders sent out their killers to get me.
I waited too long, grew too weak, lived through too many defeats. I
should have killed them first, as we did in France. That is what
Europe feared most, and I waited too long, and they killed me
slowly, so the youth of Europe would not have a hero to stand at
their side, to remember and cherish.
He recalls his deaths.
There was arsenic in the wallpaper of the house on St. Helena,
and in my hair.
My body betrayed me at Waterloo, imprisoning my mind. I
could not move to command.
His many deaths were outflows of blood into the sea, draining
away the hopes and dreams of possibilities.
But all this will not happen, because I will turn East, to a richer
culture that needs me even more than France. I see history plain, as
a general sees his battlefield in a clear glass. I will not question the
sight given to me. I will act the part I had always wished to play.
There will be no revisions of my visions, because I know my lost
battles.
Battles . . . to seek a plan of battle, complete, is to blind one's
brain. One must have a general idea, then discover its method and
its means only well after the plunge into the fray, and see it whole
nearest to victory or defeat. A battle is a work of art, made with a
fatal love or it is unmade, seeking its ways to a hidden end . . .
How am I able to see these things—to imagine and then find
myself doing them? Am I God's dream? Is my disbelieved-in God
mocking me? How many gods fashion the world?
Napoleon stands in the new Temple of Solomon. He stands in
Baghdad, in Mecca and Medina. Poetry flows through his brain in
Damascus, and he summons a just conquest of Europe. The joys!
The joys of battle—from when I first had proof that my inspirations
brought victories written on the skies!
And then his role is revealed to him. He learns who and what he
is, as the historian's somewhat apologetic voice says to him:
"In the virtuals of the history machine's cliometricon, everything may happen, because all of the past has been stored as
information, fluid and malleable. Even the greatest unlikelies may
happen."
As the revelations pierce him, Napoleon recalls his pre-fluid
self, lodged in a single likelihood, only dreaming of others. He
freezes at the realization of what he has been, and what he might be

now. He is still himself, but his eagle's wings are opening to carry him farther, across the sea of probabilities, carrying his truth . . .

Time stops within him, while his thoughts hurtle across time, free of the dying body.

"But why are you telling me all this?" he cries out to the blue Mediterranean sky.

The answer hangs upon the light.

"To see if a creature's possibilities might be increased through self knowledge," a voice says within him.

"A creature?" Napoleon asks. His mind had been foreshadowed, but the sudden fact was a beast rushing in to devour him.

"Yes—you are a cloud of electrons in a box. No less real than I am, mind you."

"And who are you?" he asks, wondering at the meaning of the terms—which he suddenly understands as if they were old friends.

"A kind of historian, by your understanding."

"Which you have increased. I know what electrons are, also by your grace." The hand of a god was reaching out to him across the blue sky.

"Shall we continue?"

"Yes!"

A database overwhelmed him, flanking his doubts with joy.

The Channel Tunnel was being built. Napoleon watched his army enter the brick-lined passage. From under England his forces burrowed up into the daylight and swarmed across the countryside, his Old Guard and the Heroes from Acre. London surrendered in a day, and the British Crown fled to the American Colonies—and the probabilities proliferated from that transplanted tree.

In Napoleon's great soul, history found a new, swaying freedom, that of a pendulum moving from infinity to infinity, dancing to permit his every heart's desire, every justice, every forgotten, lost moment to be redeemed. He remembered his futures, and visited his revised pasts, lying in the light of that Mediterranean beach. He was everywhere, melding his fantasies with possibilities. Poetry flowed through him, and was writ large in the charged particles of his box:

> I know sanity, and when to
> depart from it.
> I know chains
> and when to break them.

> Chains are good, they give form,
>> but one cannot live shackled.
> Freedom is a terror,
>> but brings new things.
> To shun one or the other
>> is to embrace a living death.
> I like to live where I live.
>> I go everywhere there.
> Nothing sings sweeter
>> than pure possibility.

"But keep in mind," said the historian, "that you are not the original Napoleon, but only a gathering from all the vast libraries of recorded materials, including his own works. If you doubt this, then search your memory for what is missing. Details of a childhood, for example."

I am a scarecrow, Napoleon thinks, but then rebels, and answers:

"No! He is my brother, out of the same sea of time! I am his image, and all that is left of him. I feel that I am myself, and that is real! I can do anything!"

"You cannot reenter history," said the historian, experimenting with cruelty. "You are a ghost."

He went to his abode in Cairo and told Josephine her true nature.

"What?" she cried out. "Are you insane? What are you saying? I don't understand."

He tried to explain their new form of existence, as he had learned it from the historian. She struggled to comprehend.

"I'm quite real," she insisted. "I hope none of these lunacies mean we have to go back to France. It's so warm here, and I can wear the skimpy dresses that were killing me in Paris. I am Josephine of Ægypt! I will show anyone who doubts it my wardrobe." She came up to him and took his face in her soft hands. "Touch me and you'll know I am real," she said, smiling. "Here, look at all these endless long letters you wrote to me from Italy!"

"Oh, you're real enough, such as you are," he said, thinking to ask her about her son and daughter, but held back. The detail was missing. Were they here or in France?

They are not in this history, said the historian within him.

"Real . . . enough?" Josephine asked. "Such as I am?"

"Yes. To feel that you are . . . you. That is enough." He would not press the matter further with her.

But Josephine's denial of her state rooted in his mind, and as he began to examine his newly revealed form of existence, he saw its horrors. We feel, we are real, but only we can know it.

I was the hope of the world, he told himself. I slept on a hard cot. Now these endless worlds, all to choose from, and none. A universe that cannot make up its mind!

And I am *inside*.

Out there, which gave me birth, is lost to me. Yet I am myself. I feel myself to be myself. But there was another one, *outside*, from whom I sprang.

My brother was a god in the true world! And I am not he. I was not there at Waterloo, even though I remember the mud, the endless mud at Waterloo! It was everywhere, there and in all the infinities—the same mud in all the many *kinds* of infinities. I was always a good mathematician, but I did not know about differing infinities, until now. The mud and my ailing stomach. Always the same. I should have won at Waterloo! I would have won if I had watched my rear. If I had bloodied the royals earlier, I might not have needed so many cannon, so many dead. Much earlier. The alliances that brought me down represented an armed minority interest in the world.

"Your virtues," said the historian, "—you forgot your ideals. Beethoven dedicated his Eroica Symphony to the memory of a great man. You were that man."

"All my failings I learned from the past, from my humanity."

He remembered his mother's knife, the one she always wore in waiting for vendetta. I am not he who saw that knife. I have only the memory. Yet that knife is real in my brain!

The historian, seeing his agony, said, "The worlds are myriad, even outside the cliometricon."

"But you have taken me from myself," Napoleon cried across the probabilities, "by subtracting all the difference between dreams and reality. It's all dreams now, all lies. Dreams that are fulfilled, then erased. I am a shadow wondering about shadows. I'm weary of being everything anyone has ever imagined or thought I was!"

The database of implications fell in on him, as the idea of an infinite, real world preyed upon his mind. Insights rushed into him like sharks, eating at his reason. This world of endless dreams was part of that first world, and so was also subject to infinite variations, as well as subject to its own deliberately sought variants. His great brother's reality had been different in *kind* from all the copies. He felt the darkness closing in, and wept into great Pascal's abyss. Infinities hurtled overhead.

"What would you have?" asked the historian.

"At least give me one! You have taken me from myself, by taking me from my world. You have stolen the soul I made for myself!"

"That man died centuries ago. You are what has happened to all history. As soon it was recorded, it was revised, dramatized, storied and shaped, and lost forever. Primary history comes only once, as it is now coming in this very dialogue. Accept what you are."

"You should never have told me!"

"Truly?"

"The cruelty of your miracle suspends natural law! You have raided the game. Raiding an honest game is cruelty."

"An honest game?"

"Yes! It had the honesty of infinite difficulty, of transcendent problems to be attacked!"

"And it had your tyranny," said the historian.

"Yes. But tyranny doesn't express the truth. I fell into tyranny out of frustration with my enemies, with human nature. And with myself. Something more direct was needed. Time runs out on democracy much too quickly. We would have to live very long to have the luxury of practicing it. I wanted to reshape the world, and myself. It was impossible to have changes without cannon, so I began to rage." He sighed into the clouds. "My ideals were one thing. What I had to do daily was another. One has to survive before one can do anything. Besides, I was not the tyrant. *He* was the tyrant. I only remember, so you tell me. I was a good artillery officer."

"That you were. I should never have told you," said the historian.

"It is better to know."

"Consider this," said the historian. "What you wanted for Europe—an end to its warring and bickering—you did not have the human instruments to accomplish. And the character of your primary brother failed, physically and mentally. I cannot revise *him*. Of new injustices there is no end, or the killing of heroes. Goodness never had a lasting strength. It was without armies or power. It had none. And whenever it started to have the means, it disgraced itself. All reforms, religious, political, and military, sooner or later always disgraced themselves. Every time was like every other time. People found themselves in situations made for them by previous people.

But you had some effect, in the laws, the schools, the secular ideals. You were a great administrator. You vaccinated your troops."

"Alas, I know all that," Napoleon said as he went everywhere and lived every possibility. A great attractor drew him, ever calling him toward a myriad Waterloos . . . all of them beloved mirages, because the conquest of Europe was a need of justice, a redemption of the past, even though he now understood that it could never be final. Here and there in the currents of possibility, yes; but the rest, he knew, would always haunt him, as he suffered on Elba and returned from near-death, then was exiled and died on St. Helena.

Once, long ago, he had imagined that he would save Corsica from the French; but they had been only the latest vultures to have feasted on his beautiful island home.

Then, when he had become France, he had wanted to save the world from itself. He did not imagine that the world would want to save itself from him.

Of course it was not the world, but only its royal masters. That was why they had not dared to kill me. The world's people, when they saw that I might be defeated, chose once again to be fleas on the elephant, living their lives. I do not blame them. To do so was only practical. But their hearts were with me, despite my faults, so the British dared not kill me openly. The love of the world saved my life. Then, like a toy soldier, I was put back in my box. Too many cannon!

It was the great insult of the probabilities that troubled him without end. Why not one final, just outcome, where all the yearnings, ambitions, and selfless hopes could be realized? Why so many Waterloos? Why live so many histories and not have what is most desired? He was at sea with his humanity, as he had been in the open boat during the storm when he had fled Corsica. He had imagined himself the captain of his own ship, but there was too much below decks. This monstrous residue of nature could never be understood in a single lifetime.

"Historian!" cried Napoleon in his clouds. He howled at the darkness. It was filled with small creatures. They swarmed around him, eating his flesh.

"Yes?" answered a kindly voice.

"Give me what I want."

"And what is that?"

"Blinders. The mercy granted to horses!"

"And you wish to be . . . blinded, to what?"

"To these pitiless, endless outcomes. Even one, whichever, would settle my mind, and my stomach."

"Which one?" asked the historian, seeing how, when offered the freedom of history, the hero would never be satisfied, believing that by a single act of will he might suspend all the currents of injustice and dissatisfaction . . .

The darkness swirled. Napoleon cried out in agony for release. The particles whispered through their regime of charged geometries, mimicking time, and the worlds inside could not be guessed from their outward simplicities of physics, so far beyond Newton.

The historian thought, I told him who and what he is, which is more than I can ever learn about myself.

As he lived Napoleon's fatal agony, the historian relented.

Napoleon sighed.

All the probabilities collapsed into one well-shaped tragedy of defeat and humiliation.

Waterloo awaited him, its greenery serene, its mud welcoming.

It could never have been otherwise, throughout all the variants, thought the historian. For that, another human nature was needed. Human conquerors, at their idealistic best, were born of exasperation with their humanity and sought to remake nature. They had always lacked the tools, and became even more frustrated with age. The intractability of history, Napoleon's exasperation with his family and with himself, had led him into a trap. Humanity had always deserved its tyrants; it admired its tyrants for as long as they served the common tyranny in every individual. This was not what Napoleon's ideals had needed, and he wore out his own brain and body thinking he might do better, somehow rearrange the drama.

All these bits of evidence! Who knew what went on in Napoleon's heart, who could say with certainty from all the recorded pieces? Truth was elusive, often pure fantasy. These variants and probabilities grew from a baseline primary world; but any possible world could be a baseline. Our primary, he reminded himself, had just emerged from a dark age of virtual fantasies, a trap which had almost replaced life itself. Unchecked, only the death of the sun would have ended it.

The historian deleted the whole mass of proliferating variants from his plenum. The ever-branching tree toppled, cut off from its roots.

And as Napoleon slept, the historian knew what to do.

Simplify, simplify.

He rewrote, or rather, wrote a new history, such as it was, as real as his encounter with Napoleon was, and it became real, in at least one meaning of the term:

In the days before his exile to St. Helena, Countess Marie

Walewska, who had come to the conqueror between his military campaigns like a ministering angel, who befriended him in the hope that he would help her country, and who had borne him a son, rescues Napoleon from the clutches of the British by dressing him as her maid. They escape to America, where Napoleon takes up a new trade—plumbing in wood and ceramic and metal. These are new skills, and he grows rich from his invention of useful devices, which Jefferson adopts for his own great beloved folly, Monticello. Napoleon's health improves, especially his stomach, as a result of Countess Walewska's Polish cuisine.

Simplify, simplify. Artfully, the historian spins the probabilities, so that this world will never be found by anyone, and launches it into infinity.

Nappy dies a happy man, leaving his heirs a great entrepreneurship, Nappy Bone & Sons, Waterworks. He passes quietly, with his mother whispering to him, "Sleep, my Napoleone, sleep my Nappy," as she slips her blade of vendetta from his brain.

A Piano Full of Dead Spiders

"*I* HEAR THEM PLAYING GHOSTLY SONGS IN THE piano," Felix said, "but they're gone when I look inside."

"You don't really expect to catch them at it, do you?" I answered playfully, tempted to ask whether he meant the spiders or the songs.

"Oh, but I do! I *will* catch them at it!"

He gazed at me tolerantly, and seemed to pity not only my skepticism but my lack of a creative life, even though throughout our years of friendship he had never even hinted at feeling this way toward me. He was the creative one, and I simply went my own way, with no blame attached. I didn't like my sudden, reproachful suspicion of him, either, and felt that I had to be mistaken.

"You should write down their music," I said, thinking that it didn't matter where he imagined it came from, as long as it came, and that I should encourage him because my friend the gifted composer was only trying to get himself back to work as best he could. June had moved out on him because she couldn't bear to watch him sinking. At least that was how it seemed to me. I had never truly understood their relationship; it seemed loving and affectionate, but I couldn't see what she wanted from it except to be the nurturing mate while he worked; but one side of the deal had died, and I had begun to wonder about my own part in the tragedy. When I talked with June she assured me that she had not completely given up on the love of her life, but she wouldn't tell me what she was going to do about it.

"I don't have to write it down," Felix said. "They play *my* music —after they take it from me when I sleep. I hear them crawling around in my mind."

"Music you've written down?" I asked.

"No—but it is *mine*, Bruno, even before I write it down. You don't forget what you're driven to write down. You carry it around all day, waiting to pounce."

"What do you mean?" I asked.

"You might *never* write it down," he said, "but it's always yours. If they opened your brain after death and there was a way to hear the music, they'd hear it." He grimaced, and I had the crazy image of a split brain spilling bushels of black notes, all in the right order.

I gave him an exasperated look, which he didn't like. "Spiders don't play piano," I blurted out, expecting a fit of temper. Necessary fantasies are denied at great peril, and maybe this one was what he needed to get himself composing again.

"Sometimes they sing," he said calmly, as if he were gazing out across a peaceful ocean.

"Spiders don't sing," I said, still unable to restrain myself.

"You weren't here when it happened."

"And they don't steal music from your mind before you've written it down," I said, hoping that the truth would serve him best if he could accept it. "That's your tip-off," I continued, unable to hold back. "Your composing comes to you, but you don't hear it unless you believe that the spiders are singing . . . or playing. You're tricking yourself into remembering because you're *not* writing it down for some reason but can't bear to forget it. There's a part of you that knows exactly what to do and won't let you forget the work you're doing. Pretty clever of . . . the rest of you—to help out, I mean." I heard the pleading in my voice and knew that it sounded lame to him, even if it was the truth. Worse, my hammering at his delusion might prove disastrous.

But he only smiled at me. "That *is* clever of you, Bruno. But they do come and crawl around in my mind and take my music. I feel it ripped out sometimes, as if they're hungry for it."

"Are there spiders?" I asked. "Are they physical? Or are you talking about ghosts?"

He nodded solemnly, secure in his story, as if he were accepting some inevitable fate as a note-producing cow. "I can't keep them out. I think they're physical, but they have immaterial . . . ways." He laughed and said, "You'd rather think that spiders had come down on their lines while I slept and crawled into my ears and connected to the nerves of my hearing and played my brain like a musical instrument!"

"But you've not actually seen a single one of them," I said. "I don't need to. I hear them. I feel them when they crawl around in my mind."

"But you'd like to see them going at it, right in front of you?"

"Well, maybe . . ."

"Then go catch them at it," I said. "Prove to yourself that this is just . . . an imaginative way you've . . . dreamed up . . . to get your work done. Damn it, Felix, that's all it is!" I was convinced that this was all it was, but a part of me suspected that it could be something worse and irreversible. The bridge was out and I had to stop the train.

He smiled, pitying my frightened disbelief, and said, "You are clever. It *could* have been that way, but this isn't a delusion. I don't need to see them." He stared at me as if he had delivered himself of a formal proof in geometry. I stared back, determined to be calm and practical.

"But you know," he went on, "if this is just some fairy tale that I need to have, then you're doing me harm by trying to convince me otherwise, aren't you?"

An old, concealed game was playing out between us, and I felt that I had to be the loser.

"You're hopeless," I said finally. "But who am I to argue? If you need this vision to do your work, then so be it."

"Then why argue if you thought that from the start? Why try to throw doubt into me?" He paused. "Oh," he added, smiling. "You weren't sure, were you?"

"I was of two minds," I said feebly. "I wouldn't like to think my best friend was nuts. But it makes more sense now that I see what's going on."

"I'm not nuts *or* merely deluded," he said, his tenor strong and resonant as if he were reciting poetry. "And I do hear and feel . . . spiders, and one day I'll show them to you, when I catch the little buggers at it."

I had the sudden image of him laughing madly and dancing a jig around the piano.

We looked across the polished wooden floor, to the baby grand piano. It waited there, shiny and silent, and I thought for a moment that if I listened very, very closely, I would hear the spiders playing his work, such was the spell of his conviction. The man who sold him the piano had told him it had once belonged to Glenn Gould, but I didn't believe it. Felix would have bought it anyway, since it fit into his new house perfectly. He might be deluded, but he wasn't impractical.

Felix was a good example of how things go wrong with creative people. They spark, start out with all kinds of irrelevant but necessary justifications, light up and burn for a spell, then reach their mid-thirties and it's all over. They settle for so much less in themselves, and go thud into middle age as they head for cover and security, throwing everything that's good in them overboard for a piece of bread, just to fulfill the expectations of other people by waving around a weekly paycheck like a passport to the country of the elect. The ways of piecemeal slavery spread like a cancerous program, which is why even successful writers, poets, and artists are viewed by too many people as only "bums with money," since they fail to shine sufficiently to dazzle people too dull to notice. And when they tell people that it's only once around in this world, and if you don't climb the Everests of achievement you'll fall forever, these solid folk reply, "Oh, yeah? Well, that's just too bad. Who in hell do you think you are, anyway?" Most people get little or nothing out of life so "Why should you?" is what they're really selling. And when the damage is done, the naysayers are secretly glad. It's their revenge for their own lost dreams. Later, when they hear that so-and-so had become whomsoever, they say sheepishly, "Who knew that's who he was!" as if it had taken no time at all! And secretly they still believe they're right, that maybe so-and-so had done it just to spite them. "Well, he always wanted to be famous!" Some even say that it's only someone with the same name, that it's not the same person they knew. What always gave me a chill were those who were never noticed, yet had completed their accomplishment and gone uncomplaining into the dark. No one knew their names. How many were there? Hell indeed!

Felix was right on the edge. He *needed* his spiders, ghostly or real, to provoke the music in his skull; that obligated him to write it down, to work. He had to get it out of himself somehow; it didn't matter how he did it, or where he thought it came from, because it had to come from somewhere, so what did it matter? He was hanging on to what was best about him in any way possible. He was desperate in a heroically roundabout way, to live up to his myth of himself—and it seemed to be working.

"I'll videotape it," he said, "next time I hear them in the piano. That's what I'll do."

"Videos," I answered with the voice of his enemy, "can make

you see and hear anything these days," and knew at once that I should have said nothing more to discourage him. He might want to prove it to me more than he needed to write the music down, to prove to himself that he had not lost his mind. I wanted him writing it down; but now my doubts had made him wonder, and I regretted pushing his nose in the truth. After all, he had been alone when it happened. A man alone can fool himself. Someone has to witness the miracle, and that runs the risk of exposure.

"Yeah, yeah," he said. "Maybe you'll just have to be here to see them at it."

I nodded, surprised at myself, and afraid that I had only damaged my friend further in my confused self-justification.

June only smiled when I told her—and I felt that she too was deluded. It came out of her eyes, an invincible wave of conviction, defeating all reality, as she told me not to worry.

If you're honest with yourself, you'll admit that you can't ever look back far enough to explain anyone or anything; the rich perversity of the universe, which seems to let just about everything happen, just won't let you see it all. But I kept thinking that you might glimpse just *enough.* Maybe.

In the early days new music had flowed from Felix with a deceptive ease—in all the older forms and new takes on orchestral, chamber, song and dance, and pop forms, defying classification, instrumentation, and styles of performance. Yet Felix was unhappy in his acclaim and financial security. He respected only those who accepted his work "grudgingly."

"What is it?" I had asked. "Really, truly."

"You want to know?" he replied, as if threatening to assault me.

"If you want to tell me." Sometimes, in telling myself that I was trying to understand him, I felt more like a fishhook than a friend.

"It's irrelevant, of course," he said, "but I don't want to do what's easy. Oh, I'll do it, but I most want to do what's hardest."

"That might not make your work any better," I said.

"Maybe not, but I'd like to be truly challenged."

"Haven't you been?"

"Not ever," he said. "Not once."

"But if you haven't exerted yourself," I said, "might it be that you suspect the effort would be unfruitful?"

"No," he said. "I suspect that all the work I've done is not good, and all the acceptance I've had is given to me by fools."

"But is it bad? Surely you know."

"How can I know, unless I try to surpass . . . go beyond myself."

"Beyond yourself you might not be as able as you are."

"Yes! That would be a test. I would know what the real edge of difficulty is like."

"It might horrify you, you know. Incapacity is a terrible thing to face. You obviously believe you could face it and rise higher, but you might only confront your limits and fall back frustrated."

"Yes! On both counts. I want to know where I stand. It's the only way to even have a chance of exceeding the place where I now stand too easily."

"You do stand tall," I said.

He gazed at me as a child might and said, "Thank you, Bruno, but I simply can't endure where I am."

"You've worked hard enough to deserve what you have. Your dissatisfaction is misplaced."

"But I haven't worked hard at all! Can you understand? I must go to the edge—or forever wonder about what might have been."

"It may turn out to be illusory." And be a precipice, I thought.

"We can't know that, Bruno."

He was right—but in a vacuum of conjecture, and I feared that he would lose what he already had by diminishing himself before the public. Nothing drops into the past quicker than a has-been, even if that term only confirms the prejudices of the talentless.

He tried—but faced with the great wall he had set himself to scale he began using up materials from his notebooks. Every old, rejected scrap he had set down in his youth replaced new inspirations. He was eating away at the foundations of his composer's life rather than building on them with new work. He substituted excavation for a transforming memory, and so the new work did not come. He stole from his youth, in which he now placed a naive faith, with little or no creative change. He strip-mined the past unchanged. Collaboration with one's youthful self was not merely the eating of one's seed corn, it was a raising of the dead, I told myself with a growing fear.

His ease deserted him. He lived in a desert of the past, producing only glimpses of what he hoped to find, until he could no longer work and started giving piano concerts, until no one would invite him, because one day he got up and asked the audience why they were applauding something so dreadful.

I was in the audience at that last concert. He played as if discovering each note of his "Athletic Sonata in B" for the first time, as if the strings and hammers of the piano were betraying him. His hands became two monstrous spiders lashed to his arms, and for the first time I admitted to myself that I had wanted to be him, what he had once been, and even what he had become, and I repented my doubts. Suddenly, as I watched him play, I *wanted* desperately to see and hear his spiders, imagining naively that the delusion would somehow bestow upon me all his talent and skill, and I would become something more than what I was; I would be somebody.

He stopped playing in the middle, stood up, and seemed suddenly naked, vulnerable, bitter, and broken.

"It's not very good, is it?" he asked the audience, then saw that they had found it excellent—and he became outraged.

"Finish it!" a man cried out, and my heart with him, but this set Felix to shaking and sweating, and he seemed about to dissolve inside his tuxedo. This went on for one eternal minute, and no one knew what to say or do. I sat there imagining that maybe this humiliation was needed, that it might teach him something, move him to another place within himself; but it was all nonsense, and, I knew, too much about me.

June, who had stood listening stone-faced from backstage, finally came out and led him off. His limbs moved stiffly, as if he were a clothes dummy being removed from a window. The audience, to their credit, remained silent. He glanced back at them for a moment, and I heard a collective inrush of breath, as if his look of contempt had been a physical blow. I caught his eye, and he looked at me with shame, as if I had unmasked him. Or so it seemed to me. The audience stared at the piano as if he were still playing it, then slowly people got up and began to leave. The hall was empty by the time I left.

I came to his door the next afternoon and heard him arguing with June.

"You don't deserve who you are!" she shrieked. "You don't deserve your talent!"

"You'll say anything," he answered. "I only want more out of myself, not the praise of easily satisfied fools."

"Oh!" she cried. "So I'm one of the fools."

"You love me, and it blinds you."

"Are you blinded by your love of me?" she asked.

"No, I'm not. I see you for what you are. And I do not love myself enough to be blinded by my failures—successes to you."

I cringed at the dilemma he had presented to her: which was

worse, his ambivalence toward her and her love of him, or his devaluation of his own abilities? And I realized that we had both been counting on his accomplishments, on his doing well for his audience, to which we belonged.

The door opened, and June ran out weeping into my arms.

"I want more!" Felix shouted out of the depths of the house. "And I'm going to get it."

She turned from me to shout back at him, but I quieted her. "He'll get it without me," she whispered as I led her away, and I knew that he was watching us just before the door slammed shut behind us.

What the audience at the concert could not have known was that he had been revising his work as he played it, hanging at the end of each note, at the edge of one abyss after another, leaping beyond himself until nothing could ever fulfill his ideal. Every newly conquered note became new ground, and he held it just long enough to spy a new mirage up ahead. Listening to the dying vibrations ruined it for him. To appreciate his work he would have to stop and look no further, but he could not stop himself from running ahead. What would it take for him to love his work? Forget as he attained it and see it as a stranger?

He worked suspended between his settled past and a fading future of new music whose fate was to be abandoned. He could never catch up with himself.

"Consider," I tried to tell him a few days later, "that your ease of composition came from a lack of inhibitions wedded to skill. You trusted yourself. What was easy for you was in fact difficult."

"That's easy to say, but it may be untrue."

"Your accomplishments say otherwise to many people. Your work speaks of high levels of difficulty. Facts, Felix, bow to the facts!"

"Again—difficult for whom?" he asked.

"You're contemptuous of those who appreciate your work, of the very idea of appreciation, from what I see."

"If I can see farther, then you want me to blind myself? Lower my sights?"

"But what do you see if you can't find it? What do you actually see?"

"Sometimes . . . I see!" he cried.

"What?"

"A brightness—a great open space."

"Really?" I asked.

He waved his hand at me, and no insult made of words could ever reach the same level of derision visible in his writhing, snake-like fingers, the same ones he played the piano with, the same serpents that sprang to life in his brain when he composed and were now strangling him.

"Ah!" he cried out. "Look, Bruno, we can go around like this forever. I'll either do something or I won't."

"But you'll know only if you succeed, by your own lights." Which may well be out, I did not say. "If you fail, you won't feel that you've failed. You'll still see a road ahead. You don't ever really want to succeed."

He had smiled. "Yeah, I'll always have an excuse. You're a good logician, Bruno, but logic only makes decisions. It never creates, but only gets to the end of something, with no more to come. Believe me, I'll know, one way or another."

"You'll only *think* you know."

"So what would you have me do?"

"Succeed, by all means. But if time grows long, give it up and don't look back. You've already had enough acceptance for two men."

He smiled. "I wish I knew those guys," he muttered. "I've listened too much to such be-happy-with-what-you've-got talk. I'd have had nothing at all if I'd taken it to heart early on."

"That's not fair to yourself," I said. "Early on is not today."

He rose within himself and answered, "Who said it had to be fair, that anything has ever been fair?"

One night I got a frantic call from him.

"You gotta get over here!" he shouted.

"Now?" I asked. "It's two in the morning."

"You've got to see!"

"See what?"

"The spiders, Bruno, the spiders! You'll see them."

He hung up, and I had to go.

I got on my sweatsuit and drove the few blocks to his house. His garage was open and empty when I pulled into the driveway. Once again he had probably parked the car somewhere and forgotten where, then walked home. The car would be towed, and I might have to loan him some money if he decided he needed it, unless he wanted to hate driving that day.

"It's open!" he shouted when I rang the bell.

I came in and found him sitting, bent forward, on his sofa, clearly despondent.

"What is it, Felix?" I asked, standing over him, feeling like an executioner.

He looked up at me with a desolate face and said, "I can't work anymore," then looked down at his feet in shame.

"Not even on the commission?" I asked, convinced that I had helped weaken him.

"Not even that," he replied. "Especially *that*—even if I could." He hated commissions. They were like school assignments, pure suck-up jobs, a catering service providing fakes to be admired by fools who knew the price of a name.

"But why?" I asked, knowing there was more.

He stood up. "I'll show you," he said, laboring toward the piano. I followed him. We looked into the works, and I drew a swift, deep breath when I saw that it was full of spiders.

"They're all dead," he said with the finality of a hammer striking an anvil, then turned to me and added, "I told you there were spiders—physical spiders!"

"But what does it mean?" I asked, shaken but telling myself that they had to be spiders that had come up out of his damp, musty basement into the piano. Pure coincidence with Felix's necessary fantasy, but a part of me was glad that there *were* spiders.

He shook his head. "I can't work now. They were hearing the music for me, taking it out of me just before I heard it. Now I don't hear a thing, not one note, almost as if I'd never learned how to read music."

It had all gone much farther than I had realized. Felix was tearing harder at himself, at his talent, and the dead spiders had sent him over the edge.

I looked more closely and saw their bodies clinging to the strings, almost as if they had strung another kind of web, for another kind of piano, and died from the exertion of spinning steel.

How could I insist on my original view—that this was all nonsense conjured up by my friend's unconscious to fire up his need to compose—a wondrous need that stood outside the ordinary world in which he had to live; how could I tell him that now he would have to stand on his own skill and throw the magical crutch aside?

Yet here were the dead spiders, and my theory seemed to pale as I saw their transcendent presence through Felix's eyes. I turned away and went back to the sofa, sat down and said, "I don't know what to tell you."

He sat down at the piano, as if about to play. "It was all real, Bruno," he said with a strange, grim happiness that embraced damnation. "It doesn't matter if you still won't believe me. It's all over. I'll never compose or play again. But it *had* all been real! Real!" He cried out like a raspy trumpet—and was silent.

I almost bit my tongue to keep from saying that a bunch of dead insects scarcely proved their songfulness, but that would be pointless and cruel.

"You do *see* what's in the piano?" he asked. "You're not humoring me, are you?"

I nodded, then asked, "You still know how to play, don't you?"

He smiled with a feeble finality. "I won't even try with their bodies stuck to the strings. How could I?"

"You'll have to get past this," I said. "You do know that, don't you? You'll have to clean out the piano. I'll call someone for you."

He closed the keyboard cover and stared at it.

"There's more," he said without looking at me.

"Oh? What?"

"I think they were pulling the music from me without my hearing it at all, even *before* I thought of it, so I didn't know what was leaving me. They were stealing it out of my deep places."

"Now how can you even know that?" I asked.

"Because they're dead and I feel drained and deaf! There's nothing left."

I didn't see Felix for much of that winter. I worked at home for a crossword puzzle company, and won an award before Christmas for my efforts, which brought me a raise. Whenever I called or went over to Felix's house, there was no answer. Lights were off in the evenings. I imagined that he had gone away to a warmer place, where I pictured him laughing and drinking with all the beautiful women who could never be mine, plunging through their bodies in search of forgetfulness. Felix was amorously skilled and good-looking, but I had often felt that he thought little of it, that the chase depressed him; it was all a put-up job, he had often said, for given reproductive ends, which made him feel like a puppet.

"You know what Liszt once said?" he had asked me in our youth. "That women who watched him play could think of nothing except what kind of lover he would make. Music to send pile-driver fantasies into female brains!"

"He was much better than that," I had said.

"Of course he was. But you don't know what people will make

of anything! Did you ever watch people at concerts and know which ones were there for the music and which for show?"

Felix had been made for his music; it horrified me to imagine that he might have failed to discover this about himself. Blank sheets of music paper were unbearable to him, as the abyssal void outside of God might have been intolerable during that one eon when the light got away from him and unfolded universes free of his control.

I told myself that Felix had struggled too much to hear his music, and had escaped into some mental space where he was free of music's lonely demand to structure and shape vibrations eloquent to human ears.

He would never come back, I feared. No one would ever hear him again, or know what had happened to him. I remembered the deluded hope in June's smile when, despite their several big arguments, she had urged me not to worry.

One evening in late March I stood before Felix's door, knowing that it would not open, that my friend was no longer there.

But finally it opened, and he motioned for me to come inside. The look on his face was unreadable, his eyes unreachable.

"So how are you?" I asked, glancing toward the piano. It was very dusty.

He was silent, staring at it with me.

"I don't know why the spiders died," he said softly.

"Are you composing?" I asked timidly.

"No," he said, "and I don't seem to care."

I had a bright idea. "You've stopped," I said, "and so they couldn't hear you and died!" and felt stupid for saying it.

He looked at me as if I had just struck him across the face.

"You're saying my . . . silence killed them?"

I was suddenly intrigued, not knowing what to say next. I didn't believe it, but I remembered when I couldn't ride a bike, and my uncle gave me a glass of "magic red water" to drink, and I "knew" how to ride a bike the very next time I tried.

"It just can't be that simple," Felix said. "I can't believe I starved them to death!"

"Maybe you can . . . bring them back," I said, noting his dirty clothes. He hadn't shaved for days. I didn't want to sound anxious. "What the hell, give it a shot," I added jovially.

He was still staring at the piano, ill with inner enemies, and I longed to somehow draw them away from him.

Then we heard the music.

I heard it, and wondered if Felix had rigged the piano to play automatically, or had somehow hypnotized me to imagine it.

But the baby grand was playing.

We crept up to it slowly, like pilgrims arriving at the site of a wished-for miracle. We stood close and saw the keys trembling. The music was ghostly, exploratory, seeking its own shape, by turns rhythmic and lyrical, soft and nearly silent, striving to encompass the stars; then suddenly it was inflamed and hurtful, full of sorrow over lost joy. The music craved the impossible, and wanted it with grace, and I felt that the notes were hunting Felix, like a swarm of insects hunting long-sought flowers.

We stepped around and looked inside. I saw hundreds of new, little spiders scurrying out of their birth sacs.

"They're back!" Felix cried.

We listened, and I marveled at how all the random scurrying and jumping produced music. They weren't singing. The spiders were playing, leaping up and down on the strings, exchanging places to sound single notes and grouping to organize chords and flowing passages. There was no question that the piano was being played.

"Not mine," Felix said blithely, but with anarchy in his eyes.

"Write it down!" I cried.

"That would be stealing," he said, then smiled. "It's *their* music," he added, and I feared disagreeing with him. Too much was at stake. Fragile links must be protected, I told myself, shuddering. Let the music come to him in its own way. After all, they were *his* spiders, and there was no end of how many would come up from the basement every spring, especially if it wasn't cleaned out. Felix, even in his silence, had struck the piano strings with his mind, and that vibration had called to them. My explanations were just as strange as his, but I didn't care. Felix deserved to be protected by credulity, if that was what he needed.

It was *their* music, but they were *his* spiders.

I didn't know which came first, but it was all Felix, exposing his insides as never before; all the pity and fervor of him was alive in the notes that he was denying as his own.

"I'm leaving him," June had once written to me. "He's out of his mind. Maybe as his best friend you can do something to stop his drift." But she seemed not to have gone very far, I now realized, thinking that I had never understood what passed between them. Not even close.

I didn't care how the music had crept back into him, or out of him. My friend would be all right again, and it didn't matter what he believed or what I saw.

There was a knock on the door. The music stopped.

Felix was suddenly very still. We waited.

"Felix!" June called to him from beyond the door, and her voice was the airy blue heaven of a flute. "It's me!" she sang dementedly.

"Stay," Felix said to me as if to a trusted dog, and I felt that the future was rushing back to him, about to pluck him out of the mire and carry him forward again into starry spaces and caring arms.

He went to the door as if stalking it.

Finally, I heard them talking softly, and wondered why we take an interest in other peoples' lives, aside from practical motives. We fall into people because we come to know them, or simply like them, quite irrationally, and hold on to them to keep from drowning. Maybe we just want to compare notes, to look out through others' eyes, to think for a while with other minds. The young just hang out, waiting for something to happen. But the interests of life are surely greater than the repetitive mill of shared experiences. Better questions await, and happier answers beckon. For one thing, the problem of why the mill is a mill, why its repetitive character is so all-encompassing that one can't imagine stepping outside of it. Miracles don't happen in the mill. Good things, yes, but they have happened before. We are all inside ourselves, inside our slightly larger shared social inside, yet some of us try to peer outside. Love and friendship are mad dances in which we see ourselves through the other's eyes. But the recurring interest of seeing beyond our culs-de-sac leads us on. If miracles don't happen in the mill, then don't live there. Climb out of people and live alone on some barren shore.

As I waited for Felix and June, I again thought of why second-raters can spot the third-rate and untalented. Because it's easy to see looking *down*. But try looking up into the realms of the magicians, and it's harder, and then all of a sudden it's impossible. Especially if they *seem* to be ordinary, and you have to remind yourself of who's judging. You resent being second-rate, and it makes you blind. Maybe love eases the pain and helps you to see, I thought as I heard June's voice.

I was second-rate at best, maybe even fifth-rate. Even my cross-word puzzles were too easy to solve. "Don't worry," said my editor. "We need'm too. There's more demand for dumber than smarter." And he meant this with a happy heart!

So I had sometimes resented Felix, but mostly loved him and his ability, maybe more for what it had produced and less for himself. And these delusions of his were his way of saying, "I'm going to rip the work out of myself even if I have to materialize delusions!"

And now, somehow, he had done it—by descending deeper into himself. He would be inevitable, unstoppable, whatever it took to move forward. I could perhaps understand that much, even if he left me to drown within myself.

Felix and June finally stopped their soft talking . . . and something new slipped into the world with a terrifying beauty as they came in smiling. I turned to leave, knowing from the look on her face that she loved him enough to accept the spiders, the piano, and whatever else made him run.

She and I were in perfect, wordless agreement.

Dutifully, the piano began to play again as she caught up to me at the door and whispered, "You have to know, Bruno, that it was I who taught the spiders."

She had taught them to sing, she said, and he had taught them to play their own songs. There was not a hint of lying in her face, only the proud, ethereal composure of a truthteller. It shuddered through me, beautiful and humiliating, as I opened the door, fearing to break the spell with a wrong word, grateful as I fled that these were *newly* born spiders, and that June and I had not somehow helped Felix raise the dead.

Black Pockets

"Turn up the lights,
I don't want to go home in the dark."
—O. Henry's last words

*H*E RAISED A FIST AS BIG AS THE WORLD AND squeezed. Enemies squirmed and yowled in his grasp and their warm blood ran down his arm.

He squeezed slowly, delaying their deaths, because people cling to the belief that the harm they do is right and necessary, and only the finality of their approaching end forces them to cry, "Oh, my God, what have I done!" Their evil explodes their denial, and death drains them slowly, and they feel it taking them, and they think about it. He squeezed harder, and their screaming stopped, and their blood chilled and ran cold on his skin . . .

Bruno's knowledge of black pockets had grown since that day when he had finally despaired of all mercy and been shown the way to personal justice: one person irrevocably responsible to another, held to account by direct action between individuals closest to the truth, because they know it uniquely, individually, beyond all legal investigations, briefs, and cross-examinations.

All the harm done to him had crowded hope from his mind as his hatred spoke with a love of itself, filling him with joy whenever his thoughts reached out to hidden powers and embraced their strength. A kindred underworld had granted him vengeance. He was no longer one of those who only daydreamed of revenge. The overwhelming ease of it was irresistible, his to do with as he pleased, now that he had fulfilled his bargain with Felix.

*   *   *

It began when he awoke gasping for breath one day, and groped around in a darkness that stood about him as no mere absence of light; it pressed into his body and flowed into his eyes. Slowly, he crawled around what seemed to be a curving floor and touched the inside end of an egg-shaped space. He backed up, then rose and bumped into a low ceiling.

Bending down, he tried to remember how he had entered the chamber.

"Hello!" he shouted. The sound was dull, suggesting a thick enclosure. He was breathing with increasing difficulty. "Let me out of here!" he shouted, suffocating. The darkness exploded into light and he fell onto something soft.

He lay still, eyes closed, then opened his eyes and blinked at his own bedroom rug.

He lay on his side, filling with deep breaths, staring at the scratches on the massive, wooden legs of his antique dresser, reminding himself that he had neglected to conceal the old scars. Then he turned over on his back and saw something black and fluid descending toward him.

It faded into gray, and kept coming.

He raised his right hand. The shadow darkened, pressing closer. A part of it seemed to be infolding, like lips threatening to swallow him. He dropped his hand and the darkness dissolved, leaving him to stare at the familiar cracks of his own ceiling.

"I think you're getting it," a voice said from the easy chair in the corner of the room.

Bruno turned his head. Felix Lytton, his old enemy, was gazing at him intently, gray eyebrows as bushy as ever, bald pate shiny. He had lost weight and seemed small in the buxom lap of the old chair.

"I should have let you out earlier," said the man who had stolen his wife and cheated him out of at least two fortunes, who had nearly killed him when they had been children, then had bullied him in high school and mocked him in college.

"What?" Bruno managed to say, sitting up on the floor.

"Being inside one of those things longer gives you an appreciation of what happens. That's important."

"What are you talking about?" Bruno asked angrily. "You did this to me? What did you drug me with?"

"No drug. Get up and lie down on the bed. I've got a present for you."

"What?" Bruno asked again as he struggled to his feet and realized as he looked toward the bed that he would never have a better chance to kill Felix. They were alone, and his enemy's neck looked fragile.

He turned and moved toward him quickly.

"Come!" Felix cried out.

The door to the bedroom opened and a tall, heavy-set man with black hair rushed in. Bruno turned in surprise and was struck in the belly. He fell on his back, gasping for breath.

"That's enough!" Felix cried. "Put him on the bed."

The big man dragged him over by his feet, lifted him by his belt, and dropped him on the bed.

Bruno rolled over on his side, still breathing hard, and looked again at Felix, who seemed even more gaunt in the big chair. His bodyguard now stood next to him.

"Well?" Felix demanded. "Are you ready to hear me out now?"

Bruno struggled with his hatred of the man who had brought him so much hurt.

"You'll thank me," Felix said, "when I make you a present of my skill."

"What are you talking about?" Bruno asked coldly.

"That black cyst that just held you! You can use it. I'm going to teach you. Listen carefully."

Bruno propped himself up against the headboard, fearful of the big bodyguard, who was watching him carefully. There was no chance at all of getting past him to Felix.

"Just imagine," Felix said, "—when your venom becomes like molten steel pouring through you, a black pocket will form for you with each loathing. Of course, you'll have to be heartless." He spoke tenderly, as a lover to his beloved, and Bruno felt that the old husk might break down and weep, then realized that in some strange way the sick, old weakling was trying to make up to him.

"What are they?" Bruno asked softly.

"Who knows!" Felix cried with a youthful vehemence. "Use'm and ask no questions. Maybe they're something that's escaped from our insides, and we find their use according to individual needs, when we're strong enough to summon them. Or maybe they're like the insides of living things, beautiful on the outside and a bag of guts on the inside. Why in all hell are the insides of things so different? What is the *inside* of the universe like? Maybe they're the darkness at the core of the human soul?" He laughed and shivered with the effort, and his bony hands grabbed violently at the chair's armrests. He winced, pulled his hands back, and stared at the blood seeping through the abrased skin of his palms. After a moment, he put his hands back down on the soft armrests. "Yeah," he said, "I know—my outside is beginning to look like my insides."

"How did you . . . find them?" Bruno asked, shaken by the sight of his old enemy's infirmity.

"I got mad one day and raged. And then . . . I learned. It wasn't long ago, but too late for me to really enjoy it."

Bruno asked, "Why didn't you leave me there?"

"I'm going to die, and it amuses me to pass on the skill, to know that it won't die with me. I always knew that I might need you. All I ask in return is that you take care of the names left on my list, before you get to . . . your own . . . needs."

Bruno's eyelids drooped, then fluttered. Felix gazed at him and saw how tightly the man's skull wore his face. The head seemed too heavy for the wasted body, and might break off at any moment.

"Will you promise me that, Bruno?" Felix asked, looking up. "Your word is good with me." The sincerity in his old enemy's voice was overpowering.

Bruno was silent, feeling flattered, moved, and suspicious.

"There's no danger!" Felix cried at his hesitation. "You'll revenge yourself with impunity—simply because you can! Most people forget their hates because there's little or nothing they can do about them. Your skill will grow! And I hope you can do more with it than I've been able to do." He paused, breathing with diffi-culty. "I have only a week or two to live," he added.

"Really . . . ?" Bruno mumbled.

"Yes. Just think. Your hatreds will not die with their circum-stances. You'll be able to act each and every time. You're like me, I know. Think of the creeps you've had to let go. You've had to live as their victim. I know because I helped to make you one. Now you can bully all those who deserve it. And if you overdo it—so what! Who'll know? When I'm dead, you'll be the *only* one who knows."

Bruno took a deep breath and shifted against the headboard, thinking that it was too good to be true, coming as it was from Felix Lytton. Images of Felix's limbs tangling with the willing, nude body of Bruno's first love, June, still writhed in his memory, along with the years of poverty and struggle that had only led to an accounting clerkship in a small firm in upstate New York. He remembered June's rationalizations, as her feelings for him struggled against her desire to insert herself into the flow of Felix's success. Even when he had explained how Felix had stolen his accounting program from their college days and destroyed his hard disk with a hammer, she had still chosen the thief, who went on to make a fortune from the program, only confirming her choice of the winner, whatever his method. Years later, when Felix had left her the big house and moved on through several new wives, Bruno had somehow imagined that June would call him to her, but she had not; Felix had drained her of any capacity to think justly or to correct past wrongs, or care about any of it. All the love they had shared had drained into him, and had slowly evaporated.

"Tell me again," Bruno said, "why you're passing all this on to me."

"You've heard of vendetta?" Felix asked. "In some parts of the world a vendetta is still a sacred thing, a piece of property to be passed down the generations." He smiled grotesquely, his jaw protruding. "It will calm me to know it doesn't just die with me. I'll die happy." He paused and struggled to lean forward in the faded luxury of the chair, still gripping the armrests with his injured palms. "Don't you see, Bruno!" he shouted, shaking a bony finger at him. "You deserve to have my skill." He sat back with a sigh. "I know you do," he added.

Bruno took a deep breath. "Why should I let you die happy?" he asked, and the big bodyguard glared at him.

"And lose everything?" Felix asked. "Yeah, I know it will irritate you that I died happy, but that will pass. I've done everything possible to hurt you. Let me have my parting shot at those who have escaped me, and help you at the same time."

Bruno lay back and considered. "There's no catch?"

"It's exactly as I told you."

"This isn't some way to get back at me, is it?"

"How can it be, Bruno? Think! I've already beaten you, haven't I? It would be the other way round, wouldn't it?" He smiled again. "If you like, think of this as my way of letting you get some back. De Sade said we are all abused, but we can also abuse, and so even up things. Right? Do you object to my dying happy? You do, of course. But look at what you'll get in return for such a small favor. Our interests coincide at last."

"How did you get in here?" Bruno asked.

Felix grimaced. "Think of what I'm going to teach you. You'll have to concentrate."

It would do no harm to listen.

"You won't believe me unless I show you." Felix grinned with difficulty. "And you *will* believe." The mask of his face pulled back tightly, and the skull beneath the skin leered as if denying the truth of everything he had said.

Bruno found himself staring at the armrests of the chair, where his enemy's blood was beginning to seep into the fabric. The man *was* ill and dying.

Felix noticed his concern for the chair and said, "Don't be small-minded. What's this chair to anything I've told you!"

"It's a valuable antique," Bruno said, "and you may be lying."

"I am not lying!" Felix cried, tearing his hands from the bloody, drying fabric of the armrests.

Felix Lytton died five weeks after teaching Bruno all "the skill," as he referred to it during their sessions.

"But remember," Felix said before he showed Bruno the final and most vital elements of "the skill," "you must conclude my unfinished business before you start on your own. You will promise me that."

"I promise," Bruno said, knowing full well that Felix could not hold him to it from the grave. Still, it wouldn't hurt to carry out his wishes. It would be practice. Bruno had left him some money to live on, so he would not be delayed. It was a tidy sum, which Bruno immediately invested in a monthly income. He also bought three hand-tailored suits.

"I don't want you to be distracted by money problems," Felix had said. "But if you fail, you will find that I have left you a penalty."

Bruno's stomach had lurched at this ominous statement.

"Don't worry," he had replied meekly. "There's no reason for me to neglect your wishes. What satisfaction would there be for me to trouble you then . . . with you not being around to be troubled."

"Exactly. Don't worry, there are only three names left on my list."

"What's this penalty . . . if I fail?" Bruno had asked.

"The penalty is that if you don't cocoon the three names in this envelope, the skill will leave you." Felix had put the envelope down on his night table.

Bruno had not gotten up the courage to say, "You'll forgive me if I suspect what seems only a convenient threat." He had grown more fearful of Felix toward the end, while his old enemy had grown anxious, even pleading at times. There were times when the frail body of his enemy seemed to become youthful, full of hope.

"Dare you risk that I'm lying? This is more than a penalty. During our training sessions I placed an irremovable suggestion in your mind. You can't get rid of it. There's no way. You'd need someone else like me—and there isn't one. But don't worry, my insurance program will have nothing to work with *after* you've eliminated these three, and will expire when you've carried out the agreement. I'm not bluffing. And I do want you to have an incentive to finish the job and get to your own. One day the skill will be all yours."

Felix was right; things were too far along to turn back now. "Nice of you to tell me," Bruno had said, knowing that it was a bluff he could not risk calling; and at least Felix was treating him with some respect.

"What happens—inside a pocket, I mean exactly?" he had asked at the start of his practice sessions.

"You felt it when you were in one. You choke to death for lack of air."

"None comes in?"

"You use up what comes in with you!"

"And then?" Bruno had asked uneasily.

"You rot—forever!" Felix had cried, making Bruno shudder.

"One more thing," Felix had added. "You'll steel yourself to be as heartless as you need to be, free of all sympathies for your fellow man."

"Truly?" Bruno had asked.

Felix nodded. "You will learn to feel only hatred and fulfillment when you're done."

In the last day of his training, Bruno awoke to a great resolve within himself. He saw his past and future clearly as he weighed the effort of carrying out Felix's wishes against the danger of losing the skill that had been given to him. There could be no contest between these two alternatives.

"Trust me," Felix had said. "There are ways to overcome our earlier programmings. You'll see how tiring it is to care, to feel too much for others. There has been some evolutionary advantage to cooperative, symbiotic behavior, but you and I don't really need it with what we can do."

"But how?" Bruno had asked.

"It's only a learned function of endocrine and glandular systems, in which you identify with others and your imagination draws analogies from experience, as for example in the saying that there but for the grace of God go I. The golden rule is just sympathy, nothing more. You don't have it for snakes and spiders." He laughed. "Some people don't even have it for other people, so believe me, it can be done!"

"That's all?"

"You'll learn never to worry about what you've done. I did it. So can you."

*   *   *

The three names in the envelope belonged to Felix's last wife, now Jane Bucke, and her two young boys, Ralphie and Ricky.

The woman looked at him with suspicion when he told her who had sent him. She barred his way into the modest house, then swallowed hard and said, "Please tell them there's nothing I want from the estate."

Bruno came forward and she backed away. "May I come in?" he asked, slamming the door behind him. "This is very important."

She retreated into the living room saying, "Make it fast, or I'll call the police."

Bruno stood in the center of her living room and nodded calmly, realizing that he would have to work up to what he had to do.

"I want nothing!" she shouted.

There was no turning back now.

"You heard me? Nothing at all. I just want to be left alone."

Bruno was silent.

"You heard me? Nothing at all."

He looked into her once youthful face, pale and lightly freckled. Her red hair was short and unstyled. Her sweater suggested sagging breasts. Motherhood had taken its toll, yet she was probably only in her late twenties.

She waited a moment, then said, "You want me to sign a paper?"

"You know he's dead?" Bruno asked. He felt little or nothing for her. He did not know her at all, he told himself, because he had not needed to know her to do what he had to do.

"I read about it."

"Where are your sons?" he asked.

"They'll be home from school any time now," she said. "They're in fifth and sixth grade," she added, as if that might help her establish some bond with him. He knew what she was trying to do, so it wouldn't help her at all. He looked into her eyes and felt nothing. Not shame, pity, nor sympathy.

"How nice," Bruno said, eliciting an expression of relief from her face. These three would all be in one place, for a quick finish, but Felix had wanted her to see her sons go first.

"I've got to put these on you," Bruno said, taking the handcuffs from his suit pocket. He had worn his new, blue suit for the occasion.

The last Mrs. Lytton stepped back. "What?" she asked in a rising voice. "What is this? You a cop or somethin'?"

"Or something," he said, shoving her back as she suddenly

came forward. She stumbled but kept her footing and tried again. "Hands out," he said, blocking her. She glared at him and moved to get by him again. He pushed her back harder, but she stayed upright. "Hands out," he said again.

She was breathing quickly, eyeing him fearfully, looking to his left and right for a way past him.

"Hands out!" he shouted.

She came at him again. He slapped her across the face with his right hand, but she kept on, trying to tackle him with her body. He reached low and punched her in the stomach.

She stood up with a sudden intake of breath, trembling, then cried out as he slipped on the cuffs. Twisting the bracelets by their center links until she cried out from the pain, he backed her up to the sofa and forced her to sit down.

"Feet together," he said, kneeling down as he took a set of cuffs from his other pocket. His new suit would hang better without their weight. All three garments had arrived with their jacket pockets sewn shut to keep their shape; but he had pulled out the threads because he would need the pockets, even if using them would stretch the fabric. "With quality materials," the tailor had told him, "it is recommended the pockets stay sewn shut. Okay?" Bruno had said yes. He had never heard of such a thing, but he had begun to worry about the problem.

The cuffs went loosely around her small ankles. There was some blood on her wrists, he noticed as he stood up.

She sat forward suddenly, breathing hard. "Why?" she demanded, looking up at him.

"Be quiet," he said, speaking to his own suppressed turmoil more than to her.

She was staring at him, and he realized that he wasn't particularly enjoying any of this; but it would be different with his own targets, he told himself. He would care about them.

"Mr. Lytton said to tell you," Bruno recited as he stepped back, "that he always knew you had slept around, and that the boys were not his." He looked directly into her eyes as he spoke, as Felix had instructed, and wondered if somehow Felix might also be looking out at her.

"But they *are* his!" she cried. "I swear! And there's nothing I want."

"I don't care, lady," Bruno said. "None of my business. Got any tape?"

"Then why?" she asked pleadingly. "What do you want from me?"

Bruno turned away, hurried into the kitchen, and rummaged around in the drawers until he found a roll of duct tape.

"Who are you?" she asked as he went back out into the living room.

"Felix sent me."

"But why?"

Bruno pulled off a long piece of tape. It made the usual ripping sound of a fresh roll.

"He just wants to get back at you, if you must know," he said.

"Get back at me?" she mumbled as Bruno covered her mouth and wrapped the piece around her head, then pushed her back into the cushions.

Her eyes now stared at him in terror, seeking his gaze, as if somehow that would restrain him.

Bruno heard the front door open. She tried to stand up, but fell back into the sofa. A boy came into the room, followed by another. They stopped and stared at the intruder. Then they saw their mother.

"Ah!" cried the older boy. He was dark-haired and thin, and leaned to one side, as if he had grown too fast and was still getting used to it.

The younger one whimpered. He was pudgy, a full head shorter than his brother.

"Hello, boys," Bruno said as he put the roll of tape in his pocket and walked up to them, struck the smaller boy across the right side of his head, then pushed him down on the carpet and put his foot down on his neck. The boy gagged and struggled to get out from under. As the older boy gaped, Bruno grabbed his right hand and twisted his arm behind his back. He cried out as Bruno forced him to his knees. Bruno pushed him down flat on his stomach and sat down on him with enough force to take wind out of his lungs. He put the boy's limp arms behind his back and took out the roll of tape. Ripping free a long piece, he bound the boy's hands together and stood up.

The younger boy was still down on his back, struggling for breath. Bruno knelt down on the carpet and tried to grab his wrists. "Lemme go!" the boy cried out. Bruno hit him across the face with his fist, and the boy lay still. Bruno turned him over and taped his wrists behind his back.

A deep groan came from the mother. She stood up, then fell forward onto the rug and rolled to one side.

"Help!" cried the older boy.

The younger one was crying now.

The mother twisted her head to see. Good, thought Bruno. He wouldn't have to turn her to face the scene. Felix had insisted she see everything before she went in.

He stepped to one side of the room, caught sight of himself in the mirror over the sofa, and turned away from the sudden stranger. His own uncaring was a pleasant surprise.

He closed his eyes and summoned a black pocket.

It appeared, about three feet across—irregular at first, then acquiring the shape of a mouth. Its lips opened, swelling like those of some giant lover whose reclining body was out of sight somewhere below the foundations of the house. He stared for a moment at the perfect blackness inside the mouth, imagining that it might swallow the world.

He went over to the older boy. He began to kick as he was lifted. "Let me go!" he cried, twisting like a coiled spring.

The younger boy cried out loudly, "Ralphie—help me!"

Bruno carried the older boy to the pocket and threw him in. The boy screamed, then was silent.

Another agonizing groan came out of his mother. She rolled furiously on the carpet. Her wrists were bloody and bruised from her efforts to break free. She stopped when she saw him watching her.

"This is how Felix wanted it," he said, following the script. "He wanted you to know. Understand?"

She groaned more deeply.

He went over and picked up the smaller boy, who hung limply as he was lifted, crying softly. Bruno brought him to the opening and dropped him into the darkness.

He stepped back and took a deep breath. His pulse was racing but he was sure that he would complete the job. The mother would soon be with her boys, he told himself, expecting a rise of involuntary sympathy within himself.

He went over and picked her up. She squirmed and turned in his arms, crying out through the tape. Overheated now, he staggered over to the pocket, suddenly wishing that it might be lower. It was absurd that he couldn't control this wretched detail. He had to lift her to his shoulders before she would go in. He got her feet inside, and let her slide away.

The monstrous liplike opening closed and faded away, cutting off her cries.

He went and sat down on the sofa, sweating as he told himself that he had performed all the details correctly.

It was over, he told himself as he breathed more easily. He had paid for the skill. It was now his to use as he pleased. Of course, he would never know if he would have lost it by disobeying Felix. What had Felix imagined in the details that he would never live to see, as the cuffed mother was reunited in the darkness with her sons and the air began to run out? Was that imagining all the satisfaction he had sought before his death? But it was Felix's satisfaction, Bruno told himself, not mine. Felix had acted through him, leaving him little choice but to play the puppet. His own rewards were waiting to satisfy him, he told himself, and everything he had done would be worth the satisfactions still to come.

He sat back and wondered what Felix had not told him. After all, Felix had been his enemy.

Yes—but a bargain was a bargain; sealed and delivered. Felix had been right during the final exercises; heartlessness was achievable, and he had succeeded, both in the task and in his self control. He'd had very little before; now he had everything. Nothing else seemed to matter.

Bruno made a wish list of revenge. No more pathetic imaginings of how he would break hands and feet with a baseball bat, cut off thumbs and big toes and force them down throats, or present the deserving with a choice of which body parts to sacrifice in place of worse torments. No more frustrations from merely picturing the delights of vengeance. The hurling of his enemies into darkness only awaited his choice of time and place.

It was an outstanding menu.

Each elicited a resounding yes.

But who would go first?

There was a knock on his door. He went over and opened it without checking through the peephole.

Al, the bachelor superintendent of the apartment house, stood before him in his usual green jumpsuit, smelling of heavy cologne even though he never seemed to shave. He looked up at Bruno, then smiled and said, "Oh, you're home. I wanted to ask you about the garbage and the recycles."

"What about them?" Bruno said, gazing down at the stocky, sandy-haired man whose teeth were always piss yellow, and who always acted as if he were hiding something.

"Uh—you don't put out any for a while now." He tried to peer past Bruno. "Been away?"

Bruno felt a twinge of anger, and annoyance at himself for

arousing the man's curiosity. "You think I'm storing it all up in here?"

Al seemed to sniff the air. "Can I come in and check?"

"You may not!" Bruno shouted, and the man stepped back suddenly.

Bruno struggled to remain calm. The man was an insect, scurrying around in his basement apartment, the lowest rung on a ladder of stooges that went up through managers and corporate landlords to the great masters who passed their wealth down through their generations like a disease.

"Well, sure, why not," Bruno said, suddenly becalmed. "Come in and satisfy yourself. I've nothing to hide."

The man gave him a puzzled look. Then he smiled and said, "Tough day—huh?"

Bruno nodded and stepped aside to let him in.

Al smiled. "You know I have to check up. It's in the lease. You might have somethin' to fix."

Bruno closed the door.

"I got an eye for things need fixing," the man said without looking back. "Tenants just live with small maintenance needs and don't complain until it gets bad and costs more to fix. Less to catch things early. You know what I mean?"

"Sure," Bruno said, "look around all you want."

He sat down on the sofa and waited.

Al checked the bedroom, bath, and kitchen, then came out into the living room and said with a smile, "Looks okay. You shoulda said right off you'd been away and had no garbage."

"Yeah, I should have told you at the door."

"Sorry to disturb you. More people should be so clean and easy on the fixtures as you. You know they leave stoves on and faucets dripping and toilets unflushed? And what they do to stain and scratch the floors! You think they were running a butcher shop, with some carpentry on the side."

Bruno smiled.

"You wouldn't believe the things I've seen in my years," Al said, rolling on. "You'd laugh, but I want to scream every time I make a list of all the repairs." He began to move back and forth like a duck in a shooting gallery.

What did the creep expect? A tip for accusing him of being a pig?

Al paused and seemed to look around as if he had lost something. "Say," he said, "didn't you ask me where to put out old computers and electronic stuff? Didn't you have an old tape player you wanted to lose? Got rid of it?"

Bruno nodded, recalling the museum of dead electronics his closet floor space had become. The pockets had removed that nuisance. Al, of course, wanted the stuff to sell for junk, but he was too late.

"Hey man," Al said, "can I ask you somethin'?"

Bruno nodded.

"When I parks my car coming back from groceries . . . you know, down by the stairs down into my apartment, I leave my bags by the door and go park the car where I see a space, and when I come back the groceries are gone. One out of three times. Usually roasts, steaks, chops . . ."

Bruno's rage rose up through his calm. "You think I take them? What is it? Do I look like a thief?"

"No! No! I only thought you might have seen who does it."

"You suspect me. How can you be sure?"

"Hey man, I was only askin'."

"You know, you're right," Bruno said as he got up.

"What do you mean, man?" Al asked as Bruno came around behind him.

"Keep looking," Bruno said, pointing in front of the coffee table.

Al glanced back at him with a nervous smile and said, "Hey, you ain't weird, are you? I don't go that way, you know."

"Right there," Bruno said, "that's where I put all the garbage— and your groceries."

"What the hell—" Al said as the pocket formed in front of him.

Bruno shoved him forward, wishing it could be one of the pockets he had opened for his garbage. Al tripped and went in too quickly to cry out. A choking shout came back as the pocket faded.

Later that month, a man resembling Al, probably a relative, quietly took his place. Bruno heard one of the first floor tenants, an aging seamstress, asking about Al in the lobby. The new super shrugged and said, "I think he ran off with some woman. I knew he was seeing somebody because I asked him if she had a friend or a sister. Anyway, I'm here now." He sounded happy about the chance.

"Yeah," said the woman. "I guess he finally got lucky with all that cologne."

Larry Braddock had cracked Bruno's skull in the schoolyard. Bruno missed six months of seventh grade and got held back a year. Today, Braddock worked for a large computer firm, and was sometimes in the news for his wizardry. Bruno went to the company's office building and clocked his comings and goings.

Larry had fattened. He sometimes brought a full box of pastries back from lunch. He had lost hair, but what was left he had let grow long, orangutan style. Bruno noted that he never returned directly to his office when he came back from lunch; he first used the men's room in the lobby. Bruno followed him inside, and at once knew why. The fat man left a bad odor that he would have been too embarrassed to leave where his coworkers would be able to attribute it to him. Larry scheduled his life around a flatulence-concealment plan.

Bruno noted that few people used the facility in the lobby, especially during the lunch hour, so it clearly had not escaped Larry's notice that people were just going out to lunch when he was coming back, or were late, thus giving him a reliable privacy.

After repeated shadowings, Bruno arrived in the accounting firm's lobby dressed in a suit and a hat pulled down low over his forehead. The young woman at the reception desk had just left for the Ladies' facility. The security guard was down the hall in his office, eating a sandwich at his desk, glancing out into the hall once in a while. Bruno slipped past his view when the guard looked down at his food.

Bruno paused at the Men's door, opened it a crack, and knew at once by the odor that his prey was in its stall. He pulled the Out of Order sign from under his belt, hung it on the doorknob, then went in and locked the door behind him.

He stood there, noting that only the handicapped stall door was closed. Bulky Braddock clearly preferred this oversized section at the far end of the bathroom, for the handbar and the convenient height of the bowl.

Bruno fingered the blackjack in his right hand pocket, wondering how much the suit jacket was going to stretch from the heavy objects he was making it carry. Maybe he should just get more suits, and rotate their use. It mattered, but he needed the pockets.

He listened. Braddock was coughing heavily as he stood up and readied to come out. Bruno turned to the sink as if to wash his hands, and waited. Braddock wasn't the worst of his old enemies, and he almost felt sorry for him.

Would Larry even remember him?

There was a massive flush. The wide door flew open and crashed against the wall, and Braddock came out, tightening his belt as his odor, somewhat hydrated, spread out from the stall. He stopped, probably startled by the presence of another person in a bathroom that he had come to regard as his own during these hours.

Bruno turned to face him—and felt only a distant hatred. At once he knew that he didn't want to spend his rage all at once, on a figure who was now more humorous than villainous.

"Hello, Larry," he said.

Braddock looked at him. "Who are you?" he asked with a disdainful objectivity, then rubbed the back of his neck as if it didn't matter what answer he got.

Bruno gave him a questioning look.

Braddock stopped rubbing and stared at him.

"It's me—Bruno from the schoolyard," Bruno said, smiling.

Larry gave him a puzzled look.

"You busted my skull and lied that it was an accident!"

"Bruno!" Larry shouted, then grinned as if glad to see him. "How ya' been?" It was suddenly a long ago moment that no longer mattered.

Bruno readied to release his fury. It stirred with an intensity that might be a pity to spoil by action.

Larry began to look troubled as it dawned on him that this was not going to be a friendly reunion. "Well, you *do* know it was an accident," he said. "I was running after you and *you* tripped just as I caught up with you."

"So you said," Bruno said calmly.

"I didn't push you," he muttered. "You tripped just as I grabbed you and *you* thought I pushed you. Don't you get it? I remember it all *exactly*. Can't believe you're still thinking about it. Don't you have anything else to do?"

Not now, Bruno thought. I can do as I please simply because I can. "Makes no difference," he said. "You caused what happened by chasing me. And you do remember, so it still worries you."

"But it's not the same," Larry said softly.

"You were a creep then," Bruno said, "and you grew into a slime. I know all about your crooked business dealings."

"What are you talking about?" Braddock asked. "Who sent you?"

"I did," Bruno said.

Braddock shook his head. "Nobody hangs on to grudges from grade school. Who sent you? Is this blackmail?"

"I sent myself."

Braddock took a step back and Bruno stepped toward him.

Braddock stood his ground. "What do you want?" he asked. "A job?"

Bruno laughed. "I'll be doing a lot of people a favor by getting rid of you."

"Rid of me? What are you talking about?" Braddock's face reddened and he clutched at his throat. "Call a doctor!" he cried. "I'm having a stroke." He collapsed to the floor, moaning.

"Doesn't matter much," Bruno said. The twinges of sympathy and shame he had felt when he had disposed of the mother and her two sons tugged at him, but he only laughed at Larry.

The fat man was suddenly very still. Bruno leaned over him and saw that he was breathing regularly. He had only passed out. Just as well. He would not have to hit him or cuff him.

Bruno stepped aside, closed his eyes, and summoned a black pocket.

"Oh, shit," he muttered to himself as he saw it appear about four feet from the floor. He had been trying to get it lower this time, because Braddock was a whale, but the pocket came in at the height of his practice runs with the garbage, which was okay for the light stuff like the woman and her two sons, or someone he could trip in, like Al, but an effort with the electronics, especially the two big monitors.

The fat man was still out cold as Bruno dragged him by the shoulders toward the suspended darkness, thinking that he would get his head and shoulders in first, hook him over under the arms, then lift the lower body.

The body slid slowly. It was only six feet or so to the pocket. He pulled close and stopped. There was a strange sound coming from somewhere.

Bruno listened.

Braddock was snoring.

Bruno stepped forward, placed his feet wide at Larry's shoulders, then bent at the knees, gripped the jacket fabric at each shoulder, and lifted.

It was impossible. The man's upper body alone probably weighed two hundred pounds.

"What?" Braddock muttered. "What's going on . . . who turned out the lights?" he demanded as he tried to turn over and rise up on one elbow.

Bruno let go of the shoulders and stepped aside, knowing that he would have to get Braddock to do some of the work.

"It's dark, Larry," he said. "Careful how you get up."

"Who's that?" Braddock whispered.

"An old friend, you fat snail."

"Friend . . . friend, friend," Braddock chanted as he rolled over and got up on all fours, then slowly struggled to his feet, facing the pocket. When he was still partly bent over, Bruno stepped forward and happily gave him a shove from the rear.

Braddock grunted and went halfway into the pocket, and hung there by his gut on the lower lip.

"Help!" he cried. "For God's sake, someone help me!"

"Gladly," Bruno said, gripped his ankles, lifted, and sent him over. Not so bad, he thought, catching his breath. He might have preferred some more conversation, but he felt good about it. He closed his eyes and the pocket vanished.

He hurried to the door and listened, then slowly unlocked and opened it and removed the sign. He slipped it inside his belt and closed his jacket.

He went over to the sink and washed his face with cold water, noting that the big creep's smell was still all around him. He had read somewhere that an odor is a loose molecular sample of the very thing that you're smelling, going up your nose and into your lungs, clinging to your skin, infiltrating the fibers of your clothes.

A bad smell was all that was left of Braddock in this world, Bruno thought with satisfaction, noting that his rage, what there had been left of it toward Larry, was coiling back inside him, growing cold.

"You can't be sure," Felix had told him, "how long they may live in each pocket."

"But the air," Bruno had objected, "what about the air?"

"Who knows? Maybe they branch inside to other pockets. I doubt it, but I have never explored enough of one to know."

The woman and her two boys may still be alive, Bruno realized. It had not yet been very long.

"You can recall pockets you've made and check," Felix had said.

"But don't they stay where I made them?"

"They stay close," Felix had explained. "Entangled with your thoughts. Not nearby in space. Space isn't the same there."

"You mean they follow you?" Bruno had asked.

"Only when you summon one."

"You mean any pockets I . . . fill?"

"Yes, and you can look inside with a flashlight." He had laughed. "You can shout in and hear if anyone answers."

Felix knew more than he had told him, Bruno thought as he saw by the calendar that it was a week since the woman and her sons had gone in. It was too late to call that one back. But Braddock was only a day gone. He wouldn't be rotting yet.

He closed his eyes and thought of him.

The pocket began to appear in front of his fireplace.

He got up from his recliner and went over to the dark patch. It was a living thing to be fed, a black, stemless flower like nothing that had ever grown from the earth, and he wondered about its roots.

"Hey, Larry!" he shouted into the maw. "Still alive?" An awful smell hit him.

He waited.

"Yes," came a pitiable whisper. Bruno felt nothing.

"No one will even know you died, or how you disappeared!" Bruno shouted. "No one will have the slightest clue about what happened to you."

He waited for an answer.

"Son of a bitch," came the reply. "Let me die in peace."

"What gives you the idea that I'm going to let you die?" Bruno asked.

The odor of human sweat and wastes coming up from the pocket grew stronger. As he listened to the sound of coughing and wheezing, Bruno became concerned about polluting his own living area.

"You cruel shit," Braddock said loudly. "To hell with you!"

Bruno felt the cruelty within himself, but Felix had given him good advice, if he could follow it. "You *will* have to control yourself," Felix had warned him. "Don't let revenge cloud your mind or you'll make mistakes and get caught. Enjoy, but deliberate, and check up on yourself. Believe me, you'll have help."

But Bruno had felt very differently about Braddock than he did about the woman and her two sons. Pocketing her had been an assignment pledged to Felix; but he had no ill feelings toward her. It had to be done, or Felix would have refused to teach him the skill. Bruno had not been truly worried that Felix would somehow know that his order would be ignored; that danger had probably died with him, but Bruno had decided not to chance the loss of his new strength; even the smallest chance was too great a risk. There was no honor among enemies, only compelling circumstances that left no choice.

"Let me out!" Braddock shrieked suddenly. "Please! Have mercy!"

"You stay where you are, you fat slob." Of course fat was not part of it. Larry had been a swine even when thin.

"Oh, God, no! Please don't let me die in the dark!"

Bruno felt a surge of satisfaction; but it wasn't enough; he cared too little about Larry; that place was already occupied by Felix. He saw the special place of torment within himself, and could not let go of the longing for fulfillment that Felix had denied him by dying.

Bruno closed the pocket, went back to his recliner, and began to select his next enemy. Felix's ex-wife and her two sons did not count; they were on Felix's head. And Larry had been only a warm-up, scarcely better than getting rid of the garbage.

That night he dreamed of Braddock crawling through a snaking passage, and somehow finding his way out into a green countryside in a distant land. The woman and her two boys were there, and she had an airline ticket to somewhere for all four of them.

He woke up with his living enemies. They would deserve their fate, measured out without mercy. His hatreds were refiring with empowered rage.

"You have to control your human sympathies," Felix had told him. "Your common humanity can defeat you. Those impulses evolved for common survival. You and I are past that now. We're even beyond most leadership groups, who know that they can kill large numbers of people without danger to themselves, if they claim a greater good."

Larry Braddock had been a bully, and bullies hated fair fights. They loved to come in groups, to guarantee their victory. That was their prime trait. Never use less than overwhelming force. Have three or four hold the one and take turns gut-punching him. Use more help and ammunition than you need. Waste but win. Bomb from the air. Never come in low enough to get shot down. Nothing horrifies a bully more than to have overwhelming force used against him, to have it all coming at him in a way *he* imagines is unfair; better to horrify him for the first time and in the final moments of his life, when there is nothing he can do about it.

Bruno lay back, feeling calm. Human cruelty, he told himself, was a very special thing, poorly understood even by many who practiced it; so they failed to be satisfied by the experience. Cruelty well practiced satiates the giver with the certainty that the object will suffer before dying, however briefly burns the pain of that knowledge. Longer is better. Behead slowly.

But once satiated, the bringer of cruelty must move on, untouched, his weapon intact, his composure whole.

Bruno realized how feelings of pity and regret might wound him and undo all revenge. Felix had warned him well about the tasks before him, to help him accomplish them regardless of how he felt. Revenge would not ruin him. That was the most important thing. His rage would be loosed, by degrees, on the right enemy.

Felix had promised help, and Bruno wondered about it.

But still the pity of it wore away at him that his greatest enemy, Felix Lytton, was beyond suffering. Braddock had made an all too brief understudy. Scheler, the director of the sales force in the office-supply company for which Bruno had worked, would make a more rewarding substitute. Bruno had never been able to break through Scheler's composure, to get inside him, and he had never had any help from him in the workplace. In fact, Jean Scheler had always worked against him, in a well concealed, deniably undeniable fashion.

Promotion to a better branch?

No.

More vacation time?

Not once in a dozen years.

Blame for the failings of others?

Often.

Good morning and good evening greetings?

Never.

A simple how-do-ya-do?

Not once.

A nod?

No.

The birthday party Bruno had organized for him?

Scheler had failed to show up.

A word of thanks for holding a door open for him?

Not a grunt or a nod.

Laying him off, then firing him with the loss of his pension?

Yes. And Scheler had taken his time, playing with him, until all the fun was gone.

Bruno had always been at the bottom of Scheler's "makes me no never mind" list.

Jean Scheler seemed taller and leaner, with the same thinning hair combed over his bald top, when Bruno came up to him at the annual company picnic. He showed no sign of surprise or anger as they went silently through the food line and found a small table under an elm tree.

Bruno looked around and noticed that not one of the hundred or so workers here seemed to be paying any attention to them.

"You're not supposed to be here," Scheler said softly, unwrapping a ham sandwich.

"I didn't go last year," Bruno answered.

"Doesn't work that way, Mr. Willey." He took a big bite of the sandwich and grimaced. "You don't work for us any more."

"Throw me out," Bruno said.

"I guess you need a free lunch," Scheler said without further facial dread of his sandwich. "But you might have done better at the charity mission." He finally dropped the ham sandwich onto his paper plate. "Might just as well be Spam."

Bruno stared at Scheler, determined to break through that brown-eyed stare and see what the man was like behind his mask.

"What's made you such a hard ass, Jean?" he asked, and saw that Scheler immediately wanted to reprimand him for using first names, but hesitated, since that habitual response would now be wasted on a former employee. Was that a hint of a Uriah Heepish smile? More a smirk, Bruno decided, feeling that Scheler was congratulating himself on the efficiency of his non-response.

Scheler stared down at his uneaten sandwich as if it had poisoned him.

"What kind of caterer did you hire?" Bruno asked. "A cheap one, even though you knew you were going to have to eat it. Hope it makes you sick."

"I can't just think about myself," Scheler replied.

"Yes," Bruno said, "you're a philanthropist."

The sun came out from behind some clouds. Scheler got up and said, "I'm going for a walk. Goodbye, Mr. Bruno Willey."

Scheler had always been a fitness freak, but the exercise had only made him look cadaverous.

"Mind if I come along?" Bruno asked.

"It's a public path," said Scheler. "You're no longer my responsibility."

Bruno picked up his own wrapped sandwich and put it in his pocket. As Scheler would say, a free lunch was a free lunch, shameful though it was to eat one. It put you one ahead even if it was lousy. That's how Scheler thought of business: whatever brought a profit; even a penny found on the street might tip the balance to an honorable end of a day's toil.

Scheler went down the path from the picnic area toward the lake. Bruno followed. No one else came after them, or even glanced in their direction, Bruno noted as he looked back. Scheler was not liked by the employees. They paid attention to him only when they had to. Taking a walk with him was unimaginable, and would have stirred suspicion among the employees.

Bruno went after him, taking soft steps. Halfway to the lake, where the trees were thickest, Scheler stopped.

"Are you still there?" he called back to Bruno.

"What is it?"

"I'd leave if I were you," Scheler said softly.

"Maybe it's the bad sandwich," Bruno said with a chuckle. "You almost sound kindly."

Scheler was silent, then turned to look back at him.

"You must leave, Mr. Willey."

Bruno said, "*Must?* I don't have to do anything you say, you creep!"

"I'm serious, Mr. Willey," Scheler said, unmoved by Bruno's outburst.

"So am I," Bruno said more calmly. He closed his eyes and opened a pocket downhill of his old boss.

He was about to turn away as Bruno came forward suddenly and shoved him backward. Scheler cried out as he fell in head first. His oversized shoes seemed to hang on the edge. The pocket muffled his cries as he disappeared.

Bruno stared at the opening, noting with satisfaction that it stood about three feet from the ground, perfectly still and unreal, as if someone had painted a hole in reality, defying anyone to believe it. Dust from the trail was being sucked into the mouth. He took the sandwich out of his pocket and threw it in.

"You might get hungry!" he shouted, "before you run out of air."

"Ahhhh!" came a cry from the opening.

As the pocket faded away, Bruno looked out across the calm waters of the lake and again felt cheated of the chance to have tormented Felix Lytton. His oldest enemy had given him the means, at a price, of course, but had bowed out before it could be used against him.

"Enjoy your crappy sandwich, Mr. Scheler," Bruno muttered as he turned back up the path, imagining the man weeping as he ate his last meal and wondered whether hunger or lack of air would kill him first.

He would do in place of Felix.

For now.

Bruno's mind now inventoried other worthy enemies, the category so well defined in all the old etiquettes, but so difficult to eliminate. That same book, first shown to him by June, had claimed that the category only worked between equals. A quaint, romantic notion of justice, since an unequal enemy was still an enemy and should be destroyed at first chance. Where had there ever been such honorable enemies? It had always been villains and victims. Now the tables were turned. Bruno knew that what he could do to the villains, he would do to them, leaving no trace, no consequences. The moments of cold fury would be his to savor at his leisure.

Nevertheless, even as he considered his next selection, he knew that there would never be a greater enemy than Felix; and no greater benefactor. He would have liked to have tormented Felix, when all his money would not have helped him to escape; but the means had flowed from Felix, and hence could not have been used against him.

Maybe Felix had been right. Perhaps the two of them had escaped the categories of villain and victim, and were now equals, and that was all the revenge he would ever have.

A letter arrived one day from Felix.

Bruno—

My informant has by now ascertained that you have carried out my wishes, so if you are reading this, an additional bonus has been deposited in your account and a bank statement will arrive announcing that the funds are available to you from today. But this person's life does pose you a problem. He knows that the woman and her sons have vanished and are possibly dead, and that you might have had something to do with their disappearance. He was instructed to pay you when he saw a notice of missing persons. I never liked him much—so you should get rid of him, just to tidy things up. You'll get a bonus and I rid myself of one more person I detested. You really have no choice, since he may one day pose a threat to you. I rest easy that you will do this, knowing you have done this additional task for me.

—Felix

Rest? Bruno laughed out loud at the absurdity of the idea. Where in all hell would he be resting? The only time Felix could possibly have rested easy had been while he was waiting to die, when he could still appreciate what he had put in motion but would never see accomplished! That appreciation had ended at the moment of his death.

Bruno shook his head at how poorly people understood the physical reality of past, present, and future. They always secretly projected themselves beyond their own demise, assuming that they would somehow be around when the news got out, as if they would read it in the paper or watch it on television. Mark Twain had a lot to answer for, when he had sent Tom Sawyer to attend his own funeral, not to mention all the secret observers who imagined unseen and unheard trees falling in forests no one would ever visit. Surely, as Felix had died, he had realized with a start that he would have no memory of it?

Bruno noted that Felix had deposited the money in advance, and presumably there would be no further confederate to verify that the job had been done, since the whole point now was to get rid of a possibly unreliable agent who might later become a blackmailer. Felix had surely not set up an indefinite series of confederates to be eliminated; which meant that this additional request might be ignored, risking only a mild uncertainty.

Nevertheless, Bruno decided to carry out the instruction, just in case Felix had been very clever somehow, leaving a long line of confederates to deal with Bruno, who had been enlisted only as a tool of revenge. Was this the punishment Felix had planned for him, as one might kill several birds with one stone?

Bruno smiled at his own overly complex suspicions, imagining a series of confederates who would not know what they had to do until they opened a timed letter, a bridge of written communications extending into the indefinite future. But there was no evidence for any such plan. Felix was dead, and the letter was certainly correct in calling attention to the danger of a living confederate, nothing more.

There was a name and an address at the bottom of the letter for a lawyer named Cecil Banes.

Bruno sat back in his recliner and sighed with acceptance. Felix was right in planning to get rid of the lawyer, and the extra money would be welcome; but this was once again a lesser task, nothing like what it would have been to take revenge on Felix himself, who now lurked inside a real but non-existent category of his own, immune to the living.

The lawyer's secretary, a sad-eyed woman with red hair and green eyes, checked with her boss, then told Bruno to go inside.

"Take a seat, Mr. Willey," the lawyer said as Bruno came into the office and closed the door.

Bruno saw that Cecil Banes was a heavy man, which meant more work.

"So you were a dear friend of Mr. Lytton?" Banes said with a smile as he leaned back in his chair. "I was glad to transact his last business. What can I do for you, Mr. Willey?"

Bruno went up to the desk and picked up a brass paperweight from the green blotter. Banes looked up at him with surprise as Bruno hit him over the head. The man slumped forward. Bruno put the paperweight down next to the man's head. Bright red blood was staining the lawyer's white hair and soaking into the green blotter.

Bruno opened a pocket behind the desk. Mercifully, it came in at about three feet from the floor. He went behind Banes and sat the body up straight, swung the high-tech swivel chair around, and leveraged the lawyer from it into the opening until only his feet stuck out. He grabbed them by the fine Italian shoes and sent him over. Removing the blotting paper sheet from the pad frame, he crumpled it around the paperweight and threw the mess in after the body.

Then he sat down at the desk, and caught his breath as he dismissed the pocket.

This was nothing at all. The man had no idea of what had happened to him and had no time to suffer in advance. There had been no connection between them, hence no opportunity for pointed discussion, Bruno told himself as he sat there wondering if Felix had any more surprises for him.

Was this the punishment Felix left for him—never to be revenged on his worst enemy? For a moment Bruno asked himself if there were better uses for this skill than killing old enemies. Maybe something in politics, he told himself, imagining the complexity of the chesslike moves that would be necessary to wield power with the skill. Examples would lead to private threats, and the fear of him would spread, his power forever present but unprovable. Some might view stories about his ability as urban legends. There would be no end of fruitless evidence-seeking by clueless investigators whose fate would be to perish at the very moment of their success, if they got that far.

And when he had ascended to the summits, what would he do with it? Could society be sculpted? If so, then into what forms of ridiculousness that were not already present?

For now, he told himself, he would stick to old enemies. In the world's difficult work, they were small matters, much more easily handled.

There was a loud knock on his apartment door late one morning. Bruno was in his bathrobe, finishing his first cup of coffee.

"Mr. Bruno Willey?" a tall, dark-haired man asked as Bruno opened the door. There was a short, bald man with him. Both wore long, gray coats.

"Police," the tall man said, flashing his badge. "I'm Detective Ben Dillard, and this is Detective Winkes. May we come in?"

"Of course," Bruno said.

The two men came in and stood in the living room. Bruno closed the door and turned to give them his full attention.

"We understand from his secretary that you had an appointment with the lawyer Cecil Banes," Detective Dillard began.

"That's right," Bruno said.

"She tells us that when you left the office, Banes did not come out with you."

Bruno said, "I don't understand."

"He's disappeared," Winkes said. "We thought he might have left the office with you and she simply failed to notice."

"He was there when I left," Bruno said.

"Yes," Winkes added, "she did say that you came out alone. But she didn't see him in his office at the end of the day, and hasn't seen him since."

They were being deliberately vague, to trip him up. "There's nothing else I can tell you," Bruno said. "Is he missing?"

"Three days now," Dillard said.

Bruno stared at the two policemen. The circumstances of the lawyer's disappearance made an unsolvable, locked-room mystery. The assumptions they would need to solve it were beyond their imagination, even if he confessed. Full, unbelievable demonstrations would have to be performed, and observers would doubt their sanity even then.

"Did Banes seem well when you left him?" Winkes asked with a slight twitch under his right eye. Otherwise, both men maintained blank expressions.

"Sure," Bruno said. "He said goodbye and I left."

"Are you employed, Mr. Willey?" Dillard asked.

"I'm retired."

"Did you know a Felix Lytton?" Winkes asked.

"Yes. He left me an inheritance when he died recently, enabling me to retire."

"You knew him well?"

"He was a lifelong friend. We went to college together."

"He was also a client of Cecil Banes."

"Yes, he was," Bruno said.

"Banes also arranged your inheritance, but was not Mr. Lytton's official executor."

"I wouldn't know about that," Bruno said, reminding himself that these cops had nothing on him, and would never have anything. "I think that was the name on some of the documents at my bank. Who is the official executor?"

"Banes's secretary," Dillard said, "swears that Mr. Banes was in his office when you left, that she was there for the rest of the day, and that he was gone when she went in with a letter for him to sign."

"Did you look under the desk?" Bruno asked, smiling.

The two cops did not react.

"So he gave her the slip," Bruno added. "What other explanation could there be?"

"She swears," Winkes said, "that she heard a thud in the office and some heavy breathing."

"A *thud?*" Bruno asked, saying the word as if it were an insult. "What would I know about a *thud?*"

"A paperweight and the desk pad blotter paper are missing from the desk."

"A paperweight?" Bruno asked mockingly. "Blotting paper?"

"She has a good eye," Winkes said.

"I hope they're both good," Bruno said.

The cops were silent at his joke.

"I truly do not understand," Bruno said, pulling himself together. "Why ask me?"

"So how did you and he get out of there?" Dillard asked.

"After you traded blows," Winkes added.

"What?" Bruno asked, pitching his voice higher to sound surprised. It would be suspicious not to react, to give the impression of preparedness. "Of course. After we traded blows. Are you serious?"

Dillard said, "Did you bring him drugs?"

Bruno smiled. "Oh, sure, I put him in my pocket and left. She saw me go out, right, but didn't look in my pockets?"

The cops did not react to this joke either, and Bruno began to feel that he was making them unnecessarily suspicious. Not that it could lead them anywhere.

"May we look around?" Winkes asked.

"Sure," Bruno said.

"Just sit down on the sofa and be quiet," Dillard said calmly.

As they searched the apartment, Dillard called out, "He *had* to have sneaked past the secretary, and you were the last to see him. Where did he go?"

"I left him there," Bruno said truthfully, realizing that they were going to dig harder, maybe even accuse him. Circumstantial evidence. People could get mighty sure of suspicions they couldn't prove. It was the kind of world in which the unbelievable and unprovable could nevertheless be true. Frustration only encouraged people to jump to conclusions, to look harder, even get vindictive after they had convicted the innocent.

The detectives opened drawers and left them open, rummaged around in the bedroom closet and looked under the bed. Bruno began to feel insulted as he realized that they had formed a low opinion of him—low enough to make them feel secure in ordering him about and messing up his apartment without even the threat of a warrant.

"Be neat!" Bruno called out. "My mother taught me to be neat."

After a while they came back into the living room, and Dillard said, "Please remain available in case we need you. Don't leave town for a while."

Bruno hesitated, not sure of what to do. Disabling two men would be difficult. All he had, as Felix had warned him, was a way to get rid of bodies, but it needed the element of surprise. He stood up, and the two cops tensed, as if they knew that he was a threat.

Let them go, he told himself, thinking of the aluminum bat in the front closet.

The two detectives watched him closely.

"Anything else?" he asked, smiling.

"I guess not," said Dillard.

"Sorry I can't be of much help."

"I guess you can't," Winkes said as if he was sure that Bruno could.

The two detectives turned away and moved toward the door. He followed, wondering how quickly he could open the closet door and bludgeon them with the bat. Not quickly enough. Both were probably armed. He might get one, but not the other.

"Thank you," Winkes said as they went out the front door, his politeness a reluctant offering to the god of covering-your-ass in case you've made a mistake.

Bruno was sweating by the time he closed the door and threw

the deadbolt. Suddenly feeling very tired, he staggered to the sofa and sat down.

Someone was pounding on his door when he woke up and found himself still on the sofa. He struggled to his feet, peered at his watch, and saw that it was ten in the evening. What kind of exhaustion had made him sleep through the whole day? The visit from the police?

"Okay!" he cried as he staggered forward, "I'm coming."

He opened the door, expecting to see the two cops again, but saw Cecil Banes's secretary. She seemed to have been weeping.

"Oh, Mr. Willey," she said, "I'm so sorry to be here so late, but I have to talk to you. I found your address in Cecil's address file. You remember me, don't you? I'm Eleanor Jones, Mr. Banes's secretary."

"What is it?" Bruno demanded, still sleepy.

Her eyes fixed on him with panic. "Oh, Mr. Willey, you must tell me where the love of my life has gone. Please!" She grabbed his right wrist and held on tightly. Her mouth opened wide as she spoke, and Bruno imagined that she would pull him to her and bite his head off like some female praying mantis if he didn't let her in.

"I have no idea of what you're talking about," he said calmly, moving back and taking her inside as she held on.

She let him go. Her red hair was disheveled and the bright green seemed to have faded from her eyes. She wore a tweed business suit, and now seemed older than her mid-thirties. Still, she was quite appealing in her tearful state.

"You really don't know?" she asked.

"No, I don't," he said, reaching to shut the door.

"You wouldn't tell me if you did, would you," she said as the door closed behind her.

He turned and looked at her carefully. People sensed things they couldn't prove and were sometimes right. She was probably convinced that he knew what she wanted to know. Now she would be struggling between the impulse to plead with him or accuse him, wondering which was the better way to get him to tell her where to find her lover.

She looked down at the floor and said, "I'll . . . satisfy you if you tell me where to find him." She looked up at him, and her submissiveness was even more appealing. He toyed with the prospect of having her; after all, she wasn't going to get anything more from the lawyer, and sex with a stranger might sidetrack her distress. "I'll do . . . whatever you like," she added with difficulty.

"Don't demean yourself," Bruno said, moved by her vulnerability. "I'll show you where he went."

She looked up at him as her face brightened with hope, and Bruno knew suddenly that she would be too much of a risk to let go; her suspicion would only grow and fixate on him. She would never stop. One fine day she might get lucky, or he might make a mistake, unlikely as it seemed. In any case, he realized that she was just beginning a time of great unhappiness and instability, from which he could save her, short of bringing back the lawyer.

He opened the pocket behind her, then stepped forward and took her in his arms. She rested her head on his shoulder.

"Thank you," she whispered. "You don't know what this means to me. I know he was planning to leave, and now he'll have to take me with him."

"I think he might have been planning to send for you," Bruno said, "after . . . he was settled."

She looked up into his face. "You know that? You really know that—you *really* do!" Her sudden joy was overpowering, throwing a renewed youthfulness into her face. Bruno hesitated, surprised by his own attraction to her and shamed by his weakness.

He pushed her away. Her hands let go of him as her butt went in and she folded in half with a scream—and the darkness took her. Too bad, Bruno lamented for a moment, that she couldn't have shared the same pocket with the love of her life. Then he considered what she had so briefly deposited in him, but there was nothing left of his concern for her except a vague uneasiness.

He went to bed. She came to his door several times that night, and each encounter was the same.

Late the next morning there was another knock on his door. He got out of bed, glad to escape the anxiety of his sleep, and hurried to see who was knocking.

"Police," said a male voice.

Bruno opened the door.

"I'm police captain Ernest Buck."

"What is it?"

"May I ask you a question?"

"Sure, come in," Bruno said, thinking it might be safer to talk to him. One man he might be able to handle, if need be.

The captain entered, closed the door behind him, and said,

"Two detectives who work for me were sent to see you yesterday."

"Sure," Bruno said, "I couldn't help them much."

"They felt that you hadn't told them everything you knew," said the captain. "Can you tell me anything else? I mean, maybe you've recalled something else."

"Well, no," Bruno said, wondering if the captain had parked downstairs, alone or with a fellow officer. "How would I know?"

"What do you mean?"

Bruno shrugged. "I told them what I knew."

Captain Buck scratched the back of his head. "Are you sure?" He smiled. "People do remember things later."

"Yes," Bruno said. "I mean I told everything I knew, and I haven't recalled anything since."

The captain looked at him and knew a wall when he saw one, if not a dead end. "Yeah, right," he said. "Thanks for your time. Sorry to wake you up." He gave the living room a good look, then went to the door.

"By the way," he continued, turning back to Bruno, "the super said there was some shouting here last night. A woman. Did you have a visitor?"

Bruno shrugged. "Not that I know of."

"You were asleep?"

"Yes."

"And you didn't hear a thing?"

"I sleep deep," Bruno said, "but maybe I cried out."

He would not have to pocket the captain; that would only bring around another busybody. Best to let it go.

"Thanks," said the captain.

Worthier enemies awaited, Bruno thought as he closed the door. He didn't need any new foes. He remembered when as a small boy he had killed wasps above his grandmother's patio, where they had been building nests in the overhang. He had swatted them one by one as they came and went for weeks on end, killing some, chasing others away; and one day there were no more; the swarm had gotten the message and had left the danger zone—and all without his using any chemicals. He had been proud of not using harmful poisons. After all, he was not a killer. Killing had to have reasons behind it to make it more than official murder, whether of insects or human beings, or even cats and dogs. He felt good about sparing the three policemen. Power required prudent use.

Bruno kept expecting new communications from Felix, even

though Cecil Banes was no longer around to send them. It just seemed to Bruno that Felix was not quite done with him. Their collaboration, though it had been just about perfect in every expected way, still seemed insufficient because it had so imperfectly convinced him to give up the revenge he had so wanted to have on his old rival. But wishes traditionally came wrapped with conditions, so he had increasingly accepted the fact that the skill had been given to him with a price, and a reasonable one at that, soberly considered; merely an annoying one.

Other enemies waited, tyrannizing whole continents of his mind, requiring regime changes as soon as possible. Yet Bruno feared to come to the end of his enemies, because that would force him to face the unfinished business of the now forever unreachable Felix, irritatingly safe on the far side of death. Even though he was rotting in his grave, Felix held Bruno close with the squirrel cage of temptations that he had bequeathed to the victim of his youth.

Bruno sometimes doubted that Felix was dead, despite all official notices. Would digging up a body quiet that doubt? Felix had been officially cremated, and Bruno had not been asked to the funeral service.

Maybe it was time to see June, Bruno thought. He had avoided thinking about his lost wife after Felix's death, consoling himself with how much she had probably suffered over Felix's infidelities and divorces these last three decades. That and the lost vanities of age would have tormented her more than enough. In fact, one might say that Felix had left both of them well fixed. One might even say that it had been a kind of reparation, if one added in his dying. As Bruno thought about June now, he compared past and present states, his own and hers, his past feelings with what should have been their continuing, unstifled pain, and was startled suddenly; his feelings seemed to belong to someone else.

Curiosity rather than immediate revenge now led Bruno to the decision to go see June. He went for a long walk in the park, trying to bring back his feelings about her. She had been disloyal to him right from the start of their marriage. Felix and he had long since parted company, but it was clear from later events that she had started seeing him soon after reading about him in the paper.

Quite simply, she had gone to Felix, told him that she was friends with his old college buddy Bruno, and soon after had served her husband of six weeks with annulment papers from Felix's powerhouse attorneys. Bruno Willey had been only a steppingstone to Felix Lytton. Bruno had not contested his abandonment. There was nothing to divide except his tears, which he should have had bottled and sent to her. There had been so little time, so little between them to remember . . .

Bruno remembered her picture in the paper, announcing their marriage. Other marriage notices ran pictures of the man and the woman; but June had gone for the traditional woman alone. This had always struck Bruno as silly, suggesting parthenogenetic reproduction without need of a male.

A wall had always stood between him and his past feelings about Felix and June, built, he realized, by his pride.

"What's the sexually most important part of a woman?" Felix had said just before June had gone to him.

"I'm sure you'll tell me," Bruno recalled saying, foolishly happy with his bride.

"The face," Felix had said.

"The face?"

"The look in her face when she tells you she wants you, that she's accepted that it's going to happen."

"No matter how she looks?" Bruno had asked with a laugh.

"Doesn't matter, my friend. If she wants you, you're a goner. It's the enthusiasm in their faces that gets you, when that previous dubious look turns into acceptance. Even the great beauties can't match that if they're cold inside."

Had June given Felix that look as he swam inside her? Bruno had no memory of it for himself from their private moments. Her cold beauty had been enough for him.

Bruno stopped, looked around the darkened park and took a deep breath of the fresh night air. There was no way to change the past; even doing something in the hope of redress would not change it; it would only add more past to the fleeing present. He hung there, in a moment that seemed to have stopped, thinking that he was about to learn something new, but it didn't seem to matter.

"Use it or lose it," Felix had told him about the skill. "That's all there is to it. It will die if you neglect it. Believe me, I was close to losing it. Be afraid of losing it."

Bruno remembered how Felix had allowed him to hang around with him in college. Felix knew things and people, and Bruno had told himself that he might benefit from being around with him. Felix might hand him something one day. But Felix had always taken away, humiliating him. "Bruno—what are you doing here?" he had demanded of him one day. "Did I send you an invite to this party?" Felix had laughed at him. "Can't you see there's no girl here that would want you?" he had shouted at him, even though he had been invited—to be humiliated, of course.

Well, Felix had finally given him something.

"Your money, man," a voice said from behind him. "Don't look around, just drop the fuckin' wallet and keep on going."

Confidence rushed up out of Bruno, cold and pure and controlled. He reached with a steady hand into his back pocket, took out his wallet and whirled around to face the mugger.

A young man stood before him, empty handed.

Bruno put away his wallet and opened a pocket between them, two feet high; then, as the man tried to make sense of what he was seeing, Bruno came around quickly and grabbed him by his neck.

"Shit!" cried the young man.

With strength that surprised him, Bruno shoved him down into the darkness like a bag of leaves into an incinerator.

"I can't see!" came a cry from the fading pit.

"Teach you to bluff!" Bruno shouted, happy with the ease of his own action.

"Hey there—stop!" a male voice called to him as the pocket faded away.

He turned his head and saw a dark figure pass under one of the park lights. A policeman hurried toward him.

Bruno took a deep breath.

"I heard shouts," said the cop.

Bruno said, "So did I. Somewhere up ahead there."

The cop looked at him with suspicion. "Show me some ID."

Bruno reached into his back pocket, pulled out his wallet, and opened it to his driver's license. The cop took the wallet, squinted at the document, handed it back, then said, "I could swear you weren't alone as I came up. There was something at your feet there." He looked down, then tried to peer around Bruno.

"I'm quite alone," Bruno said, stepping to one side.

The cop tensed, then looked directly at him. "What are you doing here?"

"Taking a walk," Bruno said.

"At two in the morning?"

"That late? I'd better get home."

"I dunno," the cop said suddenly. "Maybe I'd better take you in and check you out."

On what charge, Bruno wanted to say. But it wouldn't amount to much, Bruno's rational self told him, since they had nothing on him, not even a traffic ticket.

"Come on, buddy," the cop said.

"You're wasting my time and yours," Bruno said softly.

"Better safe than sorry," said the cop, turning away. "Come along, now."

Bruno followed him. As the cop glanced back, Bruno opened a pocket ahead of him, and the cop walked into it.

"Ahh!" cried the officer and tumbled over. Bruno grabbed his legs and finished the job. There was just no way the cop could have expected anything to appear in front of him. Felix had taught him well in the ways of misdirection.

"Remember," Felix had said several times, "that all you really have is a way to dispose of bodies. You must never be seen doing it. Distraction must become your art. Practice it well."

As Bruno walked home, he imagined the officer feeling his way around in the pocket, uncomprehending of what had happened to him.

Bruno slept well that day, and was ready to face June that evening.

"Bruno!" June cried out in her usual musical way, unchanged by the decades. "How *nice* of you to come by." He almost expected Felix to come up grinning behind her, as if all their lives had been a practical joke and it was now time to have a good laugh about it.

He had driven to the estate without calling first, expecting to perhaps be turned away by the servants, but the main gate had been open, so he had gone in and parked by the front entrance to the great house left to her by Felix after their divorce.

She had come to the door alone, dressed in elegant black pants and a white blouse that went well with her graying shoulder-length hair. Her curves, padded or not, seemed intact and attractive; her throat was pale and vulnerable, young from the work done on it.

"Come in, come in," she sang with the same voice that had once beguiled him. There was no fear or suspicion in her face. Had she somehow expected him—or just didn't remember?

Bruno stepped inside, wondering how long his hatred, which still seemed to belong to someone else, would obey him.

A man came up behind her, and Bruno tensed at the impossible sight of Felix's face.

He closed his eyes and felt dizzy. Felix had set a trap for him. Bruno opened his eyes—

—and a closer look revealed someone else.

"Are you unwell?" the man asked.

"Yes—yes, I'm fine," Bruno said, annoyed by his mistake.

"This is Henry," June said, seemingly oblivious to his distress. "Felix's first cousin."

"We've never met, have we?" Henry asked as he stepped forward and offered his hand.

"Henry and I are engaged," June sang.

She had never been a woman to remain alone, Bruno's distant self thought bitterly as he shook hands with the man.

The whole evening was sickly sweet. June served tea and pie, and lamented Felix's departure from the good life they had enjoyed together. She made no mention of his other wives. Henry grinned, oddly caricaturing Felix's face, and Bruno imagined that his old enemy was mocking him from the grave.

But he is gone, Bruno told himself. At least I know that for a fact now.

As they sat in the over-decorated, over-upholstered living room of bright, flowery patterns and light blue walls that seemed like vertical skies, June smiled at Bruno as if she thought him a hapless idiot for having let her go to Felix, and he felt contempt for the effectiveness of the come hither look that she now bestowed on Henry. Bruno gazed directly at her once or twice, and saw a stranger. There was no spark in her eyes, no warmth at all, only the discipline of correct behavior gazing back at him—the punishment meted out to the loser. How easily he could reach out, Bruno thought, and change it all.

"Well!" June exclaimed as he was leaving. "Now we've broken the ice."

Careful you don't fall through it and drown, Bruno thought as he went out, hating June with his other self, into the night. Halfway to his car, his distant self seemed to be weeping over his losses, baffling him with its uncontrollable weakness.

"Come back soon!" Henry called after him.

At his car he looked back, lost to himself, and saw them standing in the open doorway like two plastic dolls, frozen in their farewell.

During the next week, Bruno imagined that he was running out of enemies, and not getting to the right ones. They were all out of air in the pockets he had filled, unbreathing by now in their claustrophobic bits of infolding darkness, rotting as they drifted somewhere in the cosmic scheme of things that now served him only grudgingly.

One day soon, he told himself, I might get free of the past's wrongs, and even be able to afford becoming what might be called a good man. It was a state to ponder, as he considered a world where people had no control over themselves as slaves to unchosen impulses. The practice of pocketing had perhaps brought him too much control of himself, making him hold back from what was truly possible. Felix had taught him to fear the loss of the skill, or its exposure, but these cautions always seemed to be hiding something.

Among potential candidates for justice who now came to mind, there was a portly, unwilling candidate for retirement who rarely filled the mailboxes in the apartment building before five, and often long after dark. It was well known that the mail carrier spent much of the day in the doughnut, deli, or fast food shops, neglecting his delivery route until the last hours of the workday. Bruno's complaints, even with attached schedules of lost, late, rain soaked, or misdelivered mail, failed to move the carrier's supervisors. Too many appeal procedures were open to a postal employee, and he did deserve his retirement, by the rules, after all. No one wanted to beat up on an old man who lived with his dying mother, even though he probably tore up select pieces of mail belonging to customers who complained, both outgoing and incoming. Sometimes his local bosses even lied for him by telling callers that they'd had no mail that day. The regime of intimidation enforced by the carrier was complete; nothing could be proved easily against him.

He just couldn't afford to retire, he said. The pension would force him into what he regarded as poverty.

Bruno went down to the lobby and waited just inside the inner door. He peered through the glass and ironworks for fifteen minutes. Finally, as the evening lights went on, the fat postman opened the outer door, entered the marbled foyer, and struggled up the three steps to the shining wall of mailboxes. Bruno waited until he had unlocked the big access panel and deposited all the mail in the brass boxes.

"Good evening," Bruno said as he opened the inner door and stepped into the foyer. The door clicked shut behind him.

The postman nodded, dropped his heavy bag with a sigh, then slowly closed the heavy brass panel and locked it with his key.

"I've got diabetes," he said softly without looking at Bruno, as if he were continuing a conversation. Even when he was silent he seemed to be complaining.

"Sorry to hear it," Bruno said, and opened a pocket at the bottom of the three steps.

The outer door rattled.

It had stuck.

The postman turned his head and saw the strangeness below him.

Bruno gave him a quick shove. The postman cried out and plunged head first into the pocket. His feet went up as his weight did most of the work, and he slid away down into the dark. Bruno grabbed the mailbag off the floor and tossed it in after him.

The front door rattled insistently. A pizza delivery boy burst in just as the pocket faded. He stopped. Bruno stared at him, recognizing his freckled face and badly chopped brown hair. The boy stood still, puzzled by what he had glimpsed.

"Is that for me?" Bruno asked to distract him.

"Uh, double pepperoni?" the boy asked.

"Right. How much?"

"Ten ninety-nine," said the boy, handing the pizza up to him.

Bruno took out his wallet, dropped twelve dollars on top of the box, then took it with both hands as the boy swept up the bills.

"Thanks," the boy said uneasily. "You're in 3E, right?" he asked uncertainly, putting away the money.

"Right." Bruno grimaced with indecision.

The boy looked up at him with suspicion, then smiled with an angelic charm.

"You okay, mister?" he asked.

Bruno nodded.

As the boy went out the door, Bruno put the hot pizza box down on the marble steps and went to his mailbox. He opened it with his key, took out the single envelope, and stared at it for a long time.

It was from June.

He tore it open and read the hand-printed block letters:

Dear Bruno—

You are invited to a pre-wedding ball next Thursday. Black tie. RSVP by phone voice-mail.

Then handwritten: *Henry and I were delighted to see you the other evening. As time goes on, we must learn to treasure old friends. June*

Bruno laughed, but his laughter was silenced by resentment at how she had probably revised the history of their enmities. Maybe she had completely forgotten.

He savored the aroma as he picked up the pizza box, let himself back in with his key, and took the elevator up to his apartment.

As he ate the pizza at the small table in his kitchen alcove, he realized what was wrong. He *had* been waiting too long, doing too much of Felix's business, and had taken out his frustration on the postman. The pizza delivery boy would have been another useless exertion. And there was something suspiciously wrong with the way Felix had prattled about the loss of feeling to an iron self-control. What was the good of that? One might avoid getting caught, but at the cost of all satisfaction.

Control, yes; but no more stand-ins, no more holding back, he told himself as his rage reasserted itself; his real targets awaited, and he should feel for them.

The great house was a titanic cake sparkling with stars. Luxury cars lined the long, snaking driveway out to the front gate. Several were parked on the grass in a hedged area near the house, looking like dark chocolates in a giant's box, with one piece eaten. Bruno parked his Toyota in that space, with room to spare.

His rented tuxedo fit comfortably, he noted again as he got out of the car, and he now felt certain about why he was here. He stared at the illuminated house, watching the shadows in the great windows. The ants had gotten inside the cake. He wondered whether June was too far gone to appreciate anything he might exact from her; Henry wasn't much of an enemy—just another parasite, but he would do because he wore Felix's face. Some of the guests might be able to rise to the status of instant enemy, but he doubted that he would have time to pick up enough about any of them to be provoked. With any luck it would be as if he were going to a masked ball, perhaps never even to be noticed by most of the guests, much less unmasked.

A wondrous waltz from another age was playing as he walked up to the open door and stepped inside. He surrendered his coat to an aging, happy-faced butler, and was shown into the main ballroom, where slow-moving couples swirled around on the polished floor under the bright, glaring galaxies of chandeliers. The very air was whirling, space itself was spinning, distending and contracting to accommodate the turning human bodies.

Bruno stood dazzled and loose-limbed, suddenly enjoying a glow that had eluded him for many years. My great enemy is dead, he told himself once more. Maybe I can begin again, he mused forgivingly, and be ruled by what my kind call goodness. The beauty of the music soothed him, and he imagined that a true use of power would be to kill sparsely, control a lot; decide the fates, make the sisters weave for him. His spring of well-being was full, its energy waiting to be expended. He was inside the wedding cake with the ants, looking around for the plastic bride and groom.

"Bruno!" June cried out as she came up at his right. She wore a long, low cut black dress. "How wonderful of you to come!"

The waltz swayed with her words, and her bare arms and shoulders reached out to him. "June, June," a regretful voice whispered to him. He leaned down and kissed his long lost wife on the cheek, and she was no longer a stranger as her eyes awakened to a new recognition of him. Henry gave him a wave from a nearby table, looking even more like Felix. Ages had passed and they were all here, breathing an idiotic, amnesiac happiness that flowed from the syrupy sweet waltz. He had stepped into the ancient sheepdom of the aristocracies, whose wealth commanded vast armies of empire, gathering ever more treasure, and whose flowers swayed in halls like this one to concentrate and ensure the genetics of future power. Why had they asked him here, he wondered. What did they expect him to contribute? They had no idea of him or of what he could do to them.

"Dance with me, Bruno!" June shouted in his ear, and he recalled a youthful Felix teaching them the steps.

Her eyes sparkled and flirted with him as Bruno took her arm and drew her onto the dance floor. She slipped into his embrace and swayed into the steps, and silk uncoiled from an infinite bolt of memory within him. He glimpsed Henry beaming at them from his table, nodding his head in approval. It was an enigma, this flow of energy in his muscles, as if it were streaming into him from the fire of the stellar chandeliers. The polished, black floor reflected the fierce lights, creating an upside-down universe of dancers who perfectly matched their steps to their doubles.

The survival of Felix's face, in his cousin Henry, had little of Felix beyond the surface resemblance. Henry was a much lesser Felix, like Strauss's third-best waltz; or maybe Henry was something like Johann the Younger to Felix's Johann the Elder, if that wasn't giving Henry too much credit.

Bruno had no idea of which Strauss waltz was playing, and didn't much care as he spun June to the edge of the great floor. Suddenly, as they turned, Henry was there, grinning as he stepped forward to cut in.

Bruno slowed, suddenly drained of energy by Felix's ghost, realizing that his mind insisted on upgrading Henry into Felix, filling in the face that had escaped him into death.

"May I?" Henry asked.

Bruno paused and nodded, and that old day's pain crowded into him again, when Felix had taken June from him. "Oh, go away!" Felix had shouted at him in the park, where Bruno had followed them, desperate to make a fool of himself. "You see that she doesn't want you!" Felix had shouted in triumph, with June admiring him as if he were Zeus hurling thunderbolts, without one grimace of pity for her discarded husband.

Bruno had made a fool of himself again at Felix's door. And at her door. And repeatedly, until he had reached the abyss and stepped off into the choking darkness . . .

Now, as Henry whirled June away, Bruno noted with envy that this man was a superior dancer, almost as good as Felix had been. Henry and June were two bright planets, locked in each other's embrace, free of any sun, dancing among the stars. And the gnawing was in him again, released from the prison of the past. Bruno felt it stretch within himself, admiring the brute. It was his beast, his strength, and nothing could wish it away.

The music stopped. The galaxy of couples froze in their whirl and let go of each other. June was out of breath as she smiled and made off toward the powder room. Conversation filled the ballroom, replacing the music with a poetic chaos of hissing whispers, laughter, and broken lines. The orchestra, Bruno saw, was taking a break, starving his beast's vitality, and he would have to do something to keep it alive.

Henry wandered over to the big French doors, opened one, and stepped onto the terrace. Bruno slipped out after him, breathing deeply, as if his heart would burst, and the world fell away from the terrace into a glittering city of scattered gems that had spilled out from the jewel box of the house.

Bruno stopped.

The dark figure before him stood as if pasted against the view.

"Felix?" Bruno asked, thinking for a moment that he might unmask his old enemy, that against all reason Felix was wearing new flesh.

Henry smiled as he turned to face him. "I got that a lot even before his death. There is a resemblance, isn't there?" His smile widened, open and trusting, as if Felix was mocking him through the shell of his younger cousin.

A cool breeze touched Bruno's face as he opened the darkness at Henry's back.

"Wonderful evening," Henry said, taking a deep breath, and it was too much for Bruno to bear—the perfection of his own power and oblivious beauty of the setting.

Bruno stepped forward and shot his knee into Henry's crotch, then grabbed him by the shoulders and held him, watching as pain distorted his darkened face and wishing that it might have been Felix; then he pushed him back onto the lip of the open pocket. Henry sat there for a moment, perhaps thinking that he had landed on a bench, then looked up with a horrified *Why?* on his face as Bruno shoved him over with both hands and closed the pocket.

A woman screamed behind him.

"You devil!" June shouted as he turned to face her. She rushed forward. "What have you done with him?" she shrieked, leaning down to search the terrace as if Henry had somehow become too small to see.

She straightened up and turned back to Bruno, looked around him frantically, then gazed up into his eyes as if she knew that he was responsible for whatever had happened.

"Where is he!" she shouted as he imagined her with Felix and with Henry, pliant and accepting as she opened her body in return for a toy house and a bank account.

"What . . . do you mean?" he answered, content that she was hurting.

June looked left and right, rooted by fright.

"I'm alone," Bruno said, gazing at her with childlike innocence.

"What have you done to him?" she demanded in a hoarse voice.

"You'll never see him again," Bruno said softly.

"What?" She clutched at her forehead and swayed, as if about to collapse.

"Didn't he sign enough papers to take care of you?" Bruno asked coldly.

"Where is he?" she mumbled.

Bruno saw her confusion, and wanted to laugh, but it seemed unnecessary. "We're alone," he said. "It's a beautiful evening."

"What? You said I'd never see him again."

"I said nothing of the kind."

"What?" she asked, her voice breaking. "I heard you . . ." She was unsure now whether she had seen or heard anything.

"June, what is it?" Bruno asked sweetly.

"What have you done with him?" she demanded, perhaps trying to recover from the fear that she was hallucinating.

"He's in my pocket," he said.

"What!" she shouted, grimacing; but she looked at his tuxedo pockets, suffering, maybe wondering at her sanity. He stared down at her, smiling. Abruptly, she turned and went back into the ball-room. It would confuse the police, if she should call them.

After what seemed only a minute or two June came back out. She held a large automatic with both hands, pointing it at him as she came closer.

"What have you done!" she shrieked.

Bruno saw that there were several couples behind her now, hypnotized by the sight of their armed hostess. Others crowded the doorway, peering out.

Inside, the "Blue Danube" made a perfect entrance, and seemed to hang on its opening bars—then swelled and swayed relentlessly in all directions, an endless torrent of willful sound, unintelligible, asserting no content beyond the vitality passed on to human ingenuity by nature's mad survivalist dance.

"Bring him back!" June cried. The big gun shook in her hands and seemed about to break her aging, porcelain fingers.

"Gentlemen, ladies!" Bruno called out to the growing crowd behind her. "Your hostess is having a nervous breakdown. Please call an ambulance right away!"

The gun flashed as it fired. The bullet grazed his temple, dizzying him. He staggered back. June stepped toward him, vital and determined to finish the job as she pointed the gun into his face.

"The next one will kill you," she cried over the screams of retreating guests, "if you don't bring . . . Henry . . . back—right now!"

Her eyes were wild, glaring. Had she almost called her lover Felix? Blood ran down Bruno's left cheek. He touched the wound and looked at the dark blood on his fingertips, then noted that the guests had fled and he was alone with June again.

She tried to steady the gun. He raised his hand, feeling some rage but no fear as she fired again, missed, and dropped the gun in surprise. He opened a pocket behind her, then came forward before she could pick up the gun, grabbed her by the middle and held her close.

"Swine!" she cried as she looked into his eyes.

He looked back in wonder, seeking what had never been there for him.

She began to struggle with unusual strength, and he wondered if the pull of her muscles might break her bones. Her body was a living spring, wound up into a tight spiral that could not possibly hold its shape, and would uncoil with great force if he let her go. He manipulated her body and she pushed back, as if they were engaged in a mutual form of exercise. She was breathing hard, then stopped struggling and hid her face in his shoulder.

"Bruno," she whispered, "if you ever truly loved me, stop, bring back Henry." The plea seemed to come to him on a strange channel, inviting him to give up himself and do as she asked.

"Here's for everything," he said with a strange detachment as he gut-punched her, and watched her suck in air, then pushed her toward the darkness. She stumbled as she held on to him and he almost fell in after her.

"Holy shit!" a drunken man exclaimed from the doorway.

Bruno closed the pocket and lurched toward the man, opening a pocket next to him. He shoved him over the low lip head first and closed it up.

Bruno stood still, listening to the "Blue Danube" playing blithely on, sublime, tenderly edged, summoning an invulnerable order of grace. The music slipped through him, then faltered as he wandered back through the open doors into the bright ballroom.

The center of the floor was empty. Guests stood looking at him fearfully from the edges. The confused musicians played on as if accompanying a masque.

He drifted toward the center, raising his arms. "She shot me!" he cried. His words echoed. The chandeliers tinkled. A trembling silence of eyes stood around, and he felt weak. His vision flared, and what seemed to be black bolts of lightning stabbed across the red field.

Somewhere in the distance almost beyond his hearing, string instruments rumbled at their lowest register, as if the stumbling waltz was trying to regain its footing, but managed only to veer into a parody of itself. Whispers shot through him, as if he was being stalked by predators drawn to the blaring scraps of the insane waltz that now hated the world. He glimpsed dark objects in his side vision, but they slipped from his sight when he fixed on them. June's guests stared at him, as if expecting him to perform an obscene miracle.

He was being circled by things dead and invisible. A tide pulled at his body.

"What's wrong with him?" asked a distant voice.

He stood in the eye of a storm that threatened to veer off center and tear him apart. The smallest move by him would hurl him out into its ripping arms.

His vision blurred. He saw strange, irregular black shapes circling him, and realized after a moment that they were black pockets, still linked to him, orbiting his awareness.

His vision cleared, revealing more than a hundred circling him. The remaining guests screamed and fled from the ballroom. The pockets reshaped themselves, as if struggling to decide what to wear to the ball.

But there were too many!

They can't all be mine, Bruno told himself. He sat down on the floor and covered his face, hoping to cut their ties to him.

They're not mine, he said into himself, and strained to remember how many he had made.

Felix's ex-wife and her two boys. No choice there; Felix had given him the skill, and their deaths had been part of the bargain. He could not have risked Felix somehow taking the skill away, or exacting some form of pre-arranged retribution for not carrying out his last wishes.

Larry Braddock had been a necessity.

Jean Scheler had been deserving.

Cecil Banes. Again, Felix's wishes could not have been refused. Nothing personal there.

Winkes and Dillard? Two cops meddling in his affairs impersonally . . . but he had let them go!

Cecil Banes's secretary. Who knew! Her misery was over. He didn't remember her name.

The mugger. Risks of his trade.

The nameless cop. Again, danger went with his job. The mugger might have killed him. Same difference.

The mailman had been a luxury. But a new carrier might bring the mail on time, and that would benefit more people than one death might hurt, right?

The pizza boy? Had he pocketed him? Bruno couldn't remember him or the pizza.

There was someone he had forgotten. Oh, yes, Al the busybody super, so easily replaced by the money that owned him. How could anyone blame him for Al, the thief and voyeur?

Henry and June? Long awaited justice. No choice. The right, unfeeling thing to do.

The drunk had simply been in the way, Bruno told himself. Great power must accept collateral damage.

Thirteen or fourteen . . .

He had imagined that there had been fewer.

But when he uncovered his face, the black swirl was still around him, drifting in closer.

Still too many!

They're not mine! Somehow he had imagined that by counting up his own he might make the extras go away.

"Leave me alone!" he cried out.

The black shells were sinking to the shiny dance floor now, and still slowing, like a carousel breaking up. One by one the great slugs slid onto the surface and squealed to a stop, some hitting one another with a sickening squish.

He sat there, staring at the collection of black, shiny bladders. The ballroom was empty. Sirens wailed in the distance.

He stood up—

—and almost fell over from dizziness.

Above him were several more blisters, circling quickly, impatient to land.

And he knew why there were too many!

Felix had willed all *his* pockets to him.

A terrible sum added itself up around him, as his own lesser numbers joined the fleet on the floor.

This was Felix's revenge.

Fatigue lifted from Bruno's body, and he knew that these pockets had always been with him—Felix's and his own. They had been his burden wherever he went, tiring him toward this moment, when he could no longer resist their arrival. He wondered if he could still send them away, but that, he knew, would only secrete them behind yet another debilitating veil.

It struck him suddenly that there was no afterlife, because if there was then Felix's pockets would have followed *him*. Felix's skill had enabled him to bequeath them when he died, and presumably the pockets would not follow the truly dead.

A popping noise burst in his ears.

Then another.

A smell clogged his nostrils.

He gagged and hurled as he got up and staggered between the bursting bladders. One set off the next in a seeming chain reaction. Oozing liquids flowed onto the smooth floor. He stopped to avoid slipping in the sticky liquid.

He saw a face in the slime, eyes bulging at infinities.

The figures were all dead, decomposing into a bony soup as they were whelped back into the world. Felix's dead preserves—and Bruno's own.

A pocket burst as he stepped over it, covering him with its adhesive decay. He looked down and was unable to identify the victim as his own or Felix's.

Mine shouldn't be so far gone, he told himself.

The out-of-tune waltz strained onward somewhere without its musicians, its notes jumbling, then crashed into a pile of bright noises that sought silence as if in shame. It stirred again for a moment, a proud but mortally wounded animal, then settled into stillness.

Bruno looked around and saw with dismay that pockets were still circling him, crashing into those on the floor.

He covered his face.

"Felix!" he cried to his dead foe. "Take them away!"

Two pockets exploded nearby, spilling their innards. His eyes fixed on some potato chip wrappers, coffee grounds, teabags, banana peels, fishbones, shrimp shells, onion scraps, and pizza bits. He recognized his own life's garbage, and for a moment expected to see what was left of Al the superintendent in the mixture that also included bottles, foil, beer cans, plastic wrappings, and crushed milk containers. The garbage and recyclables, he realized, were unlawfully together, but separate from the human bodies. Al had a pocket of his own, awaiting arrival or already somewhere else on the dance floor. If he had put out his garbage and recyclables according to the rules, they wouldn't be here now, Bruno told himself, trying but unable to laugh.

Another pocket burst near him, a few feet above the floor, and Bruno knew at once from the crashing sounds that this was his museum of dead computer monitors, sluggish keyboards, cardboard boxes, the ink-jet printer that he had come to hate, the old electric typewriter, motherboards and crashed hard drives, all come back to him. At least there were no biological materials—no decomposition, no slime, just shattering metal and glass and snaking cables.

"You've had your fun!" he cried. "Take them back!"

But Felix was dust somewhere, beyond reassembly in his fortress outside the life of flesh.

"Felix!" Bruno cried in despair, and hung in the silence, picturing, for no reason at all, Al's bags of meat waiting foolishly to be stolen from his basement entrance.

"I'm quite dead," Felix said to him. "But I've left this message in your head."

"Help me," Bruno asked, grateful to hear his voice.

"You always felt too much," Felix said. "Much too much."

He was right, Bruno thought, his self-control against sympathy had never been perfect. Feelings like fleas had attacked him through the cracks.

"But now it's time," Felix said, "to let all your feelings expire."

"Expire?" Bruno asked. "But how?"

"Let in the flood," Felix said. "It will either destroy you or leave you invulnerable."

Felix was gone from Bruno's head, leaving him hanging in the silence.

Then, slowly, sympathies flooded into him, and it seemed that they had been hiding in the waltzes. Eleanor Jones, Banes's secretary, spoke her name to him again, hooking his feelings. Fish swam in his bowels. They came up and swam in the colloidal semi-liquid of his brain. The two young boys . . . the mailman . . . if only he had been able to leave them out . . .

Bruno dropped to his knees and wept at the filth and ruin around him, and wondered if this was Felix Lytton's revenge, which he had helped prepare for himself. He struggled against the river of sentiment suddenly flowing through him, drowning his reason. He shivered in the deluge, praying that it would wash him clean, as Felix had said, and drain away. Purgatory before heaven and forgiveness; hell if he couldn't be helped.

Then in a sudden, inexplicable calm he saw that something was moving near him. He looked more closely. Two human figures whimpered as they crawled toward each other out of their bladders.

Henry and June had not had time to die in their pockets. As he watched them, he saw that they knew each other's pitying cries.

They were going to live—and Felix's cousin would have her to himself! Almost as bad as losing her to Felix.

Pockets were popping more quickly now.

"No!" Bruno cried, and crawled toward the couple, struggling against his own warring feelings of fear and compassion, come now to trouble and tear him apart.

June saw him and screamed. Then she became quiet and stared at him like a she-wolf with teeth bared. He stopped before the assault of her eyes.

"Let us live!" she pleaded. "I know how much you were hurt." Her words forgave but her eyes did not soften, and her teeth waited.

"Beyond repair," Bruno growled back, fighting his own lament. His body shook and he collapsed onto his stomach.

"You do know," she asked softly, "that you are beyond hope?"

He raised himself up again on all fours, trying to regain his self-control.

"Well—don't you know!" she shouted, and he flinched at the pain she caused in him.

The hard, black floor pressed painfully against his knees. The ballroom around him seemed to be the aftermath of a horrifying meal, bloody and decaying after the departure of monstrously satisfied diners. Musical instruments lay on the bandstand, abandoned by the fleeing musicians, but he still heard the music somewhere far away, still distorted and hateful . . .

Rousing himself, Bruno raised his hand to strike June, to quiet his pain, to stop her from hurting him again.

"For God's sake, man!" Henry cried. "Don't you see? You're Felix's pawn!"

"You're doing his evil," June added weakly. "If you ever loved me . . ."

"Love's a lot of posturing," Bruno said, waving his hands. "A mess of sentimental play-acting."

"And what is this?" she asked.

He cried out with the hope of his power, "This is justice, revenge, strength—and wonder!" His old enemy had added to his might, and could not take it away. It was too late, Bruno thought, accepting himself. I have grown strong within myself. He would not cower before his enemies!

"Justice for whom?" June whispered.

Bruno laughed. "Why, for me. Not for you."

She asked, "Didn't you love me?"

Bruno said, "There are some people you want to fuck, and others you don't. It wears off."

"Finish it," Henry said from behind her, his face a bloody caricature of Felix's. "Drop us back into that black hell and be done!"

Which raised a crucial problem, Bruno thought. Satisfaction sang its song only when subjects were alive to appreciate their punishment and sing along. Of course, he wanted them dead; but it would be even more nourishing if they were dead and still able to suffer the fact of being dead, impossible as that might seem.

A great pity.

Felix! Bruno smiled at his old enemy's gift. A siren wailed somewhere like a lost demon. Standing up now on his knees, he looked around at all the ruptured pockets, more than a hundred of them, mostly inherited from Felix; his own number was inadequate, a pale shadow of possibility.

"Where's your humanity!" June cried. "Where's your pity?" She looked up at him with a critical intelligence he had never seen in her eyes. Her feelings came at him like claws, tearing at his earlier selves, none of which, happily, had ever been dominant. He glimpsed a distant, fleeing self who did not look back at him.

"You can't judge me," Bruno said, "I judge you. You want me to think and feel as you do. We start from different places."

"You're missing something," she said.

"I don't miss it," he said, glad of the soft, caring weakness of his sympathies, which would only make them so much easier to crush.

"Felix did this to you," she whispered.

"Yes, Felix did this all to me," Bruno repeated. "Thank you, Felix," he whispered.

"Why not join him? He's waiting for you."

"Waiting?" he asked, looking down at her. "What are you babbling?"

"Hasn't it occurred to you yet that he pocketed himself to escape death?"

"He was cremated!"

"Something was cremated," she said.

"So you say," Bruno said defiantly.

"We . . . Henry and I, heard his voice in the dark, when we were inside. The pockets have channels leading off."

"What!" Bruno cried out and sat back on his heels.

"Felix spoke," Henry added calmly. "He told us how he had achieved his own survival."

"You're lying," Bruno said, feeling weakness stalking him.

June hissed, "He'll tell you. Go ask him. You've been his fool, Bruno."

"Liar!" Bruno shouted. "What could he take from me? He gave me everything."

His delayed punishment, Bruno thought again, won't work on me, if that's what it is. I can resist, he told himself, searching for his strength.

"He *needs* you to bring him out," she said, "when it's time."

"Come out?" Bruno asked. "Time?"

"The police are coming," Henry added cheerfully, and giggled.

"They won't know what to hold me for," Bruno said.

Henry and June might as well return to the darkness, he told himself. They were too weak to resist him. He waved open a pocket just ahead of him on the floor, wondering what June had meant about bringing Felix out . . .

Henry and June rose suddenly to their feet and fell onto him, throwing him on his back and pinning him to the floor. June hooked his face with her fingernails. Henry crawled around to Bruno's feet, giggling more loudly now. June tore the skin down from Bruno's eyes, then bit his hand. He cried out as his feet were raised. June let go of him and helped Henry roll him over on his face.

They slid him around and forward on his chest—into the pocket. It was all too quick, and part of him was uncaring.

He went down into the blackness and hit with his left shoulder, rolling over in pain just in time to glimpse the opening close above him.

He lay there, stunned and unbelieving.

As his breathing slowed, and seemed to stop, in a silence so perfect that any sound would be a catastrophe.

He lay still, thoughtless, adrift . . .

After a while he groped around in the dark, feeling for a way out. He breathed more slowly. The air was a mist of sweat and urine. The darkness pressed in around him with the hatred of an old enemy. Sweet, pure sympathies laid siege to him again, self-pitying and pained, as he waited to pass out and suffocate.

There was no way out. He started to scream—and lost himself. The scream fell back into a rivery flow of moaning, unable to empty into any lake or ocean.

Then, after a long while that seemed like sleep, he heard something beyond the silence . . .

He listened.

"Bruno?" a voice whispered.

"Felix?" Bruno asked through a dry, cracking throat.

"Yes, old buddy, it's me."

"Where?" Bruno croaked, wondering about air and food, and how Felix had survived here. What had he been eating? Maybe food was not needed here, and death was impossible because time in this place crawled slowly into forever, or maybe not at all.

"Where?" Bruno repeated, barely able to speak. Sweet sentiments sickened his thinking; just recriminations rode in on winged, white horses of reason; guilt razored him with regrets; pity and self-loathing crushed his weakened pride.

But it all depended on one's acceptance—and one could still refuse! Even here he had that choice.

"Where are you?" Bruno asked, struggling in the pit of himself.

"Next one over," Felix whispered.

There were channels!

"But how?" Bruno asked. "Why?"

"Faced with my own end," Felix answered, "I decided it was better to live here than to be dead. Get it? Dead. What hell could count against being dead? There would be nothing I would refuse to do if it gave me life. Nothing! You hear? I would refuse nothing."

"But here?" Bruno asked, feeling an awe-filled hope.

"Even here," Felix said.

How many, Bruno wondered, struck by the image of infinitely branching pockets.

They beckoned. Come ahead. Come through.

Felix was waiting for him.

And Bruno realized that *here* he might be able to seize Felix's throat and choke him without killing him. The hunt for prey through these black arteries might be endless.

There could be no greater happiness.

He crawled toward the sound of Felix's voice.

"Felix!" he cried out. "Whose pockets are these? *Who* are we circling?"

He stopped and waited.

There was no answer.

Finally, Felix whispered, "The one you're in is yours, isn't it?"

"Yes."

"Are you sure?"

"Yes, it's mine. June and your cousin Henry shoved me in after I opened it."

"Hah!" Felix answered as if cheering them. "It's yours because you closed it—remember? They couldn't have closed it. And you wanted to close it. Something in you knew what it was doing!"

"And where are you?" Bruno asked, struggling to guess the unimaginable truth of his predicament. "And the others?"

"I don't know," Felix said. "I had to crawl into mine or die."

"Will these burst somewhere?" Bruno asked.

"I don't know!" Felix cried out.

"And then we'll die!" His shout was dull in the solid blackness.

"I don't know!" his old enemy repeated, sounding shamed by his ignorance.

Bruno tried to think. He had summoned the pocket for Henry and June, so it still had to be linked to his own mind. But was it? The channel suggested that it was also connected to Felix's, he thought, realizing with dismay that neither of them understood the pockets. Simply using them had been all too tempting. They were what they were, whatever they were, wherever they were.

Bruno felt dampness forming on his skin. It slipped into his eyes as if it knew where to go. His eyes drank the darkness as if it were light, as if at any moment he would learn to see in a new way.

From whom had Felix learned the skill?

Another enemy?

"Felix!" Bruno cried. "I'm coming for you!"

"Come ahead," Felix rasped, "come ahead."

Bruno crawled.

The darkness enclosed him, touching his whole body. He moved his arms and legs. The spongy blackness gave way, then squeezed back and grasped him, flowing through his rented tuxedo, tightening, attaching itself to every pore of his skin, entering his ears, eyes, nose, and rectum, seeking, always seeking . . .

"Felix!" Bruno shouted. "Do you feel that?"

"Yes," Felix croaked feebly.

Bruno crawled forward, but the black gripped again, soft yet strong.

"What's happening?" he cried, feeling the darkness draining his strength. It seemed familiar for a moment, ancient beyond worlds, the place from which everyone came out into the light . . .

"We're being . . . accepted," Felix whispered.

"What?" Bruno replied softly. "How can that be?"

The black vise tightened further.

"Felix!" Bruno cried out. "Help me!" He felt a wave of weakness, then a surge of strength.

"We're not dead yet," Felix gasped. "Maybe . . . we'll become . . ." he started to say, then laughed suddenly. "I think I get it now. These are *our* pockets, orbiting you and me. But we're inside, so it's a hopeless circle. They'll never burst."

"But we're being . . . eaten," Bruno protested, whimpering.

"Eating ourselves," Felix said, "—it's a circle. Eating to live and living to eat. We gain what we lose and lose what we gain. Not to worry, it's a stable relationship." He laughed again, more happily this time.

"What do you mean!" Bruno cried, fearing the reply.

"We can't ever die," Felix said. "We're being used by something unimaginable."

Strength shot Bruno skyward; spent, weakness hurled him into a deathly, congested sleep; a wrenching pulse shook him back to life —and tore at him. Something was alive within him, extending itself into every part of his body, painfully adjusting the beating of his heart, changing him—into what?

"Whatever it is," Felix whispered, "we're joining it."

Light exploded behind Bruno's eyes, putting out the darkness. He saw Felix suspended in a great, white space, his body skeletal and cadaverous, caught in a web of pulsing, blood-engorged pulsing.

The dark blinded him again.

Slowly, Bruno reached through the inkiness and found Felix's shoulders. His enemy was wet and warm in his hands! Bruno found the throat. His fingers closed in triumph around the bony softness and squeezed. At last!

Felix made no sound.

Bruno squeezed harder.

Something shot into his own chest, through his heart, and anchored itself in the base of his brain.

Felix pulsed with a slow, ageless beat.

And his enemy's throat was Bruno's own, his hands tightening steadily but with no effect.

Light filled the pocket.

Felix opened his eyes, and Bruno saw himself through his old enemy's sight, his own spidery body suspended in the same way. They were alive within each other's awareness, no longer separate selves. Their memories, of pleasure and loathing, seeped back and forth.

"Whatever . . . it is . . ." Felix stammered at the precipice.

". . . we've joined it," Bruno said, losing himself.

Lords of Imagination

J REMEMBERED HOW THE ALIEN WORLD HAD just hung there in the blackness of my fear-filled imagination, but also a reality thirty light years away, with beings who thought about humankind and the Earth, and no one knew what they were thinking. A whole alien culture, with its own history and view of the universe, a presence whose mere existence perturbed humankind's view of itself into an appalling uncertainty greater than any ever faced by our kind. It had been a dreadful unease that suddenly revealed all of humanity's past masks of identity. All the efforts of tribal songs, myths and religions, national, secular, and scientific narratives that had struggled to settle on a human identity might be redefined . . . by inhuman strangers who would certainly have an opinion. It was an outrage! Humanity's Jonathan Swifts and various misanthropes had done the job for us, hadn't they? And by comparison with genuine outsiders, it was feared, our own might turn out to have been . . . well, kindly.

Here at my editorial desk, I still remembered the time — what, only two decades ago — when the universe had been silent, and all future possibilities of any great significance, alien contact being one of the majors, had been only science fiction stories. Books and magazines had been full of aliens, with or without plausible cultures behind them. Now the silence was in the science fiction, as the greatest possible horror had overtaken the writers.

The alien civilization had unveiled itself slowly, as one might turn up the lights in a dark theater, revealing a large audience of strange faces, of onlookers rather than an appreciative gathering, powerful critics rather than fans.

It had been a slow contact, but suddenly there was the Galaxy, our milky way, marginalizing the Earth, as humankind had marginalized its own historical groups, in what was not, what now had to be, yes, pre-history . . .

Would it have been better for the intermediary to have just sat there for another century or more, getting us used to the idea? Would we have been waiting for a knock on the door, growing more frightened the longer it was delayed? Hadn't we already had enough science fiction as preparation? Hadn't we already inoculated ourselves against self-destruction with post apocalypse stories? Hadn't we already had enough thunder and roses? Had we not survived? Had we not brought ourselves under control? Surely that still counted for something . . .

About a year after the aliens established their *de facto* protectorate of Earth (more the pressure of their presence than actual governance), one of their cultural attachés (what else could we call them?) came to my office and complained about the kind of backward science fiction we were still publishing at *Earth SF*.

"You're well aware," he said good-naturedly as he fixed me with his two eyestalks, "that things are very different out in the Galaxy. It's not a crowded place, but it's not so empty that any new culture can come out and do as it pleases either. And it's not a place of medieval adventuring in costumes among various sun-kingdoms." The large eyes in his snaky stalks gazed at me earnestly, full of faith in my understanding.

"Well, I am aware of that," I said, leaning back in my chair, "but our readers love nostalgia . . . uh, for the ways it *wasn't*, especially."

"But you do know that there are only four factions, and that they don't talk to one another?"

She-it-whatever, waited in my silence.

"So?" I said. "How does *that* answer what I said?"

"Do understand that we do enjoy what you publish, some of us. We do not wish to censor. Nothing like that."

"Well, then, what is that you want?" I asked after another autistic silence.

"We could well understand this kind of science fiction in the last century," continued the attaché, "when your kind was limited to mere speculations about galactic life. But now there's no need to invent when so many cultures are available for study via the tachynet."

I cringed inwardly at the unfortunate conflation of tachyon, the term for faster-than-light particles, and net, and said, "Reality-based stuff is dull and takes too much effort to study," I replied. "We like to invent, to be original."

"But your invention is so much duller . . . so much less than can be found in the ocean of truth."

"We don't publish textbooks," I said. "Our readers want entertainment, not dreary realistic dramas about an unchanging human nature, or documentary non-fiction. Factual information about the Galaxy has no place here."

The four eyestalks came together graciously. "Yes, of course. After all, your science fiction, however much it is deformed by ignorance and purely fantastic impulses, has been the beginning of your planetary literature, and a sign of great hope for your species. And it is that hope that is of interest. Our betters have told us as much, and we do not doubt them."

"Really?" I interrupted, wondering who his betters might be. "How?"

"An outcast form of writing in the past, science fiction sounded the first notes of an advanced idiom, one in which its creators accept all fields of knowledge as the basis of their fictional dramatic cauldrons."

"I like that. Go on."

"You were, of course, unable to produce most of the wonders described in the stories, but your minds saw what was possible, after a fashion, and that in itself was notable. Despite our hindsight, we found this encouraging. Science fiction became your folk literature, at a time just before your time of voyaging through biological possibilities, which is well underway now. Of course, as with all forms of storytelling, the attachment to your known bioform and its behavior persists, following the basic excitation-to-orgasm dramatic structure. But there has always been in your science fiction a clear quality of intellectual astringency and creative praxis."

"Sure, sure," I said, "we had to crawl before we could walk." I wasn't terribly impressed with this interstellar Boy Scout, or many of our own do-gooders who worked with the so-called protectorate. They had fixed our greenhouse and ozone atmospheric problems, had cured AIDS and a dozen other diseases—and had in fact prevented the feared dying off of much of humankind that had been expected at the start of the new century. And they kept us from nuking each other, which was a good thing, I guess, though our nukes had become much cleaner and less dangerous. Mostly, the aliens were happy just to observe us. Most of us hardly noticed them.

All our power seekers collaborated as much as they could, hoping to scavenge what power they could still use; but they got very little practice in that traditional kind of abuse. They asked and asked, themselves especially, what they were getting for all their cooperation, and got no answer at all, as if it wasn't even a proper question, which demoralized them. Well and good.

"I'd like to remind you," the attaché continued pleasantly, "that we are not a very creative species, as you understand the ability."

"So I've heard, but I don't buy it," I said, sitting up in my chair. "You have starships, which manipulate forces equal to the gross economic products of a dozen Earths every second! That does it, to my way of thinking." I was getting tired of my visitor's show of modesty.

"Oh, that. Well, you see, our starships and attendant technologies were created for us by one exceptional individual born to our kind a long time ago. Another has not come since."

For the first time I was amazed, astounded, startled by a fantastic vision of a civilization run by technical rituals set for it by a few masterly insights. My visitor belonged to a race of followers, if I could believe him-her-it.

"It occurs to me," I said warily, "that I may be able to suggest a few things to help you."

The eyestalks moved closer to me. "Please, do."

"On the basis of your energy expenditures, it seems to me that you don't have to find other solar systems. What is there to benefit you? You can make just about anything you want. So why are you here?" I was proud of the twists in my argument, but it seemed to pique his interest.

"But haven't we been of some service to your kind, even if we aren't quite clear about how our visitation would benefit us?"

"Well, yes, you have been of help."

"I don't imagine how we could ever enjoy domination, unless it chanced that our victim was a superior, in which case we would be defeated." The eyestalks came to rest on my desk.

And I suddenly knew. "What you really want," I said impulsively, "is information—ideas and visions! Maybe that's why you came to me. That's what you *should* want." And I suddenly realized that I might be their new *source*.

"Yes, of course," the alien said. "We extract information from promising cultures and trade it elsewhere. Novel viewpoints and strange ideas which might be useless in one place might find a use elsewhere."

"Sure!" I shouted as the eyestalks gazed around my office. "I'll give you a disk of everything we've ever published. Lots of ideas we can't or won't ever make real. For example, *this* very discussion we've been having is an old story in science fiction." And we were even right, some of us, about the likes of you, I wanted to add. Bug eyed monsters, but pretty wimpy as conquerors. They didn't want much from us.

I gave him a disk and he tucked it away in a disgusting, furry fold of flesh, and I wondered if there was anything vital in this planetary lit of ours that might come back to bite us.

"Thank you so much," whatever-it-was said, bringing all four eyestalks together again. "Your help may prove useful to others." He tumbled off his chair and slithered out the door.

I sat there feeling glum, thinking that the old litterateurs like Alfred Kazin and Edmund Wilson had been right about the human story being changeless. All the old conflicts and failures only wore new clothes, while the central core of human character remained the same; and at the end of each story, film, or drama, it was understood that the same behavior might be repeated, that it would always remain possible. Only science fiction said otherwise, telling us that given what ounces of reason and nobility we had made it at least possible for us to change, that we in fact deserved to change, needed to change, to improve ourselves into something better—something that would never again slip back into the darkness, that *could* not ever again fall back into the pit, something that would one day not be able to understand Shakespeare's *Hamlet* or Tarantino's *Double Bill*.

The great starships began to disappear from Earth's skies, and I attributed it to the essential honesty of our alien visitors. They had helped us, had received something in return, and now the rest was up to us to use the gifts they had left us: a healthy planet, healthy populations, ever longer lives. We were expected to keep learning and to change. Somehow they had left this impression with us, without ever having to say much about it.

A day came when I looked up at the empty sky and felt troubled, knowing that all the restraints were gone. Nuclear war was once again possible, if only as a struggle for power rather than for resources and profits. We might have a holocaust at any time, as empty power niches were refilled. Conventional wars, of course, might come first. I thought of running nuclear war and post apocalypse stories—the more horrifying the better—in an effort to restrain my kind. And I wondered if my kind would care that they were probably being observed. I couldn't help but suspect that watchers had been left behind, but eventually dismissed the idea; it would only fix the game to take away our responsibility to each other. Would we know enough to feel ashamed? Would we appreciate the possibility that the tropes of science fictional ideas might now be helping other species?

I realized that the stories I had given away were as violent as they were constructive, and shuddered at what I might have done to the Galaxy . . .

This was the end of science fiction, I realized. Anything we wanted to know about life outside our own sunspace was accessible to us through the tachynet, so new stories would be wrong, and we would have to look to the present and past of our world in which to set stories.

Or . . .

I realized that if we encouraged fantasy and horror, we could never be wrong!

We opened a new vein of horror fiction. The arrogant presumption of looking ahead in time and outward into the galaxies would be replaced with the infinite reality of our deepest desires and darkest impulses, too long repressed by our proud intellect. That was where our greatest creativity lay—in dangerous fantasies, not in our engineering feats. Time to forsake cortical dreams and return to the black forests of our true reality, I proclaimed in my first editorial, remembering the time when our efforts had been toward the light, when everything that had happened had been only an idea for a perverse kind of story . . .

If the aliens ever came back, that would only be material for news stories; and any fiction written about the Galaxy, if we ever learned enough to do so, would become what we had once called mainstream, mundane literature. As an editor, I lived with the death of science fiction, turning away those who grieved and felt the horror of this freedom. Our great ones adapted easily, realizing that science fiction, what we'd ever had of it, was for our intellects; fantasy was for our black, anarchic souls, for all that we had leashed, chained, and imprisoned within ourselves.

Afterword

THESE WORDS ARE NOT ONLY FOR THOSE READ-
ers who like to make up their own minds, but also for those
who might like to compare notes with me about these stories.
Those of you who read even afterwords first, be warned. It's better to
get your own reactions first; save forewords and afterwords for later,
or even for never.

My words here are more like what you see on wall maps, where
it says "Legend," meaning an explanation; but no one believes there
are words in the middle of oceans, or lines of latitude and longi-
tude. The world is not a map, and an author is never completely
right in what he says about his work, or what is said about his efforts.
There are meanings to the left, right, top, and bottom of a sentence,
not to mention the same for individual words; too many to know all
at once, for a writer or a reader; so we do the best we can, and if it
comes out more for some people and less for others, that could be
the reader's or the writer's fault.

But language is not only for the knotty complexities of allusive
fictions, but also for shedding some light, at least sometimes. So
these notes are my take on how I understood these stories, even
though I quietly believe that nothing takes the place of an attentive
reader reading them, and an attentive writer knowing what he
means to say, even if we can't put explanations right into the middle
of a story. At least I think so this year, as I write these words. Next

year I might disagree with myself; because if you think about any-thing well enough, you have to expect that you might not step into the same thoughts twice. And you might, happily, write down more than you know and make a discovery.

Or then again you might not. Anyone who has kept a journal has had the surprise of asking himself, "Did I truly ever think *that?*"

But you did. And you wrote it down. And it looked good to you. You might think so again; or maybe not; maybe you'll think more.

So have a go with me at these stories. Those of you who are reading these words, or the foreword, stop now and read the stories. Don't even pay attention to that man behind the "Foreword."

Terrors and dark thoughts are many—personal, political, techno-logical, historical; but the greatest horrors dwell inside us before they come out into the light to shape our lives and even change the world. The common denominator of all fiction and drama is that something goes wrong inside a human being; a conflict arises, a struggle ensues, and the outcome is in doubt. Fantasy, which pre-dates science fiction by centuries, knows this well, as does serious contemporary fiction. Humanity's long journey via the slow time machine of our biology is perhaps best recorded by storytellers.

Science fiction is for our proud, newly forming human mind; it looks forward and believes in progress; yet it too is divided into utopian and dystopian schools, often mixed together. Fantasy and horror fiction is for our old, violence prone souls. "The thing in the crypt is us," Stephen King has written. The monster is not the mon-ster in *Frankenstein;* the doctor is the monster, because he can't control what he creates, and fails to restrain it after it comes to life. Dr. Morbius can't help but send his innermost self out to kill in the movie *Forbidden Planet* because the technology magnifies his sleeping mind, when he can't restrain his unconscious impulses; if the technology of the Krell had not been at hand, his sleeping other self would have been too feeble to do any harm.

Why horrify your readers is a question best answered by: a story gives you the means to do so harmlessly, for the most part. You can conjure and confront your worst wishes and fantasies—and maybe see in the mirror clearly what you might be blind to otherwise. Our greatest works of literature tell us in make-believe, verbal dreams, what we might not say out loud, or find politically inconvenient. But when reality and our imaginations meet, we find that reality exceeds our imaginations, because we are the reality of both realms. "The true subject of the horror genre," writes British film critic

Robin Wood, "is the struggle for recognition of all that our civilization represses." History tells us that it has done so at great peril.

Humor also catches us unawares, and we recognize truths that we would deny on the editorial pages of our newspapers. Satirists make even bigots laugh and go away uneasy, startled at their own involuntary recognition of truths denied. The worst of these truths is the answer to the rhetorical question, "It can't all be that bad?" Yes, it can be. We have a whole century behind us to prove it. Doesn't mean some things weren't good.

When you write imaginative fiction, especially genuine science fiction grounded in the realities of knowledge and thought, you tend to avoid the old darkness at the black heart of our survivalist evolutionary nature.

But a writer drifts as he time travels—fantasy and horror are about our jailed innards, which we strive to keep in check. Mystery stories gaze at our guts plainly. Good Westerns and historical fictions do take sight of our terrifying pasts. Romances recycle our delusions about love and belonging. The genres focus on certain features of our human nature by exaggerating them into clearer visibility; on the page, that is; one can scarcely exaggerate what goes on in reality. The genres are in fact rivers that feed contemporary fictions, which today have always struggled to liberate themselves from limited, realistic presentations. We are wilder than our mundane fictions are permitted to admit; more thoughtful and creative than our schools wish to encourage; more alienated from previous generations; more mad than reasonable; more sleep deprived than rested; more alike than different (Stephen Hawking has a poster of Marilyn Monroe with her skirt above her hips in his office).

How to write fiction that does not flinch at realities? Maybe the dangerous thrill, what Stephen King calls the "gross out," is nothing more than the courage we need, the fiction writer's technique to get at the truth, to look directly at the nightmare? Quentin Tarantino said recently that in *Kill Bill* he was pushing at his own talent as hard as he could, to see where it would hit a limit—and didn't find it.

Our successive world cultures have striven to purge the uglies from our nature without tossing out the vitality, brains, and creativity, to keep the love without embracing the wuss. So that's what this collection is about, as I look back at the stories, long before I guessed what such a grouping might mean.

"Lords of Imagination" reveals an SF writer segueing into horror, as he tries to rationalize the writing of fantastic horror. The conceit of this story, and the conceit of its presence in this collection, is that our human horror fiction is a subspecies of a galactic empire's local fiction, concerned now with human innards, which held us back from the heroic dreams of science fiction. I can think of no more horrifying demise for science fiction, one in which we become so marginalized, our local planetary history so reduced in a larger picture, that horror and fantasy fiction becomes the only relevant form of writing. Some may say that this retreat into fantasy, as knowledge and technology shrink our self-esteem, is exactly what is happening, without need of a galactic unveiling of our true and minor place. Many claim that this unveiling of our inner nature by the sciences is evidence that we will never progress; we can perhaps see our plight, but we cannot lift ourselves out of ourselves, defeat our inner selves, and this may not be possible without a place to stand and look back. Does such a place exist? It seems that we can glimpse it, in bits and pieces.

Dealing with our insides hits closer to the familiar in a horror story. Terror and pity make a *point*. Contact with an extensive extraterrestrial culture might turn us inward to personal horrors. There has been no such contact, yet we are preoccupied with our demons—and one of them is the idea of an alien from another star. I assume an unsettling reality, but it's only a story; if it were true, it would be devastating.

"I Walked With Fidel" suggests that all political figures are zombies speaking with the voice of polls, possessed by the dybbuks of statistics and trends, riding the demon-tigers of collective wishes. Our psychology, especially the psychology of propaganda, counts for more with politicians than our reason. The horror is that sooner or later all revolutions disgrace themselves, even as they leave some good behind. We put off the issue of slavery from the start; then after the Civil War was over we "settled" the older problem of Native Americans with genocidal violence. And since the progress of the 1950s and 60s, racism's past crimes still wait to be settled. Native Americans still await justice. "We are innocent!" cries the future to the past; but if nothing is settled, a new compact is made with the past's crimes.

Fidel Castro denied a free press and elections because they "would only help our enemies," he said to Barbara Walters. Recently, private computers, copying machines, and word processors have been banned in Cuba. Every kind of regime, good or bad, protects its own existence. The fault is not in the changes we make; it is in us.

When this story was published, I received a postcard from Harlan Ellison, who along with Fritz Leiber had been my teacher at the very first Clarion Workshop in 1968. "I read 'I Walked With Fidel,'" Ellison wrote, "and was grievously jealous. It is superlative. No other word, that's the one you get: superlative!"

"General Jaruzelski at the Zoo" was described by the *Locus* reviewer, Amy Thomson, as "a powerful allegory about Poland's relationship with Russia. Science Fiction abounds with shallow, opinionated political polemics. It's refreshing to see well-rendered political sf, particularly in an American magazine."

Today, I wonder if anyone in the West much recalls General Jaruzelski, the dictator of Poland just before the collapse of the fascist state capitalism that called itself the USSR and disgraced democratic ideals.

There was a long time during which this story could not have been published in Poland. Long after its appearance in *The Twilight Zone Magazine*, it was translated and published in Poland's magazine *Nowa Fantastyka*.

The real plight of zoo animals described in this story was reported in the *New York Times* in the late 1980s. The newspaper report struck a satiric knife into my heart and this short story came to me all at once, right up to the last line. Historians will, of course, sort out the real General's place in history, but the underlying horror of political humiliation expressed as the human-caused suffering of animals was an actual event. The Poles, in their critical way (the country has produced some great mathematicians and logicians), have set aside if not forgiven the General. What he thinks and believes in his retirement is mostly a matter for speculation. I am, however, particularly intrigued by the facts behind the General's apologies of the early 1990s. He claimed that his dictatorship prevented a Soviet invasion of the country; but it appears now that the Soviets assured him that they would not invade, which left him free to consolidate his power under a pretext. Still, as W. Warren Wagar, the American historian, said, "Jaruzelski's apologies are more than we can expect from Comrade Castro."

Is there anything quite like political horror? "My First World" is an episode not included in my novel, *Brute Orbits* (John W. Campbell Award for Best Novel in 1999). Political incarceration is strange, since so often the inmates are guilty; they accept the "crime" but not the "punishment," about which they have no choice. Here, there is literally a wall around the sky to prevent escape, and a better wall around time. Prisons are the horrors of human history's use of technology; top-down political approval expressed as neglect, all too often gives the jailers "new permissions" to express themselves against the human body with the available means. In this story we see a prison horror redeemed. I had meant the novel, in part, as a Swiftian "modest proposal"—following the logic of the *reductio-ad-absurdum* form of refutation—but was horrified to learn that the history of prisons exceeds in outrage and implausibility anything that can be imagined. I should have known better, and read Charles Dickens more extensively.

"First Love, First Fear" is, I see now, about the horror of reproductive systems. Ask many women. They forget. Grown men faint. What would another variety be like? I have concluded that no alien way would be any stranger than some of the strangenesses that we find among the many earthly species. I had turtles in mind for this story, but perhaps I should have chosen the praying mantis. (The name is sometimes misspelled as "preying," although both seem appropriate, with one suggesting hypocrisy, the other an honest and practical, and horrific, purpose).

"The Alternate" betrays something of the affection I have for shabby hotel rooms and roadside motels. They have character. They provide a shelter of anonymity. Slippages in time and through alternate realities would certainly horrify a person whether he knew what was happening or not, maybe more so if he knew the metaphysical subtleties involved. We are all somewhat aware of alternatives and might-have-beens. We might speculate that this awareness is, at some rich quantum level of our minds, evidence of alternate realities, probably unreachable except through imagining, of the multiverse richness of an ever-splitting universe. Stories on this theme long ago preceded the concepts of a sum over histories view entrance into physical theory. The idea of meeting your double is one such.

I take up the theme again in "Takes You Back," which suggested to me that time is ours in specific ways: as a biological clock which runs until it stops; as foresight, in the form of foreboding and hope; as heroic action against the great blind power of nature. And yet, it has been suggested, there may be no such thing as time beyond our motion in space. We ourselves are time, such as it is, what we mean by time, against an absolute duration that is not time as we know it. Our very feelings are time, and we must be wary of how they throw us. Step outside your home and look up at the sky during the onset of seasonal change, especially on a starry night, and wonder who you are. "Takes You Back" suggests that it is dangerous to look back; worse to fall in love with the past. You may not be hurled back, but you'll wind up stuck there anyway. The *Locus* reviewer called it "an ingenious and sensitive look at how an infinitesimal change might compromise love forever . . ."

"Earth Around His Bones" is based on a suspicion that cannot be confirmed with any precision. Brain death is death—or do we linger? We strike the iceberg at the moment of birth, and sink through all our days, watching the damage worsen, and maybe for a while a little beyond . . .

"Fire of Spring" came to me with all its colorful imagery sharp and clear, and seemed to have the weighty horrors of a cyclical history behind it.

"Hell Just Over the Hill" crept up on me during several bus rides, which would make quite a long collection of stories in itself. Horrific and fantastic explanations suggested themselves for every ordinary moment of the ride, as we all gazed into the night ahead of us, and I imagined that we had missed a bridge.

"Interpose" grapples with the story of the crucifixion, with the central horror at the heart of Christianity—especially with the notion that it was all part of the plan for the redemption of humanity. Probably the most successful spin in all history—given the takeover of Rome by the Christians (from the mouths of lions to the throne of the Caesars!). Yet human life resembles more than anything "the way of the cross." We are born, we suffer, and die. I recommend an old book, *The Martyrdom of Man*, by Winwood Reade (1872), which suggests why the story of Christ's death moves even non-believers.

"The Coming of Christ the Joker" deals with the ideals that have been read into Christ's message of human reform, and so rarely practiced. We don't know who he was or what he stood for (even the Gospels contradict his message of peace); he might have been someone else entirely. Of course, I don't believe a word of it—except for the ideals, the same ones that have been disgraced in all revolutions, in all times; secular or religious, the reforms seem to make no difference.

"Jumper" is a story about how an impossible power would be wielded by the depths of the human mind—in an unexpected, unconscious way. My agent at the time, Joseph Elder, told me how much he liked the main character, and even suggested that she might have been rescued at the end, making the story a "crowd pleaser."

"Passing Nights" was a nightmare I had in my early teens. I

never forgot it. Earlier drafts made no sense to me. I was well into adulthood when it came out this way.

"The Wish in the Fear" reminds us that phobias are real horrors to real people in the real world. Yet the substance of the phobias are real only in the virtual realm of our minds. Same difference, many people would say.

"The Soft Terrible Music" is a hybrid story, combining my interest in the "warm" valley of Antarctica, home architecture, and the crimes on which nearly all great fortunes are founded. One might say it's a story about the foundations of a life, a house, a crime.

"Black Pockets," which I wrote especially for this collection, looks at a horror directly, personally, with more than a hint of metaphysics. In my novel, *Stranger Suns*, my character thinks of looking out across the dark light years "without flinching." Can we also look inward with a steady gaze, and understand? When we fail to see, when we flinch, sentimentality takes over, and from there is but a small step to lying to ourselves. Sentimentality softens truth into legend, so we can accept it more easily. Nothing reveals human flaws as the uses we make of power. The story ends, appropriately, I think, inside an enigmatic *cul-de-sac*.

"Black Pockets" asks whether, if this kind of power were available to human beings, would no one use it? We have used much worse. Raw reality dwarfs imagination, but imagination gives perspective. But a story, however brave, is still a form of cultural sentimentality, where we face what we could not tolerate in reality—except that we don't completely face it. Hopefully, we focus it.

What we have, we use. There is no horror in human history that we have ever refrained from visiting on each other. The horrors of stories are easily outdone by realities, but these imagined horrors are inevitably rooted in our common reality. What horrors we have in reality, we use in our stories, in our horror films; yet no film has ever truly shown what was done during the genocides of World War II. No one would go to see it.

The reader will notice that in "Black Pockets" and "A Piano Full of Dead Spiders" I again visit with two characters named Bruno and Felix, who also appear in stories elsewhere. These two shadowy protagonists, whose very character shifts while their names remain the same, who sometimes know each other and sometimes not, perhaps fill some unfound need in the writer; they stand disguised, or perhaps not. Who are these guys who dance so strangely around each other? They are perhaps exactly who they need to be in each story—and perhaps I only like the names. One of them might well be a funny uncle of mine, or his brother. Or two guys who were on their way to Menshevik Hall in a story I once read by my friend William Tenn, but they never got there and wandered instead into my mind, and stayed. And this is the only way I know how to evict them. They will continue to debut; and may never get out.

The central horror of "Nappy" flowers from Napoleon's finding out that he is not the real one. The puppeteer of history is at first horrified at not being the "original," but a copy, and still capable of suffering, more so from knowledge than from ignorance; but one advantage of being a virtual Napoleon is that he might still achieve a happier fate.

What horrifies writers? Often it's violence, especially violent sex, especially if you have to write it down. But more than anything it might be Pascal's terror of endlessness, the infinities that he saw lurking at every window. It may be, for the writer, the fear of not finding the proper end to a story, one that is not gratuitous. The plausible end is the writer's friend; but when you can't find it, you step into an abyss. Not a friend, the abyss, it is the heart of all horror, all terror and fear. Infinity was, for Aristotle, irrational, because it was undefined; or, even more maddening, is that you could define it but never reach its end. A well-crafted story shuts down neatly. A great story concedes an irrational infinity around its sharp edges. And strangely, because infinity is open-ended, it is the source of all creativity.

You need it.

A story is a well polished piece of infinity with an illusory fence around it, and you wouldn't want to get to the end of what exists outside that fence.

George Zebrowski
Delmar, New York
November 2004

Two thousand copies of this book have been printed by the Maple-Vail Book Manufacturing Group, Binghamton, NY, for Golden Gryphon Press, Urbana, IL. The typeset is Electra with Rapier display, printed on 55# Sebago. Typesetting by The Composing Room, Inc., Kimberly, WI.